From Dream to Reality

Dragons and Dreamphasers Book Two

Jen Robyn

Published by Jen Robin Kaltman

First paperback edition September 2013

Cover designed by Melody Simmons of eBookindiecovers.com
Cover model Jimmy Thomas, image licensed under Romancenovelcenter.com
Elf image by George Mayer licensed under Fotolia.com
Staff image by Oliver Lenz licensed under Fotolia.com

ISBN-10: 0989449211
ISBN-13: 978-0-9894492-1-2

This book is dedicated to

My "dream knight"

Thank you for being in my life

Acknowledgments

Thank you to my Mom for her editing assistance during the read-throughs.
Your patience, helpful advice, and support are greatly appreciated.

Thank you to my Dad for helping to get the word out, and the suggestion for a web page.
Your support is also very appreciated.

Thank you to my good friend who encouraged me to self-publish my novels.
Your inspiration helped make this possible.

Additionally, a thank you to the cover lady for the beautiful covers for Book One and Book Two. Your work is amazing. Thank you to a friend for designing an excellent web page for the books. Your help was so important in making it look great. A thank you to my friends and family. You have all contributed something wonderful to my life.

And a thank you to my readers. May you enjoy reading the books as much as I enjoyed writing them.

Chapter One

The silver dragon heard the butler yelling long before he approached the room, yet tried to ignore him, while continuing to stare at the parchment he'd discovered quite by accident upon awakening from his recent nap.

"Sir, I tried to stop him, but he wouldn't listen!"

"Well then, both his behavior and yours are no surprise as usual," growled the man who strode ahead of him into the room.

Though many years older with white hair, there was no mistaking the strong presence of Chaos Westbrooke, especially since irritation was creating a visible aura around his head. Evidence of his being a rare multi-abilitied supernatural, more than capable of building up and overseeing the island they resided on.

As he reached the dragon, he sighed heavily, struggling not to let his ire get the better of him, since Chaolyn was one of his oldest friends. Regardless of the times he tried his patience, including now, since the dragon was pointedly ignoring him.

"When last I checked, this was still my study," Chaos reminded him.

"*Which you said I could borrow to nap in...*" mumbled the dragon, curiously gazing from one side of the paper to the next.

"Oh, and how is this napping?"

The dragon shrugged. "*Well, I woke up.*"

"Exactly. So why don't you go find something to do elsewhere, while I get back to my work."

"Sir, that's exactly what I told him!" the butler chimed in. "He's being deliberately disagreeable!"

Finally lifting his head, the silver dragon turned to him slowly. *"And do you think you're someone who should be lecturing a dragon on manners?"* Chaolyn asked with an audible growl. As his gaze fell on the butler, his eyes began glowing a fiery red.

Visibly shaken, the butler nearly tripped as he fled the room.

Immediately after, Chaolyn's eyes returned to normal and he began chuckling. *"There are days I love being able to do that."*

His aggravation fading slightly, even Chaos couldn't repress a smile.

"You never mentioned you were working on another building project," the dragon told him.

"That's because it's not a formal one yet," he replied, "and nothing to concern yourself with." As he tried to roll the parchment up, Chaolyn's talons halted this.

"It's not a typical home like those you've built. It almost looks like a small castle. Wait... is that a **nursery?"** He gasped sharply in realization. *"You're already planning a home for Dominick and his future bride?"*

Chaos rolled his eyes, mentally promising himself to revoke the dragon's privilege to nap here in the future, possibly keeping the room locked.

"Yes, yes, a tentative one," he admitted. "If you must know, I'm preparing the best home possible, so my grandson won't reconsider living on a world light years away with his bride and future children."

Chaolyn raised one talon. *"Um, Chaos, I think you've been misinformed about the distance. Earth is only millions of miles away, while a single light year is actually more than five trillion miles..."*

"And when's the last time our world dealt with technology, much less space travel? One tends to forget."

"I just thought you should know…"

"Fine! My point was, so he won't reconsider taking them **millions** of miles away to live on another world. Now mind your own business."

The silver dragon's enthusiasm deflated instantly. *"Old friend, I'm wounded. I only inquired to prevent you from getting yourself into difficulty."*

"There is no difficulty here. One can plan ahead."

"True, true. But even you must admit this is an unusual circumstance."

Unusual indeed, Chaos mused.

Over the past month, his longtime bachelor grandson had finally fallen in love with a woman he wished to marry. Something that would have thrilled Chaos completely, if not for the problem that she resided on another world… namely Earth.

Their own homeworld of Chavernos existed on the other side of the sun, surrounded by magically-enhanced mists, making Earth oblivious to it. Magic was prevalent on Chavernos, and especially with the supernaturals on the island of Barokka who had inborn magic abilities.

It was Dominick's supernatural ability of dreamphasing that enabled him to visit Earth astrally, where he actually met his fiancée Julianna in her dreams. Amidst a variety of different dream scenarios, several romantic, within a short time they'd fallen in love, and now they wished to be married. Knowing that could only happen if they could be brought together in reality, Chaos suggested Dominick seek out the dragon sorcerer Lendric, and hopefully he could provide a solution.

"To say the least," Chaos agreed, "however, given our world's reputation for proving things are not always as impossible as they seem, I learned long ago that ways are often found where there seem to be none."

"Oh, and reasonable optimism is understandable. In this case though, don't you think you should at least wait until you know the young ones **can** *be brought together?"*

"Wait for what?" came an amused voice from the doorway.

"Dominick..." Chaos called out meaningfully, while both he and Chaolyn hastily shifted some papers to obscure the parchment from view. Several papers errantly flew from the table to Chaos's chagrin, causing him to roll his eyes as he turned towards his grandson. "You're back sooner than expected."

The younger man's deep blue eyes grew curious. "Am I interrupting something?"

"No, not at all," replied Chaos, eager to change the subject. "Did your parents come back with you?"

"Yes, and they'll wait to see you before heading home."

Chaos nodded, striding over to him, with Chaolyn following close at his heels. "Well, don't keep us in suspense, boy. Did you speak with Lendric?"

Dominick nodded. "Yes. And there is a way."

Smiling, Chaos turned to Chaolyn knowingly. "There, you see? What did I tell you?"

"But... there's also a snag."

The dragon clicked his tongue. *"And this is what* **I** *tried to tell you."*

Glaring at him, Chaos gestured to a pair of nearby leather chairs which he and Dominick occupied immediately. His demeanor became cool. "Now, explain."

Running a hand through his raven black hair, Dominick sighed heavily. "Per Lendric's request, what I tell you must stay between us. He has a rare magical device, called the Myzalik Teleportation Staff, which is capable of teleporting the bearer and others with the bearer between worlds. He's even used it to travel to Earth before."

Chaos spread his hands. "So then what's the problem?"

"The problem is, Lendric loaned the Staff to his brothers, and they've been missing for several months. There's no knowing where they went, which could be anywhere in the universe. Even expert dreamphasers Lendric sent out were unsuccessful in locating them, in spite of our vast range of travel, which is why he sent out a pair of demon allies instead. Hopefully they can both locate and bring them back safely."

"Dreamphasers are one thing, but demon allies? With their unpredictable nature, a device of that magnitude would likely be more of a temptation than a mere rescue mission."

"*It depends,*" Chaolyn interjected. "*Dragons don't trust demons lightly, and especially since these are his brothers, I'm sure Lendric is wise enough to only send those he would trust with his own life.*"

Dominick nodded. "Lendric assured us that he does."

"*Then it is likely only a matter of time.*"

"It can't happen soon enough," sighed Dominick, half to himself.

He certainly treasured every moment he shared with his spirited red-haired companion, the constant sparkle in her warm brown eyes echoing their shared love. However, being limited to only seeing each other in the dream realm, constantly being pulled away from each other with each dawn, was not without its frustration. How he wished she was already here on Chavernos, where he could show her the beauty of the island, enjoying the sunshine together by day, and walking beneath the stars at night, knowing they had all the time in the world with nothing to keep them apart.

Chaos shook his head with a smile. "I must admit, even now, it's hard to believe you went and fell in love with a woman from another world."

"*Yes,*" replied Chaolyn. "*It's not every day you find the love of your dreams… quite literally in your dreams.*"

Without realizing it, their positive words softened Dominick's inner frustration. "You're right," he said. "And believe me, I'm grateful I did."

Sensing something else, Chaos's expression changed. "Are you still concerned about that ex-boyfriend of hers?"

"Roger Collins," he supplied. "And yes I am. Recently, he's been trying to insinuate himself back into Julianna's life, regardless of how badly things ended between them, and I certainly don't trust the man not to hurt her emotionally again."

Inspired by his earlier dealing with the butler, Chaolyn turned to him with a grin. "*You could appear as a dragon in his dreams and scare him into leaving her be,*" he suggested. "*I find that tactic works wonders.*"

Dominick stifled a laugh. "I don't think Roger would give up that easily, though I'll keep that thought in mind."

The dragon cocked his head to one side. "*Speaking of which, there's another person here who won't be too happy when she discovers your engagement.*"

"Sionne," he agreed, turning to his grandfather. "You know, I can't figure out whether she's really infatuated with me or not, but I've never encouraged it, and she knows I don't reciprocate it. I respect that her late father was a good friend to you, and I understand the loyalty which convinced you to allow them to live in the palace all these years, but there are times it's very uncomfortable visiting when she's here. I strongly doubt it's going to improve when Julianna arrives."

Chaos nodded thoughtfully. "Her father saved my life, so yes I felt I owed him and his family that much. Although her sister Sireni moved out awhile ago, I've let things be, since for the most part, Sionne and her mother have kept to themselves."

Not always, Dominick thought, shaking his head. "It didn't help matters when you tried to see me betrothed to her."

"I merely thought it was time you married," protested Chaos. "I'd initially thought that you and Sionne might be a suitable match; however, time has clearly proven otherwise. You needn't worry; Sionne will just have to find someone else."

"I'm glad you understand that now."

"So then the only real issue remaining is to bring your Julianna here."

"Not... quite."

Chaolyn's ears perked up. *"There's something else amiss?"*

"Yes. I got in a fight with Dual Arrovill at Lost Limbo earlier today."

"As if there's not enough to deal with," Chaos growled. "Dominick, I've told you before to stay away from him. He was trouble even before that incident with his late fiancée happened."

"Dual blatantly provoked me, Grandfather. You can ask Zantarl the bartender if you don't believe me." He frowned. "Worse still, he knows about Julianna."

"Hmmm, I'm guessing from your engagement announcement in the dream-state."

"Exactly," he said. "Considering how much animosity he's always borne since he blames me for the death of his fiancée, there's no telling what he might do in retaliation."

"I'll alert the palace guard to double security."

"That's fine for here, but I'm more concerned about Julianna."

"She should be safe from him in the dream-state. After all, he doesn't know where she lives."

Dominick shook his head. "That's not a guarantee. Riff managed to follow me there in astral form to find her."

"He did **what**?" Chaos's eyes narrowed. "Oh, now I remember. You told me something about that earlier."

Chaolyn gave a low whistle at that but said nothing.

Dominick instantly regretted reminding him. Although he hadn't formerly told Chaolyn of his mischievous older brother's visiting Julianna, he wasn't surprised the dragon already guessed why. As had been the case with other girlfriends Dominick had known, Riff thought he could seduce Julianna. Fortunately, he hadn't succeeded, but that didn't stop Dominick from giving him one hell of a fistfight. Afterwards, Riff apologized for his actions and vowed to back off. He hadn't caused trouble since.

"He... wanted to meet her, since I wouldn't say much about her at the time." That much was true, although Dominick had to force the words out, given the actual incident. Even Chaolyn looked skeptical, but the younger man shook his head. "The point is, if Riff could follow me to find her, Dual could do something similar."

"Maybe," said Chaos, "but now that you're aware of this, Dual will find it much harder. An alert dreamphaser is not easily followed."

"Oh, I assure you I'll be mindful when I travel."

Chaos placed his hands on his grandson's shoulders. "Then let this go for now. You're doing all you can."

Dominick nodded. "There is one other thing I wish to speak with you of privately. That is, if Chaolyn can give us a few minutes."

"*Of course*," agreed the dragon. "*I'll be back later*

to finish my nap."

Chaos shook his head after him. "So long as you stick to that!" he shouted.

Chaolyn's chortling laughter was his only reply, shutting the door with his tail as he exited.

"What was *that* about?" chuckled Dominick.

"Oh... never mind," mumbled Chaos. "Now, what else did you wish to speak with me about?"

Keeping his promise of secrecy to Lendric, Dominick revealed what the dragon sorcerer suggested regarding having Julianna and her sister Crystal meet a Chavernian family that Lendric had sent to Earth many years ago. They were a family of dragons, a couple and their son, appearing in human form as all Chavernian dragons could. The couple's son, however, was brought there as a child with no knowledge of this, in order to protect him. His violet eyes were both the blessing of a future gift of greater magic, and a curse since there were dark ones on Chavernos who would exploit or destroy those bearing this gift.

"This will prove our existence to both Julianna and her sister," Dominick explained, "and it should ease their doubts until I can go to Julianna myself."

"Any help to this situation is welcome. It was good of Lendric to share this with us."

"Agreed," Dominick replied, his gaze spying a portion of the building plans that some of the fallen papers left revealed. "I didn't know you were working on a new construction," he commented, walking over to see better.

"Uh... it's a private project really," Chaos said quickly, rushing over. "Nothing you need concern yourself with."

Dominick moved a few of the obscuring papers aside and his eyes widened, turning to him incredulously. "Is this what I think it is?"

The elder man sighed with a nod. "I wanted it to be a surprise for you and your bride. It's probably not as spacious as the dream castle you created for her, but it will have the same look and feel in reality." At Dominick's continued silence, he added, "It's tentative, of course. If you wish it modified, or something else entirely, I'll understand. I just felt that whether you choose to live on Chavernos or not, you'll still have your own home here."

Slowly, Dominick smiled. "It looks wonderful, Grandfather," he said gently, earning a relieved look from him. "This really means a lot to me. Thank you for keeping an open mind."

Chaos smiled a rare warm smile. "I realized that regardless of my wanting you both to reside here, your happiness is more important."

Moved beyond words, Dominick stepped forward to give him a strong hug, which Chaos gladly reciprocated.

"This calls for a celebration," he decided enthusiastically. "It's been ages since we've had a good island feast, and it's certainly time for one now."

"Now, Grandfather..." Dominick protested. "Announcing our engagement in the dream-state was premature enough for the time being."

Chaos warded this off.

"So we won't give a reason why. We'll know the truth. That's all that matters. Let me go track down our esteemed butler and see if we can arrange this for tomorrow night."

"Tomorrow?" questioned Dominick, trailing after him. "I don't know..."

"Perish that thought, and leave everything to me."

As Chaos opened the door, Riff fell forward as he was clearly about to knock.

"Leave what to you?" he asked in bewilderment.

The elder man's eyes narrowed, as he folded his arms. "Ah, I was about to look for you next. Just what were you thinking visiting Dominick's fiancée in the dream-state?"

Riff's green eyes opened wide with a mixture of shock and anger.

"Phase!" he exclaimed in exasperation. "You said you wouldn't tell him about that!" Before his brother could dispute this, Riff turned back to Chaos. "Grandfather, I swear nothing happened. It never went beyond a kiss, and it won't happen again."

Chaos's own eyes widened at that, while Dominick shook his head with an 'I tried to tell you' look.

"He... didn't tell you about that, did he?"

"No, he didn't!" snapped Chaos, his eyes gleaming angrily. "But *you* will!"

Riff groaned, eyeing Dominick witheringly. "I guess this means the dancing girls are definitely out for the wedding?"

Chapter Two

Sionne started instantly upon hearing a door open below. From the familiar voices to the ensuing agitated comments of the castle butler, it was apparent that Dominick was back.

Fluffing up her golden hair once, she immediately hurried down the stairs to greet him, but halted upon seeing Chaos walk out with him. Lowering to hide behind one of the pillars beside the banister, she huddled silently to better hear what was being said.

"So all can be arranged to our mutual satisfaction," Chaos laughed as he clapped a hand against Dominick's shoulder. "You get to marry the girl of your dreams, and I finally see a chance at acquiring a few great-grandchildren."

Sionne's eyes narrowed. *What girl?* her thoughts demanded. *Surely not the same viper that held a claim to Dominick's nightly thoughts.*

"Yes, but not immediately," he sighed. "It could be some time before Lendric's brothers return with the means to bring Julianna here. I still say it might be best not to prepare a celebration in advance."

"Details, details," mumbled Chaos. "Don't bother me with technicalities. I have enough of those with the running of this island. In the meantime, I'd best see your parents off, so I don't incur your mother's wrath. Warp never likes to be kept waiting." Smiling knowingly, he shook his head upon leaving. "A lack of patience which you'd do best to curb yourself in regard to your awaiting Julianna's arrival."

Dominick muttered something under his breath, but didn't interrupt Chaos's departure. Heading for the stairs, he caught sight of a rustle of silk, setting one foot on the bottom step before peering upwards.

"Aren't you a bit old to be playing hide-and-seek, Sionne?" he asked.

Standing to walk down the steps towards him, she raised her chin. "And aren't *you* a bit old to believe in fairy tales? After all, there's no guarantee that this supposed dream girl of yours is all she seems, let alone that she'll choose to come to Chavernos."

"Ah... eavesdropping as well, were you?" He smiled slightly, but without humor.

"Why shouldn't I be concerned with the affairs of my future betrothed?"

Dominick's expression darkened. "Sionne, I am *not* your future betrothed, and never will be. Don't you think it would benefit us both if you accepted that now, rather than wait until my true bride arrives to resign yourself to that reality?"

Smiling weakly, she replied, "You're not one of the rare mystics, and hence even you can't know the future so definitely. Things might change."

"*Nothing* will change," he replied assuredly, leaning against the nearby wall. "I love Julianna for all that she is, and I have every confidence that she'll choose to come here to our world one day. If she wishes otherwise, then I intend to reside with her on Earth instead. Either way, we'll be wed in reality one day."

Remembering some advice Sireni had given her earlier, Sionne took the final step down to Dominick's level, gazing into his eyes. "You turned from me on account of the rumors which labeled me a marble statue without emotions," she said bitterly. At his surprised look, she continued, "Oh yes, Dominick, I know what they say behind my back. And the only real reason why that other woman holds your interest is for how well she warms your bed each night, like any other common tramp."

His eyes glittering warningly, Dominick came close to slapping her face, but instead bit out a reply. "Julianna is a warm and loving soul, and certainly not a tramp. Only a cold-hearted wench like yourself would proclaim otherwise, thus proving the rumors true, and gladdening my heart that I found Julianna instead."

Flushing angrily, Sionne hissed, "So you think I'm cold as ice, do you, Dominick Westbrooke? Then allow me to prove you a liar." She launched herself at him, digging her hands into the shoulders of his jacket as she pressed him back to the wall, her mouth claiming his in a fierce kiss.

Caught off-guard, he was momentarily stunned, granting Sionne a brief feeling of triumph as she attempted to melt the barriers around his resistance. The feeling was short-lived when he abruptly thrust her aside, causing her to stumble to the floor, clutching the banister.

"By Chaos, don't you *ever* do that again, Sionne!" he growled, startling her with his adamant fury. "Because my grandfather was a good friend of your late father, who was a most trusted ally, you and your mother remained under the palace roof and I was respectful of this. But so help me, Sionne, if you dare come at me like that again, I swear you'll be sent packing to live elsewhere."

Rising up slowly, she shook her head. "You'll not get rid of me that easily, Dominick. If I was the ice maiden you say, you wouldn't have reacted so heatedly, would you? No. And therefore, you must feel more for me than you claim."

"You're the most stubborn, infuriating woman on the planet," he said, barely keeping a rein on his anger.

Oblivious to this, Sionne smiled winsomely, stepping closer to touch his cheek, ignoring his flinch. "But in the same reality as you, my arrogant suitor."

He brushed her hand away, about to cast off her last words as false, just as an arising scuffle at the door drew his attention. "What in blazes," he exclaimed, striding over to a fair-haired woman who was speaking rapidly to the butler. Two children chattered beside her, while she did her best to quiet them. "Laelea," he gasped loudly, gaining her attention.

"Dominick," she sighed in relief. "Thank the stars I've found you." The butler seemed to agree, excusing himself to find Chaos.

"Oh, now really, this tops the cake," Sionne sneered behind them. "First a fool's notion of a red-haired dream woman, and now you bring elven mistresses to the door!"

"Cease your ranting!" Dominick snapped, whirling to face her. "This is my good friend Alarius's wife, and a sweet lady who deserves no disrespect from anyone, let alone you." Sionne fell silent, but glared at him. Turning back to the bemused Laelea, he frowned upon noting her awkward stance. "Dear heaven, you shouldn't be traveling about with your child nearly born. Here." Pulling forth a comfortable chair, he helped her into it. "You should have sent Alarius instead."

"Alarius..." she bit out, "is the reason I'm here." Clasping Dominick's hand, she continued uneasily. "He's been kidnapped. A note from an unknown messenger arrived this day to inform me of it." Reaching within her cloak, she withdrew a thin paper. "This will explain it."

Taking the letter from her, Dominick read it silently, a muscle twitching in his cheek as he read the last. "Dual," he hissed. "Damn him, when will that bastard ever learn?"

"The odd part is, he didn't mention ransom money. He merely stated that you're the one that must come for him, or he'll be killed this evening." Laelea's eyes lowered as she twisted her hands together. "I wish I didn't have to burden you with this, when you've already done so much to help us."

Dominick shushed her gently. "You had no choice," he assured her. "If I'd had any idea that that demon-spawn Dual would get involved, I'd have sent assistance to help Alarius procure the treasures. As it is, I'm surprised he went searching for them at a time like this. He mentioned needing money with the new child on the way, but I naturally assumed it could wait until after it was born." As Laelea's expression grew more somber, he looked at the children in realization. "Where's Daric?"

"He's home. A family friend is with him."

Dominick reached out to hold her hand. "What aren't you telling me?" She sighed heavily, explaining Daric's condition, and how he'd taken a turn for the worse. A doctor was needed immediately. When she finished, Dominick shook his head. "I had no idea Daric was sick. Why didn't Alarius tell us?"

"You must understand my husband's thoughts in this matter," she said. "He's a proud man, and he had enormous trepidation over simply accepting your gift of the map. He felt he could not ask for more, when we could offer only gratitude for now, and wished to be responsible in finding the treasures himself."

"You, Alarius, and the children are like family to us," he declared. "We'll come up with some way to dispel any ideas Alarius might have of debts later. But in the meantime, you tell that physician to get to work saving Daric. The money you require will go with you. And as soon as he can safely be brought here, you're all to come stay at the palace until the treasures are rightfully reclaimed and all is resolved."

"I beg your pardon!" barked Chaos as he strode in with the butler, narrowly missing Chaolyn who poked his head in the room as well. "Dominick, I know I once told you this will always be your home, but since when did I condone running a relocation program through the palace?"

Dominick sighed. "Alarius is being held hostage, so further explanations will have to wait. But look at it this way, Grandfather. You have a soft spot for children, right?"

"Well..." he mumbled, eyeing the two children who were now racing about with exuberant yells. "I suppose..."

"Exactly," finished Dominick. "So since your plans for our next generation are on hold right now anyway, it's the perfect way for you to adjust to the future prospect." Leaving no room for argument, he headed to the front door. "While you take care of granting Laelea the money for her son's doctor, I'll go roust Riff out of whatever corner he's hiding to help find Alarius."

"But... wait a second!" sputtered Chaos, just before the door slammed in his face. "Impertinent youngster," he murmured.

"*True,*" agreed Chaolyn, clicking his tongue. "*Can't imagine* **where** *he got that trait from.*"

Glaring at him, Chaos turned to Laelea sympathetically. Patting her hand, as she sat with an unusually grim expression, he smiled. "Don't you worry, my dear," he told her. "I have the greatest confidence in my grandsons, and Alarius is as good as rescued already. Now if you'll allow me to help you up." Laelea's face abruptly blanched.

"I think I'd best wait right here," she replied, one hand rising to her stomach.

"Is the child restless?"

"In a matter of speaking," she said uneasily. "I believe he or she wishes to join us immediately."

"*What?*" exclaimed Chaos, his eyes alighting on the gaping Chaolyn instantly. "Well, don't just lie there like a carpet of scales! Go fetch a doctor... or a midwife... or whoever else in blazes should be here!"

"*Right away,*" said the dragon, turning to Laelea. "*In the meantime, try and keep him calm at all costs.*"

"I highly doubt the child will remain so!" snapped Chaos.

Chaolyn turned his head towards him. "*I wasn't referring to the child,*" he amended. "*I meant* **you.**"

*****

"Haven't I had enough of your damn curses regarding women in the past?" blasted Riff, not having let up once during the past hour from berating his brother for interrupting his pleasant activities with a beautiful fair-haired damsel.

"At your obvious reluctance to leave, at least this one didn't need a frog spell to get rid of her," murmured Dominick, smiling slightly. "She seemed to understand well enough upon hearing the tests weren't in yet regarding your... medical problem."

"Damn you, Phase, if you needed me for a rescue mission, why didn't you just say so?" his brother snarled in reply. "It would have been a hell of a lot easier to explain to Luscious, unlike that pack of lies you dropped on me!"

"Luscious?" laughed Dominick. "With a name, and a possible reputation from that, I think you're lucky I saved you from Kiri's inevitable wrath."

Riff's mouth curled into a sneer. "As if you wouldn't be the first to tell her about it anyway!"

"Maybe I won't have to, if you cooperate," he said.

"Right. When demons live in harmony!"

Seeing a light up ahead, as well as hearing voices, Dominick abruptly shushed him. "That looks promising," he said quietly. Riff nodded, with a smirk.

"Dual's obviously off the ball tonight," he replied. "Posting only two guards at the door."

"There's probably an army within," said Dominick.

"Maybe... but Alarius needs us, right? Besides, I'm in the perfect mood for rattling a few lame-brained idiots, so let's go."

At the door, the guards held their crossbows loosely, too busy chatting to hear the brothers sneak up beside them while placing their swords against their necks.

"Pardon us, boys," Riff chuckled. "We're a bit late for

an appointment with our old friend Dual. Surely you won't let on to him that we're here, will you?"

"N-no," stammered one man. "Of course not."

"But we will," announced another man, one of several striding up from hidden posts. Distracted, Dominick and Riff turned to face their attackers, while the crossbow men recovered to aim at their backs.

Moments before they could fire, a loud screech rang out, causing all to drop their weapons to cover their ears, including Dominick and Riff.

"Blazes, Psych!" shouted Buddy, emerging with a sword. "We really need to discuss your methods of fighting!"

"Oh, be quiet, angel-boy," said Kiri, jumping out of her own hiding place with Jarissa and Inferno, all wielding crossbows of their own. Riff could only gape at her as she strode up, keeping the guards at bay. "Word has it you've found yourself a... Luscious lady in my absence." As Riff gave a weak laugh, she raised her crossbow towards his eyes.

"Happy to see you too, hon," he joked, carefully pushing the weapon aside. "Mind if I ask what you're doing here?"

"A good question," she replied with a forced smile. "But I suppose I was trying to save your sorry hide from your more foolish maneuvers of attack."

"Hey, it was all Dominick's idea!" he protested.

His brother rolled his eyes with a groan. Some things *never* changed. "Seriously though," he said, "how *did* all of you get word of this so soon?"

"Chaolyn sent us out, while he went to fetch a doctor for Laelea," explained Inferno. "That dragon's as fierce as your grandfather when he wants something done." Sharing a grin with his friend, he clapped a hand on his shoulder. "Besides, that's what friends are for. Now, let's see to wrapping up the guards here, so we can deal with Dual and free Alarius."

With Buddy and Jarissa's threats to summon more allies

from the guardian spectrum to deal with the guards if they didn't surrender, the one problem was soon literally tied up, but leaving another in its wake.

"The door's locked," Psych informed the rest. "Anyone got a skeleton key?"

"But of course," said Jarissa, gesturing to the sky to materialize her trusty pitchfork. Pointing it at the door, she warned, "Stand back," moments before a heat ray shot from it, shattering the heavy wood into splinters.

"Nice trick," said Buddy, nodding. As she smiled, he continued, "Do you focus your temper into that thing to activate it?"

Her eyes narrowed, her smile becoming devious. "Why don't I let you judge for yourself?" she hissed, sending a beam zapping at his feet. While his boot began to smoke, along with his ensuing curses, Jarissa gestured to the open doorway. "All hotfoots take up the rear," she laughed.

As they entered, Buddy whispered to Inferno, "I'd like to kick her in her..."

"I get the idea," his friend interrupted, with a smile.

*****

There were fewer guards within, only sparking everyone's wary curiosity. It wasn't like Dual to make anything simple for his adversaries, but thus far, it had been just that. The going concern was that Alarius had already been killed, since Dual was ever unpredictable.

Fortunately, it was a voice within one door that convinced them otherwise.

"Your trusted friend has less than an hour remaining to come for you," it hissed. "Elsewise, your family will be mourning you tomorrow."

"Why that...!" began Jarissa, ready to barbecue this door as well.

"Wait," interrupted Buddy. "Why don't we try the more

reasonable approach? Observe." Knocking on the door casually, he gave a surprised look to the gaping faces surrounding him. "Well, it works for the traveling salesmen."

There was a muffled sound within, followed by a harsh set of curses, but no further reply. "Yes, but we're not selling anything," sighed Kiri, stepping forward, while gesturing for the women to join her.

Riff grabbed her arm. "Now what the hell are you doing?" he demanded.

"You had your chance," she replied, shrugging his hand away. "Now let us try it our way. Ladies?" Gesturing again to the pair beside her, the trio of females instantly kicked their booted heels into the door, opening it. "And *that's* how you get things done." Smirking at Riff, she strode in.

"Kiri, look out!" he yelled, moments before her head snapped about, in time to see an arrow plunge into her chest.

Letting out a pained gasp as she eyed the kneeling executioner still holding his crossbow, she sank unconscious to the floor, stopped only by Riff's arms catching her.

"Chavernos, no!" he shouted, all too aware of how the arrow protruded perilously close to her heart, as he lowered her carefully. Lifting his gaze to the man responsible, his eyes shot fire. "You're next," he said coldly.

"Fool!" snarled the masked executioner, standing slowly with deep laughter. "If you kill me, I'll be replaced by fifty others."

"Then we'll deal with them as we will you!" hissed Riff, hurling a concealed dagger like a spear at the man's chest.

It struck him dead-center, while his allies with crossbows made sure their aim was equally precise, changing the executioner's laugh into a gargle as he crumpled to the floor. Turning haunted eyes upon Kiri's pale face, while the others ran to aid Alarius, Riff touched her cheek.

"By Chavernos, Kiri, don't you leave me now," he

implored.

"She won't," assured Buddy, aided by Jarissa in removing the arrow as quickly yet smoothly as possible. Even so, Riff flinched when they did, noting that Kiri remained silent. Glancing up at his guardian companion, Buddy placed one hand over Kiri's wound, speaking somberly, "I may need your help."

"Already one step ahead of you," she replied, placing her hand over his. Nodding agreement, both shut their eyes to begin the healing process, while Riff clasped Kiri's lifeless hand with a silent prayer of his own.

"It looks like the executioner took the execution himself this time," said Inferno, shaking his head as he removed the dead man's mask. "But it certainly isn't Dual."

"So much for wishful thinking," said Dominick, removing the gag from Alarius, who immediately breathed easier. "We'll have you free in a minute, old friend," he said reassuringly, cutting the ropes free from the half-elf's arms and legs.

Due to the lack of food and water having weakened him considerably, Alarius slumped forward when no longer tied to the chair. Dominick, Inferno, and Psych caught him quickly.

"Thank you," he gasped. "Dual left awhile ago. Dominick... I must tell you where... He's going to... to..." A moment later, his head fell forward, unconscious.

Dominick's eyes narrowed fiercely. "Dual had best run for his life if he values it," he said, his gaze softening afterwards. "But for now, we need to get Alarius back to his wife." Glancing over to Riff, he prayed that Kiri too would be all right, for both their sakes.

As lights cascaded over the wound, Riff smoothed back Kiri's hair, pressing her hand against his heart. "Come back, sweetheart. You still have a lot of living to do here before departing from this plane." Not gaining any response, he shut his eyes and kissed her hand. "And I swear there won't be any other women, if you'll just open your eyes and wake up. Please, Kiri."

"Sounds pretty drastic to me," she whispered.

"Nothing's more drastic than you dying, and..." He abruptly stopped, opening his eyes to see her gazing weakly at him. "You're alive!"

"Yes, and you're getting tears all over me," she protested gently, though squeezing his hand which still held hers.

"Kiri, when that arrow struck you, it felt like it went through me as well," he said quietly. "I've never experienced anything like it."

"Definitely not the kind of experience I'd recommend repeating," she replied. He leaned his forehead against hers tenderly for long moments. "But as for that promise you intend to keep..."

"We'll discuss it later," he interrupted, reaching out to hug her. "Right now, I'm just glad you're all right."

Smiling against his shoulder, Kiri saw Jarissa mouthing something that looked like, *"You should have thought of this ages ago,"* confirmed by the clear thought in her head. As her friend added a wink, Kiri simply shut her eyes happily.

*****

When they returned to the palace, a doctor was already there to attend to Laelea, but took a quick break to make sure Kiri would be all right. It was obvious she would be though, as soon as she began arguing with Riff when he appreciatively noticed how pretty the doctor's female assistant was.

Ignoring the butler's usual protests, both Dominick and Riff then helped a newly revived Alarius into the palace. Even in his weakened state, the half-elf was alert instantly upon hearing an unexpectedly familiar cry.

"Laelea!" he shouted, trying to push free of the pair aiding him to head towards the next room. At the attempt, his legs started to go out from under him, but both brothers were ready at hand to help him to his destination.

"Alarius?" his wife queried, her eyes widening as he appeared in the doorway. "Thank the blessed stars, you're all right." In moments, he was beside her, clasping her hands with new worry creasing his brow.

"'Tis you I'm concerned for, love. The child's coming a mite early, is it not?"

"Aye," she said, her grip strengthening on his hand. "But at least you returned in time for it, safe and sound. That's all that matters for now." She cried out again as another pain lanced through her. "And in another minute, I believe our child will agree with me."

Not soon after, Laelea's words were proven, when with the encouragement and help of the others, their new daughter emerged into the world, screaming out in demonstration of her healthy half-elven lungs. The adults surrounding her could only smile and laugh in warm celebration of her birth.

As the infant was placed in her mother's tired arms, both she and the proud father lost their hearts to the tiny bundle, enwrapped in the ever awe-inspiring miracle of new life.

Turning to Chaos, who looked nearly as worn out as the child's mother, Dominick and Riff both bore proud smiles. "Got to hand it to you, Grandfather, you've certainly proven your ability to handle any crisis with a flourish," said Dominick. "This certainly wasn't on your typical island itinerary."

"When one needs to keep a cool head on one's shoulders, one does," Chaos replied curtly. "You'd both best remember that someday for your own benefit."

"Dom's right though," said Riff. "We're not usually present when the island's inhabitants add new additions."

"I was referring to needing the knowledge for your *own* future children!" barked Chaos, causing both men to turn away with innocent whistles. "Blazes, I only hope your future wives Julianna and Kiri can get through those stubborn minds of yours."

From Dream to Reality

When Riff began arguing that Kiri was by no means his future wife, contrary to Chaos's machinations along those lines, they carried the debate outside, while the butler mentioned something to Dominick. Grinning, he walked over to the new parents again.

"I have good news. Chaolyn's just returned to inform us that Daric is undergoing the necessary medical procedure as we speak," he said, earning relieved looks from them.

"I just hope he'll be all right," murmured Alarius.

Laelea squeezed his hand reassuringly. "He's strong like his father. He'll survive as surely as you always have."

"Aye, and as you have as well," he said, shaking his head to dispel any negative thoughts, turning to Dominick. "In the meantime though, there's the matter of the offer Laelea says you made earlier. And while the both of us surely appreciate it, we cannot accept..."

"Alarius..." interjected Laelea, tugging at his arm. He warded this away to continue.

"Furthermore, as things stand, we believe the treasures when recovered should be returned to you, in payment for all you've done."

Dominick quirked one eyebrow up. "Payment?" he laughed. "After your clever assistance got us out of many disputes over the years?" Clasping a hand on his shoulder, he continued, "If anyone owes a debt around here, it's mine to repay. And with all the unforeseen trouble I've caused, I believe it's only justified that you be granted a respite here until we can see to granting your family a more suitable home."

"If you still feel doubtful," he added, "we can always use an extra loyal hand at taking care of the island, and Chaos can surely find steady work for you here, for as long as you wish it."

Laelea smiled up at her husband's softened expression, knowing what Dominick's words meant to him.

"I know not what to say," Alarius said finally.

"Then say you'll join us here," replied Dominick, holding out his hand. The half-elf shook it with a broad smile, all thoughts of debts erased in an instant.

"We'll do that," he agreed.

"Splendid," Laelea said brightly, earning a gurgle from their new daughter. This prompted her to contemplate an undecided matter. "Now that you've both set your male pride to rest, I would think our daughter is curious as to what her new name will be."

Both men laughed. "I must admit my thoughts haven't been solely dedicated to that subject recently," said Alarius. "My head's still reeling from the abuse it took over the past few days. I hope you might have a possibility in mind."

"As a matter of fact, I debated it while Chaos informed me of our friend's dream companion. Dominick, you never told us you planned to marry in the near future."

"I preferred to wait until my bride-to-be is here on Chavernus," he explained. "But what has this to do with your daughter?"

Glancing down at her, Laelea smiled. "I asked Chaos who your dream companion was, and once he told me, I decided that if my husband agreed, I should like to name our child after her, if it was a girl. And seeing as she is..." Turning to Alarius, she asked, "Would you mind if we called her Julianna?"

Her husband nodded. "A beautiful name indeed for our precious one."

Rendered nearly speechless, Dominick smiled as well. "I'm certain my own Julianna will be most pleased, and more than honored to meet her namesake one day."

"By all means, we'll look forward to meeting her as well," replied Laelea.

None of them noticed Sionne, who had remained hidden outside the door, listening to all that was said. Her eavesdropping didn't go unnoticed for long.

"Why a crease in such a fair complexion?" asked a voice. Turning with a gasp, she exhaled a sigh of relief. "Quell," she murmured. "I'm glad it's you." Casting a glare towards those in the other room, she asked, "Did you hear all that's been said about that Julianna witch?" He nodded. "Then you know my feelings. How dare they treat that dream tramp as if she's royalty!" she snapped.

"Sionne," he began, "have you ever considered that maybe Dominick's not worth the money and the title which you seek? For he surely isn't in love with you while that other woman exists in his life."

A sly look crossed her features in remembrance of a secret discussion she'd had with Sireni's companion Dual. He'd been most sympathetic to her plight regarding Dominick's dream lover, and promised that this night she'd pay for her interference to Sionne's happiness.

"I wouldn't worry about that much longer," she replied, heading from the castle. "Not after tonight." Though he didn't know what she was referring to, Quell followed after her, somberly wishing she'd give up her determined scheming.

During this time though, as Dominick told Laelea more of Julianna, a sudden dark thought filled Alarius's own mind. Something he'd forgotten.

"By Chavernos... Dual!" he shouted, startling both, and causing Dominick's cheerful expression to change instantly into concern.

"He'll be dealt with later," he said with forced quiet.

"No, you don't understand!" Alarius interjected. "When I was being held by him earlier, I remember him saying that he was using me as a diversion to keep you from your future wife in the dream realm."

His friend's face drained of color. "No..."

Alarius bit his lip. "At the same time, he made it quite clear what he planned to do, since one of his allies managed to locate her for him. He was merely waiting for sunset to go after her."

"***Damn his soul!***" shouted Dominick, racing into a secluded room to concentrate on sending out. A minute later, his brother joined him, locking the door and earning his anger. "Not now, Riff!" he hissed. "Julianna needs me!"

"I heard the end of your conversation, just before you left, and I told Chaos to let no one interfere with us, since two dreamphasers are better equipped to handle that demon," said Riff, his own expression somber. "Besides, I owe her one for that misunderstanding before."

Dominick took only moments to consider this. "All right," he agreed. "I just hope I can trust you for once."

"Hey, are you kidding?" he laughed. "The Chavernos Cavalry is on patrol!"

Nodding quickly, Dominick shut his eyes. The sun had set awhile ago, but Julianna had sometimes stayed up late in the past. Hopefully, tonight was one of those evenings.

*****

Something's wrong, Julianna decided, having difficulty pushing her way through a score of tangled vines.

Originally having waited quite some time for Dominick in the castle, she finally decided to search for him around the castle's perimeter. When that too failed to reveal his presence, she went deeper into the forest, only to find endless rows of these hindering vines. In fact, considering some seemed to spring up from where she'd just come from, it only fueled her confusion.

"Dominick!" she called out, still gaining no response. *He'd better have a good excuse for being late*, she thought, just before it struck her that he might be sick. Sympathetically, she hoped not.

"Just who the devil is this Dominick?" asked a voice behind her.

Whipping around, Julianna felt her breath catch. "Roger?" she gasped uncertainly. "What are *you* doing here?"

Dual smiled from beneath his façade. It had been all too easy to read her thoughts to find out about Dominick's rival, and even easier to transform into his likeness. What better way to confuse his betrothed?

At his silence, Julianna's eyes narrowed. "Oh, I get it," she murmured, her voice rising with anger. "And I'll tell you, Dominick, this isn't one of your more amusing jokes! Just because I let you get away with some of them, don't think I'll put up with *anything*."

Roger's expression darkened, as he strode forward purposefully. "Dammit, Julianna, I've had enough of this foolishness of yours! What will it take to get through to you that your supposed Dominick is merely a dream?"

Further confused, she backed up warily. Whoever this might be, it certainly wasn't her dream companion. Had she conjured him up over some misguided thoughts of Roger?

"Who's to say you're any more real than he is?" she retorted, eyeing the vines surreptitiously for an escape route.

"Damn you, I will *not* put up with your imaginary men anymore!" he shouted in reply. "I'm as real as you are, sweetheart, and if it's proof you need, I'll more than gladly give it to you."

"Look, Roger, if you'll calm down, maybe we can... ouch!" She tripped forward, clasping her ankle. "Oh, now what I done?" she lamented. As expected, he bent closer, giving her the perfect opportunity to connect her 'injured' foot with Roger's stomach.

Not looking back, despite his low groans, Julianna took a way out she'd spotted, doing her best to push past newer vines that abruptly sprang up before her. Hearing Roger's mocking laughter as he apparently recovered, she thought quickly. A faster means of travel would help. Or maybe...

In moments, a large knife materialized in her hand, allowing her the freedom to slice away at the vines, slashing a path through them easily. Even so, the fact that she was becoming more lost with every step wasn't doing her much good.

"Looking for a way out?" taunted Roger's voice, sounding like he was directly behind her.

Not having much experience with teleporting, Julianna knew it to be her last viable option, shutting her eyes in silent concentration. Feeling wind sweep up around her filled her heart with hope. It was working!

Moments later, she found herself once again within the castle, racing upstairs to the bedroom, and slamming the door shut behind her. Even for a dream, she was breathing heavily, yet inwardly thankful to be safe once more. Pressing her ear against the door, she could only hope the Roger lookalike hadn't followed.

"That anxious to see me, sweetheart?"

Upon hearing the familiar voice of her beloved, Julianna turned immediately to rush into his arms, burying her head against his shoulder.

"Dominick, thank heaven it's you."

"Well, who else would it be?" he chuckled, patting her back.

Clutching him tightly, she shut her eyes in remembrance. "Before I came here, I ran into Roger." Feeling him stiffen, she added quickly, "It wasn't intentional. In fact, shortly afterwards, he started chasing after me through endless vines. I know it couldn't be the Roger from my world, but he still scared me. If I hadn't teleported here to safety... oh, Dominick, I can't thank you enough for showing me how."

"My pleasure," he said, hugging her tighter as his eyes glittered. "I'm sorry you had to deal with that, Julianna," he continued, "but you see, occasionally even a dreamphaser can't completely prevent a nightmare from taking hold."

Remembering several other occasions of when this had happened, namely the spaceship and the story monster, Julianna could only nod against him. Yet still, a thought nagged at her. "You weren't here when I arrived," she told him. "Where were you all this time?"

"I was unavoidably detained on the island," he replied. "But as soon as I got here a few minutes ago, I began searching the other castle rooms for you. If I hadn't found you in another minute, I'd have continued the search outside."

"In another minute, that Roger imposter would have caught me," she retorted, her voice catching. At the pained look in his expression, she relented. "I'm sorry, Dominick. I know it wasn't your fault. But still, what if he somehow follows me here?"

"Shhh... hush, my jewel," he whispered reassuringly, his hands stroking down her back before pulling her closer. "You're safe with me now. That other one won't disturb us anymore tonight."

"How can you be sure he won't?"

He silenced her protests with his mouth, kissing her until she slowly relaxed completely in his arms. Picking her up, he brought her over to the bed, resting her upon the covers only seconds before climbing in beside her, as if not wanting to part from her for even a moment.

Julianna was surprised by the unusually savage demanding nature of his kisses, but could only assume it stemmed from what she'd told him of Roger. Clinging to him as he moved atop her, his hands trailed along her soft curves, all the while never relenting from his kisses. Left breathless, she wanted to gently tell him so, but wasn't given the chance as he tugged her leg about his waist, pressing their bodies closer together.

Equally unprepared for the rough caresses of his hands through the soft fabric of her outfit, Julianna cried out sharply in pain at one point, pushing against him until he did back off.

"Dominick, you're hurting me!" she protested, breathing heavily while ignoring his puzzled look.

Touching her cheek softly, he shook his head with a smile. "I'm sorry, Julie," he chuckled in apology, not noticing the way her expression suddenly changed at his unusual usage of her shortened name. Continuing to stroke her, he kissed her again. "It's just that you're such a tempting morsel, I sometimes lose control. Come... let's resume where we left off, my sweet wench."

A tempting morsel? Had she heard him correctly? And his sweet *wench*? Dominick knew how much she hated that appellation. Suspiciously, she pushed him away again, clasping his face in her hands.

"Are you drunk?" she asked quietly.

Mirthfully, he brushed her hands aside. "Of course not," he replied, resting his hand at her waist. "I've no need of alcohol while I have you to keep me warm. Why would you say such a thing?"

"I... I don't know. You're just acting peculiar."

Her blood froze as she faced him again, seeing something she'd missed. It was his eyes... they weren't the warm blue that captivated her, but instead, an unfamiliar darker gray. This wasn't Dominick at all!

Steeling her expression to appear oblivious to this, she gave a smile, moving away from him carefully. "You know, Dominick, I wasn't feeling too well earlier, and it hasn't gotten any better now. I think maybe we should simply call it a night, and try this again tomorrow instead."

Edging closer to her to draw one finger along her back, he gave a short laugh, while she couldn't hide a shiver. "You've picked an unusual time to play the shy flower, my love. There wouldn't be any... *other* reasons why you're not in the mood, would there?"

"Of course not," she said, a bit shakily. "I'm just tired, that's all."

Without answering, his palm rested against her neck, moments before he took hold of the back of her dress, pulling her backwards sharply. Through a choked gasp, she glanced up to find him poised above her again, his gray eyes filled with an unreadable expression.

"Dominick... what are you doing?" she whispered.

His smile intensified into something akin to cruelty. "The same thing we always do obviously," he replied with a husky laugh, silencing her with a forceful kiss.

Unable to free herself any other way, Julianna reached forward to grab a handful of his hair, tugging hard until he pulled back with a low cry. Sliding out from beneath him, she jumped from the bed and raced from the room.

Running down the hall, Julianna only reached the upstairs rail by the staircase before the imposter Dominick grabbed her from behind to slam her back against the rail painfully. Crying out, she stole a glance over the edge, the distant floor below seeming much further away.

"It's a long way down," the imposter murmured close to her cheek. "Especially if an unfortunate damsel was to fall from here... headfirst." Pressing her backwards, so her waist leaned against the rail precariously, fear took hold.

"Don't!" Julianna cried out. His ensuing laughter only kindled rage within her. Glaring at him with hatred, one thought of who this might be came to the surface. "Damn you, Riff! You've had your fun... now let go of me!" As he only looked more amused, she inwardly chided herself upon remembering something else. Riff had green eyes, not gray. Not to mention, Riff had never threatened her life, and somehow, she knew he'd never hurt her. But then who short of the devil was this?

"Many have labeled me the devil, sweet thing," said the imposter, "and you're obviously not so well versed in the dream-state to know how easily minds can be read. Otherwise, you'd know exactly when I realized you'd caught on to my deception as your betrothed. But if you want to know who I *really* am, then allow me to show you."

The likeness of Dominick melted away, revealing a less welcome face... Roger's. "You see, my dear. That man chasing you earlier was none other than me."

"That may have been you, but you still can't be the real Roger, since he's no dreamphaser. So who *are* you?"

His eyes grew cold. "Someone out of your worst nightmares," he replied, his hold tightening on her as he pressed his mouth against hers. Feeling waves of revulsion course through her, Julianna lashed out in the only way she could... biting him. "Ouch!" he snarled, moments before pulling away to rub his wounded mouth. Seeing the defiant vengeful look in her eyes, Dual's own expression darkened as he slapped her face hard. "Witch!" he hissed.

"Bastard!" she retorted, kicking him. As she struggled to free herself, he recovered swiftly, keeping a tight hold on her to prevent her escape.

"Fine, let's end the façade, shall we?" His grin resembling that of a demon, as indeed he partly was, Dual dropped his illusion of Roger to reveal his true self, startling Julianna anew.

"You're the man from the engagement party," she realized. Once again, she noticed the resemblance between him and Buddy.

"I'm no angel," he said darkly, reading her thoughts.

"But you said you know Dominick."

"Oh, I do. But I never said he was my friend. Quite the contrary actually, which is why I came to visit you." She tried again to escape, but his hold was tighter. "There's no need to rush off," he insisted, running a finger along her neck. "You know, this isn't the way I want it, of course. I'd much prefer to continue our pleasant loveplay of earlier, if you'd but say the word."

"Burn in flames!" she spat. "I'd sooner break my neck than be touched by your slime!"

He smiled malevolently. "That can be arranged." Clasping one hand about her neck, he pushed her further over the rail, so her feet left the floor. She gasped sharply, trying desperately to concentrate enough to teleport free of her predicament. To her chagrin, it didn't work. "Think your weak mind can match the strength of mine?" he asked. "No, dear wench, you can't escape that easily. If you fall from here, I guarantee it will be both hard and painful." His eyes narrowed. "But I tire of this game. Either submit, or go over the side headfirst. Choose."

Julianna wouldn't reply, still attempting to break free.

"Hmmm, since you're so reluctant to choose, maybe I'll do both. It could be most satisfying to render you helpless before taking you."

Screaming as he lowered her another several inches, a voice suddenly called out, "I wouldn't, if I were you!"

Dual's head whipped to his left, seeing Riff standing a few feet away with a sword. His irritated look became amusement once more. "Well, well, if it isn't little brother's antagonist himself. Why the scowl? Since you enjoy sharing his women as well, surely we can take turns with this one tonight."

"Wrong!" snapped Riff. "*This* one is under our mutual protection."

"Why, Riff, I didn't know you had it in you. Does Kiri know of your threesome?"

Reminded of Dual's machinations which had nearly killed Kiri, his expression darkened even more. "Let her go, Dual," he hissed in reply. "She's done nothing to earn your venom."

"Venom?" chortled the assassin. "Interest is more it."

"Release her!"

"Oh, very well," he sighed, casting a sympathetic look at Julianna. Her tear-filled eyes clamped shut as he caressed her cheek regretfully with his free hand. "A disagreeable lout, isn't he? Most unfortunate for you."

Giving her a slight push as he released her neck, he grinned as Riff rushed forward too late to correct his error. She fell with a scream.

Darkness started to close in on her, just before a sharp jolt jarred her senses. Yet not the bone-crushing type she'd anticipated, but instead the immediate encompassment of warmth.

"I told you I'd protect you if you ever fell," murmured a familiar voice.

"Dominick," she breathed, as her eyes flew open. He smiled, but before he could reply, he found her staring at him most strangely. She smiled back upon finding the answer she sought. "Blue eyes..." she whispered, clinging to him fiercely. "Thank heaven, it *is* you."

Perplexed by her cryptic words, he asked, "Was there ever any doubt?"

She nodded quickly, pointing upwards. "That other one... he made himself look like you, and..."

Before she could speak another word, Dominick set her on her feet and raced up the stairs. "By Chaos, Dual, I'll toss your bones to the hellhounds of Chavernos!"

"Meaningless promises," responded Dual, while keeping Riff at bay with his own sword. Raising one hand, he rose up towards the ceiling, transforming into a black dragon. Facing Dominick with red eyes, his voice deepened with a rumble. *"Your interference this night will cost you, my enemy,"* he hissed. *"Mark my words, you'll pay for it."* Glancing down at Julianna, his grin became menacing. *"As for you, fair beauty, we'll meet again soon. And when we do, things will most certainly heat up between us.*"

Shooting a silver flame at her, she tried to dodge the blast, but it came too quickly, consuming her as the force of it pressed her against the floor.

Just as quickly, Dominick and Riff cast ice blue beams in her direction, melting the inferno instantly. When she looked up to face them, there was no trace of burns upon her.

"You're outnumbered, Dual," Riff stated evenly. "Best leave now while you still can."

"*Empty threats,*" spat the dark dreamphaser, disappearing in a black fog to swoop down.

Julianna immediately stood to run for the staircase, but only got a few feet before she found her throat constricted by an enormous black snake. Unable to scream, she scraped her nails against the tightening coil in an attempt to free herself, but the snake only squeezed tighter, turning her face an ashen color. Reduced to a whimper, she stared into the threatening reptilian eyes and shook uncontrollably.

"Well now, pretty ssssiren," hissed Dual, "let's ssssee how quickly your neck can be ssssnapped in two."

"Yours will be severed instead!" yelled Dominick, raising a sword from behind to slash it down towards his head.

Dual quickly vanished, giving the dreamphaser only a split second to stop from accidentally striking Julianna. Dropping the sword with a loud clatter to pull her sobbing form close, he glanced up in time to see an unidentifiable winged creature hovering over them.

Amidst eerie laughter, the creature called out, "Consider yourself lucky this night, dreamphaser. The true nightmare is just beginning for you and your lover!"

"It'll be your own, if you ever return!" snarled Dominick, answered by more of Dual's amused laughter.

That was all Riff was waiting for.

From the staircase, he let loose a shot from a crossbow.

The arrow pierced Dual's form dead center in the back, bringing forth a roar of pained rage from him. Turning to face Riff, he bit out, "You'll pay for that last insult!" A moment later, his form evaporated before everyone's eyes.

"Egotistical bastard," said Riff.

Returning his gaze to Julianna, Dominick spoke soothingly as he held her. "It's all right, love. The danger's passed."

"Yes," she said, "but for how long?" He shushed her gently, but she refused to let it go. "Dominick, who *was* that Dual? You and Riff obviously know him."

All too well, he thought.

Still, he didn't want to distress her further with the details tonight. "I'll explain it all to you tomorrow when we have more time," he assured her.

"Dual's the scum of Chavernos, end of story," replied Riff, startling Julianna as he appeared behind her.

Gripping her chest, she inhaled sharply. "I don't think I'll ever get used to your methods of teleportation," she said, "but thank you both." Reaching out, she hugged Riff too, just before Dominick told her briefly of where he'd been that night. "Then Alarius is all right?"

"Alive and well to be present at his new daughter's birth," Dominick agreed, squeezing her hand. "They named her after you."

Surprised, she shook her head. "But they don't even know me. Why would they?"

"They know enough, and will certainly meet you one day in the future." Seeing things misting over, he raised an eyebrow knowingly, before hugging her one last time. "I promise I'll make this up to you tomorrow, love," he murmured. "No power on Chavernos will keep me away then."

Julianna said nothing more as the dream faded into reality. Sitting up in bed, she clutched the blanket to her.

From Dream to Reality

"Unless that Dual shows up again," she sighed, brushing a hand across her eyes.

She just missed noticing the blink of light, which had paused to overhear her last words before vanishing into the concealing sunlight.

Chapter Three

"You really got Almira steamed over yesterday," said Marybeth, not stifling a laugh. "I haven't heard language like that with some of the men I've dated in the past."

Julianna nodded, toying with the pencil she was sketching with. "I wouldn't worry about it," she replied. "After all, I've never heard of stomach pains being a fireable offense. Besides, considering how highly she regards 'Mr. Collins', deep down I'm sure she's just as glad I stood him up at the table."

"Speaking of Mr. Collins, has Roger the Renegade shown up again at our happy business domicile yet?"

"Not that I know of, but I'm sure the guard dogs will start barking when he does. Or should I say, Almira?"

"Rather harsh treatment for a renegade, ladies."

Both whipped about to find Roger standing a few feet away, arms folded. Julianna cast him a meaningful look. "If you don't like the way we do business, feel free to leave, Mr. Collins."

"Not likely, **Miss** Sherborne," he retorted, doing a double take upon seeing the paper on her desk. "Now what are you up to? Plotting a grievance letter against me?"

"A letter like that would take a week, and I have better things to do with my life."

Glancing over her shoulder, Roger's expression changed from curiosity into irritation upon seeing her sketch. "Do I even need to ask who **this** is a portrait of?"

"You can ask, but I don't have to tell you," Julianna replied.

"So when do I get a chance to meet this Dominick who

seems to have captured your thoughts?" he inquired.

"And me too," added Marybeth. "After all, if he has a cute brother, maybe..."

Julianna's blood went cold at their words, but she managed to keep her composure. "That'll have to wait, since Dominick's out of town for a while," she replied finally. *Out of this world more accurately!* "As for his brother," she told Marybeth, "he's interesting, but not quite what you'd expect. And he does have a girlfriend of sorts anyway. You'd do best to stick with your current boyfriend."

"I suppose so," she sighed. "Just a thought. Oh, by the way, Julie, what time should I pick you up tonight, so we can check out that club I told you about?"

Seeing her attention diverted back to her drawing, Roger backed off, but not before overhearing the details of where Julianna and Marybeth were going tonight. After having taken a bit of ribbing from the boys back at his office over her skipping out on him during lunch yesterday, he'd been only too eager to correct the matter today.

And now with this Dominick of hers conveniently out of town for now, there wouldn't be a better opportunity to start rekindling their former relationship. After all, why shouldn't absence—**Dominick's** absence—make Julianna's heart grow fonder, though not for her missing companion.

With newfound determination, his mind began planning the evening ahead.

*****

Beneath the evening sky of Chavernos, the crowd surrounding the bonfire cheered along with their clapping in rhythm to the music, while the women dancing to it twirled their colorful sashes in perfect accordance with each other. Kiri, Jarissa, and Psych applauded with the crowd, just before seeing how observant their companions were.

It was only when the men started whistling at the

dancers, earning appreciative smiles from them, that the silent gals finally found their tongues to interrupt.

Needless to say, the ensuing mayhem brought amused laughter from the crowd.

Sionne, however, kept her thoughts on other matters. Mainly, how to steer one certain man's attention away from his dream woman from another world.

Dual certainly hadn't been any help last night! she thought angrily. All he'd done was push Julianna into Dominick's arms even more than before. If only those half-elves had kept their noses out of the situation, maybe Dual's ploy would have worked; but alas, it hadn't.

Now, it was all up to her once more.

Turning to Dominick as he sat beside her, he looked as distracted as he'd been all day. No doubt thinking of his red-haired harlot! One look at Chaos, who was gleefully enjoying the festivities, indicated just how far the Earth woman had interfered. He'd just told Sionne earlier that since things with Dominick hadn't worked out, he'd find another way to compensate her for this.

Compensate her! her thoughts echoed. A good ruler he might be, but his tact often fell short of the mark. It had taken all of her careful training to steel her expression to remain civil. She could all but see the images of future great-grandchildren dancing in his eyes, but those of Dominick and Julianna instead.

Chaos was in for a surprise if he thought she'd bow out gracefully though. She intended to fight with whatever means necessary to bind Dominick to her instead, and tonight seemed the best time to do just that.

"Aren't you going to eat something, Dominick?" she asked sweetly, hoping to shake the vacant look from him. When he failed to respond, she waved a hand in front of his eyes, the twinkle of her blue star ring catching his attention.

He shook his head, forcing a weak smile. "No thanks,

Sionne. I'm really not hungry now."

Tact, she reminded herself. After all, their brief argument earlier hadn't helped. "Dominick, I've been meaning to talk with you about yesterday. I didn't mean to start a fight between us."

"Forget it, Sionne," he sighed. "Things have a been a little crazy for all of us these days. And incidentally, I do apologize for that crack I made the other day about my reference to you and my grandfather. You're a very beautiful woman who could surely catch any man's eyes."

Sionne beamed. This was certainly a turn in the right direction from him! "Even yours?" she asked softly.

Dominick clasped her hand. "Mine are elsewhere," he replied meaningfully. "However, I know that when you find the right one out there, he'll be able to appreciate you far better than I ever could."

Her cheek twitched, but she maintained her smile. "I've found the right one already," she decided, squeezing his hand.

His eyes dimmed. "Sionne, don't..."

"You just haven't considered things enough," she continued. "If you'd give us half a chance, you'd see how right we are for one another."

"Sionne, listen to me. If there's one thing I've learned over the years, it's that a person can't force love to exist in another's heart. It's either there, or it isn't. I couldn't condemn either of us to a marriage which would end up making us both suffer."

"But, Dominick..."

"Look, not to interrupt you, Sionne, but these loud festivities have given me a headache. I think I'd rather be by myself for a while right now."

"But..."

"Please, Sionne," he added with finality, rubbing his temples. "We can talk later if there's something else you need to tell me. Good night."

"Dom?" questioned Buddy, just before his friend vanished in the direction of the palace stables. Having witnessed this, along with Sionne's disheartened response, Chaos relinquished his drink to follow after him silently.

As both walked off, Sionne nearly stamped her foot in frustration, having lost her own appetite now. How in blazes was she ever going to get that stubborn man's attention? He was being surprisingly difficult, considering his future wife wasn't here to fulfill his physical needs, but still, sooner or later he'd come around. A man like Dominick wasn't bound to remain celibate forever in reality.

From where he watched in the shadows, Quell fairly gnashed his own teeth at the sight of Sionne lost in her scheming again. Considering his own feelings for the spirited woman, he was ever annoyed at relinquishing her to the ignorant man who'd walked off alone.

Despite his chosen profession as an assassin, Quell had certainly once cared deeply about his sister when she was alive, and thus could appreciate not wanting to hurt someone one loved. So he did have some modicum of understanding in Dominick's point of not wanting to betray his future wife.

But Sionne was more the issue here. What would it take to stop her foolish infatuation with the man? If it was indeed infatuation. For all Sionne's beauty, there indeed lurked a calculating mind beneath it. It could very well be that she was chasing a title and gold instead.

And if that chase ended unsuccessfully?

Perhaps sooner than later, she might need someone to turn to, he considered, smiling at the prospect. Not to mention, his hidden share of the treasures would satisfy her craving for money. Maybe tonight, he should play this trump card and go for broke. After all, if Dominick wasn't interested in Sionne, she should know that someone else close to her felt otherwise.

From Dream to Reality

With a nod, he disappeared into the darkness again.

*****

In the stables, as soon as Dominick came into view of a particular black stallion, the horse tossed its head with a welcoming neigh. "I know, Windrider," he chuckled, patting his neck. "A beautiful evening like this is meant for soaring with the wind, not sitting idle at festivities." Windrider snorted once as he took care of the saddle.

"He seems to agree with you, lad," laughed the older stable hand behind him.

A man with the ability to travel vast distances on foot with amazing speed, Traverse had traveled widely across Chavernos, being equally famous for his tales brought back. Tales that he'd often told Dominick and Riff as children, earning their longstanding friendship. Due to his love of horses, he'd easily become the head trainer in the palace stables, and had once taught both how to ride long ago.

"Will you be gone long?" he asked.

"Maybe," replied Dominick. "But you don't have to wait up, Traverse. I'll take care of Windrider later. In the meantime, why don't you go join the others at the bonfire? I'm sure they could use their favorite storyteller there."

"I just might do that."

"Oh, but before you go, have you received word on the subject we discussed a few days ago?"

Traverse instantly brightened. "I was hoping to have the chance to tell you. She arrived yesterday."

"Wonderful," Dominick replied, following him to a farther corner of the stable. Upon seeing them approach, a pure white mare with a silver-gold mane stepped closer to the stall gate before her.

"She's a beauty, isn't she, lad?"

"Yes," he said appreciatively, reaching one hand beneath her chin. The mare nuzzled it tentatively with a soft whinny.

"She's exactly what I was looking for. Does she have a name?"

"Aye, it's Starbeam." *Perfect*, Dominick thought, before Traverse continued. "She's as gentle as you please, and will no doubt be perfect for your lady."

"I'm sure Julianna will be pleased with her when she arrives," he agreed, flashing Traverse a smile.

"Really?" Chaos inquired, gaining their attention. "For one who told me not to assume anything regarding her arrival here, you seem unusually prepared."

His sarcasm couldn't dim Dominick's spirits. "You'll have to forgive me, Grandfather," he chuckled. "I just wanted to prepare a special gift in advance for my future bride-to-be. What do you think of her?"

Glancing at Starbeam, Chaos nodded. "The mare is splendid. But perhaps you should have heeded your own words before and waited on bringing her here."

Clasping his shoulder, Dominick grinned. "Best be more positive, Grandfather. Remember, the sooner Julianna gets here, the sooner we can see to those great-grandkids you want so badly." Mollifying Chaos long enough to escape via Windrider, neither man noticed the two blonde-haired females hiding nearby.

"This situation is getting serious," murmured Sireni. "If you wish to marry him before that Julianna sinks her hooks into him, you may need magic to lure him to it."

Irritated, Sionne's eyes narrowed. "With the assets I have, I don't need to use my powers to outdo a red-headed witch from another world!" she snapped.

"I'd think twice on that if I were you, dear sister," replied Sireni. "He's already spurned you several times by normal tactics. It seems logical that the time for pretty words is over, and action is called for."

Sionne sensed the truth in her words as she glanced over her shoulder, silently watching as Dominick and his steed disappeared from view.

*****

As Dominick rode towards the beach, the familiar sound of wings drew his attention. Glancing up, he gave a quick wave to the blue dragon hovering above.

"Why is it you always prefer riding those grounded creatures when you can soar to the stars with us?" asked Roderlin, clicking his tongue.

Obviously irritated, Windrider cast his dark head up to the sky with an angry snort. Dominick patted his neck once. "Sometimes I prefer to remain where the ground's a comforting surety," he replied. "I don't imagine you fancy being up there when hurricanes brew."

"Maybe not," said the dragon, *"but there's certainly no storm brewing tonight."* Eyeing his friend knowingly, he added, *"Except, I would imagine, for the storm raging inside you over your distant maiden."*

Dominick's levity faded. "A matter which remains unsettled, but which shall be remedied as soon as possible."

Cocking his head to one side, Roderlin cast him a curious eye. *"Why do you linger here when you can go visit her?"*

"It's too soon. Besides, I have other things on my mind."

"Like wanting to beat a certain dark-haired dreamphaser senseless?" inquired Roderlin. Dominick's expression spoke volumes. *"I would gladly set my talons upon him to dispel the son of a demon, but I'm afraid he has a great many followers, and you know what happens when one of their own is killed."*

"They send dozens in revenge," agreed Dominick. "Point taken, although not a satisfying one."

Roderlin nodded. *"Alysadaria is awaiting me elsewhere, but we'll drop by again soon to see you. In the meantime, are you sure I can't tempt you away from your stallion for a quick flight?"*

"Thanks, but not tonight, Roderlin," he said quietly. "Tell 'Lysa I said hello."

"I'll do that," replied the dragon, clicking his tongue again. *"Say, how many miles to the hoof does that thing cover?"*

This time, Windrider gave an angry whinny, only gaining laughter from Roderlin as he vanished towards the horizon. Dominick smiled after him, wondering if the dragon would ever stop irking his intelligent steed. Probably not. But if a magic spell could grant Windrider a human's speech, that might even the odds somewhat.

Something he'd have to keep in mind for future reference.

Shortly after securing Windrider nearby, Dominick strode along the beach. Watching the darkening night set in, he reclined upon the sand, his mood oddly somber. He knew that he'd be with Julianna soon, which should have comforted him, but still... moments like this brought to light the all too pressing distance separating them. Was it asking that much to wish reality wasn't so cruel as to keep his intended wife from his arms?

Leaning back against one arm, Dominick began to drift into a pleasant relaxed state. Although he wouldn't go to find Julianna just yet, he couldn't help conjuring up images of her in his mind. Images with memories which became more and more vivid.

He was holding his arms out to her, while she ran to him with laughter... they embraced with kisses filled with desire... they were entwined together on the soft sand as passion consumed them...

Her kisses became stronger still, as she climbed over him, pressing closer as she wrapped her arms about his neck.

"Julianna..." he murmured, eyes still closed as he felt her gentle hands loosen his shirt, exposing his chest to the salty sea air, before she ran her hands across it.

"Dominick," came the soft whisper of a familiar voice. Against his closed eyes, he could feel the still gentler presence of a pair of hands touching his face. *Ah, Julianna*, he thought, lost in his musings for long moments before the truth hit him.

He *was* still in reality!

So what in blazes was affecting his mind so to believe otherwise? *Sionne*, his thoughts concluded, starting instantly as he sat up, shrugging away the intruding hands. "Look, Sionne, you know how I feel about Julianna, so why don't you just..."

"Dominick, for heaven's sake, after all this time, don't you know me?"

As his eyes focused, his face paled and his mouth dropped open. Sitting beside him, amidst bubbling laughter at his bemused expression, was Julianna. There was no mistaking the reddish-brown curls that played about her, nor the adoring eyes that had captivated him so easily from the start, and especially not her teasing voice.

He couldn't even move as she edged closer. Tentatively he raised his own trembling hands to touch her waist. Moments later, his grip tightened, and a thankful smile of wonder creased his expression.

"You're real," he said, moving one hand up to caress her cheek. She smiled at his touch, fairly purring in delight.

"As much as you are now, my Dominick," she replied softly, leaning closer to kiss him lightly on the mouth. Slowly, he responded, yet even as he did, he sensed something wasn't right here. She was soft as ever, and nonetheless enticing, yet...

His mouth moved away from hers, despite the fact that she continued kissing him. "This is impossible," he whispered, shaking his head slowly. "We don't have the means of teleportation yet."

"I found another way to reach you, my love," she told him. "But let's not speak of that now. All that matters is that we're finally together."

She was about to kiss him again, but Dominick remained hesitant. While his body raged against his stubborn mind for not catering to its desires, his gaze was unendingly drawn to Julianna, his thoughts flashing back to the many times he'd been with her like this. Her love, her laughter, her blue star ring...

Her blue star ring? he thought with alarm.

That certainly didn't belong to his future wife, but he *did* know who the true owner was.

Abruptly he stiffened, reaching up to clasp her wrists tightly while wrenching her back from him to stare deeply into her suddenly bewildered eyes. "Dominick, you look at me so strangely."

"*Do* I now, love?" he hissed, his grip tightening even more on the hand bearing the ring. Pulling it forward, he held it in front of her eyes. "Since when did I give you *Sionne's* ring, my dear deceiver?"

Totally at a loss, she blinked rapidly, fighting for her voice. "Dominick, I don't know how it got there. I just..."

"*You* know, Sionne!" he exclaimed, shaking her once. "Damn it all, woman, haven't I made my feelings clear to you by now? I don't know how you managed to imitate her voice, let alone learn of her appearance as you have, but it doesn't matter. Your illusion magic can't change the truth. I love my true fiancée completely, and nothing... *nothing* will ever change that."

"Please, Dominick, if that's the way you want it, I won't ask you to. Just grant me one night first."

"One night!" he scoffed. "I see your mind's workings too clearly. Time enough to make it possible for you to get pregnant with my child, and then demand that I marry *you* instead of the woman I love. I think not, Sionne. Because I will *never* betray her with another woman. Not you; not anyone."

"Haven't I proven I can be just as pleasing as she can?" she insisted. "I made you forget once, and I surely can again!" Emphasizing this with a kiss, her appearance temporarily disoriented him, but his resolve remained firm.

Unwilling to betray his Julianna, Dominick pushed her back to stand, brushing a hand across his mouth to erase the telltale lipstick from it.

"It's apparent I can't reason with you anymore, Sionne," he said with forced calm. "And given your unwillingness to accept the circumstances, I think the only solution is obvious. You'd best get your things together and move out of the palace."

She hadn't expected *that* response. "Move out?" she gasped, her illusion fading to reveal her genuine shock. "You're throwing me out of the home I grew up in?"

"You aren't giving me any choice, are you?" he growled. "If you think I'm going to subject Julianna to your constant barbs and venom when she comes to our world, let alone have to keep fending off your nonstop advances myself, you're sorely mistaken."

"You have a funny way of treating a woman who loves you!" she spat.

"You've never loved me, Sionne, and you damn well know it. You've only ever been after control of the island, the status, and the money that's attached to it." At her blanch, he shook his head. "Did you think you blinded me as easily as my grandfather? Even he's suspected you on occasion, although your abilities as an actress often dispelled this."

"I don't have to sit here and take your insults."

"A smart move, since you'll no doubt have endless packing ahead of you at the palace."

Narrowing her eyes, Sionne stormed off to her hidden horse, calling out angrily behind her, "You'll be sorry for this humiliation, Dominick Westbrooke! I swear you will!"

"Blazes!" he swore, heading towards Windrider to make sure the spiteful female didn't spin more lies in his absence. As he reached his stallion, he overheard the sound of a clicking tongue, turning to find himself staring at another familiar face. "Sireni," he sighed wearily. "I might have known, since you two tend to stick together."

"Twins often do," she replied with a shrug, casting him a mischievous look. "I'd say it's about time my poor sister finally wised up about you."

Suspicion filled his eyes. "Did you send her out here like this?" he asked.

"Sionne has her own mind, as do I!"

"And your similar knack for causing havoc and finding trouble," he replied, climbing upon Windrider as a new realization seized him. "You know, Sireni, since you're a dreamphaser and your sister isn't, I can only assume you're the one who gained the information on Julianna's appearance and voice so Sionne could imitate it." His eyes darkened. "Unless of course, you gained your knowledge from another dreamphaser."

"Are you accusing me of something, Westbrooke?" she demanded.

"You sound more and more like Dual every day," he hissed, earning a look of surprise from her. He cast her a crooked smile. "Don't think I'm ignorant to the rumors regarding you two. It only makes me twice as glad that you'll no longer be roaming about the palace, any more than your scheming sister will."

Sending Windrider in the direction of home, he ignored Sireni's scathing reply.

*****

The palace butler took one look at the arriving Dominick, and then a cursory glance at Sionne's ranting mother, before deciding this feud could commence without him, racing off to find Chaos instead.

"Give me one good reason why I shouldn't take a sword to you for breaking my child's heart!" snapped Sionne's mother.

Dominick stared back at her with folded arms. "Of late, I've come to learn your daughter doesn't seem to have one," he retorted. *A trait her mother shares*, he considered. "And I have reason enough, since I happen to love another woman instead of your precious Sionne."

The woman's face turned red as she stepped forward, waving her finger angrily. "You keep a civil tongue in your head around me, you arrogant, dreamphasing, skirt-chasing devil!"

"I never did like you very much as a child, and in case you haven't noticed, I'm not an eight-year-old boy you can intimidate anymore!" he shot back. "This palace belongs to us, not you. We only continued to let you live here out of deference to your late husband. I'm only surprised he didn't have a heart attack sooner from dealing with you."

Her face turned a shade closer to purple as Riff's laughter interrupted whatever she was about to say. "There you are," he said meaningfully to Dominick, clapping a hand on his shoulder. As his brother eyed him suspiciously, he whispered, "You must have a death wish to be antagonizing the dreaded demonlady."

"I heard that, Riff-Raff!" she snapped, causing him to roll his eyes at the ceiling. "You're almost as bad as your no-good brother."

"Almost?" he exclaimed. "Phase, I do believe I've been insulted."

"As for *you*, Dominick Westbrooke," Sionne's mother continued, "you'll pay dearly for this outrage!"

"Like mother, like daughters," Dominick murmured to Riff.

"If you think you can get away with tossing us out of our home without a second thought, I'll see you dead first!"

*"**Really** now?"* boomed Chaos as he strode in with Chaolyn beside him.

Sionne's mother blanched, instantly containing her anger under forced civility. "Your pardon, Chaos. I didn't mean the words quite the way they came out."

"My dear woman," he interrupted, "I can assure you that death threats against my family are never taken lightly. Upon hearing of the situation between my grandson and your daughter, I'd thought to contradict his words that you move out. But now that I clearly see the animosity you bear him, I can only agree with him."

Her expression darkened. "My husband was a loyal friend to you and saved your life!"

"Hence, I've seen to granting you and your daughters all the comforts of the palace while they grew up. But seeing as they're both over twenty-one, with Sireni already living on her own elsewhere, I see no great difference in granting you another home of equal comfort somewhere else on the island as well. You'll still be well provided for. Simply not under the palace roof."

The woman's mouth curved into a malicious smile. "And what's to protect your precious family from any... 'accidents' that might occur afterwards. One never knows where danger could lurk unexpectedly."

"Oh, I've no doubt such exists," Chaos agreed. "Which is why Chaolyn here, along with Roderlin, Alysadaria, and their other faithful dragon allies will be sure to keep their eyes out for any troubles you speak of. Won't you now, my friend?"

"A dragon's sight never fails in cases like this," replied Chaolyn, his eyes reddening as they focused on Sionne's mother. *"Thus if they're wise, most people rarely tangle with those we loyally protect, my lady."*

"Quite so," said Chaos, his own eyes narrowing. "And if any harm **does** come to anyone in our family, you'll immediately be suspect, and hence lose the comforts you're so used to, perhaps ending up banished from the island entirely." Her expression paled. "Yes, my dear woman, it would seem you understand quite well. As for your new residence, I'll see to the arrangements immediately, while you pack your things."

As she stormed up the stairs, Chaolyn turned to Dominick with an amused smile. *"I suppose I should watch my step with you, young Westbrooke, lest 'moving day' come upon me as well."*

"Chaolyn, you're family," he chuckled, patting his head. "You'll be welcome here as long as the palace stands. After all, your kind have never caused us any trouble."

"I should hope not!" he snorted, his gaze turning playful. *"We dragons have the most well-bred of manners despite some of the humans we deal with frequently."*

"Before you cast your eyes upon me," growled Chaos, "you'd best remember that *I* have the final say about who remains in this palace."

"You know I was just kidding, Chaos," he apologized. *"Should I head for the sunset too?"*

The elder man's irritation faded. "No," he sighed, patting the dragon's shoulder. "This place would be too quiet without you. Just try not to undermine my authority in front of others, all right?"

"Will do, o' Mighty Ruler," Chaolyn replied cheerfully, earning another growl from Chaos.

"Brother, Phase, you must really love Julianna to take on a demon's wrath like that," laughed Riff. "Her fangs were bared and everything!"

Dominick shook his head. "No matter. I'd never betray Julianna, and I'll make sure nothing and no one ever comes between us."

From his hidden vantage point outside one of the palace windows, Dual could only smile darkly at his words. Somehow, he vowed to discredit them in the days to come. Not just for Sionne of course, but for his own vengeance.

As he disappeared unnoticed, Riff grinned. "When you speak of her, she sounds like one in a million, Dom. I'll be glad when she can join us here on Chavernos."

"So will Chaos, no doubt," he murmured, never forgetting the elder man's constant hints about great-grandchildren.

*****

Shortly afterwards, Quell found and comforted an upset Sionne at her sister's house, although he was inwardly relieved that she'd no longer be living in such close proximity to Dominick. Maybe now, she'd get over him.

"I'll always be here for you, Sionne," he promised, stroking her back as he held her.

Pushing away from him gently, she touched his cheek. "You've always been a good friend to me, Quell," she replied, not noticing the way he flinched at how she'd titled him. "But I still can't let Dominick get away with this."

"Why not?" he retorted. "Sionne, he's not worth the time and effort you've lavished on him. He's obviously in love with that Julianna woman from Earth."

"No!" she shouted, covering her ears.

Pulling her hands free with gritted teeth, Quell continued, "Sionne, he doesn't love you! What in blazes is it going to take to convince you?"

"Damn his eyes, I don't need his love! I just need him!" she snapped before she thought.

Releasing her instantly, Quell shook his head, while she stared back at him regretfully. "At last, you finally admit the real truth. All you want from Dominick is the guarantee of furthering the lifestyle you're accustomed to. Well, sweetheart, you don't need someone like him to get that, when there are others just as capable."

From Dream to Reality

Blinking in surprise at his vehemence, Sionne wondered—as she had several times before—at the feelings lurking behind his words. Could he be thinking of her as more than just a friend? she wondered. If so, she'd be tempted to forego her earlier plans and to blazes with Dominick.

But of course, that was an impossibility. He was as ever, just being a caring friend.

"Quell..." she began brokenly.

"Is it jewels you want, Sionne?" he queried. "Fortunes aplenty? Fine! Then allow me to prove Dominick's not the only one who can give them to you!"

Reaching for a pouch at his side, he loosened the tie and dumped the contents on the floor as she could only gape. Large blue sapphires and green emeralds tumbled out to shine up at her, along with diamonds and other gems worth a king's ransom... or at least a prince's! Raising a hand to her mouth, Sionne turned to him with wide eyes.

"Quell, how did you get...?"

"That's unimportant," he interrupted. "What *is* important is that you see that I do have the means to give you what you want, along with something he never could. Sionne, I love you. I have ever since I first set eyes on you as a young girl at the palace."

For the first time, real tears blurred her vision. "Why didn't you tell me, after all these years?"

"I didn't want to drag you into the lifestyle I'd carved out for myself, allied with Dual in those assassination missions of ours. I felt you deserved better. If Dominick had treated you as you desired, maybe I would have remained silent, but since that's not the case anymore, all that's changed. For you, I'd be willing to give up my former dark career and try to start a new life. Marry me, Sionne, and I'll do this, and build you a whole new world elsewhere, away from this island and the people who've ended up bringing us both nothing but pain."

"I want to," she whispered, lowering her head. "You can't know how much. But surely you've heard the rumors of me. You know how I've been known to react around men, even regarding simple kisses."

"Yes, I've heard," he agreed, "but perhaps someone with experience in these matters could change that. Someone who considers a kiss as far more than just simple."

Before she could think, he pulled her to him with a scorching kiss. He felt her tense immediately, but refused to allow her fears to reach the surface. Running his hands upwards in a leisurely caress as he held her, Sionne's resistance abruptly melted with a sound akin to a purr. Having heard Sireni act similarly when teasing Dual, Quell smiled upon realizing what so many fools had not. His so-called 'ice princess' was indeed capable of passion after all, as he'd always suspected. After all, she couldn't be *that* different from having a twin like her most chased after sister!

As he broke away from her slowly, she gazed up at him with newfound wonder. *This* was the same man she'd once had a crush on when younger, whom she felt certain was *just* a friend?

"Now that I've merely begun to disprove your theory, will you marry me, and give me a chance to prove just how much more you might find you've been wrong about?"

Sionne was silent for long moments, before a look of genuine happiness crossed her face. Since her loving father died, she hadn't felt loved by anyone else... not even with Chaos's grandfatherly affection. Reaching up to place her arms about Quell's neck, she asked softly, "Would tonight be soon enough?"

Quell's eyes lit up, much as hers had, lifting her off the floor. "It's about time!" he said jubilantly.

She laughed, before sobering a bit. "Of course... I wouldn't mind if you showed me a few more of those kisses I've been misinformed about, before we leave," she told him.

"Sweetheart," he replied, leaning closer. "Prepare to discover what you've been missing."

*****

"Oh, come on, Julie, give it a try," urged Marybeth. "Do you think those guys sing any better, screens with words or no?"

"It's anyone's prerogative to jump off a bridge too, but I don't see many takers for that one," Julianna retorted.

"I hardly think karaoke and bridge jumping should be lumped into the same category. Besides, it's not like there are hundreds of people in this place."

Julianna cast her a quick smile. "So why don't you go up and try it?" Coughing once, Marybeth picked up her drink to muffle her response, earning a laugh from her friend.

Shortly afterwards, Marybeth looked up. "Say, that looks like Elaine and Bobby from college over there. Julie, can you excuse me for a second?"

Before receiving a reply, she was already up and gone. "No problem," Julianna said, rolling her eyes as she glanced back at the stage where a man was doing his best to stumble through the tune he'd chosen. Fortunately, the crowd here was courteous to all types, pros and amateurs, although perhaps a few drinks had helped their music approval.

Inwardly, she'd been tempted to give it a try herself, having always enjoyed singing along with the radio in private. But still, to get up in front of a bunch of strangers... that was something else.

"Hey there, pretty thing," said a male voice beside her. Glancing up, she saw two men standing there. Great... of all the times for Marybeth to vanish. "Can we buy you a drink?" the one who'd spoken asked.

"Thanks, but no," she replied. "I'm just waiting for my friend to come back."

"In that case, we'll keep you company," he decided, sitting at the table with his friend.

Slightly irritated, Julianna tried to ignore them, until the man who'd spoken touched her arm. Slapping the offending hand, she snapped, "I said I'm not alone!"

"Doesn't look like your friend's returning anytime soon," he laughed, echoed by his friend.

Pushing in her chair, Julianna stood hastily to find Marybeth. As the two men got up to protest, another voice broke into their conversation. "I'd leave the lady alone, guys."

Julianna could only gape. "Roger, what are you doing here?"

"I told you I'd just be a minute, hon," he said, eyeing the other pair darkly as he slammed a beer bottle on the table. "I'm sure you two boys can find your way back to your table, can't you?" Grumbling under their breath, the pair left without another word. "You were here first, I believe," he told Julianna, gesturing to her chair.

She sat again hesitantly. "Were you following me?"

Roger gave a mock sigh. "Alas, the knight protects his maiden, and as a reward, she rails at him."

"You're not exactly a knight, Roger."

"And your Dominick is?" he sneered, leaning against the table. "Would you have felt any better if I'd simply stood back and let them harass you?"

Realizing she *was* being a bit hard on him given the circumstances, Julianna visibly relaxed, shaking her head. "No," she replied. "Thank you for getting rid of them without a fistfight."

"Don't think I wouldn't have if necessary to protect you."

"You're dying for that 'knight' title, aren't you?"

"Well, maybe..."

"Roger, look out!"

Her warning prompted him to duck a bottle aimed at the back of his head. Getting to his feet as the bottle shattered harmlessly against the table, he faced the two men from before, as well as a third. So much for words!

Ducking as another man threw a punch, he returned it instantly, knocking the dazed man to the floor. The others presented no great problem either, mostly because they'd all had their share of alcohol, dulling their movements. When one edged towards Julianna again, she gave a surprised cry, but quickly recovered to use a move she'd learned in a self-defense class to deal with him, earning a quick look of admiration from Roger.

Shortly after, the security in the place jumped in to escort the drunken instigators from the scene. Sporting a bleeding mouth and a few minor bruises, Roger sat down again, newly surprised when Julianna dunked a napkin in water to dab against his wounded mouth.

"Have I earned the title of 'knight', since you've turned into a concerned nurse?" he asked.

"Don't make me wish I'd poured alcohol on this napkin instead," she retorted, although without much conviction. "Oh, Roger, how is it that you always get yourself into these things? You have for as long as I've known you."

Taking her hand, he said meaningfully, "Maybe I wouldn't mind being your knight in shining armor that you've always proclaimed you wanted."

Not replying, but casting him a little smile, Julianna glanced up when Marybeth returned. Her friend was stunned at what she'd missed—having been tempted by Elaine and Bobby to see his new sports car—but quickly saw that the friction between the pair seemed to have abated somewhat.

"I'm sorry I left so abruptly, Julie," Marybeth told her. "We should have both gone over to my friends' table to begin with. Are you all right?"

"I'm fine," Julianna replied.

"Listen, why don't you come with me, and I'll introduce you."

"Thanks, but I think I'd rather get going. I've had enough excitement for one night."

Marybeth's expression dimmed. "Now?" she asked.

Sensing her unwillingness to leave her other friends, Roger stepped in. "I can drive you home, Julie. As you said, I was really just looking for you tonight anyway." At the wary glance she shot him, he asked, "Haven't I proven myself trustworthy enough?"

"I suppose so," she agreed. "All right, o' shining knight, let's go."

*****

Roger made it a point to walk Julianna to her door, even though she insisted it was unnecessary. Having chatted more amiably on the way here than they had in ages, Julianna found it hard to remember all the reasons she'd been angry with him before.

"Thanks again for bringing me back," she said, reaching for her key.

"For my lady, anything," he said, with a bow.

Reminding her briefly of Dominick in his manner, Julianna's smile faded. What would once have been the most welcome thing on Earth to her, now brought a wave of regret. If he had been like this before, maybe things would be different today.

In any case, what *might* have been was no longer possible. She loved Dominick now, and could no longer feel what she once had for Roger. Memories of seeing Marilyn come out of his room weren't so easily forgotten.

"Good night, Roger," she said simply, turning towards the door.

"Uh-oh, ice wall alert."

Turning to him with a bored look, she sighed, "Look, Roger, I only accepted a ride home. I never said…"

He suddenly pulled her to him, his mouth finding hers,

while her shock changed quickly to annoyance. Her protest was muffled as his arms tightened about her, but she still managed to break away from him, breathing heavily. "Roger, stop it! You know I'm seeing someone else."

"So I've heard," he replied. "But if he cares about you so much, then where is he? I mean, who's to say he's not two-timing *you* with another woman?"

The color drained from Julianna's face. "Like *you* did?"

"Julie, I didn't mean…"

"Good night, Roger!" she said again, much more icily, as she opened the front door to dart inside.

"Julie, wait. I only wanted…" The door slamming in his face cut off his last words. "Damn!" he bit out in self-reprimand. "Well, Julie, I guess we're back to square one again," he said, walking back to his car. "But that certainly doesn't mean I'm giving up," he added on an afterthought, before driving away.

*****

A scene of bright white greeted Crystal's eyes, causing her to blink, just before the blinding light faded to reveal she was seated at a table with another empty chair. Other than how she suddenly got here, the only other unusual thing was the table's location, since the ocean was but a few feet away.

About to pull her chair safely back, a male voice swiftly interrupted her. "There's no need to move. The ocean in this realm isn't the same as that of physical reality."

Turning slowly to face who'd spoken, Crystal took one look at him and blanched with a gasp. "It can't be..." she murmured, pressing a hand to her mouth in disbelief.

Smiling gently, the dark-haired man took the vacant seat across from her. "Aye, my lady. It can. In case you're uncertain who I am, although it appears you know already, I'm Dominick Westbrooke of Chavernos." Crystal nearly fell backwards from her chair, but he caught her arm first to prevent this. "Your sister reacted much the same way at our second meeting," he chuckled.

"This is impossible," she breathed, regaining her composure gradually. "You can't be real."

"I could say the same of you, you know."

Crystal's expression turned more skeptical. "And how can I be sure that I haven't just conjured your image up, due to my conversations with Julie lately?"

"You can't," he said, shaking his head once before spreading his hands. "Thus, it seems we're at an impasse."

"So knowing this, why would you bother coming to see me?" she asked uneasily.

"Ah, because it only *seems* impossible to prove my reality to you," corrected Dominick. "In truth, I've found a way to prove the certainty of my existence, not only to you but to Julianna as well."

Crystal gaped at that. *What curious dreams to conjure up!* she thought.

"Not curious dreams, my lady," he said. "Merely ones difficult to believe, 'tis all."

"You read my mind," she whispered. "Just like..."

"As Julianna no doubt told you I can," he replied. "This is indeed so in the dream-state. Not reality, of course, since I do have some limits to my magic powers."

"You said you had a way to prove your existence."

Smiling, since by listening she was already starting to believe him, Dominick told her exactly what Lendric had.

*****

Not too long after he finished his explanation, Crystal was finding it more conceivable that Julianna had told the truth after all. And if that was true, one day they might indeed be welcoming Dominick into their family.

"I'll confirm this with her tomorrow to see if you're telling me the truth," she decided. "But what if I can't remember?"

"If you don't remember it all, she will, since she's grown accustomed to remembering our meetings. In any case, your information will coincide, since she'll be learning it tonight the same as you are."

"If you're planning on seeing her, shouldn't you get going or something?" asked Crystal.

"I will shortly. But first, there is one thing you could do for me," he replied thoughtfully. Her eyes became wary. "Would you mind telling me about Julianna's former association with Roger Collins?"

Crystal's suspicions faded instantly. "I imagine she's already told you what happened." He nodded.

"She told me of his deceptions, but I'd be more interested to learn of their earlier background."

"I understand," she agreed, turning to stare out at the ocean. "They were very close once," she began. "Julianna met Roger when she was a teenager, and I'm afraid she developed a crush on him right from the start. Although I'm sure he meant no harm at the time by his ignorance of this, he never gave her reason to believe otherwise."

"But he never displayed more than friendship for her then?"

Crystal thought for a moment before turning back to Dominick with a weak smile. "He did at least once," she said, earning his full attention. "Although I hadn't been present that night, I found out the next day. When Julianna was fifteen, Roger climbed up to her bedroom via the ledge outside her window. Upon hearing something, our father opened her door to catch them together on her bed."

Dominick's eyes flew wide open at that. "They were *where*?" he shouted. *Julianna had certainly never mentioned this before!*

"Nothing happened between them," Crystal interrupted quickly, filling in the missing details. Gradually, he relaxed again, chiding himself for having assumed the worst before hearing the rest. "But although they were both dressed and in plain sight above the covers, all our father saw was their compromising embrace and kisses. He threw Roger out immediately."

"I can't blame your father for how he reacted," replied Dominick. "If I had a daughter that age, I'd be just as protective, if not more."

"After hearing about it, I lost a great deal of respect for Roger, since being several years older, he surely knew he was taking advantage of Julianna's innocence. I'm just glad our father found them before he'd ended up hurting her both physically and emotionally with his selfish motives. At fifteen, she was too innocent to know what he'd wanted, and afterwards, couldn't see what we'd been worried about." Crystal sighed heavily. "Julianna confided in me then that Roger promised he'd return in a few weeks to see her."

Dominick's jaw clenched at the thought of Roger's attempt at seducing a much younger Julianna. Given her innocence when he'd met her, it wasn't hard to picture her similarly at fifteen. Yet if Roger had succeeded that night, to him it would have been just a conquest, while Julianna's trusting soul could have suffered irreparable damage from it. Heaven knew he'd brought her enough grief recently.

"And did he?"

"Yes, but only as a friend. During his absence from Julianna, Vicki overheard that he'd found another more amenable girl to cater to his... needs. He was very clever at hiding this from her with fake smiles."

"Thus history repeating itself when they were older," whispered Dominick.

Crystal nodded, just before clasping his hand. "But now that Julianna has you in her life, she's much happier than she ever was with Roger. Surely you've seen that, since we've all noticed the welcome change in her." As he quirked one eyebrow up, she realized what she was saying. "You're very convincing. I just hope you're as real as you seem now."

"Very much so," he laughed.

"Then maybe I should go tell her of our meeting, to put her mind more at ease."

"I'd ask if you'd postpone that until tomorrow," he said. "After all, I haven't had a chance to give her the information I've told you. And also because I promised to make up for an incident regarding last night."

A smile crossed her mouth. "A lovers' quarrel already?"

"Not exactly," he sighed in grim remembrance.

"No matter. I'll abide by your request."

Standing, Dominick took her hand, squeezing it once. "Thank you, Crystal. Your sister was right in that you have a most understanding heart. Perhaps one day, you and your family might be able to visit my world as well, so you can see just how real it truly is."

"No doubt my son would appreciate that. His mind is often in a perpetual fantasy world like Julie."

Dominick couldn't help grinning. "So she's told me," he replied. "I look forward to meeting Sammy too eventually."

"So... how do we get out of this dream now?"

He shook his head. "You'll remain, my lady. After all, this is *your* dream. It is merely I who must leave. Farewell, until I reach your world one day."

As Crystal blinked her eyes, he vanished into thin air, sparkling lights glittering and fading where he'd stood, just before her former dream took precedence in her mind once more.

Chapter Four

Julianna walked onto the familiar castle balcony, leaning against the stone parapet, while watching the full moon shine its radiance upon the ocean below. Every star was visible in the beautiful night sky, though no rainbows tonight, she thought.

As she began to wonder what was keeping her companion, worried from the events of the prior evening, a brightening glow on the beach drew her attention.

Her expression lit up as swiftly as the rainbow now arcing across the sky.

"Dominick…" she whispered.

"One rainbow, just as my lady wishes."

As she felt the comfort of warm arms surround her, she turned to see his blue eyes gazing back. The memories of last night faded into nothing. Turning completely in his embrace, she met his welcoming kiss, her heart filled with happiness for long moments. *If only this could be real.*

When he finally drew back, brushing a curl from her cheek, she immediately chided herself, hoping he hadn't caught her last thought.

His knowing expression indicated otherwise, though he smiled. "Having doubts about our future?" he inquired softly.

"Of course not," she said. Frustrated when her words lacked conviction, she reached out to hold his hand. "I'm engaged to the man I love, and I know it's only a matter of time before we'll be together in reality. Why should I have doubts, since I trust you with my life?"

Giving him a lingering kiss, she tried to dispel any

reservations, earning an appreciative look from him when they broke apart.

"You're very convincing, love," he replied. "But you wouldn't be human if you didn't have doubts, since we've only met in dreams. However, thanks to a good friend of mine, there may be a feasible way to remedy this which I've already set in motion."

At Julianna's quizzical look, he paused only momentarily before continuing. "My grandfather would prefer I wait to share this with you, but given these doubts are clearly upsetting you, I'd rather you know what's going on since it does affect our future together. On my world, there's a dragon sorcerer called Lendric, whom my family has known for quite some time. After visiting him recently, he said there may indeed be a way for me to reach you on Earth."

Her heart skipped a beat, while her eyes fairly glowed. "Dominick, that's wonderful!" she exclaimed. "How soon?"

"That is where the problem lies," he sighed, turning away from her hopeful gaze. "You see, the means Lendric spoke of involves a Teleportation Staff which he'd given to his brothers temporarily. They were due back months ago, and there's been no word from them since."

"But where could they have gone?"

Dominick spread his hands uncertainly. "With a device of that magnitude, they could be anywhere in the universe. Believe me, Lendric and his sister are both concerned about their prolonged absence, and they've even sent out a pair of demons to find out what happened to them."

"Demons? I wouldn't have thought their kind took on the roles of helpful detectives."

"Usually they don't, but Lendric swears they're loyal. The best we can hope for is that his brothers can be found and returned to Chavernos safe and sound, along with an intact Teleportation Staff." Clasping her hands, Dominick faced her again. "Can you be patient awhile longer, love?"

"I'll wait forever if I have to."

He smiled. "I'd hoped you'd say that. But there's more to it. Namely, a way has been revealed that I can prove to you my existence and Chavernos." Julianna's eyes widened in surprise. "My only condition in telling you this information is that you keep silent about it, with the exception of your sister Crystal."

"Crystal?" she asked. "I'm afraid I don't understand." Squeezing her hand, he explained everything as Lendric had told him, leaving Julianna a bit bemused. "Let me get this straight. You visited Crystal so she'd have confirmation of this address you've given me, so that she can't say I made it up. And if we go to find this Oliver Dragend, he'll..."

"No," he interrupted quickly. "Remember what I told you of Lendric's conditions. Oliver must never hear any of this, since he's not to learn his true identity and heritage yet. You can only speak of it with his parents."

"I'll remember," she promised. "And if I understand correctly, they'll be able to confirm all of this, since they're complete strangers to us, who've lived most of their lives on Chavernos."

"Even Crystal will believe you when she hears it from them," he concurred.

"I'm sure I'll be glad for that. But I'll be gladder still to hear the truth for myself. It's not easy living with doubts when they revolve around someone you desperately want to believe... and already love very much."

Understanding, Dominick pulled her close, cradling her head gently against his chest. "It's more hope than we had before though. And with the Teleportation Staff a viable possibility now, it's only a matter of time until our separation will end."

"Unless something's happened to his brothers and the

Staff itself," she whispered, feeling a few tears creep into her eyes.

"No matter. If that way becomes impossible, I swear I'll find another." She nodded against his shoulder, even as he brushed away her tears. "Now, enough of this unnecessary melancholia. Tell me how you've fared on your world since we last talked."

Julianna told him of Roger's appearance at the club earlier, along with the minor brawl which followed. Afraid of what she'd see in his eyes over the mere mention of Roger, she was surprised to find tenderness there instead.

"I'm just glad you're all right, love," he said finally.

"I thought you'd be angry."

"Certainly not with you," replied Dominick. "If you went to the club with Marybeth, it's not your fault he decided to trail after you like a bloodhound. Granted, I'm not thrilled it was Roger who was the resident avenger with those bar drunks, but I understand that." He shook his head. "The only thing I *don't* understand is why you went home with him."

Pushing away from him, Julianna's gaze met his without faltering. "It was purely innocent," she insisted. "Marybeth wanted to stay and chat with some old friends of hers, and Roger was merely trying to help by driving me back early."

Dominick's own gaze became defensive. "But apparently, he had more than an 'innocent' gesture in mind since he kissed you afterwards."

She stared at the parapet, remembering her exchange with Roger at the door. "He forced that kiss on me!" she reminded him. "As soon as I broke away, I stormed into the house and slammed the door in his face."

Dominick's eyes sparkled a bit in amusement. "*That* I'm glad to hear," he said. "Roger deserved it for taking advantage of the situation." Moments later, he clasped her shoulders tightly, searching her eyes questioningly. "But blazes, love, why couldn't you have avoided this by simply calling for your family to pick you up?"

She considered his words silently, but couldn't refute his logical suggestion. "Maybe I should have," she agreed softly. "But I was tired, and I didn't feel like belaboring my past arguments with Roger tonight. He offered to drive me home, and that's *all* I accepted from him."

Dominick nodded, giving her a hug. "I believe you," he murmured. "I just hope it's the *last* favor he offers you." Wishing to mend the uneasy tension still lingering, he changed the subject. "So... when are you going to go back to try a song at that place?"

Her eyebrows raised in confusion as he released her again. "I never said I was going to."

"But by the way you spoke of it, you're interested in trying," he interrupted. "Since I've glimpsed you singing alone in your room while your music played, you can't deny you're tempted." At her surprised look, he shrugged. "Although I must admit I would have preferred being with you in your dreams sooner on those nights, I still enjoyed listening to you."

"I'm flattered," she replied. "But it's different when you try it in front of a bunch of total strangers."

"So imagine they aren't there," he suggested, covering her hand with his. "Imagine it's only you and me instead."

"Well... since Marybeth and I might go to the club again tomorrow anyway, I'll think about it."

"You'll have at least one admirer in the audience." She laughed at the impossibility of that notion, never noticing the mischievous gleam in his eyes. So she doubted he'd be there, did she? He'd see about that later. "As far as Roger goes though, just promise me you'll be careful around him. I'd sooner you trust an impish fairy than the likes of him."

More amused than irritated now, Julianna smiled. "I'm glad you've been so understanding, but you really shouldn't be jealous regarding him. He's the one who stands the right to be jealous. After all, I chose you over him, didn't I?"

Dominick sighed heavily. "Julianna, you can ask anything you want of me, and I'll do my best to comply. But as far as the millions of miles separating us are concerned, don't ask me to stop feeling jealous over Roger. He's where I most want to be, able to be around the one I most want to be with. I think I have reason enough to feel envious of that."

"But not of him," she said, shaking her head. "I may be on Earth physically, but my heart is only where you are." Seeing the steadfast question in his eyes, she continued, "And as far as your mentioned concern over me goes, you needn't worry that I'll be careful, my overprotective fiancé."

"Better overprotective than ignorant and devious like Roger the Shark."

As he pulled her close, Julianna couldn't resist laughing at the former memory, only one of many. Thanks to her unearthly companion, this other world had become a virtual paradise to her, full of new wonders every time she closed her eyes. Although, she suspected, perhaps anyplace would seem like paradise as long as she was with him.

Sensing if not completely reading her thoughts, Dominick was glad he hadn't let quick anger overcome him regarding Roger. What he and Julianna shared shouldn't be ruined by someone like him. She never ceased to fascinate him with her endless imagination and curiosity. In fact, he mused, she might have been a most apt dreamphaser. Not that it would have made the slightest difference in how he felt about her, but it was an intriguing notion.

While his thoughts were elsewhere, she caught him off-guard moments later.

"Dominick, what happened to that other dreamphaser, Dual, whom you and Riff sent away last night?"

"He's likely fled for the time being," he replied evenly,

hoping the rumors he'd heard were indeed true.

"Maybe... but what if he finds us again?"

"It's unlikely," he told her, meeting her gaze. "I imagine Dual must have other sport he can prey on for the evening." Kissing her forehead to allay her fears, she still seemed ill at ease.

"He was so full of hatred towards you. Has he always been like this?"

"For most of the years I've known him," Dominick confirmed. "From what I've heard of his past, he's been a cold-blooded assassin for countless years." She nodded.

"Still..." he continued on an afterthought, "I believe there was a time when he still had some shred of humanity. You see, in the beginning, we were friends."

"What?"

"It's true. It was many years ago, and only for several months, but when we first met, he actually helped me find a good solution to an island problem, and we had drinks at Lost Limbo afterwards. At the time, I didn't know of his assassin missions, and he was very intelligent and likeable. He actually was helpful for a time on the island when he visited."

"So what happened to change that?"

"He fell in love with a young village girl in outer Chavernos whom he was willing to set his dark ways aside for. Her name was Caralei."

"Caralei," she murmured. "What happened to her?" She could feel him tense up at her question, moments before he moved away to lean against the parapet, staring out at the ocean. Instantly concerned, she followed him, placing a comforting hand on his shoulder. He seemed to appreciate this as he turned towards her, though his responding smile still looked troubled.

"He asked me in secret to stand up for him at their wedding, which I agreed to do. She was a very kind woman who taught the village children, and one you would have liked. But shortly after I arrived, the village was set ablaze and all hell broke loose. Dual told me to get Caralei safely away, which I was prepared to do, but she wouldn't leave without the children at the orphanage. I went to help her get the children out and we got as far as the forest, but we were ambushed. I distracted them so she could escape, but she went back for Dual before I could stop her. By the time I reached the village, she'd been captured by more of the assassins."

"But why did they attack at all?" she asked.

"From what I'm to understand, Dual's dark dealings caught up with him. Although Caralei was innocent of any wrongdoing, it was enough that she was a pawn his enemies could use against him.

"When I got there, the assassin leader told Dual that I'd helped them, which of course was a lie. Though I tried to protest, he believed their words. I wasn't close enough to intervene, although Caralei's brother Quell was and tried, but the assassin leader was quicker, slashing the girl's throat before our eyes, killing her instantly."

Julianna winced at the thought. "I can't imagine how one copes with something so horrible."

Dominick stopped her gently, setting a finger against her lips. "And with your forgiving heart, I know what thoughts fill your mind, but hear me out. Make no mistake, Julianna, what happened to Caralei was horrible, and I don't deny for a moment what scars that would cause anyone, including Dual, to see one they love cut down so mercilessly. Rumors say he was more a mercenary than an assassin in his earlier days, but he apparently killed someone that brought about this catastrophe. To make matters worse, in his mind he still blames me for her death, having declared me his enemy, even though I did all in my power to protect her."

His eyes became steel. "But the truth is, I found out later that he trained to be an assassin, and became a more completely ruthless assassin ever since, preying on and eliminating not only hired targets, but anyone else who stands in his way. He thinks nothing of the lives he destroys, either of his victims or those left behind to suffer the grief of their losses. He even shows no pity or remorse towards victims who, as Caralei was, were innocents. He's taken a great many lives of such victims over the years."

Remembering Dual's personal attack on her drove Dominick's point home. The sufferings of Dual's past didn't give him the right to inflict misery and destroy the lives of others.

"How long has he had this personal vendetta against you?"

"For many years, ever since Caralei's death. But if there is anything positive out of this, lately our encounters have been brief ones. I hardly see a reason for him to change his ways now after all these years of contests of will."

"I hope you're right," she whispered. "But in the past, I've always developed sudden chills when something's wrong. Look." Touching his cheek, she surprised him with the physical truth of her words, for despite the warmth of the dream-state, her hand was cold. "I don't recall this ever happening when I was asleep."

"Ah, but then you're not used to having some control over your dreams," he reminded her. "It's probably harmless pre-wedding jitters."

"Harmless?" she questioned, rubbing her arms. "I feel like ice."

Dominick gave a comforting smile. "Well then, my lady, allow me to melt it away," he offered, hugging her closer with a kiss. His simply cradling her against him easily warmed the chills from her. At the look of expectation on her face when she glanced up at him, he laughed. "It would seem I've created a most insatiable little temptress."

She blushed, struggling to free herself from his grasp to no avail. "Don't tease me," she protested. "After twenty-five years of repressed emotions, I can't help it if I like being free to express them with the one I love." She flashed him a grin. "Something that you've never minded in the past, I might add."

"Believe me, I'm not arguing," he chuckled. "I only thought after last night you might like a change of scenery." At her curious look, he gestured towards the parapet. "Our horses await us below."

"Our what?" asked Julianna, glancing over the edge, nearly gaping at what she saw. "Wait a second..." she murmured suspiciously. "Dominick, that white mare looks just like my former steed Duchess."

"Really? Must be a coincidence."

Shooting him a disbelieving smile at the possibility of *that*, she then eyed the velvet black stallion standing beside Duchess. "I've never seen *your* horse before," she continued curiously. "What's his name?"

"Oh, an appropriate one, I suppose," Dominick replied nonchalantly. "I call him Duke."

"Where did you *ever* get an original name like that?"

"I was *inspired* by a temptress," he replied.

A bit subdued by the height as she stared at the horses, Julianna sighed in resignation. "I know you like showing off your powers as a dreamphaser, but would you mind if we use the stairs to get down this time instead of jumping?"

"It wasn't showing off," he insisted. "I just wanted to show you there was nothing to be afraid of. When it comes to you, Julianna, you get the red carpet treatment. In fact..." His eyes suddenly twinkled mischievously. "It can be any color you like."

Before she could ask what he meant, a large carpet did appear, floating over the parapet to hover beside their feet. Its colors shifted and shimmered with all the colors of the rainbow, as if it had been woven from the very fabric of it.

"It's beautiful," she breathed.

"Well, I had someplace else in mind for tonight, but it's one way to take the rainbow with us."

She turned back to him with a smile, placing her arms about his neck. "My ever-thoughtful dream knight. I think you might have more of a creative imagination than I do."

"Now *that* is a compliment," he replied, kissing her, just before gesturing towards the awaiting carpet. Once they were settled upon it, Dominick placed his arm around her waist, the carpet rising as he did. Even so, she gasped as they moved over the parapet, safely flying away from the castle. "I think our horses can find their own way home," he decided, waving a hand towards them.

As if they'd heard him, they whinnied down below, racing off together across the shore.

Her fear gave way to amazement. "Playing the part of a genie now?" she asked.

"Hmmm... that might be interesting," he considered. "Care to have any wishes granted?"

Leaning against his shoulder, she nodded wistfully. "Only one," she said, "and until Lendric's brothers return, it's impossible at the moment."

Knowing it was a wish they shared, Dominick's expression sobered, stroking her back tenderly as they continued away in silence.

*****

Later, the rainbow carpet remained fairly stationary, hovering over a cloud high above the beach below.

Dominick had brought them to this wispy-seeming—yet fully tangible—cloud, once again surprising Julianna with what was possible in a dream. They'd shared a picnic in this unconventional locale, from a basket that held more food than it seemed capable of. Whenever she asked for something, he would produce it from the basket, making her smile at the way he did it with a magician's dramatic flourish.

From Dream to Reality

Several feet from their carpet, Dominick now reclined leisurely on his side, while Julianna sat beside him.

"There's nothing to be nervous about tomorrow," he said reassuringly. "Lendric told me that the Dragends are very nice people."

"Don't you mean dragons?" she retorted.

He shook his head. "Dragons can be a hell of a lot more trustworthy than some humans. Having had a close friendship with Roderlin for the past fifteen years or so, I can clearly attest to that."

Julianna shot him a questioning look. "Didn't you once say his wife—or rather, his mate—might have shaken your trust in dragons?"

"Alysadaria," he sighed. "I'll never forget the first time we met."

"What did she do? Singe your boots?"

"Not exactly. When I first met her, she appeared as a beautiful human woman with lustrous, silver-brown hair. Unfortunately, as soon as they arrived in Barokka, she became jealous of my friendship with Roderlin, since we spoke more frequently back then. Thus, she carefully set about a plan to sever this, so she'd have him to herself again. In short, she attempted to seduce me."

Julianna gaped with wide eyes, moments before they narrowed. "I'm not so sure I want to hear the end of this."

"It doesn't end the way you might think," he continued. "You see, Alysadaria thought that if she managed to trick me into a compromising situation, and then arranged to have Roderlin 'conveniently' show up in the middle of it, he'd deal with me in a less than friendly manner."

"That she-demon!" hissed Julianna. "Roderlin might have killed you for that."

"Yes... that was probably what she had in mind," said Dominick, shaking his head at the memory, but with more amusement than grimness. "Ironically enough, it was Riff who came to my rescue."

Her expression became still more skeptical. "I find *that* very hard to believe."

"It's true though. While Alysadaria tried to work her charms on me, Riff burst in on the scene, giving his familiar wolf-whistle to her. As usual, his ego assumed that he could easily charm her away from me, but 'Lysa had other ideas. I tried to get rid of him, but you know how my brother can be around women."

"I do seem to recall one of his less shining moments."

"In 'Lysa's case, when he tried to kiss her, she was so angry, she changed back into dragon form. Riff jumped back ten feet, while she started making threats that she'd make permanent changes to his male anatomy if he so much as touched her again. As he left before she could see to making good on her threat, I was a bit shocked myself, confronting her with why she didn't tell me the truth to begin with.

"Changing back to human form, she was still angry with me, but had become a bit more reasonable upon seeing my attempts to defend her rights when Riff started bothering her. When she told me in no uncertain terms that she wanted me to stop interfering with Roderlin, I couldn't help laughing at first. After all, I was the one who first suggested the notion that he might try searching for a mate."

"So she dropped the seduction ploy then?"

Dominick shrugged. "After finding out she was Roderlin's mate, I'm afraid that *did* break the mood irrevocably."

Folding her arms, Julianna asked, "And if Roderlin—or any other dragon—hadn't been involved? Would you have reconsidered her earlier offer?"

He glanced up at her with a mischievous look. "I suppose that should be obvious. After all, she is quite stunning as a human."

"Oh, really? Maybe it would please you more if I tried transforming myself into a dragon then..."

Dominick pulled her down beside him, causing her last words to trail off. "Don't... even... think it," he admonished gently.

Raising her chin with a pout, she asked, "Is that a threat?"

"I'm not into threatening women," he replied. "And certainly not impish red-haired sprites who seem to think dragon scales are the latest fashion statement. I merely don't feel you need any other enhancements, since I happen to love you exactly the way you are."

Julianna's defiant look softened, gazing into his eyes. "You do know how to keep a girl off balance," she whispered.

His blue eyes twinkled as he grinned. "Well, my lady, as long as that woman I keep off balance is you, I must admit it does have its advantages on occasion."

Drawing her close, as he lowered her back against the cloud with a fiery kiss, Dominick then took great care in proving this to her.

*****

Enwrapped in a velvet blanket, and each other's arms, Dominick kissed Julianna's forehead, toying with her hand loosely as he gently saw to reminding her of her task ahead regarding the Dragends.

"You're sure you have the address correct to confirm with your sister?" he asked.

Julianna nodded, watching the stars glitter. "Yes," she replied. "My memory's always been undeniably accurate regarding my time with you when I'm awake. I'm just glad this Oliver's home is only a short trip into the next state. If he'd been halfway across the country, it wouldn't be so easy to just drop by for a visit."

"A small good fortune to aid our plight," he agreed, "but any unexpected help is certainly appreciated." Shifting to face her, he added, "And speaking of unexpected events, I'm sorry I was a bit late getting here originally, though I'm glad you found your way safely to the castle."

She shrugged. "It's gotten easier than I thought it would. I guess having such lucid dreams every night helps."

"Maybe. All the same, I'm glad you didn't find yourself caught by the usual unpredictable nature of dreams."

She shook her head, freeing her hand to draw lazy patterns on his chest. "I don't mind the normal, occasional nocturnal adventures we find ourselves in," she told him. "After all, it certainly does keep things interesting." Smiling, she lifted her eyes to his. "Between the two of us, we do make a pretty good team in dealing with problems in the dream-state, don't we?"

Cuddling her closer, while nuzzling kisses against her neck, he chuckled, "I believe so."

Julianna's expression turned curious. "By the way, since you *were* a bit late getting here—on account of my sister, I presume—would you mind explaining what went on?"

Halting his kisses abruptly, a puzzled look crossed his face. "What 'went on'?"

"Well, obviously you spent a long time with her, so naturally I'm curious about what happened. Anything I should know?"

Dominick nearly retorted that he wouldn't have considered anything more than platonic around her sister, but sensing he was being baited by her query, instead he chose to stare at the sky thoughtfully.

"She *was* a rather beautiful woman," he admitted, sounding a bit more interested than he should. "You know, if she hadn't been married, and if I'd passed through her room first originally, who knows what might have..."

His words were cut off by a sharp gasp, as his body involuntarily gave a jolt. Whipping his gaze back to Julianna, she blinked at him innocently, while her hand remained where it had deftly traveled beneath the blanket during his speech.

"I'm fully attentive," she assured him, her eyes brimming with amusement. "You don't have to stop on my account."

"Julianna, I was only kidding," he said, a bit uneasily under the circumstances. "We merely talked. That's all. Granted, she is an interesting woman to converse with, but..." Once more, his words were cut short. "Julianna..." he groaned, eyeing her seriously, "I swear I wouldn't chase after another woman, let alone your sister. Give me a little credit. I'm not *that* kind of a rogue."

Giving him a mollified look, Julianna nodded. "I'm certainly glad to hear that," she murmured, slowly withdrawing from her teasing. Before she could free her hand completely though, she felt Dominick clasp it tightly, his eyes darkening with desire.

Smiling, he replied playfully, "But since it seems I'm most certainly *attentive* myself at the moment, love... you don't have to stop on my account either."

*****

Crystal sat down quickly, upon digesting this new information. Yet how could she deny the truth? Having told Julianna about her odd dream involving Dominick, she'd also been about to give out the address for the Dragend family, but her sister had prevented this.

First, she'd insisted that they should both write down the addresses they'd been told. Therefore, neither could claim prior knowledge of it. As soon as Crystal put both addresses on the table, they matched identically. How could they both know a fictitious dream address, unless...

Dominick Westbrooke does in fact exist, and Julianna's story must be true!

"I was a bit surprised too at first upon finding out that Dominick was more than just an illusion I'd conjured up in my mind. But as you can see now, I was given just cause to believe in his existence."

Crystal looked up at her incredulously. "Then this address really does lead to people from another world?"

"Yes," said Julianna, wondering if the Dragends were indeed as their name implied... dragons. "At least Dominick swears it does. And since he's been right so far, I trust him on this too. I understand you might be a bit more hesitant, but since you're open-minded, he decided you should know the truth as well so I needn't carry the truth of our relationship all alone."

"This trip to the Dragends will take several hours, you realize. Even if we know where we'll be heading, there's no guarantee these people haven't moved."

"According to Dominick, Lendric says they wouldn't move without informing him, since he's supposed to be bringing them back to Chavernos in another few years."

"That would make sense," she agreed, brightening. "So, did you have an interesting 'chat' yourself with Dominick last night?"

Remembering all too clearly the way she'd blushed at her dream companion's way of teasing her during the evening, Julianna felt her face redden again. Not that they hadn't shared a most pleasurable time afterwards, until the dawn eventually brought a halt to this, but still... that wasn't something Crystal needed to hear about!

"I think we'd better get going while we've got sunlight to travel by," Julianna said finally.

"Yes," her sister replied, smiling, "and before that deep shade of red becomes a permanent addition to your skin tone."

Julianna's expression spoke volumes.

A certain dream knight was going to get it for his part in this embarrassing discussion later.

From Dream to Reality

*****

Julianna's nerves were on edge during the entire trip as she and Crystal drew nearer to the unfamiliar destination. In spite of Dominick's visit in her sister's dreams last night, she was surprised at how readily Crystal was complying with this trip, although at least it wasn't *too* far into the next state.

It hadn't been impossible for her sister to arrange an excuse that they were visiting an old friend of hers, even though Sammy initially protested their leaving him behind with Vicki. Although he'd heard some of the story regarding Dominick, both sisters deemed it best to keep this matter to themselves, since the others would surely see this trek as crazy at best, paranoid at worst. Not to mention the fact that Julianna reminded Crystal of her promise to keep this visit between them.

"You realize of course we're probably caught in a wild goose chase," said Crystal.

"If you believed that, you wouldn't be driving us there."

"How can I not?" she sighed. "For both of us to dream of this unknown location on the same evening? If there isn't some truth to this Dominick of yours, I'll be more surprised than not."

Glancing down at the map she held, Julianna said quietly, "If some of the things I've heard are true about this couple, you'll be more than surprised." Not responding to Crystal's curious stare, she leaned back in her seat and couldn't help but wonder again. Were the couple in question really dragons?

Chapter Five

Crystal double-checked the address she held. "If my memory for dreams is accurate, this should be the place."

"Mine says the same, so it should be." Stepping forward, Julianna rang the doorbell, feeling a sharp chill race through her.

Even knowing they would have to be in human form to keep their heritage secret from their son, this would be the first time she met some of Chavernos's dragons. But if Oliver wasn't home, would they transform to greet them in their scaled forms instead? she wondered.

Moments later, the door opened.

The physically fit, middle-aged man that stood there certainly gave no indication that he was anything other than human. Neither his dark brown hair nor his mustache showed the slightest indication of gray. Only his eyes held that, being a grayish-blue, and they now looked amiably upon the two women.

Glancing from one to the other, he asked, "Can I help you?"

Julianna swallowed hard. "I hope so, sir," she replied. "Are you Bruce Dragend?"

"I am," he said with a nod.

"Then we have the right place," she sighed with relief, extending her hand cordially. "I'm Julianna Sherborne, and this is my sister Crystal."

He took her offered hand, nodding again to both. "Charmed, I'm sure, but I don't recall your names."

"We haven't met before," supplied Crystal, "but after

receiving your name from a reliable source, we've come a long way to see you over a matter of personal importance."

The man shook his head. "Since I've never seen you before, I highly doubt that's possible. And if you're using a new sales pitch technique, I assure you my wife and I aren't interested."

"Who's at the door?" came a voice behind him.

Realizing that the best tactic was the truth, Julianna asked, "Is that Sheila?" The man's eyes narrowed.

"How do you know her name?" he asked, not masking the warning in his voice.

"I know a lot more, although right now I'm afraid only you can confirm it. To cut to the chase, Mr. Dragend, I'm here on a matter concerning information of your true homeworld."

Bruce's expression didn't change, although Julianna could have sworn his eye twitched. His wife appeared beside him, her own face equally devoid of recognition. Remembering Dominick's description of the woman, she might very well be the same one, since she did indeed have the blue-green eyes and ebony hair mentioned. The only difference was that her long hair had been trimmed short, curling about her ears.

"Our true homeworld?" she asked, smiling. Julianna could sense the caution within her voice. "My dear, I believe you've been reading too many science fiction magazines, or you'd know how ridiculous that sounds."

"I know it does," said Julianna. "But you see, I had no choice, since someone of your world has been visiting my dreams recently, and he's told me that only you can provide the proof of his existence."

As she mentioned the word dreams, the woman's face seemed to pale a bit. Coincidence? Perhaps not. "I hesitate to tell you the complete truth, only because I'd rather hear it proven beyond a reasonable doubt from you. But if you'll allow us a few moments, maybe I can tell you part of it, so you'll more easily understand."

"I don't think that's necessary, Miss Sherborne," the man said quickly. "All this talk of other worlds may be interesting to some, but we ourselves..."

"Bruce, wait," interrupted his wife, resting her hand against his shoulder. Her gaze was like steel as she faced Julianna. "You speak of dreams. Pray tell, exactly what do you mean you've been *visited* in them?"

"Just as it sounds," she replied. "My companion has a power which enables him to travel into my dreams each night. A supernatural power which has given him the title of a dreamphaser."

Sheila gasped sharply, the rigid look fading instantly from her eyes. Even Crystal could see how Julianna's words were beginning to strike a few chords.

"A name surely derived from a figment of your imagination," retorted Bruce. "Dreams often seem real enough to be truth, but naturally are not."

Julianna's eyes narrowed, anger lending her strength. "Why are you so against hearing of your homeworld? Do you despise it that much, or is it simply fueled by your wish to hide the truth from your dragon son?"

"*Dragon*... son?" breathed Crystal.

Abruptly, Julianna found her shoulders clamped painfully by the man's large hands, as he shook her hard. "You *dare* speak such lies of our son in my presence?" he snarled. "Young woman, I could very well have you thrown in jail for your slanderous and most irritating accusations! Surely they'll find you a psychiatrist to rant your delusions at instead. And if you persist in this tirade, I can assure you, you'll regret it."

A wave of fear shot through Julianna as she heard the underlying deep tones that might very well come from a dragon. And was that a hint of red in his eyes? Not having incurred a dragon's wrath before, she wondered if his hands would become talons and rip through her vulnerable flesh.

Frightened as she was though, the face of her beloved countered the angry man before her. If she backed down now, she'd lose the chance of gaining proof of Dominick's existence, losing Crystal's belief, and perhaps ending up questioning the soundness of her very being.

No. She wouldn't be cowed so easily.

"I'm not lying or delusional," she declared. "You can threaten me all you like, but it won't change the truth. My dreamphaser companion referred us to you from the dragon sorcerer who brought you to Earth. And although that sorcerer can't be here at present without his Myzalik Teleportation Staff, I doubt he'd be too pleased with your treatment of two people whom he specifically sent to you."

"Then that's just too bad, because you're leaving now!"

"Bruce, let the girl go!" Sheila exclaimed, tugging at his wrist. "I wish to hear the rest of this, and I won't have you arrested for harassment."

"*They're* harassing us," he growled, "*not* the other way around!"

"Dad, what's wrong?" came an unfamiliar third voice. "Do you need help?"

Cursing under his breath, Bruce pushed Julianna from him, turning to his son. "No, nothing's wrong, Oliver. These women are just... here over a neighborhood concern. It doesn't affect you."

Stepping into view, it appeared that Oliver Dragend matched Dominick's description as well. Sporting neatly cut brown hair that was a bit lighter than his father's, he was quite possibly twenty or twenty-one years old, with an air of intelligence about his expression. Most importantly though, his eyes caught both sisters' rapt attention. Even behind his glasses, they were a bright violet, appearing unearthly in their nature.

Maybe he really *was* from another world, they

considered.

Nodding once to Crystal politely, Oliver's gaze traveled to Julianna, lingering there as he smiled warmly. She nearly blushed under what looked to be interest in his eyes, although she knew it wasn't so unrealistic with their being close in age.

"You are?" he asked.

"Julianna Sherborne. And you are Oliver?"

His swift curiosity faded quickly. "Ah, you must have overheard," he realized thoughtfully. "Did you just move in around here?"

Unsure how to answer, Julianna was spared by Sheila. "They're from out of town, just visiting relatives here, but have taken some time out to help them spread the word of an upcoming neighborhood meeting."

"Oh... that's too bad," he replied softly. "Do you visit frequently, Julianna?"

Seeing wary trepidation in the younger woman's eyes, Sheila quickly intervened again. "Oliver, are you finished with that college paper you've been working on?" she asked.

"Not completely," he admitted, "but I can always get back to it later."

"Which is why you're always up at all hours of the evening," she said knowingly. At his sullen look, Sheila brightened. "But if you work on it now while we finish our discussion of the neighborhood situation, perhaps later Miss Sherborne and her sister would care to join us for dinner."

Neither sister looked quite as surprised as Bruce, who regarded his wife with open astonishment. "Sheila, you can't just invite two strangers to dinner."

"And why not?" she asked, a gleam in her eye. "I believe we can be very accommodating when need be." Bruce wouldn't reply. Turning to the awaiting pair, she gestured cordially. "Won't you come in?"

*****

From Dream to Reality

If not for Dominick's assurance that most dragons on his world didn't choose humans for a menu, Julianna wouldn't have felt at ease with the couple's mention of joining them for dinner, but as Lendric himself was a dragon, she figured she'd best get used to them now.

They were most convincing in human form, she decided, since their appearance bore not even the slightest difference to betray their true identities.

"Before we discuss another word, I wish to make it quite clear that none of our conversation is to be repeated to our son," said Bruce, eyeing both sisters sternly. "There are things he's not meant to know until a later date, for reasons of our own. Will you swear to keep silent?" They voiced agreement, earning a weary sigh from him as he sat beside his wife, across from them. "I sincerely hope you're as genuine as you seem."

"We wouldn't have come if not for the need to prove this uncertain situation," replied Julianna. "Nor have we discussed what we know with anyone."

"It would seem you'd best change that with us."

Nodding, Julianna relayed a brief accounting of her first meeting with Dominick, and the subsequent ones that followed two months later, all the while being careful to omit his last name. "We fell in love," she explained, clasping her hands as she stared at them. "Obviously that presented a challenge right there, but even more now, since we wish to get married."

"Why so soon?" asked Sheila. "You haven't known each other all that long, if I'm to understand correctly."

"I can't explain why really," she said honestly. "If you ask that, you may as well ask why some people in the world enter into arranged marriages with partners they've never seen. Or why some claim the existence of love at first sight, and sometimes marry immediately. At least with Dominick, we know each other fairly well now, and we're mutually compatible in all respects."

"Love always makes it seem that way at first, my dear," she laughed, "yet there are bound to be trials along the way. Only time can prove whether a marriage is truly meant to be."

"And our long distance separation is certainly a trial," said Julianna, shaking her head. Unable to bear her inner curiosity anymore, she faced Sheila imploringly. "You seem to accept what I've told you as truth, so can you give us the proof we seek? The name of your homeworld, or the dragon sorcerer, or even if you've heard of Dominick before. Please, Sheila... I need to know once and for all."

The woman stood, walking to the window to glance out at the sunlight, pressing her hand against the pane. "So beautiful it is," she murmured. "On our world, it's much the same. And yet, there are times when I've missed our true home over the years. The ever-changing colors of our skies, the easier pace of life instead of the hectic nature of things here, and of course being among those of our own kind. If not for the complication of Oliver's birth, we wouldn't have left. But it was that, or smother him with protection for over twenty years as he grew to adulthood."

"Your world..." whispered Julianna. "The hidden planet?"

Sheila turned to her, with a nod. "The often hidden planet due to its outer mists known as Chavernos." Julianna shut her eyes, uttering a prayer of thankfulness, even as Crystal nearly fell from the sofa. Bruce helped steady her, just before both he and his wife returned to their own sofa again.

"I apologize for my earlier actions," he told them, "but surely you understand why we can't disclose this information lightly. If we did, and were believed... well, let's just say Chavernos only knows what trouble it would cause for our situation, let alone our world. And even outside of that, I doubt those of Earth would deal well with the reality of dragons, nor believe that we'd not harm anyone."

"Likely not," agreed Julianna.

Crystal shook her head. "Wait a minute. You've lost me again. What is all this talk of dragons on Earth? You're as human as we are."

Before her sister could explain, Bruce stood slowly. "Things are not always as they appear," he said, raising his hands as his eyes closed. A glow surrounded him, clouding his appearance, until it abruptly dissipated, revealing not their human host... but a gleaming purple dragon of ceiling height.

"What in the name of heaven?" shouted Crystal, scrambling to her feet to stand behind the sofa. Even her sister gasped sharply before settling into silence. Growing suspicious, Crystal's eyes narrowed. "Julianna, did you know of this?" she demanded.

"I was told of it," she admitted, "but I was afraid you might decline coming with me if you knew the truth, and I didn't want to make this journey alone."

Moments later, Bruce returned to his human form. "Does she not know of Lendric either?" he asked.

Julianna whipped about to face him. They knew the dragon sorcerer's name. Another truth proven. Regaining her composure, she nodded. "Yes, she does, but there's a big difference between knowing of dragons, and seeing one in person."

"I'll say," sighed Crystal, still clutching her racing heart.

"You've nothing to fear," Sheila said comfortingly. "We would never attack anyone in either our dragon or human forms, except in the case of self-defense." Smiling, she added, "I would find it especially awkward, since I'm half human myself." Before Crystal became too confused, she explained the rest of the details.

"Our son isn't meant to find out his true identity until we return home in a few more years," said Bruce. "When the time comes, Lendric is supposed to return for us. But if it's as you say, and Lendric's Myzalik Staff is missing with his brothers, I hope they'll be found and bring it back by the allotted time."

"What if they don't?" asked Julianna.

"Then we're stranded here until further notice," he replied. "The arrangement was for approximately twenty-five years here on Earth, allowing Oliver to grow up safely while the power of his violet eyes developed. It would seem we all share the hope that the Staff is returned to Lendric as soon as possible."

She could only nod in agreement, listening quietly as the couple revealed more details of Chavernos.

*****

"I guess you've just about proven everything we came to hear," Julianna said awhile later, "though I must admit it will be easier to accept completely when I see Dominick here in reality."

Sensing the underlying meaning to her words, Sheila said softly, "This dreamphaser of yours sounds familiar, my dear. I wonder if it's the same one we met in years past." Julianna immediately became more attentive. "Several years before we left Chavernos, and well before Oliver was born, we visited the island of Barokka you mentioned. There, Lendric introduced us to some of the people, including its ruler Chaos. Do you know of him?"

"Yes," whispered Julianna. "Through Dominick, I did meet him in my dreams once."

"A fine man," stated Bruce. "A stern figure, but well capable of handling the many responsibilities of the island. I remember now the meeting of which you speak."

Sheila nodded. "On the day of our visit, we were greeted by an unexpected celebration. When we questioned what it was for, Chaos invited Lendric and us within the palace to a room on the second floor. A dark-haired boy of about two or three years nearly tripped us up on the way in, but despite the boy's laughter, we knew he couldn't have meant any harm. His father seemed to think otherwise."

Sighing with remembrance, Bruce shook his head. "I don't know why, but I got the notion his father was onto something."

"Now, Bruce, we've argued this before. Riff was just a child."

"I still say Riff-Raff was a more fitting title," he growled.

"Riff-Raff?" asked Julianna, her eyes brightening.

"His mother called him Riff," explained Sheila, "although I can't blame his father for being a bit short-tempered, with her having given birth to their second child but a few days prior. The celebration was being held in honor of their new son, whom she was holding in her arms. Of course, they'd named him..."

"Dominick," she finished.

"Dominick Westbrooke, to be exact," said Sheila. "The second of Chaos's grandsons, who are both the future heirs to the island." She smiled. "I can only assume by your enthusiastic response to my words that I've correctly identified our world's Dominick as your own."

"Yes," agreed Julianna, unable to resist leaning forward to hug her. "Mrs. Dragend, you have no idea how grateful I am to hear what you've told us. You've just proven what I kept praying was the truth, and now I can remain engaged to the man I love with a clear mind."

Sheila patted her back, pulling back gently. "I'm glad to have helped, my dear. I hope for your sake that you'll be reunited with your loved one as soon as possible. And who knows... maybe our paths will cross again one day on Chavernos. But in the meantime, let's see to having a pleasant Earth dinner right now."

*****

"She did *what?*" exclaimed Dominick.

"Stop playing deaf, Dom," chided Buddy. "You know you heard me full well the first time. Sionne ran off and eloped with Quell last night, and they've left the island. Her mother's been having fits all day since Sireni found the note she'd left."

Inferno flashed a broad grin to Dominick. "I guess that means you're finally off her marriage hook." Curious at his silence, he continued, "Isn't that what you wanted?"

Dominick looked up abruptly. "Of course it is," he replied. "If she's happy with Quell, then they're welcome to each other. I'm merely surprised they got married so quickly."

Both men shot him surprised smirks. "*This* from the former confirmed bachelor who proposed to his Earth maiden after a handful of weeks?" laughed Buddy. "Hmmm, you know, maybe I should take the hint and go to Earth someday, so I can find one there too."

"Not if you value that forked tail of yours!" came a familiar lilting voice from across Lost Limbo.

"Stop eavesdropping, Jarissa!" Buddy called back. "That stubborn female only makes me more certain I should go find someone else," he mumbled.

"Cheer up, Buddy," said Inferno. "There's always the dragon legion." The guardian glared at him in reply, just before a loud cough earned their attention.

"I'm afraid the dragon legion's out of business, boys," amended a familiar gold-haired man. Dominick was on his feet instantly to face him with wide eyes.

"Lendric," he exclaimed, "what are you doing here?"

"I have news regarding that matter we discussed. That is, if your friends won't mind my borrowing you outside for a few minutes."

"You're excused," Buddy said amiably, "so long as you come back here to share a drink with us afterwards."

Lendric raised an eyebrow. "You're buying?"

"Of course."

"Well, then!" he laughed brightly, clapping an arm around Dominick's shoulder. "We won't be long."

From Dream to Reality

Once outside and away from other people, Dominick's pent-up curiosity reached its limit. "I certainly wasn't expecting a visit from you this soon, Lendric. Has there been word from your brothers?"

The dragon sorcerer fairly beamed before nodding. "They're back, alive and well," he confirmed.

"Thank Chavernos! You and your sister must be greatly relieved."

"Er, well..." murmured Lendric, "considering the way they were last seen raiding the pantry at my home, I'm not so certain of that one. Zaruldar doesn't usually eat too much, but Pyro has a bottomless chasm for a stomach."

"Maybe you should try a magic padlock," suggested Dominick, folding his arms. As Lendric seemed to consider this thoughtfully, he added, "But tell me, what happened to them all this time?"

Lendric groaned, giving indication of his opinion of the situation. "Apparently, it seems my younger brother Pyrozill had a tad too much to drink on one of the planets they teleported to. While some of the others with them found him amusing, Zaruldar got annoyed with his antics and decided to teleport them somewhere else. Without realizing what he was doing, Pyrozill accidentally bumped into Zaruldar while he was in the middle of the teleportation spell, disrupting his concentration, and sending them to an unknown and much more primitive planet instead."

"Oh no. How primitive?"

"The word Neanderthal comes to mind." Dominick groaned this time. "My sentiments exactly. And unfortunately, this was a planet where magic was *much* less conducive. The Staff couldn't recharge, and before they could leave, they were attacked by the natives, who stole the Staff to satisfy their curiosity."

"Hmmm, two people materializing out of thin air might

startle anyone, let alone primitive natives," he agreed. "Why didn't they transform into their dragon forms to get the Staff back from the start?"

"Pyrozill was too sloshed to transform into a *mouse*, much less anything else!" Lendric growled in obvious annoyance. "Especially with Pyro out of it, Zaruldar didn't want the Staff accidentally damaged. The sheer number of the natives overwhelmed them and they were herded into a primitive prison.

"To make matters worse, Zaruldar discovered that they couldn't even transform properly without risking injury. When he attempted it, with his magic ability hampered by the atmosphere's resistance to magic, the effort proved too slow and painful and he nearly ended up stuck between human and dragon form. With Pyrozill's encouragement, he managed to get back to human form again, but not easily. After that, they decided to remain in their human forms for the time being, until a safer solution could be found."

"That would explain their being there awhile," said Dominick.

"Things did improve for them after a time. Somehow, they managed to gain the natives' trust and were accepted into the group, but the natives still didn't wish to give up their prized treasure. My brothers made many attempts to retrieve the Staff, but the natives turned out to be cleverer than they thought, and each attempt failed.

"Most recently, when Zaruldar finally came up with a workable plan to reach the Staff, and they succeeded in getting it, they still couldn't get it to charge properly and so they were subdued again. They were trying to reason with the angry natives, when my demon allies finally found the pair.

"Fortunately, demon magic works outside the realm of a world's atmosphere. In some ways similar to guardians, since they can also teleport themselves but not others, though their range isn't as limited. They were successful in frightening off the natives in order to obtain the Staff, and with their combined magic, were able to charge it so my brothers could use it to return home at last."

"So," began Dominick, "does that mean the Staff..."

"Also came back safe and sound? Yes, dear boy, it does," confirmed Lendric, "which is why I raced here to tell you. Even on our world, it will take several hours to charge, of course, but I thought perhaps I might see to it." He smiled knowingly. "That is, in case you want to make a trip to Earth tonight to finally meet your bride-to-be in reality."

Dominick shook his hand with deep gratitude. "Lendric, I'll never be able to thank you enough."

"Save your thanks until we get there," he replied, "although I will take personal charge of this teleportation, so I doubt there'll be any problems. As we speak, Carilya is keeping an eye on the Staff—and Pyrozill—to keep my younger brother from doing something foolish again. In the meantime, you'd best tell Chaos where we'll be, since your bride may wish to take a few days in bidding her own family good-bye, if she's to come live on Chavernos."

The younger man's expression grew somber at the thought. They hadn't really settled that issue, although Julianna *seemed* to want to live here from their last few discussions.

"Dominick, is something wrong?" he asked, picking up on his hesitation.

Shaking his head quickly to clear it, Dominick brightened again. The main thing was to reach Earth and his fiancée. He and Julianna would work out the other details when he got there. "No, of course not," he replied, satisfied. "You're right though, Lendric. We'd better plan for a brief stay on Earth, in case Julianna needs some time to adjust to this sudden development."

Leaning closer, the dragon sorcerer whispered, "Has she spoken with the Dragend family yet?"

"She was supposed to go there today with her sister, so I

would imagine it's likely she knows the truth now."

"And she'll see the proof of it when we arrive to greet her on Earth tonight," added Lendric, glancing down at a small orb on his outfit which began to glow. "What the wyverns... Oh, blazes! That's Carilya's signal. Pyrozill must have rankled the demon child awake or something, since his parents left him with us for a few more days. If you'll excuse me, Dominick. Oh, and please tell the others I'll join them another day for that drink."

"Wait," he interrupted. "What about the details for our journey tonight?"

Lendric nodded, warding this off. "Now, don't cast nightmares into your dreamphasing mind, my dear boy. I'll bring the Myzalik Staff here, fully charged, sometime later this night. We'll perform the teleportation inside the castle to avoid outside witnesses. In the meantime, you might do best to see Julianna in advance to inform her of your impending arrival. There's no sense in shocking her when we appear outside her house. At least traveling at night should minimize the risk of the neighbors noticing."

"How will I know when to return?"

"I'll send Chaos or your brother to fetch you," he replied impatiently. "Now, really, Dominick. I have to go, lest I find my home incinerated in my absence. And that certainly won't help your case if the Staff goes up in flames with it."

"I understand," he said, just before the dragon sorcerer vanished.

Dominick sighed once, before his positive enthusiasm quickly returned. *Tonight, Julianna and I will be together in reality!* he thought exultantly.

His change of mood wasn't lost on his friends when he went back to them. While he was outside, the gals had joined their table. Speaking quietly so the other patrons wouldn't overhear, he told his friends that Lendric had found a way to take him to Julianna tonight, and that in a few days he'd be bringing her to Chavernos with him when he returned. While the others respected when he wouldn't reveal the method, they'd heard enough of Lendric's magic to believe it possible.

Buddy clapped a hand on his shoulder good-naturedly. "Congratulations, Dominick. You'll finally get that dream girl of yours, and we'll have a new addition to our little group."

"I'm sure she'll fit right in," said Psych.

Kiri smiled at Dominick, surprising him as she clasped his hand. "Be sure and bring her back soon," she told him. "After what we've heard from you and Riff, she's bound to miss her family and sisters, so you be sure to tell her not to worry. She'll have three adoptive sisters ready to welcome her, so she'll feel more at home."

Dominick kissed her hand thankfully. "I'm sure Julianna will be most grateful for your understanding."

"A toast then," Buddy replied, allowing the others to raise their own glasses in salute. "To the soon-to-be newest addition to our group, Julianna Sherborne. May she and our lifelong friend have only good fortune together from this day forward."

The others clinked glasses, knowing the time for a full celebration was nearing; but in the meantime, a private one among friends would suffice.

*****

"Whatever happened today, you look like you're on cloud nine," commented Marybeth, grinning at her friend.

Once again at the club this evening, Julianna was leaning against her arm happily, staring at the ceiling. It was all true, and Crystal had been a witness. Nothing on this Earth could have brought her more happiness... short of Dominick coming here.

Just thinking of him prompted a yawn, as if her entire being wished to speed up their meeting later tonight.

"Yawning again?" laughed her friend. "You've certainly been doing that a lot lately. This Dominick you mentioned wouldn't happen to have anything to do with that, would he?"

Blushing, Julianna was spared from answering upon seeing Roger come up behind them. "Evening, ladies," he said cheerfully.

"Well, well," drawled Marybeth. "The irrational spy has tracked us down again."

Ignoring her, Roger was surprised to find Julianna fairly beaming as she gestured to a chair. "Feel free to join us," she offered.

"Are you feeling all right?"

"All's right with the universe," she replied. This time, it was Roger who was prevented from further conversation, as the local karaoke announcer called up an unexpected participant.

"One of our local rookies, Julianna Sherborne, wishes to give this a shot. Would you care to come up now?"

As Marybeth gaped, Julianna swept past her to step up to the front. Roger was still more amazed. Remembering how shy she'd once been, he had to admit she'd changed since their younger days.

Despite her momentary bravado, Julianna was as nervous as anyone else might be, waiting long moments as the coordinator found the song she'd requested. As she stared past the sea of unfamiliar faces though, she saw something else.

Blinking in surprise, she realized she hadn't imagined it. There **was** a shimmering star-like light in the back of the room, apparently unnoticed by anyone else. As if sensing her eyes upon it, the light flashed once. Knowing only one logical explanation for that star-like presence, she smiled with newfound determination.

If Dominick wished to hear her sing that much, then she'd certainly oblige him to the best of her ability. After all, he'd inspired her to come up here, and she'd thus chosen her song accordingly meant just for him.

As the first strains of music filled the air, Julianna glanced at the video display where the song lyrics to a love song began to appear. Moments later, her voice filled in the melody, earning an attentive quiet from the audience.

Having only faltered slightly at the start, Julianna rapidly proved to Dominick that she did have a beautiful singing voice, staying fairly well in key, and leaving Marybeth and Roger with looks of stunned awe.

Oblivious to them, Julianna gradually lifted her eyes from the display, keeping them focused instead on the not-so-distant light. It was more than a knowledge of the words that had Julianna pouring her heart and soul into the lyrics she sang. She was singing for one man alone, who was with her now in the only way he could be, voicing that her heart belonged only to him.

When the music drew to a close, Julianna could feel a few tears in her eyes, but the crowd didn't seem to notice as they granted her applause, along with Roger and Marybeth.

Amidst the applause, Julianna cast a knowing look to the light in the back which blinked several times. "That one's for you, Dominick!" she called out. The star flashed brightly, almost seeming as though it would float over to her, but as if thinking twice, it abruptly flew through the ceiling and disappeared. Smiling after it, Julianna missed seeing Roger's scowl at her last words. She moved to sit beside Marybeth, who clasped her hands excitedly.

"Why didn't you tell me you could sing?" she demanded. "All these years you had me believing you couldn't!"

Julianna shrugged innocently, saying nothing. Apparently, she'd disproven that theory tonight, and thank goodness, due to her unexpected audience from beyond.

*****

Finding herself formally dressed outside the dance hall again, Julianna's curiosity was piqued. Dominick only seemed to bring them here on rare occasions. What could be the reason for it now? she wondered.

Gazing into the room to see if her companion was amongst the dancers, she was startled to hear his voice just behind her, turning with a gasp.

"So the songbird has finally returned to grace me with her presence," he said, grandiosely dropping to one knee to kiss her hand. Blushing, she couldn't speak before he grinned, revealing a bouquet of red roses he'd held behind his back. "I believe this may be a custom our worlds share to congratulate a performer."

"You've been brushing up on your Earth knowledge. I'm impressed."

"Nay, fair maiden," he replied, shaking his head. "It was I who was impressed this night, when you exceeded all my expectations. I think you might have another talent besides your supposed knack for trouble. Although I already believe you have yet another talent with children."

Lending her his arm to lead her inside, Julianna accepted, apparently pleased. Placing her flowers on a nearby table, he then led her to the dance floor.

"You really think I'm not bad as a singer?" she asked.

Pulling her into his arms, his loving gaze spoke volumes. "Sweetheart, I think you could charm dragons from the skies on Chavernos, let alone anyone else you chose to enchant. Heaven knows, you've already spellbound me for life in every way."

As she kissed his cheek for the compliment, he was barely able to conceal his jubilation over the timely news he'd just received, which was part of the reason he'd arrived so early. "Darling," he said finally, taking her hands in his, eyes twinkling with enthusiasm, "I have the most wonderful news."

"Oh, so do I," she interrupted, her own eyes lighting up. "I can't wait to tell you." At first, he seemed about to protest, but then gradually nodded for her to continue. After all, he had a bit more time left before he'd need to return to Chavernos.

"Dominick, you were right. Crystal and I went to the Dragend family, and they confirmed everything. Now she believes about you and Chavernos, and I no longer have any remaining doubts either."

"I'm glad you both know the truth at last, sweetheart," he replied softly, stroking her cheek. "Things have been going well on Chavernos too. Sionne's apparently eloped with someone she's known for many years, and left the island with him last night. Rumor has it that Dual seems to have disappeared as well. And most importantly..."

"I'm glad to hear Sionne married someone else, considering how she seemed so willing to drag you to the marriage altar herself," admitted Julianna, without noticing the increasingly frustrated expression on her companion's face. "But since she's no threat to us now, I suppose I can wish her happy."

"Julianna!" he broke in.

Quieting instantly, she asked, "Am I talking too much again?"

Kissing her quickly, he shook his head. "Normally, I wouldn't mind, love. But you see, as I've been trying to tell you, tonight we can finally..."

"Well, well, well!" chimed a familiar voice. "Westbrooke and his doxy have returned."

Julianna glanced up with surprise, only to whisper, "Oh no... not again." She overheard her companion groan behind her.

Covering his eyes with one hand, Dominick couldn't help but wonder... was there a curse on him, preventing him from getting out one simple sentence to the woman he loved?

"What the blazes do *you* want now?" he snapped, allowing Daffordshire to take the brunt of his frustration. "I thought we'd settled this before over a glass of punch. Or rather, the whole punch bowl."

As the crowd started laughing, Julianna stifled a laugh

herself with one hand. Daffordshire's face reddened as he reached one hand within his coat. "I doubt you'll find *this* quite so amusing, Westbrooke!" he hissed, pulling forth a pistol.

The crowd gasped, while Dominick pulled Julianna behind him. "Now look, Daffy,... I mean, Daffordshire," he said, "can't we use a more peaceful method to settle things? After all, murder isn't going to help your reputation with the ladies."

"You already destroyed *that* during our last meeting!" spat Daffordshire. "Both you *and* your redheaded wench!"

Julianna bristled with fury behind Dominick, silently vowing that this was the *last* time she'd take being called *that* term again. Immediately, she began to search her mind for a suitable form of retribution.

Sensing her thoughts, Dominick praised her clever spirit once more. All he had to do was keep ol' Daffy occupied, and maybe... "Why don't we just declare a truce?" he suggested. "You leave us alone. We leave you alone. No bloodshed, no murders, no tabloids tomorrow."

"Oh, do be quiet!" snarled Daffordshire. "You know, Westbrooke, you really aren't quite so high and mighty when staring down a revolver, are you? Maybe I should shoot your doxy first, just to make things more interesting."

Dominick's expression darkened. "Over my dead body."

"Since you insist, I can go along with that idea," chortled Daffordshire, releasing the catch on his gun.

Julianna cursed her imaginative mind for failing her when she needed it most. *If only my dog Shadow was here. **She'd** certainly fix that foul-mouthed egotist!*

Picking up the thought from her mind gave Dominick all the ammunition he needed. "Julianna, focus all your thoughts on that dog," he whispered quickly. Curious, she looked askance, but followed his instructions.

Moments later, a loud rumble shook the room, causing people to start screaming. "Do you think a mere earthquake will stop me?" yelled Daffordshire, still waving the pistol. "Think again, Westbrooke! I'm not so stupid that I... I..."

Julianna's eyes narrowed in confusion upon seeing Daffordshire's face turn white. "What's come over him?" she asked Dominick, just noticing he was now staring behind them with an amused look.

The room shook again as a very loud set of barks nearly deafened everyone. Recognizing the sound, Julianna spun about, and her hand flew to her mouth as she saw what seemed to be her dog—or rather a ten-foot version of her dog—bounding into the room.

"Dominick!" she shouted above the barking, "Are you crazy? Shadow'll step on us, if not eat us!"

"Would she do that to her doting mistress?" he replied mirthfully.

The dog began wagging her tail upon sighting Julianna. She waved up at Shadow warily, saying, "I just hope she doesn't expect us to conjure up a dog biscuit that large."

"Say, now there's an idea," replied Dominick, raising his hands to form a megaphone. "Hey, Shadow, would you like a new chew-toy to play with?" he called out. Looking down at him in amusement, the dog barked once, as if in agreement. "Well then," he continued, pointing ahead, "why don't you go fetch that tasty chicken of Daffordshire over there?"

Eyeing the morsel in question, Shadow licked her chops. Daffordshire let out an ear-piercing scream, dropping the pistol while turning to run for the outdoors. Thinking it to be a game, Shadow promptly reached down and grabbed Daffordshire by his tailcoat, lifting him into the air. Wagging her tail at Julianna again, she began bounding off the way she'd arrived, smashing through the wall and heading towards the horizon.

Julianna could only gape as the crowd and Dominick broke into laughter, obviously taking great amusement in this. Seeing her annoyed look, he turned to her questioningly. "I know he may deserve that," she told him, "but to feed him to my dog?"

Recovering from his laughter, Dominick sobered. "You're right, love. Shadow might get indigestion. I'll take care of it. Observe." As she turned to watch, moments later, the dog in the distance literally vanished, dropping a shouting Daffordshire to the ground. Following his rather undignified landing, he started cursing anew, apparently unharmed. As Dominick waved his hand in an arc, the wall repaired itself as if nothing had occurred. "Better now?" he asked with a grin.

"Yes," she replied, not hiding a smile. "After all, ten-feet or no, she's still my puppy."

He pulled her close. "If *that's* a puppy, love, you'd certainly better cut back on the dog chow," he advised. As she groaned, he smiled. "But in order to keep an eye on her, how would you like me to come to Earth tonight to help you out?"

It took a few seconds for his words to sink in, but when they did, Julianna turned to him with wide eyes. "Does this mean...?" she began.

He nodded, clasping her face in his hands gently. "Lendric's brothers returned safely with the Staff, which he came to tell me this afternoon. And if all goes well, I think it's safe to say that by the end of this night, I'll be joining you on your homeworld Earth."

Unable to speak through her happiness, Julianna let out a joyful cry, while Dominick picked her up to spin her about. The crowd watching them was a bit perplexed, but since they had at least some appreciation for romance, they enjoyed watching the happy pair.

Only one silent figure watched them coldly with narrowed eyes from behind the back of another. As the crowd was distracted, he abruptly vanished.

*****

"Pyro, for the thousandth time, you can't silence a

demon child with tape!" yelled Carilya. "They bite right through it and aim for your fingers as well."

"Okay, got a large pillow we can stuff in his mouth instead?" suggested Pyrozill.

Their voices only raised into a louder shouting match.

Sighing as he overheard the commotion, Lendric left the charging Staff for a minute to run interference, using the calmest voice he could before the demon child let out another ear-piercing screech.

"Blazes, *give* me that tape!" he snapped at Pyrozill. Confused by the shouting, the demon child began torching the room. "*And* a fire extinguisher!"

While they were occupied, a pair of shadows silently appeared at the end of the hallway, swiftly forming into the shapes of two men. As they became fully tangible, though still obscured by magic, the first pointed to the room holding the Staff, and they both entered swiftly.

"Is this the device you wish me to take care of?" the second man asked in a deceptively calm voice.

"Yes, and be quick about it," hissed the first. "We only have moments before that meddling sorcerer returns."

The second man eyed the Staff appreciatively. "Hmmm, I do believe my master would much prefer our bringing him this instead."

"You can't do that," protested the first. "I had this plan all worked out!"

"Silence!" snarled the second. "My master *always* takes precedence over trifles." Before the other could say anything else, the man reached forward to grasp the Staff, just before a crackling sound caused him to draw back his hand in alarm. "By the netherworld, that demon sorcerer has placed a protection spell upon it, so I can't touch it!"

"There, you see?" sneered the first. "Now in deference to your master Zmalyrithe, don't you think that if *he* can't have the Staff, the dragon sorcerer and his ally should suffer for it, just as we planned?"

"Agreed," the second one replied grudgingly, rubbing his sore hand. "Your request shall be granted, if only to pay back that miserable sorcerer for my injury. Even if I can't touch it physically, at least my *magic* will still work on this blasted thing."

Raising his fingers towards it, he began reciting a solemn incantation, slowly causing a dark cloud of smoke to envelope the top part of the Staff. He murmured a name amidst the spell, bringing forth a brighter glow for a few seconds. Then, the glow faded into a deep maroon, seeping within the object. As the man closed his hand, all semblance of the smoke was gone, leaving the Staff appearing untouched as it continued to charge.

"Our work here is done," he said, gesturing to the first man. "I expect full payment for my services upon returning us to Dark Haven."

"You'll receive it," he promised, grinning darkly. "And my annoying enemy and his bride will receive quite a shock, when he tries to reach her tonight."

Nodding, the second man waved his hands, causing them to fade back into shadows, just before vanishing.

"Do you smell something cooking?" came Pyrozill's voice from the other room.

"You and your stomach again," sighed Zaruldar, just before the others began chiding him similarly.

*****

Julianna leaned against Dominick's shoulder as they danced, enjoying this last opportunity before their separation would be at an end. After that, either when awake or asleep, nothing could keep them apart again.

"The music here would have a rock snoring!" a man yelled, disrupting the mood of the room, though the music kept playing.

Dominick rolled his eyes, while Julianna fought back laughter.

"Hey, Phase," Riff said jovially, waving as he walked over. "How's it going?" Before his brother could say anything, Riff turned to the woman beside him. "Oh... the bride-to-be," he said cordially, grinning at Julianna, before swooping her into his arms. "So how have you been, my future sister? Has Phase been hassling you about wanting the honeymoon before the wedding again?"

Julianna laughed openly this time, just before Dominick interceded, eyeing his brother with a meaningful glare. "Did you come here just to give us another reason why we should stay on Earth to avoid living on the same world as you?"

"Ugh!" he groaned, gripping his chest. "My brother knows how to wound his doting family." Sobering instantly, he continued, "Seriously though, Lendric wants you back on Chavernos. He seems to think you might want to undertake a nighttime excursion to Earth, and said to mention that Julianna might want to watch for your arrival just outside of her house. Until you get home, of course, I'll gladly keep my future sister company in your absence..."

"You're coming *with* me," insisted Dominick, turning to Julianna to clasp her hands. "It won't be long now, love. Soon our patient waiting will have its sweet reward."

"I can't wait," she replied, leaning closer for him to kiss her.

"She'll have to, unless you get a move on, Phase," interrupted Riff, tugging on his brother's shoulder to pull him back.

Cuffing him with another glare, Dominick squeezed Julianna's hand. "Wait for me by your window, love," he said softly. "I promise I'll be there shortly."

Kissing him quickly before Riff could interfere, she whispered to him, "I'll be counting the minutes until your arrival."

*****

Having already said a temporary farewell to his family and close friends, Dominick stood beside Lendric in a vacant palace room on the lower floor. As the dragon sorcerer held the now glowing Staff in his grasp, concentrating on getting them to their destination, Dominick couldn't help glancing out the window at the vibrant colors of his homeworld. By Chaos, no matter how temporary, he knew he'd miss it as soon as they left.

Moments later, lights began to cascade around them, as the Teleportation Staff swept them up in its spell. The last thing Dominick saw from the window was the look of calm resignation from his grandfather as he appeared to wave a final good-bye to his much loved grandson.

Then all became a glow of pure white, and Dominick could see nothing more.

*****

Having awakened at least an hour ago, Julianna couldn't help pacing restlessly about her room, constantly glancing out the window for some sign of Dominick's arrival. Dear Lord, there were times she wished they could communicate across the distance by telepathy! Where *was* he?

Pressing her forehead against the window in silent frustration, Julianna shut her eyes with a sigh. Maybe something else had detained him. Maybe there was a problem with the Staff. Maybe he'd changed his mind...

Feeling something bright penetrate her closed eyes, she opened them carefully, her breath catching as she caught sight of a shimmering glow pouring towards the ground outside like a waterfall of light.

Almost immediately after, the light began to fade, revealing two shadowed figures standing in the middle of it. When the glow faded completely, both glanced about at their surroundings, while one finally turned to Julianna's house,

- 112 -

stepping towards it slowly.

As the streetlight illuminated the person completely, she could see by the glittering light in his eyes, the same look of recognition she felt.

"Julianna!" he called out, just before she flung the window open. At this, a grin spread across his face. "I'm sorry to have kept you waiting so long, sweetheart."

"You certainly did," she agreed. "A whole lifetime to be exact."

Dominick gave a short whistle. "That would seem to be quite an offense," he chuckled. "Any hope of a reprieve, long enough for a distant traveler to get a kiss of welcome from his loving, patient, future bride?"

"Give me five seconds, and I'll hold you to that kiss," she replied, disappearing from the window to emerge from the front door below. Racing towards Dominick, he was way ahead of her, catching her up in his arms to kiss her passionately, giving no indication he'd ever release her.

"Even dreams can't compare to this reality," he murmured, raining kisses all over Julianna's face, as his hands newly traced her soft contours, as if just holding her for the first time. A true enough fact. Glancing down at her attire, he added knowingly, "I'd imagine it's a bit chilly for you to be out like this, but you do look wonderful."

Only now realizing that in her excitement, she hadn't bothered to change out of her nightgown, Julianna blushed at his words.

"Don't worry, love," he said softly, taking her face in his hands. "I've seen you in less than this."

Before he had her blushing again, a look of wonder crossed Julianna's eyes. "I just can't believe you're really here."

"Believe it, love," he replied tenderly. "*This* is most definitely real." Kissing her again, neither noticed Lendric, who stood watching with a satisfied smile.

Ah, young love... It was moments like this that made him glad to have such a useful teleportation device. Glancing at the Staff he still held; however, his expression slowly grew wary upon hearing an odd hum growing in intensity from it.

Strange, he considered. *It's never done that before.*

As if just remembering his presence, Dominick broke apart from Julianna to gesture to the puzzled dragon elf. "Sweetheart, this is Lendric. The one responsible for making the impossible a reality."

Smiling, she walked towards him, Dominick following a few steps behind her. *So this is Lendric*, she thought. As with the Dragend family, she never would have suspected that he was truly a dragon either, judging by his present form.

"I'm certainly glad to meet you too, Lendric," she said. "Dominick and I both owe you..."

An abrupt, high-pitched sound cut off her words.

"Blazes, look out!" shouted Lendric, dropping the Staff to race from it. As soon as it hit the ground, a blast of pure energy shot forth, striking the first one it came in contact with. A scream was lost amidst the ensuing blast that deafened all of them, the force of it knocking them to the ground.

A sound that soon had several lights in the neighborhood turning on, as people ran to their own windows to see the reason for the unexpected noise.

Coughing as the blast's resulting cloud of smoke dissipated, Dominick pushed himself up from the ground, feeling shaken but in one piece. Glancing across from him, he could see Lendric rising as well. He was all right too.

As the smoke cleared further though, another sight chilled his blood.

"Julianna!" he exclaimed hoarsely, beside her still form in moments. Pulling her into his arms, he lifted her head.

His heart stopped as he saw the blood on her forehead, mingling with a series of black burn marks. Her thankfully unblemished eyes were shut loosely, but her skin color was now a deathly white. To his endless remorse, Dominick could all but feel her spirit draining away in his arms.

"Dear heaven, sweetheart, don't leave me now," he pleaded, cradling her tightly, as if he could somehow physically prevent her soul from leaving. "Come on, love, wake up," he added insistently. "Julianna, you've got to open your eyes. Please, open them." As her heartbeat grew fainter against him, he sensed he was losing the battle.

"By Chavernos, Julianna, what have I done to you?" he whispered brokenly. Tears of helpless frustration squeezed from his eyes as he cradled her lifeless form against his chest.

Chapter Six

"No..." Dominick declared a moment later, raising his head with determination. "Dammit, Julianna, after all we went through to be together, I swear you're not going to die on me now. Lendric!"

"I'm right here," assured the dragon sorcerer, having come running as soon as his shaken thoughts cleared. Touching Julianna's forehead lightly, he grimaced. "This looks bad," he said. "Whatever hit her was equivalent to a lightning bolt, and it couldn't have picked a worse place to strike."

"By Chaos, you don't have to tell me what I already know!" he retorted in desperation. "Just *do* something to heal her before she slips away forever!"

"Yes, of course," he agreed, reaching for some spell components. "There should still be time to save her, if I use just the right amounts of this."

Praying his friend's magic wouldn't fail him, Dominick shut his eyes, clasping Julianna's hand as her head leaned against his shoulder. Lendric called forth the necessary magic, waving his hands over Julianna's injury.

Somewhat reluctantly, Dominick opened his eyes to gaze down upon her, but was relieved as the burn marks gradually grew fainter, while the bleeding on her forehead stopped and then started to clear.

Keep her with us, Lendric, he thought, uncertain if he was merely imagining Julianna's heartbeat growing stronger and the pallor fading from her face.

"Julianna," he said, gaining no response at first. After another few attempts though, he was rewarded by a soft groan from her. "Thank heaven," he breathed, waiting until Lendric finished the spell before trying to speak to her again.

When the dragon sorcerer drew back, somewhat drained, but pleased that Julianna's wounds seemed to be healed, he and Dominick both watched silently as she started to open her eyes.

As she gazed upward at the man holding her, Dominick's relieved expression was the first thing she saw. "Welcome back to the living, sweetheart," he said quietly, brushing a curl back from her now unmarked forehead. "You gave us both one hell of a scare, love," he continued, as she merely blinked at him. For a reason he couldn't name, Dominick felt a sense of unease at this. "It's not like you to remain speechless, love," he said good-naturedly. "Aren't you going to say something?"

Julianna licked her lips once before speaking. "Who... are you?" she whispered.

"After all this time, you even need to ask?" he replied, his relief fading. Her blank stare never wavered, only causing his heart to sink with a new desperation. "Julianna, it's me... Dominick. Your soon-to-be husband."

"My what?" she exclaimed, struggling against him, confused by both of the faces before her. Where was her family? Where were her sisters? "Crystal," she began to call out.

"Julianna, calm down," urged Dominick, unable to stifle the very genuine fear in her eyes.

"Crystal!" she shouted louder. "*Crystal!*"

Her cry didn't go unanswered, as Crystal and Jerry had already been awakened by the loud blast from the Staff. Pushing the front door open to run outside, Crystal's questioning look soon turned to shock upon seeing Julianna in the helpless company of two strange men.

"You bastards, get away from her!" she yelled, as Jerry caught up with her, wielding a baseball bat, in case the men wouldn't cooperate peacefully. As Dominick lifted his head to meet Crystal's gaze regretfully, her hand flew to her mouth.

"Ohmigod..." she gasped. "It's you."

"It's *who*?" asked Jerry, surprised at the look of familiarity in her eyes. "Dammit, Crystal, do you *know* these men?"

"Only this one," she said, still staring at the man in question. "You're Dominick, aren't you?"

He nodded slowly, while Julianna stopped struggling momentarily. "You know this man?" she asked, before glancing towards an equally confused Jerry. At the attempt, she winced, suffering from a most painful headache. Not too surprising under the circumstances, considering what she was wearing and how cold it was outside.

Good heavens! she realized, glancing down at her nightgown. As the man still holding her refocused his attention on her, she began to fight him. "Let me go, you lecherous beast!" she shrieked, "and keep your eyes to yourself! Jerry, do something about this!"

"I intend to," he said, glaring briefly at his wife. Reaching down to take Julianna from Dominick, the other man only shrugged away from him, while dodging the retaliation of the woman in his arms.

"Julianna, stop it!" he demanded, shaking her once. "It's obvious you can't remember who I am right now, but you don't have to treat me like an attacker!" Gradually, both she and Jerry lost some of their anger.

"Who *are* you?" she asked again.

"I'm Dominick Westbrooke," he said patiently. "I came here across a great distance to be with you, so we could be married. Don't you remember any of this?"

She shook her head. "I don't even remember how I got out here, let alone what I'm doing with the likes of you. All I know is that my head is pounding. Now please, if you don't mean any harm, just let me go."

Seeing Dominick's jaw tighten with inner frustration, Crystal quickly remedied the situation. "Dominick, I think both you and your friend should come inside the house, before the neighbors start heading over here with their own questions. Then perhaps you can explain to all of us just what in heaven's name happened tonight."

"I wish I knew the answer to *that* one myself," Lendric mumbled, tentatively retrieving his now dormant Staff. It didn't seem any worse for the wear, but still, he hoped no further harm would come from it.

Nodding, Dominick began to stand, lifting Julianna with him. Instantly, she began to beat her hands against his chest.

"Crystal may know you, but to *me*, you're a total stranger!" she protested. "Now let me go!"

"Whether you know it or not, you're in no condition to walk right now," he insisted, silencing her with an equally stubborn look. "But if you'll stop fighting me, I'll get you inside and set you down safely on a chair as you seem to so fervently wish!"

Chagrined by her abrupt compliance, Dominick followed Crystal and Jerry into the house, the latter still looking skeptical as Lendric joined them too. *There was bound to be little sleep tonight*, he thought.

*****

"Of course I know you," sighed Julianna. "You're my sister Crystal, and that's your husband Jerry. Why are you looking at me like *I'm* the one who's crazy around here?" She pointed an accusing finger at Dominick. "*He's* the one who's falsely claiming I know him."

"But that's not what you were saying for the past month or so," her sister explained calmly. Turning to Dominick, she steepled her hands. "Now, I know who *you* are. But I'm afraid this man with you is unfamiliar."

"Of course," he said, gesturing to his friend. "This is Lendric. One of the most highly skilled sorcerers on..." Eyeing Julianna's skepticism warily, as well as Jerry's, he added slowly, "our homeworld of Chavernos."

"*What*?" exclaimed Jerry.

"Well, at least *one* of you seems to agree with me," said Julianna, folding her arms, just before flinching from another head pain.

Seeing her grip her head, Dominick wanted to comfort her, but knew full well how she'd react if he did. "It's quite true," he told her. "Your head injury was sustained because of an unforeseen malfunction to Lendric's teleportation device that brought us here."

"What do you mean head injury?" she asked, running her fingers across her forehead. "I don't feel any bruises or scars. Crystal, do *you* see anything?"

Her sister shook her head. "No," she admitted.

"Proof again that this man is lying."

"You wouldn't be saying that if Lendric hadn't healed your head wound with magic," countered Dominick. "Before regaining consciousness, you were burned and bleeding, near death. We couldn't call for assistance just to prove you were injured, since you might not have survived then."

"Magic!" she retorted, with a short laugh. "There *is* no magic on Earth, and I *don't* have a head injury." A sudden throbbing pain in her temples sought to refute this, but she said nothing.

"Masking your pain doesn't change the truth," he said quietly. "Maybe it's true that your physical head injury was healed and is no longer visible. However, it seems the damage went deeper, affecting your memory."

Julianna's eyes narrowed. "Just because I don't know *you* doesn't prove a damn thing. I know my family, I know my name is Julianna Sherborne, and I know where I live. All things which discredit your amnesia theory."

"Maybe... but not if you sustained *partial* amnesia."

Before Julianna could argue, Crystal interrupted, "Wait a second. Perhaps there's a way *I* can shed some light on this possibility." Walking across the room, she retrieved something from behind a table and brought it over to her sister. "Take a good look at this drawing, Julie, and tell us what you see."

Sighing wearily, Julianna took the paper from her, almost immediately glancing up at Dominick. "If I'm not mistaken, it's a drawing resembling him."

Looking over her shoulder, understanding lit his features as he realized where this was leading. "It's a very good likeness, rough as it may be," he said. "I'm touched to have been deemed a worthy subject by the artist."

While he was distracted by the portrait, Julianna glanced up at him again, surprised when her heart leaped. No doubt from his close proximity. Yet reluctantly, she found herself privately admitting that he *was* a handsome man. With that wavy dark hair, attractive physique, and eyes a most intriguing deep shade of blue...

Eyes that suddenly caught hers with silent question.

Chiding herself as she turned away, she broke out, "Regardless of its artistic merits, I don't see how this is relevant to anything, Crystal."

"You should," she said evenly. "*You're* the one who drew it. Vicki, my son, and I were present when you did."

Julianna gaped, shaking her head abruptly. "No," she whispered. "That's not possible. I've never seen this man before in my life. How could I draw a complete stranger?"

"Because Dominick is *not* a stranger to you," insisted Crystal. "At least that's what you swore before tonight." Seeing the lost look filling her sister's eyes, she placed a comforting arm around her shoulders, hugging her. "I know you're confused. I think all of us would like our own answers to what happened.

But for now, I think you'd do best to get some sleep, and we can discuss it further in the morning. All right?"

Nodding, Julianna allowed her sister to lead her upstairs to her room, carrying the portrait absently as she departed. All the while Crystal was gone, Jerry eyed the two strangers warily, but waited until his wife returned before questioning them.

"Maybe Julie's not up to hearing the rest of this tonight, but I certainly am," he said. "Now I think it's about time you both explained just who the hell you are, and what you were doing outside with my sister-in-law in the middle of the night?"

"Fair enough," Dominick agreed. "But in that case, I think we'd all better sit down. This might take quite awhile to explain."

*****

"We're most fortunate that Julianna's sister and brother-in-law are being so understanding," said Lendric, glancing about the guest room Crystal had granted Dominick. Another room across the hall had been temporarily arranged for himself as well. "I just wish I knew what in blazes happened to the Staff."

"Does it really matter now?" hissed Dominick, slamming his hand against a table in frustration. "Of all the obstacles to befall us, why *this*? Julianna was completely innocent, yet for all the trust she placed in me, she's lost part of her memory!"

"She knows her family," his friend reminded him. "At least she doesn't have complete amnesia."

"She does regarding *me* though!" he snapped. Running an agonized hand through his hair, he shook his head. "We'd have been better off if I'd never come here at all tonight."

"And how long could you have continued your long distance relationship otherwise?" asked Lendric. "Come now, Dominick, we both know this was the only way you and Julianna could have found true happiness together."

"Yes," he said, forcing a bitter laugh. "Too bad it had a very *nasty* side effect, isn't it? Do you have any idea how it tore my heart out to see her look at me as if I was her worst nightmare come to life?"

The dragon sorcerer nodded. "I imagine it must have been devastating," he agreed. "However, there's nothing more we can do tonight. I suggest we both get some sleep. Perhaps by morning, she'll begin to remember more."

At his obvious reluctance, Lendric rested a hand against his shoulder, his expression attempting to be more understanding. "Either way, try and be comforted by one truth. At least you're physically here with her now, even though she may need time to recover her lost memories."

Dominick sighed, staring at the ceiling. "I appreciate your optimism, Lendric, and I am truly glad we're on the same world finally. But right now, all I can see is a much greater distance looming between us than ever existed before, when we were merely separated by worlds. A distance that no magic on Chavernos can ever change."

As he sat on the nearby bed, he never noticed Lendric leaving the room. His head falling forward, Dominick's eyes squeezed shut against his grief, wondering silently if the woman sleeping so near—and yet so far away—would ever look upon him with recognition again.

*****

"How is she this morning?" Dominick asked Crystal, while she cleared the breakfast table. "When you spoke with her, did she mention remembering anything yet?"

She sighed heavily. "I'm afraid not. The best I can tell you is that she seems fine now physically. The aspirin we gave her seems to be helping her headache pains from last night."

Shutting his eyes, he nodded. "I'm glad for that, if nothing else," he said.

Leaning forward to clasp his hand, Crystal smiled. "She'll remember," she replied. "After all the words of love she described you with before, I doubt memories like that can be lost forever. In the meantime, you're welcome to stay here as long as you need to."

"I certainly will," he vowed. "And I swear I'll do everything possible to help her get those memories back, starting today."

Pushing his chair in, he strode towards the stairs.

*****

Glancing out the window, Julianna was a bit miffed by the clouds in the sky. They seemed as foggy as the clouds supposedly blocking her mind. Not that she believed that, of course, since she felt perfectly fine. Obviously, at least one of the strange men was suffering delusions.

*My future **husband**!* she thought. Not that she couldn't see how a woman might want a man like that for a husband, since he was certainly attractive enough. But with such a stubborn temperament... *that* quality was certainly proving frustrating.

She climbed back into bed, leaning over the side to retrieve the picture she'd deposited there. Looking at it again still brought no recognition to her. Had she really drawn it herself? she wondered. She saw no reason for Crystal to lie to her about something like that, but still...

"Ah, my fair beauty is awake," came a familiar voice.

Dropping the portrait as it was suddenly aflame, Julianna cast cold eyes upon the man who stood in the doorway.

"Not *yours*," she protested. "What are you doing here anyway?"

Maintaining a bright expression, Dominick pulled up a chair, seating himself before her. "I think, my lady, we have a lot of things to talk about. Hopefully, in doing so, you'll start to remember what memories you've lost."

"Such as my supposedly impending *marriage* to you?" she inquired sarcastically.

"Among other things," he agreed, reaching for her hand.

From Dream to Reality

She drew away instantly, eliciting a weary sigh from him. "You always did have a stubborn streak in you, Julianna. Even when we first met. Though I must admit, that endeared me to you as much as anything else."

Remembering how she'd been frustrated by his own stubbornness, she couldn't see there being appeal to that. Yet despite her best attempts to remain disinterested, his words piqued her curiosity nonetheless. "How *did* we meet?" Seeing the enthusiasm this drew forth, she added, "*If* we met at all, which I doubt."

Undaunted, he folded his arms. "That will take some explaining. But simply put, I first met you when you cried yourself to sleep late one night, about three months ago."

Pulling the blanket closer to her, Julianna's eyes grew wary. "What were you doing in my room at that hour?"

"I came to comfort you, in the only way I could."

The implication shook her, since she *knew* she wasn't the wanton type. "That's impossible! I've never slept with anyone, and certainly not a total stranger!"

Dominick shook his head quickly. "You misunderstood me. I didn't sleep with you that night. I merely talked with you... upon meeting you within your dreams."

Julianna thought herself prepared for him to say anything, but not that.

At her look of confusion, he continued his explanation. "It is a hard thing to describe, but I'll do the best I can. You see, where I come from, I'm known as a dreamphaser. Quite simply, this means that I have the magical ability to travel within a person's mind to become a part of their dreams."

Smiling in disbelief, she replied, "You've been watching one too many movies, Mr. Westbrooke."

"It's Dominick to you," he said quietly. As she merely shrugged, he went on, "And as difficult as it might be for you to believe, it *is* the truth. If you don't believe me, I can always prove it to you later."

"No thanks," she said curtly. "You're not dragging me into your mad delusions. Now... to get off this nonsense for a moment, why don't you tell me what caused my amnesia, since you claim to know so much?"

"The nonsense you speak of isn't that, Julianna. After meeting in dreams for several weeks, these times together led up to a marriage proposal, which you accepted. The only problem was that I was living too far away to reach you."

"Why should that be a problem?" she asked. "Surely planes aren't so foreign to you, if you came from another country." Her gaze became skeptical. "You don't seem to have a noticeable accent though."

"I'm afraid your world's planes *are* foreign to me," he admitted. "But more than that, I'm not from another country. I'm from another *world*, located on the other side of the sun."

Julianna sat gaping at him, only now remembering his mentioning something like that last night. "You *are* crazy," she whispered.

"It would sound that way to one who believes this is the only human-inhabited planet in the solar system," said Dominick. "But in truth, there *is* another world, a hidden planet, that your scientists merely haven't found due to its surrounding mists."

Before she could protest, he held her hand firmly. "Listen to me," he insisted. "I asked Lendric—the one who came with me—to find a way to bring us together, and he did using a magical Teleportation Staff. But for some yet unknown reason, it malfunctioned shortly after we arrived, shooting forth a bolt of energy which struck your head. You would have died if not for Lendric's timely healing magic, but I'm afraid the injury went deeper, erasing some of your memories."

"I don't know why my sister ever let you in here," murmured Julianna, tearing her hand free to back away from him. "You expect me to believe you're from another world?

Mr. Westbrooke, you're obviously living in your own *fantasy* world, and are trying to drag me into it. Well, I'm not about to let you!"

Casting all patience aside, Dominick was across the bed in moments, taking hold of her shoulders and routing her defiant gaze. "Damn it all, Julianna, for the last time, I am *not* making this up! I came here to Earth from millions of miles away, solely to be with the woman I love, even though she's stubbornly disavowing my very existence now!"

"Unhand me, Mr. Westbrooke," she hissed.

"My name is Dominick," he replied, making no move to release her. "And even if you refuse to accept who I am, you can damn well use my first name rather than treat me like your worst enemy!"

"You're certainly not acting like a *friend*!"

"You won't give me a chance one way or the other!" he argued, reaching down to retrieve the portrait from the floor. "Tell me, love... if I'm making all this up, then how do you explain your sister's confirmation of you drawing *this*?"

The portrait's tender gaze was completely different from the fiery eyes of the man before her. Trying to cover her ears to drown out his words, he wouldn't permit it, but added more gently, "Sweetheart, I know it must be frustrating not to have an answer, but don't you see? This should only prove that there might be other things you've forgotten: my world's existence, our planned marriage, the nights we shared together."

Julianna's eyes flew open, revealing a panic-stricken look. "You deceitful liar!" she yelled, tugging against his hold on her wrists. "Let go of me, or so help me I'll scream!"

Feeling no recourse but to comply, Dominick's hands fell away from her. She pulled back sharply against the pillows.

"I want you out of here right now!"

"Sweetheart, please, I didn't mean to upset you," he replied, his hand reaching for hers again. "I only meant the time we shared in the dream-state."

"No!" she shrieked, slapping him soundly, before moving to stand by the window. "Don't you *ever* touch me again! Now get out of my room!"

"Blazes, Julianna, I'd never hurt you!" he insisted. "I'm just trying to help you remember."

"You're one person I'd certainly want to forget, even if I *did* know you!" she retorted.

Stung by her words, he was about to refute them, but Crystal and Lendric interrupted this. Upon hearing the loud dispute going on upstairs, they'd both come running, the former calming her sister, while the latter tried to lead the distraught man from the room peaceably.

Forcing his attention, Lendric's steel gaze held his. "I know you want to speed up her recovery, Dominick, but it won't help matters by ignoring her wishes," he advised. "It may take time for her memories to return, and you're just going to have to accept that."

As Julianna pleaded with her sister to evict the man disturbing her, Dominick's cheek twitched with anger and desperation. "I'll leave now," he said, making sure she met his gaze before continuing, "but I promise I'll be back. I swear I'll never give up on you or the love we formerly shared. And I do mean *never*, Julianna."

As he stormed from the room, while Lendric followed, Julianna gazed after him with fear and confusion. *How could I ever have shared anything with a man like that?* she nearly yelled aloud. Obviously, she couldn't have. Whoever he really was, one thing was certain. She wasn't about to trust him alone with her anymore after this morning.

*****

Downstairs shortly afterwards, both Crystal and Lendric tried to comfort Dominick regarding Julianna's condition, reminding him that the accident had just occurred last night, so there really hadn't been time for any major changes to occur regarding her memory.

Their hopeful words didn't change the solemn look from his eyes though. *How could they understand?* he thought grimly. How often did it occur that a long distance groom arrived to find his bride bearing no recollection of him? Obviously Crystal and her husband never had to deal with a situation like that, and certainly not Lendric, who'd never been married at all.

As he stepped outside to clear his head, followed by the concerned pair, none of the trio noticed a certain man watching them a short distance away from inside his car.

Upon seeing them head to the backyard, Roger left his car to stride up to the front door of the house. After knocking, he was soon greeted by Vicki.

"Roger," she said pleasantly. "We haven't seen you around here lately. How are you?"

"I'm fine, Vicki. One of Julie's coworkers said that she wasn't in today, so I came to see how she was and to bring her these." Holding out a bouquet of flowers, he could see Vicki's curious expression melt into understanding.

"I think she'd appreciate a familiar face. That is, if she remembers you." At Roger's alarmed look, she added, "Julie seems to be suffering a partial memory loss, due to an accidental blow to her head last night."

"What happened to her?"

Vicki shook her head. "To be honest, I haven't gotten a straight answer to that myself yet, since I was asleep at the time."

Roger warded off her puzzled look. "Never mind," he said. "Where is she now?"

Vicki gestured towards the stairs, murmuring a reply.

In her room, Julianna was pacing about in agitation, having watched as Dominick left the house with Lendric and her sister. The man had some nerve trying to toy with her mind as he had! What really chagrined her was how Crystal and Jerry seemed to be going along with him, and especially her sister. Didn't they recognize a con artist when they spoke with one?

"Julie?" came another voice from the doorway.

Turning towards it, her eyes turned quizzical for a moment. "Roger?" she asked. "Is that you?"

Smiling thankfully, he entered the room, walking over to her. "I'm glad you remember me," he replied, handing her the flowers he'd brought. "These are for you, as a get-well present." Taking his offered gift, Julianna couldn't suppress a smile of her own.

"Thank you," she whispered. "They're beautiful."

"A reflection of you," he replied, earning a slight blush from her. "It's certainly good to see you well enough to be up and about. The way your sister spoke, she seems to think you have a noticeable memory loss."

"I know," she agreed, glancing out the window. "Not just my family, but a strange man who keeps insisting I know him. He claims he's my fiancé."

"Oh, really?" laughed Roger. "And what's his name? Dominick, by chance?"

Julianna's head whipped around to face him, paling instantly, as the flowers she held fell to the floor. Realizing he'd struck a minor chord, Roger's mirth faded. "What did you mean by that?" she asked.

"Nothing," he said, spreading his hands innocently, while inwardly sensing that perhaps there was something to what her sisters were claiming. In which case, he wasn't about to lend ammunition to his rival, who apparently was one of the men speaking with Crystal. Moving the flowers to a table, he thought quickly. "I heard you mention him once, that's all."

Leaning closer, she looked up at him pleadingly. "Tell me, how exactly did I speak of him? I need to know."

Roger's expression was sullen for long moments before

he answered. "You mentioned him in passing, but from what I saw, you weren't even dating the man, much less engaged to him. As a matter of fact, you and I were seeing each other just prior to your accident last night."

"We were?" she replied, her eyes visibly drawing a blank. "If we did, I don't seem to remember it."

*Hmmm... just how much **had** she forgotten?* he wondered. "What about the last time we had dinner together?" he pressed. "Do you remember that?"

Julianna searched her mind, but nothing seemed clear in that area. Shaking her head slowly, she looked up at him curiously. "No," she said, "though I feel foolish not remembering something like that."

"Not to worry," he assured her, just before placing before her the acid test. "But surely you remember my introducing you to my... cousin Marilyn at the grocery store. The one who had to stay at my place temporarily while she was looking for a new place to live?"

"No, I don't," she insisted, not noticing when he exhaled a sigh of relief.

"It's just as well," he decided. "You didn't hit it off very well, I must admit. Not to worry though. She lives elsewhere now, so you probably won't run into her again."

She was growing increasingly frustrated with the endless information she was receiving which was completely foreign to her. "I wish you and the others would stop acting as though I should know things that I don't."

"It's all right, Julie," he said, taking her hand comfortingly. "I won't throw anything else at you today, unless it involves a question you want answered."

"Thank you," she replied, sitting on the bed, rubbing her temples. "You've always been a good friend to me."

She never noticed Roger's pleased look upon realizing a very positive aspect to her memory loss. Since Julianna didn't remember the earlier reasons for their relationship dissolving, this provided him with an ample opportunity to break some much needed ground towards rebuilding a new relationship between them. It was obvious she regarded him as a friend now, and the past no longer hindered him.

Too bad for that other guy, Dominick! he thought. *The man must be furious if she can't remember him now. How ironic for her to remember only the former good times with me instead!*

He sat beside her. "As far as Dominick is concerned, don't worry about this insane notion of his that you're engaged to be married. You shouldn't rush into anything with him anyway, since you and I have been more than happy together lately. What is important right now is that you do what's right for *you*."

Julianna smiled at him. "You're very considerate. The way you speak, it would seem our friendship has only improved since we were younger."

"I'd say so," he agreed. "We were starting a relationship for the past several months. And from what you once told me, I'd say Dominick was always jealous of this, and would say anything to keep us apart, since he couldn't compare to what we shared in the past together."

"I remember a little bit regarding that. The time you kissed me, when my father found us together in my room."

"Oh, yes," said Roger, with a laugh. "All those feathers from the pillows we tossed at each other."

Giving him a mischievous look, Julianna reached back to grab one pillow. "You mean like *this*?" she asked, slamming it against his head.

"Hey, no fair!" he protested. "How am I expected to fight back against a recently injured woman?"

"You're not. Besides, you owe me one from that time my father threw a fit afterwards, making me clean up all those feathers."

"We'll see about that," he said, leaning forward to grab her. She smacked him with the pillow again, as he pressed her back against the bed. As she dropped the pillow, he took advantage of the situation by tickling her instead.

"No fair, Roger!" she laughed, tears rolling down her cheeks. "You know how ticklish I am!"

"Exactly," he replied, not letting up.

"Roger, please stop!" Her uncontrollable laughter mingled with his own.

"What the hell's going on in here?" demanded an angry voice, drawing their attention. Julianna's laughter faded, while Roger's expression only became more amused. *There's no need to ask who* **this** *man is*, Dominick thought. "Well, well," he said softly. "If it isn't Roger Collins. The former cause of unhappiness to my betrothed."

"Jealousy won't get you anywhere. Dominick, is it?" He smirked as a muscle twitched in the other man's cheek. "You'd do best to decline on titling her yours, let alone your betrothed. Julie knows the truth now, and you don't have any right to dictate what she does with her life."

"The hell you *do*!" he retorted, striding forward to pull him away from Julianna. As Roger pushed his hands away, Dominick's eyes shot fire, just before they turned upon the confused woman on the bed. "As soon as I got back, Vicki told me she'd let this bastard in, so I ran up here as fast as I could. Julianna, don't listen to a word he says. He'll only tell you lies, since he knows you can't remember everything."

"Really?" sneered Roger. "It sounds to me like you're just mad because Julie chose to remember me and forget you, obviously with good reason."

Grabbing the collar of his shirt, Dominick tugged him towards the open door, hissing through clenched teeth, "Lying time's over, *Collins*! Now get the hell out of here, lest I silence you by force!'"

"No!" snapped Julianna, pushing between them to face Dominick. "I've had just about enough from *you*, Mr. Westbrooke! How dare you threaten Roger, let alone start accusing him of ridiculous things in my presence!"

"Julianna, you don't understand what you're saying," he told her, missing the amused glint in Roger's eyes.

"No, it's *you* who don't understand! If anyone's leaving around here, it's going to be *you*!"

For a moment, Dominick looked stunned, before his eyes narrowed. "I'm not leaving you alone with this demon who'll change his words faster than a chameleon's colors."

"You have no choice!" she yelled, pushing her door open to slam it against the wall, before pointing outside. "This is *my* room, and *I'll* damn well decide who stays or goes. Now *you* get out of here! And while you're at it, you can also get out of this house and out of my life!"

"Julianna!" Crystal's voice interjected. Surprised, all three turned to her. Shooting Roger a knowing glare first, Crystal then eyed her sister. "Now… what is the problem that has you shouting the shingles from the roof?"

Julianna's expression hardened again, pointing at Dominick. "I want *this* man out of our house," she replied. "He's caused nothing but trouble for me from the moment I set eyes on him, and now he's taken to threatening someone I care about very much. Even if you *do* know him, I won't put up with his attitude anymore. Either he goes, or *I* will!"

Sighing heavily, Crystal placed a gentle hand on her shoulder. "I think you're overreacting, Julie, but in deference to this being your room, I can agree with part of your wishes. Dominick, maybe it would be better if you came downstairs for a while."

Equally stunned by her words, his anger shot out towards Roger. "And leave *him* here?" he protested.

"Please," she said insistently, her eyes bearing a determination that wouldn't accept a negative response.

Reluctantly, Dominick followed her into the hallway, allowing Crystal to draw him over to one corner. Once there, his expression bore a look of betrayal. "I thought you understood," he whispered.

"I understand more than you know about my sister," she said evenly.

"Despite the bond of my relationship with Julianna, I won't discredit you, since I know how close you are. But even so, I must argue the point that Julianna is in no condition to deal with the likes of Roger Collins."

"I'm well aware of that," she agreed. "But my sister is as stubborn as you, if not more, regarding someone she considers a stranger. I, myself, on the other hand, can remedy this quite easily. Observe."

Walking back to Roger and Julianna, Crystal interceded. "If you'll pardon my saying so, Mr. Collins, although she's better than last night, my sister *is* recuperating from a head injury. Therefore, I think it might be best if you leave as well, so she can get some rest."

Julianna shook her head. "But, Crystal, I'm not..."

"I know," she interrupted. "You're just trying to be polite to a guest, and I respect that. But your health has to come first, so allow *yourself* that much consideration." Julianna folded her arms, knowing how determined her sister could be when being protective. Casting a forced smile at Roger, Crystal deftly routed his own look of irritation. "Allow me to show you out."

Seeing that Crystal's diplomacy had the situation well in hand, Dominick headed back to his room, none too happy with the situation, but mollified for now.

It was Roger, in this case, who made no disguise of his annoyance as Crystal led him downstairs. "Not very subtle, are you?" he asked, his tone angry.

As they reached the front door, she said, "Not when *you're* involved." Her expression darkened. "Nor when you resort to sneaking past my sister Vicki, since she doesn't know the whole of your past transgressions involving Julianna, including your affair with—what was her name—Marilyn? Now understand this, *Mr.* Collins. Under the circumstances, the last thing my sister needs right now is for your interfering mind games to disrupt her recovery. You stay away from her, or else."

Roger looked amused. "Playing the surrogate mother, I see," he said. "You do it quite well. But if I were you, I'd keep in mind one simple truth. Julie is twenty-five years old, and therefore she doesn't need a guardian anymore."

"Under ordinary conditions, I'd agree with that," she replied, "but due to her partial memory loss, the rules have changed."

"Oh, not at all, my dear Crystal," Roger said calmly, reaching for the door. "We both know that Julie doesn't like being forced to do anything against her will. So if she wishes me to visit, then *that* is completely *her* decision to make, not yours."

With a smug look, he pushed the door open and strode out.

In a rare show of anger, Crystal slammed the door behind him, clasping her hands tightly to regain control.

What really bothered her was that he was right. For the moment, she'd found a ready excuse to block Roger's attention. But Julianna wasn't a child anymore, and only *she* could really decide who she wished to see in the future.

Glancing up towards her room, Crystal could only pray her headstrong sister would remember the truth soon, lest she end up welcoming the wrong man back into her life... and losing the one her heart truly wished to be with.

Chapter Seven

Basking in the warm sun in a beach chair by a sparkling pool, with tropical music playing in the background, a certain man was fully enjoying this most deserved vacation from a rough workday. Adjusting his sunglasses, as an attractive woman with striking pale blue hair in a very revealing bikini brought him a cool drink, Riff grinned at the woman.

"Thank you, beautiful," he said, taking a sip from his glass.

"You're welcome," she replied, resting one hand against the back of his chair. "It's been awhile since you last visited me here."

He shrugged. "Helping run the island keeps my mind fairly occupied. And besides, just because I'm a dreamphaser doesn't mean I don't like just sleeping and letting my dreams go where they will sometimes."

"I'm glad to hear that. I thought maybe that mind reading girl you know in Barokka might have something to do with your absence."

Riff grimaced at that, abruptly reminded of a quarrel he'd had with Kiri earlier today. If only she could accept things as they were and not keep pressuring him towards something more. He knew she loved him, and in his own way he did love her, but his feelings weren't quite where hers were. He was more comfortable with their friendship and companionship, with things less complicated. Kiri's upset reaction tonight only emphasized this.

Emptying the rest of his drink to drown out the memory, Riff shook his head, looking up at her. "What I choose to do is my business."

"I understand. So... do you like my new little outfit?"

Little is right, he thought, grateful that drinks in the dream-state worked quicker than in reality. He could already feel his tension easing. Refilling his glass, he took another sip before replying.

"It looks very nice," he said appreciatively, resting one hand behind his head. "We should only have beauties like you at the palace."

The woman leaned forward with a seductive smile, lowering her lashes becomingly. "I could come visit, if you like," she suggested. "After all, I'm not that distant a dreamphaser."

"At the moment, you're **much** too distant," he drawled, reaching one arm about her waist to pull her against him. "Ah... much better," he decided, as they shared a passionate kiss.

Deftly untying the top of her swimsuit, as things began to simmer between them, it was only when Riff opened his eyes moments later to catch a glimpse of someone casually watching them that his desire turned to irritation.

"What in blazes are *you* doing here?" he shouted.

The woman turned her head, just before gasping in shock. "'Bye, Riff," she said quickly, clasping her loosened suit close before vanishing.

"Tiaz, come back!" he protested, followed by the sound of his brother clicking his tongue.

"*Tease?*" questioned Dominick. "That's a bit unfair to her, isn't it? From what it looked like, *you* were seducing her." His brother's anger was renewed instantly.

"That's her nickname," Riff hissed through clenched teeth. "Her real name is Tiazure. Which doesn't excuse your untimely arrival here tonight!"

"Oh, I don't know. Kiri might think otherwise."

"Kiri and I are *not* a couple!"

Dominick shrugged. "As you say. I just thought you

might have had a change of heart after what happened the other night."

"Look, it's none of your business regardless," he snarled, "and I don't appreciate your chasing away someone I'm with! Do you have an urgent wish to see your bride become a widow?"

"Not likely, since she's *not* my bride."

Confusion replaced his brother's irritation. "What do you mean she's not?" he retorted. "What did you do to scare her off? Something too kinky in the bedroom?"

Dominick's eyes narrowed. "Not unless *amnesia* has become the latest rage," he replied sarcastically.

For once, Riff was rendered speechless.

*****

"Amnesia?" barked Chaos. "How in blazes did *that* happen?"

"That's a good question," said Dominick, pacing back and forth while Riff watched them both. After having heard his brother's explanation of recent events, they'd both gone to locate Chaos in the dream-state, and as could be expected, their grandfather was equally shocked.

"Even if you don't know all the facts, at least give me the details you *do* know," replied Chaos. "What happened from the point you arrived on Earth?"

"At first all went well," Dominick began. "I found Julianna, and we shared a brief reunion. But then..." He glanced at the ceiling. "Lendric's Teleportation Staff suddenly had an unexpected *malfunction*, shooting forth a blast that struck Julianna's head."

Chaos's eyes widened. "She's lucky the blow didn't kill her," he exclaimed.

"It would have, if Lendric hadn't had the magic on hand to heal her," he said, clenching his fists. "He and I have speculated that an outside source must have somehow gotten to the Staff to tamper with it. And so help me, when we find out who it was, they'll be paid back in full later."

His angry tone left no doubt as to what he'd personally *like* to do to the instigator, but Chaos silently decided to keep him from murdering the cause responsible, if necessary. *Finding* the culprit was of higher importance. One candidate readily came to mind, due to recent events and rumors.

"Dual's sudden disappearance from the island is most suspicious," he said. "Considering his many connections with dark mages, it wouldn't be beyond his means to have had something to do with this."

At the suggested possibility, rage filled Dominick's eyes. "I've considered that myself, although I have no proof yet. But if I find out that demon's responsible for Julianna's injury, I'll give him more than just a blow to the head. I'll see him decapitated!"

"And I'll gladly assist," agreed Riff. Chaos raised one eyebrow at that, earning a defiant look from his elder grandson. "I happen to care about Julianna's welfare too, contrary to what you might think."

"Oh, I don't doubt you do," remarked Chaos. "I just find it amazing that you've *finally* found something you actually agree on." Before they could begin another argument over this, he deftly added, "As to Dual, I'll have someone covertly posted near Sireni's house, since he's liable to go there at some point if he comes back."

"And knowing Dual, he won't stay away forever," said Dominick. "If not for my immediate concern over Julianna, I'd gladly hunt him down for this."

Understanding, Chaos placed a hand on his grandson's shoulder comfortingly. "In the meantime, maybe it would be best if you did come home for a while, to better think this situation through."

Stunned, Dominick backed away from him. "You'd

have me ***abandon*** Julianna ***now***, when she needs me most?" he asked incredulously.

"No, not abandon her!" he retorted. "I merely thought it might help if you both had some time to yourselves. Maybe it would improve her outlook of you if you gave her space to think for a few days, during which time perhaps her memory will return on its own."

"I see," he replied. "And if she ***does*** remember, she'll wonder why I left her to begin with. There's no way I'll allow her to believe I would disappear on her like that."

As Chaos considered this, Dominick shook his head. "No, Grandfather," he continued, more quietly. "Privately, before I went to Earth, I vowed to myself that I wouldn't return to Chavernos without Julianna, and I'm not breaking that vow. Especially not now, when she ***does*** need me, if only to keep the likes of Roger Collins from taking advantage of her memory loss."

Chaos met his gaze, folding his arms gruffly. "Oh, very well," he said. "I suppose I would have done the same thing regarding your grandmother, had such an unusual turn of events come about. Besides, it's obvious I can't simply drag you back home, now can I?"

Dominick smiled. "Not unless you've been holding out on an unknown power of yours."

"Since you're obviously set on your decision to stay, it would seem all I can offer you now is a suggestion towards remedying this mess." At the younger man's curiosity, he said, "Try visiting her in the one place Roger can't interfere, where you can start to prove the truth to her as you did before... in her dreams."

*****

Julianna's expression was peaceful as she slept, completely unaware of Dominick watching her from her bedroom doorway. Leaning against the archway as he drank in the sight of her, he was reminded of how glad he was to finally be on her world in reality.

Of course it was less comforting to remember that if she accidentally woke up at this particular moment, she'd likely rail at him again, threatening him bodily harm if he didn't leave.

Sobered by the situation, it still didn't deter him from walking over to her side, listening to her even breathing as she dreamed on in blissful ignorance of him. Unable to resist, he reached forth one hand to brush his fingers against her cheek.

Memories flooded his mind as he remembered another time, when he'd stood here similarly in his astral form, wishing for simply this.

Now of course, he wanted much more for her memory to return, he thought grimly, pulling away to leave before she could notice his presence.

Going back to his room, he shut the door and reclined on the bed, leaning his head back against his hands. Maybe Chaos was right about his suggestion to visit her in the dream-state. After all, heaven knew he had to reach her somehow, before that lying bastard Collins made things any worse between them.

Her visage in the next room haunted him now. So much like an angel while she slept. However, remembering how she'd originally reacted to their dream meetings, he knew that this particular willful angel might very well unsheathe a set of claws if he wasn't careful.

Smiling, he recalled other nights when that might not have bothered him so much.

Shaking his head, he steered his mind back to the situation at hand. If he didn't do something about it, those memories would be all he'd have left in the future. A truth he wasn't about to give in to without a fight.

Unfortunately, he suspected Julianna would be equally resolute in putting up a fight of her own against accepting the truth of their relationship.

But since only one of them could win, Dominick was determined to be that one. Only then would they both win in the end, even if she didn't know it right now.

Shutting his eyes, he reached out to the woman down the hall, silently praying her claws wouldn't be too sharp when he found her.

*****

The music had Julianna's spirit soaring, as others joined in at the chorus. How wonderful that she'd decided to come to this concert. The large auditorium made every sound echo all around her, as if she was sitting in a cathedral, the music all but visible in its colorful richness.

She was so enraptured by it, that at first she didn't notice the sudden commotion erupting to her right.

"These are *reserved* seats!" protested the irritated man beside her, getting to his feet. "You have absolutely no right to dictate otherwise."

Judging by the annoyed shushes coming from other angry spectators, Julianna could only hope this would be resolved soon. As it was, she'd missed a few bars of the song she was enjoying.

After the person he'd spoken to—apparently male—said something else, the man next to her clenched his fists. "What do you mean my wife's on the complimentary phone?" he declared. "I don't *have* a wife, and I don't know where the phone is."

"Then you'd better find it, because *someone* female asked for you by name," the other man retorted.

Julianna's eyes widened as she heard his voice. Was she mistaken, or was it somehow familiar? Suspiciously glancing over her shoulder, she saw the face of the man beside her turning red. Whoever he was speaking to might have a rearranged face pretty soon, if he wasn't careful.

"If I find out you're lying, they'll need to sing a requiem for you!" he hissed, stormily pushing past the one who'd disturbed him.

"Give your girlfriend my best!" the other man shouted after him, swiftly capturing his vacant seat while Julianna's face paled in shock. "If that's who she is, of course," Dominick murmured, smiling conspiratorially at her.

"What are *you* doing here?" she asked, just before a score of people shushed her.

"Keep your voice down, love," he advised. "These people are avid concertgoers."

Glaring at him, since she couldn't argue that, she said, "As was *I*, and you didn't answer my question, Mr. Westbrooke. What *are* you doing here?"

"Are we back to a last name basis again?" he sighed, shaking his head. "I must really be losing my touch."

Shutting her eyes to count to ten, Julianna replied finally, "*If* I use your first name, will you answer my question *then*?"

"I could be persuaded," he agreed, folding his arms amiably.

"All right, *Dominick*. Now for the last time, what..."

"I'm here to prove to you how we first met, since you seemed so skeptical when you were awake," he interrupted, earning another look of shock from her. "Yes, love. This happens to be a dream, and as I told you before, I happen to be a dreamphaser. Therefore, I can become a part of your dreams, merely by concentrating on them."

Julianna retained her skepticism. "How do I know this is a dream?"

For a moment, he considered this. "There are various ways to prove it. Originally, you were convinced when I healed myself from an injury I obtained while rescuing you from some renegade space men."

"Renegade space men?" she laughed incredulously.

"It's quite true," persisted Dominick. "Not that I can blame you for choosing not to remember *that* incident, since it wasn't very pleasant at the time."

Her amused look faded. "What happened?" Before he could answer, she warded this off with one hand. "Wait... never mind. I don't want to hear any more of your lies, since they obviously didn't happen to begin with."

"Suit yourself," he replied with a shrug. "But if you truly require proof of this being a dream, perhaps I can use that earlier method to do so."

As she watched, her attention came alive when a dagger materialized in his hand. Backing up in her chair warily, Dominick's soft laughter reassured her.

"I wasn't planning to use this on *you*, Julianna, so you don't have to eye me like I'm a murderer. I'll simply create a scratch on my own arm with it, and then prove to you how easily it can be healed in a dream."

Before he could roll up his sleeve, he was surprised when she gripped his hand holding the dagger. "Please, don't," she whispered.

"Do you believe me?" he asked.

Julianna paused before answering. "Whether I do or don't believe you, you don't have to hurt yourself to prove anything to me. I'm not the kind of person who thrives on drawing blood from an enemy, even if he plans on drawing it himself."

He dematerialized the knife, taking the opportunity to hold her hand before she could pull it away. "That's not it at all. You stopped me because deep down you care what happens to me, even if you can't remember it completely."

Her eyes narrowed at his words, wrenching her hand free. "Don't make me wish I'd stabbed you with that thing myself," she retorted, turning her eyes back to the concert. "I stopped you because I'd already figured out that you could only have materialized that dagger if this was a dream."

"True enough," he conceded. "Unless of course, I used

magic in reality."

"**Please** don't start with your lectures on magic again," she said wearily. "I already told you, it doesn't exist on Earth."

"Then explain how I got into your dream."

Julianna tried to ignore him, but his simple statement **did** start her wondering. What other explanation could there be for his appearance here? There was one, which seemed most likely. Having been subjected to his presence all day today, perhaps her subconscious had merely included him in her dreams.

"A possibility," he agreed, "but that theory won't hold much water if I visit you every night, which I may very well do, if you won't believe me any other way." As her gaze whipped back to him, he didn't seem surprised by her shock. "Yes, Julianna, through my **nonexistent** magic powers, I can read your mind in the dream-state as well."

"Oh, really?" she sneered. "Then read **this**, you arrogant jerk!"

This time, Dominick's own eyes widened in surprise. "Blazes, Julianna... Does your sister know of your very colorful, hidden vocabulary?"

"Oh, go to blazes yourself!" she snapped, as she turned away from him.

"I'm sorry, love," she heard him whisper. "I didn't tell you of my mind reading ability in dreams to make you angry. Although, it certainly did in the past on a few occasions, as I seem to recall."

Despite her best efforts, a small smile escaped Julianna.

"I'm just trying to help you remember," continued Dominick. At her determined silence, he added, "I love you, sweetheart. Why else would I be doing all this?" She wouldn't answer, leaving him newly chagrined since she still refused to face him, all amusement gone from her expression again.

"You know, Julianna," he said finally, "I'm not too surprised you came up with a dream of a concert, since we visited one ourselves on a different occasion."

Sensing she was listening, in spite of herself, he kept watching her face for a response. "I'd be the first to admit it was a great concert, in an auditorium just like this one. The music lifted our spirits, just as it docs here. We sat at the top row, which was quite vacant that night, and it was like hearing music from the heavens." A playful smile crossed his face as he leaned closer. "Then there was that time we walked up a rainbow towards the clouds, where music played, which was the perfect background for a romantic evening together…"

Feeling her face turn crimson, Julianna got to her feet, ignoring the growing irritation of the voices around her. "Keep your sordid lies to yourself, Mr. Westbrooke!" she yelled angrily. "If I hear you speak of me in that regard one more time, I'll materialize my *own* dagger to stab you with!"

As she stormed past him, Dominick began to curse silently, just before getting up to follow her. "Julianna, wait!"

Bumping into the man whom he'd evicted earlier, he rolled his eyes to the ceiling as the man's features darkened. "Still *here*, wise guy?" he snarled. "I ought to beat some manners into your con artist's head."

"Frankly, sir, you couldn't do any *worse* damage than the verbal lashing I just received from a certain woman who's now leaving," he replied, pushing past him.

Not bothering to pay him another glance, the man shrugged, delighted to reclaim his vacant seat.

*****

Striding down the final staircase, Julianna pushed through the doors leading out of the building, still angry as she strode through the empty parking lot. If this *was* a dream, where could she go now? she wondered.

She didn't have much chance to think on it, as she heard rapid footsteps catching up to her. Not turning, she quickened her pace, but that didn't deter her pursuer from reaching her.

"I'm sorry I got a bit carried away with my description of another night," Dominick told her. "It's just so difficult to believe that a memory so clear in my mind bears absolutely no meaning to you."

"Why should it?" she asked, glaring at him. "It never happened, and most **certainly** never will." Focusing her gaze ahead again, she missed seeing his frustrated expression.

"Damn it all, Julianna!" he shouted. "Your family's already helped establish that you have at least **some** blocks to your memory, and I've already shown you that this is a dream. Why are you so quick to refuse to believe me that the rest might be true too?"

Stopping short, she met his gaze without blinking. "For one thing, I'm quite certain that I wouldn't have **anything** to do with you intimately, despite your claims otherwise. And for another, this may or may **not** be a dream, disproving your so-called 'dreamphaser' theory."

"Really now?" he said, pulling her close.

"Dominick, let me go!" she protested.

"Oh, I will, love," he agreed solemnly, "but not before proving to you once and for all just how much of a dream this really is. Prepare to be enlightened, sweetheart."

Before she could utter a sound, to her amazement the world began to fade around her, leaving her reaching out for the only tangible thing she could...

*****

"Not that I mind feeling your arms around me, sweetheart," chuckled Dominick, "but you **can** let go if you wish to now."

Realizing how true this was, Julianna backed away from him, nearly slapping the grin from his face. "What have you done?" she exclaimed, glancing about the room they were now in. "Where are we?"

Moving towards the nearby window, Dominick leaned

against it, spreading his arms wide. "This, my love, is our dream castle," he replied. "A gift I once bestowed on you, on a special night we shared not so long ago." As he spoke, she walked around the room, her eyes taking everything in. "Since I know of your liking for romance and science fiction novels, I placed some in a room towards the back."

She looked at him warily. "Crystal could have mentioned that to you."

Undaunted, he gestured to the window. "You always liked the view from here," he commented. "Especially since you have an interest in the ocean." Julianna glanced outside, as he spoke. "We swam in it together several times, on separate occasions, when we weren't..."

"Please!" she interrupted, raising one hand. "I don't want to hear more of your lecherous stories."

Patiently, he continued, "I was going to say... when we weren't elsewhere in the dream-state."

Seeing honesty in his eyes, Julianna flushed. "Oh," she said in a small voice, turning around to face the four poster bed. Feeling a sudden chill as she did, she hugged her arms for warmth. Not facing him, she knew he was looking where she was, smiling uneasily. "I suppose you're just *dying* to tell me all the sordid details of what we supposedly did on that thing."

Walking up to her slowly, Dominick placed his hands on her shoulders to turn her around, shaking his head. "Nothing sordid ever happened between us, either in that bed, or anywhere else," he corrected her gently. "Anything that *did* happen between us was purely an expression of our love for each other. No matter what else you may doubt about us, don't ever doubt that."

Julianna met his gaze seriously. "I don't doubt *you* believe it," she said. "But I'm afraid *I* can't believe any of it." Gesturing towards the room, she added, "This whole place isn't familiar to me at all. And I don't want to be force-fed anymore supposed missing links by you tonight."

"I respect your wishes," he replied, earning a growing light in her eyes. "However, I happen to believe that unless you see these memories, it'll just take that much longer to find them on your own. I'm a patient man, love, and I'll wait forever if I have to. But if I can bring back your memory even one hour sooner, I have to try."

"I don't have to be a part of it," she answered.

"Wouldn't that be akin to admitting I'm right, whereas you're afraid that I am?"

Sighing, she shook her head. "If I ever need a lawyer, Mr. Westbrooke, I won't hesitate to call you."

Smiling tenderly, with a twinkle in his eyes, he held out his arm, and somewhat reluctantly, she placed her hand upon it. Wishing she'd wake up soon, but doubting she would, Julianna shut her eyes as the scene swam before her again.

*****

Once again, music greeted Julianna's ears, as she looked upon their new destination. Amazed by the scene before her, she stepped closer to get a better view, not noticing when her companion deftly waved his hand behind her.

Feeling a sudden rush of wind, Julianna glanced down with newfound wonder. She was now wearing an ivory white dress with matching slippers. Touching the soft material with shaking hands, she couldn't deny the magnificence of the gown. It fit in with the ones the other women in the room were wearing, many of whom were dancing with partners in what looked to be a waltz. The whole scene itself looked like something out of a romance novel, down to the smallest detail.

"I've got to hand it to you, Mr. Westbrooke," she said with astonishment. "No matter what else I disagree with you about, you do seem to have one hell of an imagination. After all, I..."

She stopped abruptly, upon turning to face him, since

he'd apparently changed his own attire as well. Now dressed in a formal black suit, it brought out every handsome feature she'd tried to ignore, including the captivation of his deep blue eyes. *How could any woman resist such an attractive man?* she thought breathlessly for a moment.

Just before she remembered **who** the man behind the suit was, forcibly steeling her expression again.

Sensing her inner struggle, Dominick could fairly see the ice starting to melt around her, although it hadn't remained down for long before returning. Ah well... if it happened once, it would again. Retaining his optimism, he stepped closer to her.

"Your imagination is equally admirable, my lady," he said, taking her hand while she was still distracted. "After all, you're the one who helped come up with this dream scenario to begin with." While she gaped at his words, he led her onto the dance floor.

"No," she protested. "I can't... I've never..."

"Of course you can," he insisted, placing his hand about her waist. *And you **have**,* he nearly added.

Julianna tentatively placed her own free hand upon his shoulder. As they picked up the steps of the waltz together, Dominick smiled at her look of wonder. Maybe she didn't remember him, but she certainly remembered the dance lessons he'd given her.

She seemed to sense this, her eyes questioning as the dance went on. "I showed you how to dance when we first met," he told her. Moments later, his own memory nagged at him. "Well... actually the second night we met," he amended. "Technically, we first met several months ago, when you were riding a horse called Duchess along the ocean."

"Duchess," she murmured, trying to place the name.

Growing hopeful, he asked quickly, "Is the name familiar to you?" His expression dimmed as she shook her head. "It's all right, Julianna. You'll remember one day." Before she could refute this, he continued, "I tried to forget you in the months that followed that meeting, since I must admit we didn't hit it off very well at first."

"Rather like now," she said.

"Unfortunately, yes," he agreed. "But in any case, my attempts to forget you failed, which is why I came back to see you again months later, and every night thereafter." At her uneasy look, he changed the subject. "This dance hall itself is reminiscent of yet another occasion, which bears its own significance to us."

Glancing down at her dress again, Julianna asked, "Is this what we were wearing at the time?"

"Yes," he replied. "You always did like scenes like this, which could have come straight out of one of the romance novels you read."

"Hmmm..." She smiled as her mind drifted elsewhere. "If only Roger was here."

Abruptly, he stopped dancing. For the first time, Julianna felt a hint of fear at the look of fire in his eyes, but it only lasted a moment before he shut them wearily, continuing where they left off.

Feeling a bit guilty, despite everything, she said, "I'm sorry, Dominick. It's nothing personal against you. You've got this dancing down pat, and I guess in your own way, you mean well. I'm afraid I've only ever had room in my heart for one man alone, and just because he can't zap into my dreams like you can, doesn't mean I love him any less."

Clenching his teeth, Dominick shook his head, moments before his eyes flashed open again, startling her with their anger. "I may have to tolerate many things due to your memory loss, Julianna, but listening to you praise that bastard Collins isn't one of them." Gripping her shoulders, he shook her hard. "Dammit, love, he *hurt* you!"

Julianna shook her head vigorously. "No..." she replied,

her voice gradually rising. "Roger would *never* do anything to hurt me!"

"But he *did*!" insisted Dominick. "I wouldn't be surprised if that's part of the reason you've blocked off that part of your memory regarding him."

"I'm warning you, Mr. Westbrooke..."

Ignoring her protest, his eyes bore into hers. "On the night I returned to you after my two month absence, that was when I found you having cried yourself to sleep. Upon entering your dreams, you told me yourself how Roger betrayed you, having left you for another woman called Marilyn."

"*Marilyn*?" she exclaimed, her eyes narrowing. "That's Roger's *cousin*, you idiot!"

"Since when did you hear *that*?" he demanded.

"Since he visited me earlier this afternoon."

Shutting his eyes with forced control, Dominick could feel his blood boiling. "That bloody demon..." he hissed. Before she could break free, his eyes opened again, this time with desperation. "Julianna, can't you see what he's doing to us? Roger *wants* you to believe him now, because he knows your memory has convenient gaps regarding his former betrayal. He doesn't give a damn about you. He just wants to add you to his list of conquests."

"Damn you, let go of me!" she broke in, pushing his hands aside, before storming from the room.

Behind her, Julianna could hear loud murmurs from the shocked crowd, but nothing was louder than the pounding in her head. She had to get away from that man and his lies, or else she wouldn't be responsible for her actions, whether it was a dream or no.

As she ran though, the scene seemed to transform itself, creating a set of mirrors all around her. "What the...?" she gasped, looking around desperately for an exit, but unable to find one due to the hindering walls of glass reflections.

Finally backing into someone, she let out a startled scream, quickly shushed by a gentle voice. "Sweetheart, calm down," Dominick said soothingly, feeling her shaking against him as he held her.

Nearly blinded by tears, Julianna fought against his strong hold. "Why are you tormenting me this way?" she whispered brokenly.

"Julianna, I'd never hurt you."

"Then where did these mirrors come from?" she asked.

"*I* didn't conjure them up this time," he told her softly. "I'm afraid this memory came from you." At her puzzled look, he explained further, "On the second night we met, you were running along a wall of mirrors, just like these. You were trying to find your way around them."

"Just like now," she said, glancing up at him suspiciously. "Why was I running *before*?" At his reluctance to answer, she deduced her own conclusion. "I'm beginning to see... I was running from *you*, even then!"

"No, just the opposite," he insisted, silencing her again. "You saw me here, and followed me because you were startled upon finding out I was the same man you'd met two months earlier. As for what brought this memory from your head in such an awkward way, I can only assume it means your subconscious is beginning to piece things back together, however slow this process may be."

She shook her head. "I don't believe you."

"Julianna..."

"I don't believe you!" she shouted, breaking free to race towards a nearby doorway she'd missed before.

Upon reaching the terrace outside, Julianna could no longer repress the sobs wracking her body. Holding a hand over her mouth, her eyes squeezed shut against the tears running down her cheeks. This dream was nothing short of a nightmare, and showed no signs of allowing her to escape.

From Dream to Reality

Reaching down to pinch her arm repetitively, she prayed for a quick means to end this madness, yet again, nothing erased the scene before her.

"That method doesn't always work for dreamers," came Dominick's voice.

Breaking down completely, she dropped to the floor, refusing to face him as the tears kept falling. Kneeling beside her, he gently pulled her unresisting body against his chest, holding her tightly as he stroked her back.

"I wish I could take your pain away, sweetheart," he whispered against the top of her head. "If you could only know how much I love you... how much I've always loved you... then you'd know how much it hurts me to see you this way. I can only imagine how you must feel. So confused... so afraid."

Pulling back at his last words, Julianna's eyes narrowed. "I am *not* confused, *or* afraid! *You're* the one who's causing me this pain!"

"But you *are* confused, love," he persisted. "Otherwise you'd remember that Roger Collins is the true cause of your pain. He wants to use you as he did long ago, only this time, he's underhandedly using your memory loss against you."

"And who's to say *you're* not doing that yourself?" she exclaimed, standing up to glare at him while he remained kneeling on the floor.

"I already told you why not," he sighed, wishing he could will her belief with his eyes. "Because I love you."

"I don't believe you. I could *never* believe you! If you were as trustworthy as you claim, you'd have given me time to make up my own mind, rather than using tricks in my sleep to torment me. I *hate* you, Dominick Westbrooke, and all I want right now is to be as far away from you as I can!"

As she followed through on her words, running back amongst the crowd indoors, Dominick covered his eyes with one hand, feeling a pain as great as if she'd stabbed him after all.

Even if she didn't know what she was saying, for her to proclaim she hated him... no knife could dig any deeper than those razor-sharp words.

Getting to his feet slowly, he walked back to the dance room—ignoring the many people who eyed him suspiciously—in order to reach Julianna, who'd taken safe refuge amongst a group of women.

Stopping a mere few feet away from her, Dominick nearly flinched as she turned an accusing stare upon him.

Having already sensed that he could only make things worse by staying at this point, he decided there was only one course of action left.

"You've won for now, Julianna," he said tiredly. "I'll leave for the night, so you needn't be tormented anymore as you believe I'm doing. But even though you don't believe me, you'll never be able to erase one simple truth, sweetheart. I loved you before the accident, I love you now, and I'll love you forever. You can shut me out of your life, Julianna, but I swear I'll never turn my back on you regardless. Farewell, love..."

As Julianna turned away from him, he eyed her sadly for long moments, before finally vanishing into thin air. Hearing the ensuing gasps his departure brought about, she returned her gaze back to where Dominick had stood. He was gone, just as he'd said.

Thank goodness... she thought.

Still shaking from all that had happened between them, Julianna found herself swiftly comforted by the women. Yet it was short-lived, as things grew hazy around her, returning her to the reality of the waking world.

*****

Breathing heavily as she bolted upright in bed, Julianna's eyes flew open as memories of her dream—or rather her nightmare—filled her mind with their vividness. Fortunately, it **had** been just a nightmare, she reflected, half expecting to find

Dominick sitting across from her, if his dreamphasing ability was to be believed...

Which of course she *didn't*! her mind argued.

And yet... a nagging suspicion only grew steadily in her mind as the nightmare seemed to taunt her with its clarity, each memory bearing Dominick's voice as he spoke the words...

This happens to be a dream, and as I told you before, I happen to be a dreamphaser. Therefore, I can become a part of your dreams, merely by concentrating on them.

*No... it **can't** be true!*

The voice persisted...

Your family's already helped establish that you have at least some blocks to your memory, and I've already shown you that this is a dream. Why are you so quick to refuse to believe me that the rest might be true too?

*Because **none** of it's true!*

The most unrelenting part of all replayed itself...

I loved you before the accident, I love you now, and I'll love you forever. You can shut me out of your life, Julianna, but I swear I'll never turn my back on you regardless.

I'll love you forever... forever... forever...

"No!" she cried out aloud, as if she could somehow stifle the voice which echoed in her mind.

It would seem only one thing could set this ghost to rest, she decided, pulling her night robe from its chair to storm from her room determinedly.

Striding down the hall, she reached the room given to Dominick, nearly slamming the door against the wall as she opened it. To her chagrin, he was sitting up in bed, his expression somber as he glanced over to where she stood in the doorway looking very upset.

"Is something wrong, Julianna?" he asked quietly.

Feeling her face redden at his unbelievable innocence,

she clenched her fists angrily. "*You* should know!" she retorted. "How dare you disrupt my sleep with...?"

"Disrupt your sleep?" he interrupted, with an infuriating puzzled look. "On the contrary, I've been here in my room, trying to get a good night's sleep myself, and apparently failing miserably. If you wish to take amusement from this, that's your prerogative, but I'd prefer it if you kept your laughter to your own room."

"Don't... you... *dare* play innocent with me now!" she shouted, wishing she had something she could throw at him to wipe the look from his face. "You know damn well what I'm referring to, and if you think I'm going to just let it go, you're sorely mistaken."

Folding his arms, Dominick replied calmly, "Am I to understand that you're actually *admitting* to something unusual having occurred tonight that you would have formerly believed impossible?"

Suddenly realizing the truth to his words, Julianna nearly kicked herself for her rash outburst. The last thing she was about to do was to agree with *anything* this man said, let alone to give in to that *last* admission he'd spoken of. Let the netherworld freeze first.

"No," she said finally. "Of course not. It was obviously just a nightmare."

Casting one last glance at Dominick, she turned to leave. She didn't get far before she heard his voice chime after her.

"Pleasant dreams, Julianna."

Tightening her fists to get control of herself before she ended up storming back to give a certain man a slap in the face, Julianna quickly returned to her room, slamming her door promptly upon reentering it.

Back in his own room, her display of anger brought no amusement to Dominick. As soon as he heard her door slam, his head fell forward into his hands with a heavy sigh, while his mind and heart grew increasingly distressed at the deepening rift between them that was now well on its way to becoming a full-fledged chasm.

Chapter Eight

"I'm truly sorry to hear that last night didn't work out the way you planned," said Lendric. "But seeing as the status quo isn't bound to change that much in a few days, I've decided to pay a visit to the Dragends to see how they've fared lately. I'll use a basic teleportation spell, until I'm certain the Staff is useable again."

"I don't think that's a good idea," replied Dominick, shaking his head. "What if we need you while you're gone?"

"Oh, I think among all of you, you're resourceful enough to take care of matters on your own," the dragon sorcerer said reassuringly, reaching into a side pocket. "However... should an emergency befall you that you're in desperate need of my aid, feel free to use this."

As he held out a small red object, the size of a marble, Dominick took it gingerly, looking it over curiously. "What is it?" he asked.

"It's the equivalent of an emergency flare, only it's to be heard, not seen. Don't worry. Being a device of magic attuned to my thought waves, only I shall hear it, if the need should arise."

"And how do I use it?"

"Merely cast it to the ground. This will shatter the device, releasing the necessary warning signal, and I'll return as soon as possible afterwards."

"All right," sighed Dominick, pocketing the marble-sized orb. "I suppose it'll have to be enough."

Lendric placed his hands gently upon his shoulders. "Hopefully when I return in a week, this rift between you and your betrothed will heal itself, along with her memory. But if things remain as they stand, with no change, perhaps I can return to Chavernos temporarily to try and find another solution by magical means. I doubt there is one, but I can certainly look."

"No," Dominick answered softly. "I'd much rather you didn't leave Earth just yet. Chavernos only knows how that demon Dual might find a way to prevent you from coming back later, and I don't relish the idea of being trapped here forever. Although if Julianna doesn't recover her memory, I may be forced to choose that option one day."

"Best not worry about that decision right now. It's only been a few days, and those of our world aren't expecting us back immediately anyway." At the younger man's somber expression, he added, "Deep down, you know she loves you. She'll get her memory back. Just give nature a chance to heal her."

As Dominick nodded silently, Lendric patted his arm once, before invoking the teleportation spell. In moments, he was gone, leaving a spray of magic dust in his wake.

"I only hope nature *can* heal her," whispered Dominick.

*****

"Since the gold-haired man is leaving for the time being, are you sure we should leave Julianna alone with that Westbrooke guy?" asked Vicki. "After all, she hasn't exactly gotten along with him over the past few days."

"Dominick can be trusted," insisted Crystal, helping Sammy put on his coat. "He loves Julianna very much, and I'm sure he'd never do anything to harm her. On the contrary, I believe he'd guard her with his life. In the meantime, *we* have jobs to get to today, and I have to drop Sammy off at kindergarten."

"Well... all right," Vicki said hesitantly. "I'll see you later."

As she shut the door behind her and Dominick appeared on the staircase, Crystal turned to him. "Good morning. Is

Lendric up yet?"

"Yes," he replied. "He left a few minutes ago to head over to the Dragends."

"I see," she said.

"Hi, Dominick," Sammy said cheerfully, escaping his mother to meet him at the bottom of the stairs. His enthusiasm instantly cheered the somber man, earning a smile from him. "When I come home later, can we play dinosaurs again?"

Crystal found it difficult to suppress her own smile, as Dominick knelt down to her son's level.

"I don't see why not," he said. "This time, you can use the T-Rex."

"Great!" the boy agreed, giving him a quick hug. "You're the best, Dom." Moments later, he ran to the door, picking up his toy dinosaur which he'd left there.

"I must say, you've really impressed him," Crystal said appreciatively. "Have you watched children often?"

"On occasion. Helping run an island does allow me to meet everyone, including their kids, and I've never minded helping some of them out in the past."

From this knowledge, Crystal felt her doubts ease. "I'm glad to know that," she admitted. "Our regular babysitter's away for the week, so that will help. Now, since Vicki and I have to go to work, and Sammy has school, you and Julianna will be alone here until the afternoon. Considering how things have been, will this be a problem?"

"I don't see why it should be. Julianna may have her own qualms about me, but I certainly wouldn't cause her any trouble. Besides, when Sammy comes home later, I'm sure that alone will keep her from railing at me too much."

"Let's hope so," she said, opening the door, just before her son ran outside with a laugh. "Sammy, you keep that dinosaur off the car hood!"

Smiling after them, Dominick shut the door again, just

before hearing a creak on the staircase. Without even turning, he could feel twin beams of fire upon his back.

"Good morning to you too, Julianna."

"Hmph!" she countered grumpily, walking downstairs. "Maybe for **some** of us, who weren't plagued by nightmares of people we can't stand."

"Dreaming of Roger, were you?" he asked in amusement.

Her eyes narrowed dangerously. "I was referring to **you**!" she sneered, drawing an innocent look from him which only irritated her more. "And if you say one more nasty remark against my friend Roger, I'll gladly shut your mouth with my fist!"

As she strode away to the family room, he followed at a safe distance. "The only reason Roger **is** your friend at the moment, is because you can't remember what he did before."

"Look," she said, reaching for the remote control on the television set, "I don't have to justify my relationship with Roger to anyone, let alone **you**. Now if you don't mind, I'd like to be alone for a while."

"Can't do that, sweetheart," he responded with mock regret, dropping onto the sofa leisurely. "Your sister wants me to keep an eye on you, in case you have a relapse from your recent head injury."

Groaning, Julianna was about to protest, but then realized how futile it would be with Dominick. Sitting down on a nearby recliner, she clicked the remote to turn on the television. A loud blast from it had her companion jumping from the sofa in a moment.

"What the hell is **that**?" he yelled.

Julianna stared at him in confusion. "What the hell do you **think** it is?" she asked. "It's a television."

Recovering quickly, Dominick moved to stand beside her, never taking his fascinated gaze from the chattering t.v. "I must admit, we don't have boxes like that where I come from."

"Where *are* you from?" she laughed. "Out in the wilderness?"

Turning to face her grimly, he replied, "I already told you *where* I'm from."

"Oh, good Lord... not that other world story of yours again," she sighed, dropping her head forward wearily.

"Regardless of what you choose to believe, it is true," he said patiently, "so it shouldn't be too hard for you to understand my curiosity at seeing an unusual box that houses miniature people." Ignoring her expression of disbelief, he walked closer to it, touching the glass screen, just before pulling back sharply. "Hey!" he exclaimed, flexing his hand. "You never said this device was used to zap outsiders."

"Don't be silly. You just picked up some static electricity from the carpet." When he turned to face her, the look he shot her sent an eerie chill down her spine. He *did* appear genuinely confused! *Could there possibly be some truth to his words?*

No... of course not! her mind decided.

Shaking her head, she continued, "Oh, come on, Mr. Westbrooke. You're not fooling anyone with your constant claims of being from another world." His sullen look didn't lend much to her conviction. "I'll admit there are times when a person might *wish* they were from another world, but wishing won't make it real. Whether we like it or not, we're both humans of Earth."

Suddenly feeling a great weariness descend over him from the past few days, Dominick walked to the sofa again, sitting down while absently gazing at the television. There was just no getting through to her, and right now, he was tired of trying. Maybe Chaos was right after all. Maybe he should put some space between them by going home temporarily.

For a moment only, he considered taking Julianna with

him to prove Chavernos's reality. But in her mind's weakened state, he was afraid the shock might do more harm than good. And the more he thought about it, the alternative of going home, leaving her defenseless to the lies of Roger Collins, was also out of the question.

No. For now, they were *both* staying here.

Despite the fact that Julianna's refusals to believe him were beginning to tear painfully at his soul.

He never noticed the odd way she was staring at him.

Julianna was surprised when he didn't refute her claim that he was from Earth. Maybe she was finally getting somewhere with him. And yet... upon seeing his strangely disheartened silence, she couldn't help but feel a bit sorry for him. No matter what the truth was regarding Chavernos, it was clear *he* seemed to believe it.

Not wanting to antagonize him further, she decided instead to remedy the situation, getting up to hand him the remote control. "Here," she said quietly. He looked up at her, taking the unfamiliar device warily. "Even if you are from this world, maybe you do come from one of those backwoods places that doesn't have television." *Obviously, a deserted island*, she thought.

Frowning, he ran his fingers lightly over the buttons. "I suppose that's close enough to the truth for the moment," he said. "So tell me, how does this thing work? And while you're at it... what *is* this thing?"

With more patience than she would have thought possible, Julianna explained what television was all about. Then she demonstrated use of the remote control, just before allowing him to try it himself. After Dominick accidentally blasted the volume, she was forced to shout for him to lower it again. But other than that, he was a quick learner, seeming increasingly interested in the ability to change channels instantly.

"So many choices," he said with amazement. "How on

Chavernos do you decide between them?"

Looking amused, she showed him the program guide sitting on a small table by the sofa. His eyes widened as he skimmed through the many listings. "Cable television?" he asked, turning to her for an answer. "Do you have that?"

"Yes," she agreed. "Most of my friends do too. You have to pay extra for the listed premium channels, but we do have a few of them." Pointing towards the guide, she showed him which ones, piquing his curiosity.

Punching a few buttons on the remote while Julianna replaced the guide on the table, he fairly gaped as the picture changed. "By Chavernos... is this truly *commonplace* on your world?"

Jolted to attention by the program's telltale sounds, Julianna whipped around to find a most passionate love scene nearly steaming up the television screen. *Great... that's just what **he** needs to see right now!* she thought, trying unsuccessfully to tug the remote out of Dominick's hands.

"Uh... that's why it's on a premium channel," she said quickly. "Now if you'll just let me change it."

Lifting the control away from her, he couldn't help grinning. "Hmmm, at the rate they tore each other's clothes off, it's a good thing they were already near a bed."

"*Give* me that!" she demanded, as if dealing with a mischievous child. "Mr. Westbrooke, I'm warning you..."

"Well, you said this thing was meant for entertainment," he reminded her, with a playful smile. "I just never realized how *much*." Fighting back her hands, he pulled her down beside him on the sofa. "You know, Julianna, maybe you were right in saying you can learn a lot from television."

"Oh, no you don't, Casanova!" she said, pushing free of him to race towards the television with the recaptured remote. Glancing up at her, he couldn't help chuckling as she shut the set.

"Spoilsport!"

"Skirt-chasing devil!"

"You're wearing pants, not a skirt."

Nearly reaching down to throw something at him, Julianna gradually controlled her anger, turning towards the stereo instead. Seeing as she wasn't about to relinquish the remote control again, Dominick cast a roguish look at her.

"Are you sure you don't want to put back the *educational* channel?" he asked. "You might learn something..."

This time she *did* throw a pillow at him, further ignored by his amused laughter when she missed. "And *you* could stand to learn a few manners!" she retorted, punching a few buttons on the stereo.

For several moments, he retained his curiosity, until a sharp blast of music caused both to cover their ears.

"It seems your television has something in common with *that* thing!" he shouted.

"Someone must have left it that way accidentally!" Lowering the sound, she faced him with a bored look. "You don't know what a stereo is *either*?" she questioned. Slowly, he shook his head. "All right then, come here. Time for lesson number two."

Dominick smiled warmly. This was certainly a switch from the past times when *he'd* instructed her about learning various things. How ironic that for once, *he* was to be the student.

And how fortunate he had a most pretty instructor.

"Yes, teacher," he said, walking over to her with renewed spirits.

Hmmm... maybe he was starting to get through to her after all.

*****

"Not *another* CD," groaned Julianna, as Dominick rifled

through the many titles stacked up against the wall. "I haven't even had breakfast yet, and I'm getting hungry."

"Just one more," he promised, placing a new disc in the tray. As soon as the music began, he nodded. "That's perfect," he decided, turning to Julianna. He was rewarded by her look of wonder.

"That's one of my favorite songs," she replied softly. "It's like you read my mind."

Chuckling, he shook his head. "I'm afraid I can't do that in reality, love. Although as far as one's dreams go..." Not wanting to get on *that* subject again, Julianna turned away quickly, causing his words to trail off. Understanding, Dominick gestured his hand towards her instead. "But in all honesty, I do remember you mentioning liking this song once before, which is also the title of that CD. Come here."

"Why?" she asked. "So you can continue spouting your tales of being from another world?"

"No." He took her hand and pulled her close. "So I can dance with you."

She nearly refused, but his eyes were so tenderly convincing that she couldn't speak at all. As the song played on, Julianna couldn't help blushing from the way he gazed at her. He gently pulled her head against his shoulder, feeling her own arms tighten about him tentatively.

"The title 'Remember Me' seemed appropriate," he said, beginning to hum along with the lyrics as he caught onto them. "'Please remember me. I need your love. And please say that you'll return. Please remember, all the good times we've shared. And how my heart for you ever yearns.'"

Mesmerized by his baritone voice, Julianna shut her eyes and snuggled closer. He really could be a pleasant companion when he wasn't infuriating her. As the other lyrics continued though, she couldn't help but mirror them to the present, feeling increasingly uneasy as she heard them.

From Dream to Reality

"'I think of nights that we shared, after each loving day, as the tears begin to fall. I want to hold onto you, but you're slipping away. It's like we've never met at all.'"

"No offense, Mr. Westbrooke, but I really don't feel like dancing anymore," she said.

Feeling her tense in his arms, Dominick glanced down to see the hint of tears in her eyes. "Something's upset you," he whispered. "What is it?"

She shook her head. "It's just... the song somehow reminds me of us. It *is* like we've never met each other, although you and the others insist otherwise. I just wish I knew what the truth really is."

"Shhh," he soothed, pulling her close again, while gently stroking her hair. "You'll remember when the time is right. In the meantime, just let me hold you. I promise, I won't let anything hurt you."

Clutching him tightly, as she struggled to keep the tears from falling, she felt like a child again in his arms. If only she *could* just hide from this maddening sense of loss. Gradually, his voice calmed her again, the music once more becoming the pleasant melody she'd always loved.

Silence broke through the reverie, shortly afterwards. "The song's over, love," he told her, jolting her back to reality.

Somewhat embarrassed, she pushed away from him, shutting the stereo before striding towards the kitchen. "I... I'm going to see about breakfast," she murmured.

"Lead the way," he sighed, wishing the song hadn't ended quite so soon. Too bad he hadn't had the foresight to use the 'repeat' option on the CD player.

*****

Taking out a bowl, Julianna poured in the mixture for a hot cereal, adding water and stirring it. Afterwards, she planned to heat it in the microwave. Before she could, Dominick stared at the mixture and shook his head.

"Is **this** what you eat every morning?" he asked skeptically.

"Sometimes," she replied. "Why?"

He was hard pressed to hide his amusement. "Well, to be honest, it looks more like paste than food. Are you sure you don't want to paper the walls with it?"

"One more smart-aleck remark like that, and you'll be **wearing** it," she hissed, heading to the refrigerator for a cup of milk. "I happen to like hot cereal, for your information. Now, if you can keep your wisecracks to yourself, kindly do me a favor and put it in the microwave for me."

"The what?" he asked in bewilderment.

Rolling her eyes to the ceiling, Julianna gestured behind her. "That rectangular device with numbers on it. Just push the large square button to open the door, put the bowl in, and shut it. Geez... you'd think it was brain surgery."

Not wanting to start another argument, Dominick cleverly kept his curiosity towards 'brain surgery' to himself, instead following her instructions precisely, placing the bowl inside, spoon and all.

Placing the milk on the table, Julianna walked over to the microwave, pointing out how to set the timer to cook. "Then you just hit the Start button, and that's all there is to it."

"Although it is another unfamiliar device to me, I do understand now," he agreed, folding his arms.

Pushing the Start button, Julianna barely had time to turn before a sudden strange noise gripped her attention. Peering through the glass door, she could see blue-and-white sparks shooting about inside.

"Good Lord, Dominick, what have you done?" she screamed, opening the door immediately.

Upon doing so, the smell of heated metal wafted through the room, causing both to grimace. "**That** thing is supposed to make cooking easier?" exclaimed Dominick. "**Char**-broiling is more like it!"

"It's not *supposed* to do that!" she retorted, her eyes narrowing upon noticing the problem. "Well, no wonder it went crazy," she snapped, pulling the spoon free of the bowl before dropping it on the table. "*Metallic* objects aren't meant to go in a microwave, you idiot!"

"Thanks for the belated tip," he said sarcastically. "You know, *you* were the one who left the spoon in that concoction to begin with. Besides, maybe that device agrees with me that it's not a normal breakfast for a human being."

"Mr. Westbrooke, I think you're playing your innocent act a bit too far. And until you decide to wake up to reality, I don't want you interfering with my life anymore!"

"Blazes, Julianna, I really didn't know!" he protested as she stormed from the room. "I've never dealt with a thing like this before!" Seeing her refusal to listen, he slammed the microwave door shut, chasing after her.

Hearing his footsteps behind her, she willed herself not to turn. How on Earth was she supposed to cope with that man in the house? For all she knew, he might have destroyed the microwave through his ignorance. Hopefully not, or Crystal would surely have a fit; although, *she* was the one who agreed to Dominick's residing here to begin with.

The doorbell ringing swiftly interrupted her thoughts.

Great... all I need right now is a salesman to top everything off.

Opening the door, she found Roger instead. "Hello, Julie," he said pleasantly. "I see you're feeling better today."

"Roger, thank heaven it's you. You wouldn't believe the morning I've had with..."

"I never would have guessed," Dominick interrupted icily. "If it isn't the King of Lies himself."

"And the Ace of Fools," sneered Roger, just before stepping inside. "Still here, are you, Westbrooke? You don't know when to quit, do you?"

"I could say the same to you," he replied. "But since you'll soon be leaving, I won't waste my breath."

Roger shot him a smug look. "Fair enough, Westbrooke, since I intend to take Julie out for lunch anyway."

Before Dominick could argue, Julianna interjected, "It's a bit early for lunch, isn't it?"

"Perhaps," he said with a shrug. "But since my morning meetings were canceled, I thought it might be nice to spend some more time with you."

She nodded. "Well, since my earlier breakfast was **accidentally** ruined," she began, glancing at Dominick with meaningful irritation before turning back to Roger, "I'd like that a lot. Just let me get my coat."

"Wait just a second!" said Dominick, grabbing her arm before she reached the closet. He countered her defiant look easily with his own. "Contrary to what you may think, you're in **no** condition to go traipsing about with this man. Besides, your sister specifically left you in my care until she and the rest return later."

"No matter what she told you, you are **not** my guardian, Mr. Westbrooke." Forgetting about her coat, she glared at him. "And to be honest, I'm glad to have **any** excuse to get away from you right now!"

"Not excuse enough that I'm about to let you out of my sight with **him**!" he shouted, gripping her arm tighter.

"You're **hurting** me!" she protested. "Let go..."

"Back off, Westbrooke!" warned Roger, pulling Julianna free of him. "The last thing I'll let you do is brutalize Julie, let alone fill her head with deluded lies about your past."

"I'll give you **lies**, you two-faced bastard..." growled Dominick, striding forward.

"No!" Julianna pushed him back with all her strength. "Damn you, Dominick, stop it!" The dark anger in his eyes only cooled slightly as he gazed down upon her. "Whether you like it or not, I *am* going out to lunch with Roger. And if you don't desist with this domineering behavior right now, I'll have my sister throw you out once and for all, no matter *who* you are!"

As she turned to leave, he called after her, "What about your nephew, Julianna?" That stopped her. "Don't you think Sammy will wonder where you are, if you aren't here when he returns?"

Before she could reply, Roger stepped in. "Don't worry, Westbrooke," he said with a grin. "I'll have Julie back before he gets home. Isn't it lucky for us that we'll still have a few hours together until then?"

Gritting his teeth, Dominick channeled his anger into gripping the doorframe as Roger escorted her down the walk. All the while, Julianna felt her stomach churn, although she couldn't see why. She was finally away from the cause of her constant torment, and with the man she loved instead. Surely that was nothing to feel sick about.

She opened the car door herself, warding off Roger's attempt to do so. As he walked around to the driver's side, and before she got in, a weary voice called after her. "Don't do this, Julianna. You may not trust me, but you're making a bigger mistake by trusting him."

Julianna's gaze was sharp as she faced Dominick again, unmoved by his concerned expression. "You know, you're right about one thing, Mr. Westbrooke," she replied coldly. "I *don't* trust you. And more importantly, you can't *control* me."

"I wasn't trying to. I only wanted..."

"I *know* what you want!" she snapped, narrowing her eyes. "But since you're *not* going to get it from me, why don't you just go back to your *fantasy* world, and leave me alone?"

Dropping into the car seat, Julianna slammed the door shut, and Roger's car motor completely cut off any chance of further conversation. Shooting his rival a triumphant look,

Roger sped off down the road, apparently satisfied by this turn of events. Julianna never looked back.

Nor did she see the pained look on Dominick's face from her cutting last words.

Even when the car vanished down the street, he watched after them, until finally he walked back into the house. For once, there really were no words to describe how he felt.

How could there be, since he could no longer feel at all?

*****

The restaurant's atmosphere felt comforting to Julianna as she sat beside Roger. Just being around other people again, and hearing the drone of their constant chatter, lifted her spirits. The food helped too, of course, since Dominick had so unexpectedly ruined her breakfast.

Just **thinking** about that troublesome stranger caused her to clench her fists in remembrance.

Although inwardly she felt no **real** compulsion for Roger to refute the obvious lies said about him, Julianna felt more than eager to prove Dominick wrong anyway. For the better part of the past hour, she'd tried to steer Roger away from casual conversation to learn more about **their** recent past, but for some reason, he always managed to shift the conversation away from himself.

"Roger, I'm sure my friends at work are worried about me, but I'm more interested in **us**. Now will you stop hedging my questions and give me some straight answers?"

"Haven't I always?" he asked, with an innocent grin, lifting his glass to her. "You really should try this wine, Julie. It has a wonderful taste."

"Wonderful," she sighed sarcastically, taking a sip if only to steel her determination. "Look, Roger... it's not that I'm doubting your word. Far from it. I just want to remember what the others seem to think I've forgotten. Now, about our supposed relationship, and this cousin Marilyn you mentioned the other day..."

Roger dropped his glass, spilling wine on the white tablecloth. "Oh, great... Don't worry, Julie. I'll have this cleaned up in no time."

"It doesn't matter. I just want you to tell me..."

"Waitress!" Roger shouted, bringing a woman running towards their table. "We've had a bit of an accident here, so if you could bring a few napkins or towels, we'd appreciate it."

Nodding once with a quick reply, she left to fetch them, while Julianna leaned her head against her hand in frustration. This was ridiculous! she chided herself. Why was she even bothering to ask him these questions, when she *knew* the answers in her own heart, if not her mind?

*Because I **need** to prove that stranger's wrong!* she thought.

After the waitress returned to help clean off the table, promptly leaving afterwards, Julianna leaned towards her companion. "Roger, *please* stop evading me," she implored. "I need to know the truth."

His expression slowly turned sympathetic as he reached out to hold her hand. "Of course you do," he replied. "I suppose now's as good a time as any to straighten out any doubts Westbrooke's been filling your head with."

"We were seeing each other before your accident," he began. "And as to my cousin Marilyn, truly there's not much to tell there. She stayed with me for about a month, and then went on her way. Of course, your sister Crystal has never liked me, so she doesn't want you to remember how serious our relationship was getting."

Julianna looked at him with confusion. "It was?" she asked. "But I thought..."

"You thought when you once told me you loved me, that I'd never be able to reciprocate that," he finished. "But time has proven you wrong, Julie. I'm fully able to see a relationship between us now."

She smiled awkwardly, while her mind waged a silent war. One side of her was ecstatic upon hearing this revelation from him. Roger *wanted* her now, as much as she'd always wanted him. How perfect!

How confusing... the other voice in her head argued. *How could Roger have made such a complete turnaround without my remembering something of it?* She must have taken a harder blow to the head than they'd said.

"What do you know of Dominick?" she asked, nearly unaware she had until Roger answered her.

"Not very much," he said. "I do remember you drawing a sketch of him at work, but then you drew one of me too on another occasion."

"I did? Well... where did I put them?"

"I'm afraid you won't be finding his very easily," he explained. "You see, shortly after you drew it, you had an argument with him—much like you both argue now—which resulted in your casting it aside." While she stared at the table, puzzled, he added, "As for mine, I took it home. Of course, if you want to see it..."

"No, that's all right," she said. "So there's no question that I *knew* Dominick Westbrooke before?"

"Apparently not," he concurred. "Until recently, I hadn't had the pleasure of meeting him in person, since he doesn't live around here."

Julianna looked up at that. "Did he say just *where* he was from?"

Upon sensing more behind her question than simple curiosity, he replied, "Hasn't he told you that already?"

"Well... in a manner of speaking. You see, according to him, he's not from this world."

Roger was stunned at the easy route just presented to him. Dominick must truly be crazy to think Julianna would believe such a silly story. Yet all the better for him to prove just how true this was.

Jumping upon the opportunity, he schooled his expression to become solemn, squeezing her hand. "Julianna... I'm afraid there's something you need to know about Dominick Westbrooke. You see... he may *be* from far away, but certainly not from another world."

"I've already assumed that," she laughed.

"Listen to me," he insisted, his eyes capturing hers. "I did a background check on him earlier, and some helpful people explained his condition to me."

Julianna's amusement faded into a perplexed stare. "His *condition*?"

"Yes," said Roger. "I'm afraid that's what ruined your short-term friendship, right from the start. Dominick suffers from a disorder which leaves him trapped in a world of illusions which he's created with his own unstable mind. Through this, he believes he's from another planet, and that you're supposedly his future wife."

She turned away to digest this, shaking her head. "But... my sister never mentioned his having a condition like that. Otherwise, why would she agree to let him stay at our house so readily?"

Roger thought quickly. "Simple. Because he's a friend of hers, and she's trying to find a way to handle the situation without having to send him to a mental hospital."

"A *mental* hospital?" she gasped.

"Of course." Roger released her hand to lean back casually in his chair. "He is psychologically unbalanced, as you've obviously seen, especially from his outbursts of anger recently. Why, they told me..."

Ignoring his continued explanation, Julianna pondered his words silently.

Dominick Westbrooke was *really* crazy?

Maybe his stories were a bit farfetched, and perhaps he *did* have a temper... but crazy?

It only took her a moment to reject this idea entirely.

For one thing, if one was to complain of an uncontrollable temper, she *herself* was no saint—that much she *did* remember! Second, she *knew* Crystal wouldn't condone having an unstable man living in the house—friend or no—since she had a young child to consider. Not to mention, she knew her sister would have *told* her of this, if it *had* been the case.

And disregarding any anger she felt towards Dominick Westbrooke, deep down she sensed he *wasn't* a candidate for a mental hospital. The worst he might be accused of was being a good actor and a storyteller, but he didn't strike her as being mentally unstable.

"You're sure about this?" she asked, barely hiding her new skepticism.

"Sure as I'm sitting here," he assured her. "Would I lie to you, Julie?"

His ensuing smile uneasily reminded her of a sneaky salesman she'd once encountered, who would have said *anything* to get what he wanted. She hadn't given in then, and she certainly wasn't going to now.

Still, Roger didn't need to know this.

"No, of course not," she replied, mollifying him. While he spoke of other things, a deeper-rooted fear grew within her though. If he could lie so easily about one thing, who was to say he hadn't lied about other things. *Many* things perhaps?

Once he'd admitted she had known Dominick before, which matched what her family said, she slowly realized there must be *some* gaps to her memory after all.

Knowing that at least some of his preceding words were lies, and judging by that smug look on his face—which he tried unsuccessfully to hide from her—the evidence didn't exactly lean towards his side anymore.

For this reason, she gradually began to reconsider Dominick's warnings of Roger, both within her dreams and out of them. Had *he* been telling her the truth after all? At least in regard to Roger, if nothing else?

She needed to speak with him, she decided.

"Julianna?" chimed Roger, abruptly recapturing her attention. "Where did you disappear to, sweetheart? You looked like you were off daydreaming somewhere."

"Daydreaming?" Julianna asked softly. "Yes... I suppose I was." She couldn't help but smile at that. It seemed as if a certain stranger was infiltrating *all* of her dreaming patterns recently. If only she could remember something *about* him to clear the mist away from her apparently missing memories.

Reality pulled her back sharply, as she suddenly felt Roger's mouth against her own. Her eyes flew open with shock, and... something else she couldn't name. *Repulsion?* she wondered.

Whatever it was, she immediately began pushing her hands against his chest, fighting his hold on her. He seemed oblivious to her protests, trying to gain a more intimate kiss from her. Clenching her teeth to prevent this, Julianna finally managed to break free by whipping her head aside, breathing heavily as her eyes grew angry.

"Roger, *don't*!" she protested.

"Why not? It's not wrong for a couple to express their feelings on occasion, and we *were* seeing each other before, remember?"

Julianna never answered him, as she indeed started to remember something... but not what he intended. Her mind flashed back to another time, where Roger was standing with her on the front porch of her house. He pulled her close while she was distracted. He kissed her forcibly, and she pushed him away.

Just like now.

Vaguely she remembered slamming the door in his face afterwards. And a sixth sense nagged at her that perhaps, just maybe... it also had something to do with Dominick.

In any case, the partial memory chilled her blood. After all, he'd certainly forced a kiss upon her *now*, regardless of the past.

Whether due to this, or from Dominick's words subconsciously getting through to her, one thing was clear.

"I want to go home," she whispered.

Roger's expression turned defensive. "But why?" he retorted. "We were having such a good time."

"Please, Roger," insisted Julianna. "My head's starting to hurt again, and I'm cold from having left my coat home. Besides, Sammy will be home soon, and I don't want him to worry about my absence."

No matter what else he was, Roger wasn't stupid. He could easily sense the sudden change in her attitude.

"Julie, about that kiss... I didn't mean to frighten you."

"You didn't," she said quickly, though sorely lacking conviction. "It's just... Well, maybe I *wasn't* up to going out just yet after all. I'm sorry about this, Roger."

"No," he interrupted. "I understand, Julie."

Better than she knew, he thought. Obviously he'd come on too strong, so the only thing to remedy this would be to play it cool for a while. He'd simply have to be more careful in gaining her trust first before continuing to take their relationship in that direction.

But best not to lose the upper hand while he had it, he decided, holding her hand again. "Please, Julianna... don't let this ruin what we have. Give me a chance to make it up to you over dinner. I have to pack for a business appointment out of town tomorrow, but we can get together the following evening."

"I-I'm not sure," she stammered, staring at the table. "I'll have to see if..."

"What?" he asked. "Do you have to ask Westbrooke's *permission* first?"

At that, Julianna raised her chin stubbornly, as Roger felt certain she would. "No," she replied, holding his gaze. "I've already made it clear, he doesn't rule my life."

"Then you'll go out with me?" he pressed.

Not allowing herself to consider what Dominick would think, Julianna nodded. "All right, I will."

Seeing he'd won one battle, Roger grinned. "I'll see you in a few days then," he said, silently amused at the thought of one man who'd be less than pleased when he found out later.

*****

Julianna shut the front door to her house, relieved to be home again. Apparently someone else was glad to see her, as Sammy came rushing forward to greet her.

"Aunt Julie!" he exclaimed. Happy to see him, she knelt down to give him a hug. "I'm glad you're back," he continued. "Uncle Dominick said you would be, but I wasn't sure."

Her smile faded instantly, as she pulled away slowly. "Sammy... *what* did you just call him?"

"Uncle Dominick," he repeated, tilting his head to one side curiously. "It's part of our secret, remember?"

She forced a look of calm for his benefit. "Would you remind me what that secret is?"

"Sure," he said. "No one's supposed to know that Uncle Dominick's been seeing you in your dreams, even though he already *is* here now from Kah-vern-ohs."

"Chavernos..." she murmured. *Good heavens, it couldn't be true!*

"Yup," agreed Sammy. "Say, Aunt Julie, now that he's here, are you gonna marry him, so I can tell the others he's my uncle too?"

"Not just yet," she told him, shaking her head as she held his shoulders gently. "Sammy... did Dominick tell you about

Chavernos?"

Sammy grinned. "He sure has. It's even more fun sharing the secret with him, since he knows all about dragons too."

Sighing with relief, Julianna chided herself for jumping to conclusions. Since Dominick was telling his stories to her, it wouldn't be so farfetched for him to tell her nephew the same things.

"And is this the first time you've heard of Chavernos, from your 'Uncle' Dominick?"

"Nope," he said, confusing her again. "You told me first, Aunt Julie. That's when you made that drawing of Uncle Dominick and started crying, because he couldn't come to Earth just yet."

The drawing, her mind echoed. *Then I **did** really draw it after all? Because he couldn't come to Earth just yet? Sammy wouldn't make up a story like **that**, would he? And I was **crying** over that stranger?*

Flustered, Julianna turned away from him, barely noticing when Dominick's voice rang out.

"Sammy!" he bellowed from the staircase, his amused smile betraying his mock irritation. "If we're going to play hide-and-seek, and I'm hiding, the least you can do is remember to seek." Dominick stopped abruptly upon seeing Julianna staring back at him. "Oh... all right. I guess I can understand your interrupting the game to greet your aunt."

Was it true? her mind asked for the umpteenth time. ***Could** this man have been my fiancé, after all?*

Unnerved by the odd look in his eyes, she wasn't sure just how to react to it.

"Hello, Dominick," she said finally.

Her recently uncommon usage of his first name didn't seem to affect him one way or the other, as he nodded curtly before turning to face Sammy.

"I think we've played enough hide-and-seek for now," he said quietly. "Why don't you go see if those cartoons you mentioned are on television instead?" The boy's face lit up with enthusiasm as he ran from the room to do just that. Facing Julianna, Dominick's expression remained unreadable. "How was Roger?" he asked.

Remembering their earlier dispute, Julianna's eyes darkened defensively. "He's fine. And you may as well know, we're going out again in a few nights."

Earlier, her response would have stunned him. Yet now, any anger he once held had changed into indifference over the past few hours. His normally warm blue eyes had turned a dull shade... almost devoid of color in their despondency.

For some reason, this only made Julianna feel more uneasy, causing her to involuntarily shiver.

"I myself have had enough television for a while," he told her without emotion. "But since you're back now, you can keep an eye on your nephew while I get some much needed rest upstairs. If you'll excuse me."

Without another word, he turned towards the direction of his room. Surprised by his actions, for the first time Julianna felt a strong twinge of guilt for how she'd treated him. Especially due to her less-than-satisfactory lunch with Roger. Without hesitation, she stepped forward.

"Dominick, wait!" she called out. He halted, but refused to turn. "Look, I know you're angry about Roger, but you have to understand..." Shaking his head, he kept going, without stopping the next time she called after him. "Dominick, let me explain!"

The door shutting upstairs spoke its own meaning. Her eyes narrowing, Julianna strode towards the staircase. *That stubborn man!* she nearly shouted aloud. *If he thinks he's just going to disappear now, he's sorely mistaken!*

She was halfway up the steps before she heard Sammy

shout to her from the family room. "Aunt Julie, I found some cartoons! Aren't you and Dominick gonna watch with me?"

Glancing towards the other room, and then back at the stairs, Julianna felt torn by this unlikely decision. Maybe it was just as well Sammy had stopped her, she decided finally. After all, Dominick might be angry now, but surely he'd get over it by dinner.

In the meantime, she wasn't about to disappoint one little boy with her current state of uncertainty, when she could devote her time to *him* without being questioned by everyone else.

As she walked back down the steps, she responded cheerfully, "I'll be right in, Sammy! Don't let the cartoons start without me!"

Chapter Nine

Julianna felt too shaken to sleep.

Guilt was the master of insomnia.

It had started from the moment Dominick left earlier. Afterwards, she was determined to set it aside, but it hadn't worked.

Even as she'd watched television with Sammy, the feelings of guilt over Dominick only continued to prey on Julianna's mind as the day went by. Up to a point where she sat up in bed later, unable to see anything else but the pained indifference on Dominick's face as he'd left her.

He'd barely spoken to her since.

Even over dinner, he'd steered his conversation to the others, with only perhaps a civil word or two exchanged with her when necessary. Afterwards, he'd excused himself to retire early, claiming it due to a headache he'd developed during the day. He did spare her one cursory glance, just before leaving, but nothing more.

It was enough. At the accusing look Crystal shot her upon his departure, as if silently questioning what she'd said to him earlier, Julianna grew too flustered to finish her own dinner, escaping to the comfort of her room.

That was several hours ago, and the rest of the house was asleep, so she supposed she could go downstairs now for a late night snack if she chose to. The only trouble was, she didn't feel hungry in the slightest. Her pangs of guilt seemed filling enough at the moment.

Gazing at the clock, Julianna realized just how late it was. *He must be asleep by now*, she considered.

Then again... maybe not.

After another moment's hesitation, Julianna pushed the bedcovers aside and strode to the bedroom door, for once not bothering to retrieve her robe and slippers. Padding across the hallway, a million thoughts rushed into her head. *What can I possibly say to him now?* she wondered. *'Please excuse me for forgetting who you are?'*

Obviously not! her mind chided, reaching his door. Knocking on it softly, her heart began to race. As long moments passed, she had time to rethink. *Maybe this isn't such a good idea.*

The door creaked open.

"Julianna..." said Dominick, his air of indifference returning swiftly. "What are you doing here at this hour?" She didn't reply at first. "Seeing how you consider me your worst enemy, aren't you afraid I might drag you in here to ravish you?"

"I... no, of course not," she whispered.

"A small mercy," he replied. "So then tell me, what *are* you doing here?"

Julianna began toying with her hands, but managed to keep her gaze focused on his. "I came here to apologize for how I mentioned Roger before. I was just angry, and didn't mean the way it came out."

Nodding, his expression never wavered. "You don't have to apologize for your feelings for Roger, if he's what you truly want," he said quietly. "I just wish you might have granted me the same trust you find so easily in him."

Mixed feelings shot through her over this, which she couldn't voice as he continued. "But... in regard to our dispute earlier, I won't pursue it further, if that's what you want." She could only nod in reply, confirming his words. After a moment's pause, he asked, "Is that *all*?"

Yes, she nearly answered, growing uneasier as she remained. Yet deep down, another more defiant voice rose up to silence the first.

"Well... not quite," she said. Glancing back down the hall, she added, "Would you mind terribly if I came in, before continuing? This lurking in doorways is very awkward."

"Are you sure you trust me?" he sneered. "The last thing I need is for you to step inside, just before falsely screaming to your sisters that I'm attacking you."

Sensing he wasn't about to let down his defenses easily with her now, Julianna realized how much depended on her response. Yet her decision wasn't as difficult as it might have been before, since she didn't hesitate with her reply.

"I trust you, Dominick."

A small smile replaced his somber expression, as he stepped aside to let her pass. If she was still using his first name, at least it was a minor breakthrough. Shutting the door hesitantly, while uncertain if he should, he cast a glance at Julianna. She made no move to stop him though, merely watching him silently with folded hands.

As the door shut completely, he considered it another minor victory, since at least it proved her voiced trust was genuine.

"I'm not one to keep a lady standing," he told her, gesturing towards the bed. "Please... sit down." As she did, she left enough room for him to do so as well, eyeing him intently. Reading her thoughts, he shook his head grimly. "No, my lady. I do value my reputation, so I'd prefer to stand, lest you misconstrue my actions. Now, what was it you wished to speak with me about?"

Not knowing where to begin, Julianna jumped right to the heart of the matter. "If things really happened as you say they did, then I *do* want to remember what I've forgotten, but I need your help to do that."

Sighing heavily, he ran a hand through his hair. "Julianna... you've already said you won't believe me, so what's the point in my telling you anything? It would only be a waste of time."

His words trailed off as she leaned forward to clasp his hand, lifting his head to face her eyes. He could easily read the uncertainty in them, yet still more, there was a new desperation in them. An inner need to *know*.

"I know I haven't made things easy on you," she said, her tone regretful. "But hearing all of you say that a part of my memory is missing is just so difficult to face. I feel like I've lost part of my identity."

Slowly, she tightened her grip on his hand. "Please help me, Dominick. Tell me something, *anything*, you can think of that might trigger a memory. I want to remember what I've lost."

Glancing down at her hand, Dominick felt his defenses slipping away. Such a small gesture… yet with one touch, she'd melted away his anger. If that didn't possess its own magic, he'd wonder just *what* true magic really was.

Shifting to entwine her fingers with his, he faced her tenderly. "Since this may take awhile, would you mind if I rescinded my decision to stand?" he asked.

With a genuine smile, she patted the vacant seat beside her. "I promise not to call out the armed forces," she replied.

*****

A short while later, Julianna found herself laughing openly along with Dominick, as he related several humorous incidents of their supposed past together. Whether or not they were completely true, they were certainly amusing enough.

"Maybe Sir Daffordshire was miffed when you routed him in a sword fight, but I'm certain I never wielded one of those before."

"You didn't," he agreed. "When I began to teach you fencing, we used much lighter practice foils. I must admit you were a quick learner though, since one time you nearly threatened to leave me singing soprano for life."

Julianna looked astounded. "Now I *know* you're kidding," she said. "I'd never do *that* to anyone."

He shrugged. "Maybe not intentionally, but let's just say I'm glad it was only a dream, where no true physical harm is possible."

"Well, if that *is* how it happened, then I do apologize for being too worthy a student for your own good. I won't let that happen again."

"I'm glad to hear it. As I'm sure a certain part of my male pride gratefully appreciates that too."

As she laughed with him, he related other incidents that made her smile, rather than irritating her as they might have once. Reading between the lines though, Julianna sensed what he wasn't telling her, wondering inwardly if she *had* shared an intimate relationship with him. Not that she couldn't see how that might have come about, since he *was* a most attractive—and now, increasingly interesting—man to be with.

Still a bit skeptical at his constant mention of meetings in dreams, however, Julianna managed to maintain a noncommittal look. "Dominick, if all this you speak of is true, then there is one more thing you can answer for me."

"You're certainly making up for lost time with these endless questions," he chuckled. "Ask away, love."

"What's your homeworld like?" she replied curiously. Seeing his enthusiasm dim, since he was obviously reluctant to speak of it again, she pressed softly, "Whether or not I believe you, I would like to hear more of it."

"Chavernos is very far away," he whispered, shifting his gaze to the ceiling. "It's a world similar to this one, minus most of the mechanical devices you're familiar with, such as the cars, the televisions... and of course those infuriating microwave ovens you possess."

She smiled at the vehement tone he used over that last

item, remembering the 'microwave incident' very well.

"But what my world has in place of these things is too vast to explain simply. There are places where music plays, while shimmering colors pour forth from the sounds. There are ways of traveling without the need of a horse, where you can feel the wind rush by you as you fairly float to your destination. Magic makes many things possible, not the least of which is the ability to heal and help things flourish.

"Physically, it's a land of brilliant skies of shifting colors, and in many places there are purple mountains which go on forever. And especially on the island Barokka, where I live, magic is used frequently to make daily life easier. Living so close to the ocean, one can spend a night on the sand safely—without complaint by others—leaving one free to soak up the ambience of the night's stars as the ocean sounds lull your senses."

At the serious tone he'd taken during this explanation, Julianna felt an involuntary shiver course through her. His descriptions seemed so vivid, she couldn't help but wonder. *Could* it be true?

She certainly wasn't able to refute it with actual proof.

"You sound as though you miss it a great deal, for one who's only been here a few days," she remarked.

Dominick nodded. "I do miss it. Although I've never had a chance to experience being apart from my world before, I can say now that it has a way of calling to its inhabitants who've lived there, no matter how great the distance may be."

"Then why don't you go back?" His gaze met hers with a conviction that answered her question without words. "Oh. I guess I shouldn't have bothered to ask that one."

Catching onto her uncertainty about all of this, he took her hand gently. "I understand why you did," he replied, "although I never once doubted your heart's true consideration for others, be they strangers or no. Still more, I know how this must sound to you, and I understand better than anyone why you doubt the truth.'"

Squeezing her hand, he continued, "But, Julianna, I would ask that you reserve judgment on what I've told you, until you have more time to think it through completely."

"I promise I'll do just that," she agreed. Realizing how long they'd been talking, she blushed. "I guess I'd better get back to my room. I doubt my family will understand what I'm doing here, if they catch me here at dawn." Smiling once more at him, she said, "Thank you for being patient with me, Dominick. Although I still don't remember more than I did before, I do appreciate all you've told me." Moving to stand, she added, "Good night."

"Julianna, wait," Dominick said quickly, causing her to eye him curiously. Placing his hands on her shoulders, for long moments he struggled to find the right words he sought. "Before you go, I just wanted to tell you... That is..." It soon became obvious there was no proper way to verbally express what he wanted to.

"Oh, blazes, to hell with words," he murmured finally, just before he caught her up in his arms to capture her mouth with his.

Startled, at first Julianna felt a wave of panic surge through her, as she'd felt with Roger earlier.

And yet... to her surprise moments later, as Dominick's hands began to move in a lazy caress as he held her, his kisses changing from desperation into sweet tenderness, Julianna felt a very different reaction than anything she'd ever felt before. Unable to stifle a soft moan, she shut her eyes with pleasure, raising her arms to hold him as she found herself pressing closer against him.

Dominick emitted a low groan as she did, since the thin fabric of her nightgown did little to hide the soft curves of her body. She might as well be wearing nothing for the way his own body began to react.

It was only as she began murmuring his name that a new truth dawned on him. Maybe her mind had forgotten him, but there was no doubt that her body *did* remember him. Gladdened by this simple truth, Dominick smiled against her cheek, allowing his hands to circle about her waist.

As Julianna arched back, he kissed the pulse at her throat, slowly traveling lower, until he felt her fingers entwine in his hair.

"Dominick, please..." she whispered.

"Please, what, sweetheart?" he asked.

Unable to voice what she was feeling, nor able to face the question in his eyes, Julianna tugged him closer, initiating her own kiss. What madness *held* her in its grip? she wondered. It was almost as if she knew *exactly* what she was doing now, yet surely she didn't.

Even when she felt herself lowered back against the softness of the pillows, she couldn't resist the temptation of the moment.

Dominick captured her mouth again with a series of teasing kisses, which she eagerly responded to, only fueling her curiosity as to why—while surely wrong—this felt so right. As if his kisses were creating their own magical spell over her, Julianna's rational thoughts became lost to pure sensation, while Roger faded into nonexistence completely.

Dominick's expert caresses left her unable to stifle the sounds of yearning that escaped her lips. Yet still, as he pressed his full length against her, she also couldn't prevent a shiver from running through her.

Upon feeling that one shudder, Dominick froze, ceasing his ministrations. As if attuned to her, he could tell instantly that it was fear, not passion, which caused her trembling now. Gazing down at her, he saw her eyes open wide to stare at him in glazed wonder.

Wonder and innocence... the same as their first time

together in the dream-state. Not that she'd ever truly lost her innocence technically, since they'd never shared a physical union in reality. But that one look now steeled his will. No matter how much he wanted her at this moment, there was absolutely no way he was about to give in to that desire right now.

Only when there was love—not fear and confusion—in her eyes, would he consider otherwise.

Confusion did play across her features as she watched him. "What's wrong?" she breathed.

Dominick smiled, his own breathing uneven from the flames they'd kindled. "My sweet Julianna," he whispered. "I love you so very much. Too much to let things continue this way."

"I don't understand," she said. "Was it something I've done?"

He nearly chuckled, remembering another time when she'd questioned him with similar innocence. Bless her heart, she was precious in this manner, even though he'd certainly borne no objection to her being a swift learner of romance in the dream-state.

"You could never disappoint me, sweetheart," he replied gently, kissing her once. "If desire alone were enough, I wouldn't hesitate to take us both soaring to that eternal heaven lovers share, right now."

He shook his head as he continued. "But you see... it *is* more than that here. I *love* you enough to know that it's too soon for this. You still need to find out just where your feelings lie towards me, before anything else can happen between us."

As Dominick's words sank in, bringing Julianna back to her senses fully, she couldn't help blushing at this awkward situation. Good heavens, had she really *thrown* herself at him just now? her thoughts demanded accusingly.

"I-I'm sorry this happened," she said, sliding out from beneath him to stand. "Please forgive me for bothering you like this. It won't happen again."

Before she could leave, Dominick reached out to take her hand, his expression concerned. "Julianna, there's nothing to apologize for. *I* was the one who kissed you. You only responded naturally afterwards."

Unable to accept his explanation, Julianna shook her head, breaking free of his hold. "Again... I'm sorry. Good night, Dominick," she said quickly, fleeing swiftly down the hall.

Bolting to his feet, he halted in the doorway. "Julianna, wait!" he called after her. Getting no response as she disappeared into her room, he waited until hearing her door shut before slamming his fist against the doorframe. "Damn!" he exclaimed, shutting his own door to drop back against the bed wearily. *Will there never be an end to this?* he wondered regretfully.

In her own room, Julianna had immediately climbed into her own bed, pulling the covers over her head as if she was a child again, instead of a mature woman of twenty-five. Finally admonishing herself on this count, she lowered the covers back. All during this time, she wished she could stop her heart from racing, although she doubted it was caused by merely running to her room.

No... there was no use denying it was caused solely by her reaction to Dominick tonight.

Reluctantly allowing her thoughts to replay the last few minutes, Julianna could all but feel it happening again. The way he'd held her, kissed her, touched her... all of which had left her whole being tingling and apparently craving more. If Dominick hadn't taken the initiative to put a halt to things when he did, who *knew* how far things might have gone?

Maybe he's a gentleman after all.

Turning onto her side, she exhaled a deep sigh. Well, there was at least one thing she couldn't easily deny anymore. Whatever else might or might not be true, there was certainly a spark of *something* between them.

Confronted by this unexpected truth, she then spent the next several minutes convincing herself that it must be purely physical, since she **surely** didn't feel anything for him emotionally.

Thank goodness for that, she decided.

Although...

Stopping the thought from completion, and trying not to think anymore at all, she soon drifted into slumber.

*****

The sound of the surf, mixed with her women friends' chatter, kept Julianna's spirits high as she sat on the beach beside them. It was beautiful today, with the sun warm and shining, although perhaps a bit too strong to be without sunblock, she considered, reaching for the bottle on the blanket.

"That squid from Mars seemed to think I was in the mood to tangle with an octopus," said one of her friends, while the others listened intently. "But I threatened to remove a few of his limbs for piranha bait, if he didn't back off."

"And did he?" asked another.

"Well... let's just say, he must have broken a track record as he left my apartment."

While the others laughed, Julianna tapped a younger woman's shoulder. "Not to interrupt," she said, "but could you help me put some of this on my back? I don't feel like having my skin turn as red as my hair."

"Sure thing," the blonde-haired woman replied chipperly. "Just turn around, and I'll have you fixed up right away. You'd better pull your hair forward, since it's so long and curly." She sighed upon giving a casual glance to her own very short and straight hairstyle. "I only wish mine was like that."

"Can't you just let it grow out?"

"Maybe, but that won't make it any curlier," the woman returned, shrugging. "Ah well, I guess it's back to the old curling iron drawing board again."

With an understanding smile, Julianna pulled her knees up to her chest, resting her arms upon them. *Ah, it's like heaven here*, she thought, just before she felt several drops of the cool sunblock hit her back.

"Hey, watch it with that," she laughed. "That stuff feels like ice."

Moments later, she felt a pair of hands against her back, easily warming away the chill as they rubbed the sunblock into her skin. "Mmmm," she murmured, as the hands began to massage her pleasingly as they worked. Yet even as she reveled in this, her eyebrows narrowed as she sensed something wasn't quite right.

Those hands certainly don't feel like those of a female, she thought.

"I should hope not," confirmed a low chuckle. "Otherwise, I might well develop a complex."

Gasping, Julianna turned sharply to face Dominick, his blue eyes twinkling with amusement in the sunlight. She nearly bit her tongue in surprise, since she'd never seen so *much* of him unclothed before, although one wouldn't expect any more than brief swimming attire during a hot day at the beach.

"Not that I mind an inspection from you, love," he told her, "but if you keep those sweet eyes upon me, I'll never be able to finish here, since I'll be too distracted by the desire to start something else with you."

As he never ceased his ministrations, she turned away again quickly, although this did nothing to erase the image of him. She could all but see every sun-bronzed inch of his skin, his muscles flexing as he smoothed the lotion against her back.

It was only when his hands slid around to touch her waist that she jumped away from him, eyeing him suspiciously. "I never said I needed sunblock elsewhere than my back," she retorted, noticing for the first time how the other women were openly gazing upon Dominick with devouring eyes.

"You're right," he replied, with a growing smile, "but then again, why take chances?"

Slightly irritated, she sneered, "Somehow, I doubt thoughts of my skin's safety had anything to do with those wandering hands of yours." Suddenly finding an interest in staring at the sky, Dominick's expression bore the look of total innocence... well, almost.

Within Julianna's mind, it was suspicion that held her in its grip. True, she *had* been newly surprised by his being here with her now. Yet not as much as the night before. In fact, deep down she had to admit she rather liked the feel of his touch while he caressed her back... er, as he applied the sunblock, of course.

She never noticed Dominick stealing closer to rest his chin upon her shoulder, until he whispered seductively, "If you'd like a more thorough body massage, I know of a more private spot on the beach where I could grant you one."

Her face burning red, Julianna whipped about to smack his face, earning a look of startled confusion in his eyes. "You sneaky libertine," she hissed. "Don't think I can't see through your little scheme!"

"What scheme?" he demanded. "Is it so deplorable of me to want to help your muscles relax while you soak up the sun?" Growling at her silence, he added, "You make it sound like a crime for merely wishing to touch you."

"I've heard better lines than *those* used before, pal," she replied sarcastically. "Don't think I'm dumb enough to fall for them."

Nearly cursing under his breath at her stubbornness, Dominick moved away from her to recline on his side, staring towards the ocean miserably. Even when he'd first met her, she wasn't this hard to get through to. That blow to her head must have jarred more than just her memory, he decided.

Soft laughter returned his attention to the several women

still eyeing him, having wondered amongst themselves how Julianna could spurn him so lightly. After all, he couldn't be faulted for looks or charm, now could he?

"Excuse me, sir," said an attractive brunette, capturing his gaze as she moved beside him. "Would you please help me with my suntan lotion too?"

He shook his head politely. "I don't think I..." Abruptly he stopped, upon suddenly feeling Julianna's eyes upon his back. Sensing what she was feeling was far from indifference, he smiled slowly, deciding that perhaps there was another way to trigger a response from her.

"I don't see how I could possibly resist," he finished, beaming as he took the bottle from the woman before him.

As soon as he poured some on her back, she gave a gasp. "Oooh, that *is* a bit cold," she said coyly.

Cold, my foot! Julianna thought. The woman was an outright bimbo!

Yet to her chagrin, Dominick didn't seem to mind, laughing with the woman as his hands trailed lower, giving her reason to arch back against him, until her back was pressed fully against his chest.

"We don't usually see your kind around the beaches these days," the woman said, eyeing him provocatively. "Are you seeing anyone else at the moment?"

Dominick smiled awkwardly as he shot a glance towards Julianna. "I... was," he confirmed, "but she doesn't seem to want to know I exist at the moment."

"How unfortunate," the brunette said, turning around to fairly dump herself in his lap. "For her, that is. I myself know not to let a good thing go when I see it."

Before he could put a halt to her flirtations, Julianna took the initiative to interrupt. "How amusing, Dominick. Tell me, just how many bimbos do you cater to in the dream-state? A few hundred? A thousand?"

"*Bimbo*?" exclaimed the brunette. "Some friend *you* turned out to be!"

"I never said you were a bimbo," Julianna replied blithely. "You apparently must know something about yourself that I don't."

While the woman fumed silently, Dominick casually pretended to ignore his auburn-haired companion's apparent jealousy, in favor of continuing the charade. At least jealousy wasn't indifference.

"Don't worry," he told the brunette. "That's what happens to females who don't have the proper man in their lives. They can't help feeling repressed."

"*Repressed*?" snapped Julianna, glaring at him. "How dare you call me that!"

He regarded her steadily. "Miss Sherborne, I never said you were repressed, nor did I mention your name specifically. Obviously you must know something about yourself that we don't."

While the brunette laughed, Julianna felt her anger rekindle. Getting to her feet, she stormed off, while Dominick instantly regretted his words. "Julianna, don't leave!" he called after her. "I was kidding!"

Miffed at his distraction, the brunette moved in front of his view, rolling her eyes. "Wherever she went shouldn't concern you," she decided. "Some of us here aren't running off."

Her words didn't deter him, though it took him a minute to dissuade her completely. Having no clue where to look for Julianna, he gazed towards the water. "Did she head over to the ocean?" he asked one of the others.

The blonde-haired woman who'd assisted Julianna earlier answered him. "It looks like she did, but as soon as she passed that crowd with the beach ball, she disappeared from view."

Dominick nodded, groaning with frustration.

"Only long enough to see to cooling off that ego of yours, honey!" came a loud voice from behind him, just before a cascade of icy water poured over his head.

Shouting at the sudden chill, Dominick darted away from the barrage, clearing his eyes to see Julianna staring at him with a highly satisfied smile.

"There," she said, tossing her emptied bucket forcefully into his arms. "Now it's as vacant as that arrogant head of yours."

While he fumbled with the pail, she ran back towards the ocean—gleeful that she'd wiped the smug look from his face—never noticing the renewed amusement of the women she'd left behind, including the brunette as well.

Dominick got a full dose of it though. He was on his feet in moments to chase after her.

Glancing back, Julianna broke into laughter upon seeing the sight he presented. His formerly wavy hair was now plastered against his neck, while he dripped water everywhere. If only she'd had a camera to get a snapshot of him like this! Her distraction caused its own dilemma though. As soon as they were away from the majority of the other people on the beach, Dominick managed to catch up to her, grabbing her about the waist.

"Gotcha!" he yelled, halting her flight to fall with her upon the sand. Unable to control her mirth, his own amusement began to match hers, as he held her back against the beach. "I'm glad you find this so funny, Julianna. Because in another moment, I'm going to see to adding ocean water to *your* features to fix *your* attitude for a change!"

Picking her up before she could think to move, he began striding towards the water to carry out his threat.

"Dominick, don't!" she squeaked, shaking her head as she kicked her feet ineffectively.

His own deep laughter answered her. "Give me one good reason why I shouldn't?"

As her mind sought the quickest excuse it could find, she ended up finding something else instead. Her eyes glazed momentarily as another memory triggered...

Through countless moments, she was returned to the time when she similarly tried to persuade him not to dump her in the ocean. She could see herself in Dominick's arms, laughing with him, just before they fell into the water, and the memory dimmed.

Sensing her spark of remembrance, Dominick spoke quickly, "Tell me, love. What were you just thinking of?"

"I... I'm not sure," she replied. "It went through my mind so fast. I think... you and I were in the ocean together like this."

"You remember a memory of *us*?" he exclaimed. She nodded slowly.

"It seems like it."

"That's great! And do you remember anything else?" he pressed insistently.

"And... I'm not too certain of the rest." Sighing, she shook her head. "No, that's all. It was probably nothing anyway."

Nothing? he thought. Any memory she recovered was certainly *something*. And since he happened to know the ending to that particular memory she'd spoken of, he decided there was only one logical thing to do.

"Don't say that," he said finally, a devious smile crossing his face. "Maybe if we follow through on what happened afterwards, you'll remember the rest completely."

Remembering enough to realize his intent, Julianna began shaking her head more frantically. "No, no, *no!*" she shouted, just before he 'tripped', pulling her into the ocean with him.

Upon resurfacing with a gasp, Julianna pushed the wet strands of hair from her face, finding Dominick grinning just across from her.

"Why, you no-good beast!" She sent a barrage of splashes directly at him. "I ought to drown you, you unthinking boor! If I ever hire a bodyguard, I'll have him..." Her protests were cut off as he lifted her from the water again, carrying her back towards the beach. "*Now* what are you doing?" she demanded. "Put me down!"

"Calm your vocal chords, my lady," he chuckled. "I'll set you down soon enough." Completing his journey, he lowered her back against the warm dry sand, just before dropping beside her moments later. Cleverly, he threw one leg over hers to successfully keep her from bolting. Not that she seemed inclined to do so, despite her angry expression.

"You'll be lucky if I don't unleash my full temper on you," she warned.

"I've seen it recently, remember?"

Blushing, she lowered her lashes. "And I apologized already, so don't ask me to do it again."

"You never have to apologize with me, love," he said seriously, as her eyes opened to focus upon his tender gaze. Tousling her hair, he added mischievously, "Not even though you dumped a bucket of freezing water on my head tonight."

"Well, you *deserved* it," she retorted softly, even as her eyes twinkled.

"In that one instance, maybe so, love," he replied, as he began loosely brushing her wet hair back from her forehead. "But in all honesty, it seemed the only way to reclaim your attention." At her smirk, he added, "It worked, didn't it?"

"Too well!" she agreed. "Thanks to your soaking us in an ice bath, the sun will probably take ten times longer to dry us off again."

"Hmmm..." he murmured, skimming one hand upward

along her leg. As she gasped, he leaned his mouth closer to hers, whispering against it, "Maybe I can find a way to warm us up a bit sooner."

Realizing where this was leading, Julianna began to shake her head. "Dominick, wait. You don't have to..."

His bone-melting kiss destroyed any semblance of a verbal argument from her, evoking only a breathless little cry instead. With the barriers down between them again, Julianna couldn't fight the increasing feelings he had kindled within her, nor was she about to try.

As Dominick's hands traveled past her shoulders to the shuddering rise and fall of her chest, Julianna nearly jumped when he began stroking her there through the fabric of her swimsuit. Her widened eyes drifted shut languorously as he traced lazy circles against her skin, expertly kissing the most sensitive area along her neck.

"This can't be happening," she breathed.

"Oh, it most certainly is, love," he replied, teasing her mouth with his. "And it's going to *keep* happening for many years to come... over and over."

Wrapping his arms about her waist as his kisses became searingly possessive, Julianna was surprised to find no trace of fear. Instead, she felt it wasn't enough, lifting one foot to lightly run along his leg, while her hands drifted upwards to grip his back.

His low groan indicated part of the inner struggle now raging through him. Chavernos, but it would be so simple to drown himself in the warmth of her tempting body tonight, he thought, nearly growling as she began toying with his hair.

It *was* just a dream, for pity's sake! his mind and body argued in silent agreement.

"By the stars, Julianna..." he said. "Can you possibly know how much I want you right now?"

"Yes. I do know. Dominick... I want..."

He shook his head desperately. "You want *what*?" he asked insistently. "Julianna, *tell* me now."

Against his never-ending kisses, she felt herself drifting farther still from rational thought. "I want..."

"Excuse me, you two, but this isn't your own *private* beach!" an unfamiliar voice barked sharply.

Both looked up, only to find a stern older lifeguard glaring down at them. "What is *wrong* with you kids nowadays?" he demanded. "Can't you keep your extracurricular activities to yourselves anymore?"

Turning to face each other afterwards, the pair gradually gave in to laughter, indeed feeling like a pair of teenagers. Even in a dream, the voices of propriety could still interfere on occasion—often at a most inconvenient time such as this.

Getting to his feet, Dominick helped Julianna up, just before facing the lifeguard again. "We're sorry about that," he said. "I'm afraid we just got carried away."

"Hmph! Well, just make sure it doesn't happen again, or I'll have the police carry you *both* out! Understood?"

They mock saluted him, earning a low grunt from him, just before Dominick took Julianna's hand and raced further along the beach with her. When they were a safe distance away from the lifeguard and the rest of the beachgoers, they slowed to a normal pace, still holding hands as they began to talk leisurely.

"Although you probably won't believe me now, I don't make a habit of that with strangers," she told him.

"I believe you," he replied, squeezing her hand reassuringly.

Pleased by his response, Julianna said, "You know, I can't help being a bit surprised at how quickly you've become such an important part of my life. I can't seem to picture what it would be like without you now."

"Don't worry. I'm not going anywhere. But I'm not so surprised at how quickly things have warmed up between us.

Even when we originally met, there was a strong attraction that couldn't be denied for very long.

"Nonetheless... it's as well that lifeguard showed up when he did. Otherwise, I doubt I could have extinguished the sparks we kindled before." Glancing down at her, he sought her eyes. "You're not angry with me over what nearly happened, are you?"

"Of course not. How could I be? I was as much at fault as anyone."

He abruptly stopped walking to grip her shoulders. "Attraction between two people isn't necessarily a fault," he told her simply. "There's usually a good reason for it."

"Hmmm, perhaps," she agreed. "I still don't remember that much yet," she admitted, "even though a few pieces are starting to come together. But it's obvious you're different from the other men I've known, and maybe..." She continued slowly. "Maybe I'm starting to believe you after all."

Dominick's features softened. "Thank Chavernos," he said. "Now as long as you remember that when you wake up, we'll be in business."

"I won't forget," she promised, keeping her gaze focused on his.

"And I won't let you." He embraced her again, but before he could kiss her, he pulled back suddenly, frowning at the setting around them. "Wait. This is wrong," he murmured, shaking his head.

"Why is something *always* wrong with you?" Running her hand along his cheek, she asked, "Are you still angry over that lifeguard?"

"Blazes, no," he replied. "But since I *am* a dreamphaser, I intend to do something about this blistering heat." A bit perplexed by his words, she watched silently as he waved his hand towards the sky.

Julianna couldn't help gaping, as almost immediately the

sun set, the surrounding brilliant colors fading to red before deepening into a midnight blue. To brighten the darkness, the sky suddenly lit up with the lights of a thousand stars, while a glistening full moon rose to take its place among them. When it did, time seemed to slow once more.

The beach itself was completely vacant now, while although still warm, a mild breeze played about them soothingly. In all her years, Julianna had never been out in a setting quite like this.

Blinking, she turned back to her companion, finding him staring back at her with a satisfied smile as he cradled her face in his hands. "Now *that* is a more appropriate background for two lovers," he decided.

Before she could protest, Dominick countered this with a kiss that ended all argument from her, pulling her closer as her arms wound about him.

Moving back to the sand again, their shared kisses fairly simmered against the warmth around them, while the lulling sounds of the ocean echoed their promise that they were the only ones in their private world right now.

Julianna trembled, not with fear but passion, as his hands began stroking her, molding her every curve against his body. She whimpered softly from the intimacy, and from her own body's yearning as she pressed nearer.

"Can you feel it, love?" he whispered. "Our hearts beat as one... like our bodies are one... as our very souls will always be... one."

"Yes," she breathed blissfully. "Oh, Dominick... I do feel it. I..." Her expression changed abruptly as her hand reached for his neck, and found it growing less tangible.

Alarmed, Julianna held him closer. "Dominick, what's happening to you?" she gasped. "You're... fading somehow."

He sighed heavily. "It must be morning," he told her, pulling back to touch her cheek while he still could. "Although it seems real, this is but a dream, Julianna," he continued quickly. "I have to leave you now."

"No!" she exclaimed. "I won't let you."

"You have no choice, love," he said regretfully. "But be comforted. Unlike the separations of our past, at least I'll still be with you in reality when you awaken, should you wish to find me again."

"But I don't want us to leave this place," she protested. "It's different between us here than when we're awake."

"No, love," he replied, hugging her. "Whether you're awake or asleep, nothing really changes. You'll remember our time together tonight, as will I, since in its own way, it *is* real."

Squeezing her eyes shut, Julianna responded by embracing him tighter. "I wish so much that I could remember you," she whispered desperately.

He smiled. "You will, love," he assured her. "You just need time to heal."

Brokenly, she felt tears threatening. "But if I *don't* remember... you'll leave me, won't you?"

"Never, sweetheart," he insisted, kissing her to emphasize this. "No matter what happens, I promise I'll *never* leave you, whether in your dreams if you wish it, or when you wake up. I'll always be here for you, Julianna. Always."

"Dominick... don't say anymore," she said quickly. "Please, just kiss me one last time."

"Let it be as my lady wishes," he murmured.

Taking her mouth again with passionate demand, she received him with the same eagerness. Encouraged by this, Dominick silently prayed this moment would last, uncertain how she'd react upon awakening. For now though, there was no mistaking Julianna's desire matched his, as they both clung to each other in feverish desperation.

The background grew hazy around them, but Julianna never noticed, lost to all but the man who held her. For long moments, she felt the odd sensation that her body was melting.

Almost as if, like Dominick had said... they were becoming one.

Chapter Ten

Julianna turned onto her side, stretching a hand forth absently. "Dominick..." she murmured, moments before the silence jolted her awake. Glancing up, her eyes scanned the room quickly, finding it empty except for her.

*It had all been a **dream?*** she thought with disappointment.

Turning to face the clock, she gaped at the time. Eleven o'clock? Good Lord, she'd certainly overslept! Although, she considered, she could fully understand it since one certain man had kept her mesmerized in her dreams last night.

Smiling at the memory, she decided to see if Dominick was also sleeping late this morning. Not that it would prove anything, since she still held firm to the belief that her dreaming of him last night was just another coincidence. But still, she'd be glad for his company now anyway.

Knocking on his door, she wasn't too surprised to get no answer. "Dominick?" she said softly. Still no response. Tentatively, she opened the door. "Time to wake up, Dom..." Her words were cut short, upon finding his room empty.

The bed was neatly made, as if it hadn't even been slept in, and a few recently rearranged pieces of furniture were back the way they'd been before Dominick's arrival. Almost as if he'd never been there.

Backing out of the room, Julianna's confusion built. She *couldn't* have just imagined his existence, could she?

No, of course not! her thoughts chided her.

Just because Dominick wasn't in his room shouldn't alarm her. Unfortunately, it didn't ease her mind either. Rushing to the staircase, she called out his name twice, but again there was no reply.

All right... *now* she was alarmed.

Running downstairs, Julianna went from room to room, calling his name, but each time was only greeted by silence. "Dominick, where are you?" she yelled, feeling a surge of distress. What if he *had* left after all? Even though she'd apologized for what happened the day before, what if he hadn't really believed her, and just went back where he came from?

She tried the family room, the dining room, and even the basement, but there was no trace of him. Pressing a hand against her mouth as she felt tears threaten, she backed against one wall, shaking her head at the implication.

Dominick was gone.

How could he leave after last night? After the kisses they'd shared... and the rest?

Her blood turned cold. Maybe he'd left because of that. Maybe she *had* done something wrong. Displeased him somehow, so he'd left her.

"No!" she cried out, slamming her fist against the basement door.

Walking over to the family room again, Julianna dropped onto the sofa. Hugging her arms, she shut her eyes against the tears that now fell, inwardly cursing herself for having chased away the man who'd sparked such emotions in her last night.

"He can't be gone," she whispered, shaking her head. "He promised he wouldn't leave." *But that was a dream*, her thoughts reminded her unpleasantly. Feeling sobs wrack through her at the renewed memories this conjured up, Julianna screamed out, "*Dominick!*"

She was too upset to consciously notice the back door slamming against the wall, followed by loud barking, just before a pair of strong arms caught hold of her, pulling her close.

"I'm here, love," a familiar voice soothed her.

"Dominick!" she gasped, her own arms gripping him. "Oh, thank heaven."

Unseen by her, Dominick's face was a mask of worry as he held her, feeling her body shaking in his grasp. "Dear heaven, Julianna, you feel like you're going to fall to pieces in my arms. Are you all right?"

"Yes," she sniffed against his shoulder. "I... I was just worried about you."

"About *me*?" he asked incredulously, never releasing her. "At first I thought I'd simply imagined hearing your voice while I was outside. But when I heard it again, I decided to make sure you were all right, and could hear you screaming my name from just outside the door. Blazes, I thought the damned house was burning down!"

"No, the house is fine," she said quickly, pulling back to look into his eyes. "But where *were* you? I thought..."

"I was just letting your dog outside, before Shadow could start climbing the walls," he chuckled. At the mention of her name, Shadow jumped up on the couch beside Julianna, licking her face and wagging her tail. "Where did you *think* I was?"

*All this was over **Shadow**?* she thought, blushing so much, she knew she'd surely die of embarrassment. Giving her dog a hug, since she barely felt able to face Dominick now, she confessed, "When I couldn't find you anywhere in the house, I... I thought you'd left last night."

Shutting her eyes, she steeled herself for his laughter, but long moments passed without this. Slowly, she dared to glance up at him again, finding him smiling at her tenderly instead.

"I'm touched that you cared enough to notice," he told her, brushing her tousled hair away from her face.

He nearly added that he'd already explained in her dreams the night before that he'd never leave her, but sensing she still might not believe him, he decided not to risk their fragile beginning over it. However, there was nothing wrong with asserting the truth again now.

"You don't have to worry the next time," he assured her. "Despite what you may have believed, I'm not going to leave you, Julianna. All right?" She nodded. "Good. Now, as soon as I retrieve Shadow's toy for her, we can go in to breakfast."

"Breakfast?" she asked, surprised. "Don't tell me you cook too."

"Suit yourself. I won't tell you."

Julianna could only gape as he went into the other room. Handsome, intelligent, caring, amusing, *and* he could cook?

Now she *knew* she was still dreaming.

Shadow's cheerful barking interrupted her thoughts, as the dog jumped into her lap to lick her cheek again. A bit overwhelmed, Julianna gently tried to calm her exuberant friend's endless affection, until Dominick cleverly held up a pink-and-blue toy that squeaked.

"Here, Shadow," he called out, squeaking it a few times.

The dog turned playfully, her eyes lighting up as he tossed the ball in her direction. Barking happily, Shadow leaped off the sofa to retrieve it, just before running into the next room with it.

"She doesn't seem to understand how to play 'fetch'," Julianna told him.

"I know," he agreed mischievously, taking her hand before leading them to the kitchen.

"Um... not to bring up a sore point, Dominick, but shouldn't I be a bit concerned if you've been attempting to cook again, since that last incident with the microwave?"

"I understand," he responded good-naturedly. "But last night, your sister Crystal explained what I'd done wrong, as well as the correct way to use it, so that won't happen again. Besides, she showed me how to use the stove instead, so I didn't bother with the microwave this morning. I decided to cook breakfast for you, rather than another ounce of paste."

Julianna looked amused this time. "You know, you might actually like it if you give it a chance."

He shrugged. "You may be right. But in the meantime, we'll just have to make do with what's already prepared." He gestured grandly.

Her eyes opened wide upon walking into the room. "Apparently, you did more than just cook breakfast," she remarked, eyeing the formally set table.

"I'm surprised you didn't notice it when you came downstairs before. You must have been really worried."

"You'll never know how much." Walking towards her chair, she was newly gratified when Dominick held it out for her. "I could get used to this," she warned, as he seated her.

"That's the general idea," he said, bringing over two plates of food from the counter before sitting next to her.

"Eggs, bacon, and toast?" she questioned, glancing up at him.

Dominick started at that. "Did I forget something?" he asked. "I was certain..."

"No, don't misunderstand," she interrupted. "I'm surprised since this is one of my favorite breakfasts, when I feel like cooking it."

"Thank goodness. For a minute there, I thought you were sorry I passed on another microwave adventure. And before you ask me, no, I'm not psychic too. Since I wasn't sure what you'd want, I simply asked your sister what your preference was beforehand."

"You certainly succeeded." She took a bite of the eggs. "Mmmm, this tastes great, Dominick."

"You're very welcome," he replied, pleased.

"I have to hand it to you. Between cooking this meal, setting the table, *and* having such manners over breakfast, you *must* be from another world."

Dominick merely grinned in reply, hoping he could one day show her just how true that statement was.

*****

At one point while they ate, Julianna eyed her companion with a teasing smile. "You'll never guess who I dreamed of last night."

Not facing her, Dominick wore his own amused look. "I might," he said quietly.

Having overheard, she sighed meaningfully. "It's *that* obvious?" He nodded. "Well, you're right then. I dreamed of Roger."

He nearly choked on his food, until a startled Julianna said hurriedly, "I was just kidding, Dominick. I dreamed of *you*, not him. Good heavens, I didn't mean that to happen."

"I'm all right," he assured her. "Just don't *do* that again, love. I have enough trouble dealing with the man as it is, but it's *certainly* too early in the morning for him now."

"So I see," she agreed. "But getting back to what I'd mentioned before, I *did* dream of you last night."

Dominick stopped eating to watch her. "Anything... interesting?" he asked.

The knowing look in his eyes began to unnerve Julianna, so she decided to focus on her food instead. "Just the usual stuff, I suppose," she mumbled.

"Hmmm... the kisses we shared, let alone changing day into night doesn't seem very usual to me."

Julianna's silverware chimed as it hit the floor, just before her face drained of color. "How did you know that?" she asked. "I never told you..."

"You didn't have to. I was there." Seeing her lingering doubts, he added, "I must admit that brunette wasn't my type at all, contrary to what you might have thought at the time. But that lifeguard was a real pain-in-the-neck. All that talk of extracurricular activities, as if romance was but a school sport!"

Bolting to her feet, she stared at him with renewed shock. "Who *are* you?" she exclaimed.

He gazed at her with patient tenderness. "The man that loved you enough to travel across the solar system to reach you," he told her gently. "Julianna, I didn't reveal what I know to frighten you. I merely wished to confirm that what I've been telling you is the truth."

"But how *can* it be? Someone who can get into another's dreams by magic?" Her eyes widened as another thought crossed her mind. "Does this mean you're going to keep infiltrating my dreams, until I give in to you physically?"

"By Chavernos, no," he insisted, standing as well. "Listen to me, Julianna, if this is all too much for you to accept right now, I'll back off. I won't even visit you in your dreams anymore, if this is what you want. Can I be any fairer than that?"

Julianna shook her head slowly. "I guess not," she said, sitting down.

Worried by her vacant look, Dominick sat beside her again, reaching out to hold her hand, squeezing it comfortingly. "I don't expect you to accept everything all at once, love. I just wanted to put the truth on the table for you." Glancing down at their food, he added brightly, "And speaking of tables, it might be a good idea if we finish eating before our breakfast gets cold."

She ate, but her expression never changed.

The rest of breakfast passed uneventfully. Afterwards, Dominick took care of cleaning up. Seeing she was still out of it, he inwardly chided himself for rushing in with the truth too fast. Maybe he should have waited, after all.

"Why don't you go rest while I finish up in here?" he asked. "You're still looking a bit pale."

"Why should *you* care if I stay here?" she grumbled, just before sneezing twice. "You've already made it clear I can't go *anywhere* without you following me... not even in my *dreams*."

Dropping the dish he was washing in the sink, Dominick

strode over to her to pull her chair back. It grated against the floor while she eyed him with irritation.

"Do you mind?" she snapped.

"Yes, I do!" he retorted, reaching down to lift her from the chair.

"Hey!"

Shifting her in his arms, he silenced her with a glance. "Now look, I've put up with a lot from you over the past few days, and I've been as patient as I could. But I'm through complying with your stubborn attitude against listening to me, when it's obvious you're not feeling well. You probably caught a cold when you stormed out without your coat yesterday."

"Dominick, if you don't put me down, I'll..." Her words trailed off as she sneezed again, earning an infuriating 'I told you so' look from him.

"I rest my case," he replied with satisfaction as he carried her into the family room.

*****

Julianna couldn't protest for long, since her cold grew steadily worse over the next hour, so Dominick took charge. Although she claimed it wasn't necessary—between sneezes— he fetched extra pillows and a blanket for her while she reclined on the sofa, taking time to make her comfortable before seeing to other things. Due to her endless sneezing, he brought back a box of tissues, along with some cold medicine she asked for, and then made something warm for her to drink.

As she propped herself up, he handed her a mug of tea, helping her keep it steady as she took a sip. "Be careful you don't burn yourself," he said.

Shaking her head against his concern, she moved back, clutching a tissue in her hand restlessly and looking quite miffed. "This is ridiculous. I *rarely* catch anything."

Dominick smiled as he placed the mug on the end table. "Most people aren't invulnerable to illness, love. Chaos knows

I've contracted my share of colds over the years."

She smirked. "I thought you're an *alien*, hence immune to these things."

"Why would you think that? I may not be native to this world, or an alien as you so aptly put it, but I assure you that I'm as human as you are, love, and just as susceptible to common illnesses. Even my friend Lendric—who's really a dragon—gets sick on occasion, although not nearly as often as humans."

"So you told me," she said. "I hope you won't be angry, but I'm still skeptical about that. After all, he certainly looks as human as you, with the minor exception of those pointed ears."

"He often prefers to mask his dragon form under the guise of an elf," explained Dominick. "If you like, I'll ask him to prove it to you sometime when you're better."

"Yes, well..." she stammered, "I'm not too sure I *want* to see that, if it's all the same to you."

He couldn't help laughing. "Trust me, Julianna, he'd never endanger any of us. Lendric's been a friend of my family's since before I was born. Besides, I happen to have a close bond with another dragon by the name of..."

His words were cut short as she abruptly started coughing. Not too surprising, since she'd already experienced several minor coughing fits after breakfast.

Sensing this to be an extremely bad one, Dominick immediately sat beside her to pull her close, patting her back as she began shaking.

"Don't," she protested, chagrined when he only held her tighter. "Dominick, you shouldn't hold me like this. You'll only catch it!"

"I won't, and you're more important," he countered, leaving no room for further protests.

Despite her wracking coughs, Julianna managed a weak smile. "Stubborn man," she whispered, without any real reprimand.

Comforted by his soothing warmth, the coughing fit gradually subsided, leaving her breathing easier again. Even then, she snuggled closer to him, smiling at the thought of his equal stubbornness. They were indeed a well-matched pair, she considered silently.

Unable to read her mind, Dominick merely gazed down at her, stroking her shoulder tenderly. This was a great change from a few days ago, when she'd have yelled at him if he so much as touched her. Now, although he wished she felt better, he couldn't help enjoying the simple pleasure of being free to hold her in his arms again.

The doorbell shattered this fragile peace, leaving him sighing as he stood. "I'll get that."

"I'm not an invalid. I can do it."

"*You* stay put," he insisted, his eyes challenging her to defy him. "It's probably just Sammy."

"Yes, Dr. Westbrooke," she said sarcastically, folding her arms with a smirk.

"Watch it, patient, or it's off to bed with you right now," he warned.

As he turned to answer the door, he heard her ask, "Do you mean literally *with* you?"

Freezing where he stood as he faced her again, Dominick couldn't tell whether she was teasing him or not. The doorbell rang again, not allowing him to find out.

"Ask me that again when you're feeling better, and I might just be tempted," he replied.

Satisfied by her immediate blush, he hastily left the room, lest he forget all about the person at the door.

*****

It was Sammy, as Dominick predicted, so he explained to him that his aunt wasn't feeling well and that he needed to let her rest. Sammy was agreeable and offered to help, but Dominick declined, telling the child that he'd most certainly let him know if he needed his help later.

Sammy seemed to understand, watching television and playing with his dinosaurs quietly, while Dominick continued to sit with Julianna, allowing her to lean her head on his shoulder.

For a short while, she tried to maintain her talkative nature with her nephew, but as she grew more and more tired, it didn't take a genius to see her illness was getting worse. Dominick kept a worried eye on her, up to the point when her eyes closed and she began to drift off.

"What's wrong with Aunt Julie, Dominick?" asked Sammy.

"Don't worry. She just seems to be falling asleep," he said, lifting Julianna in his arms. "Would you stay here and watch the dinosaurs while I help her to her room?"

"Okay," he agreed. "Will she be all right?"

"Of course she will, Sammy," Dominick reassured him. "She just needs to rest out this cold, that's all."

Seeing the boy give a nod, Dominick swiftly carried his companion upstairs, the jarring motion evincing a low moan from her. Carefully, he made his way to her bedroom, pulling the covers back before placing her beneath them.

She seemed oblivious to him now, tossing against the pillows as he tucked her in. As he touched her forehead with his hand, his earlier worries of a fever were confirmed.

Although concerned, he was about to go, when he heard her whisper, "Dominick..."

"What is it, love?" he asked, holding her hand above the covers.

"Don't leave me."

He kissed her hand, shaking his head. "I won't, sweetheart. I do need to fetch something to help bring down your fever, but I promise I'll be right back." He wasn't certain whether she agreed or not as he strode out to the hallway, returning shortly afterwards with some cool cloths he'd soaked in the bathroom sink.

Wringing one out over a small bowl he'd found, Dominick placed the cloth against Julianna's forehead. She moaned again, her eyes squinting shut.

"It's cold," she said weakly.

"Yes, but you have a fever," he replied, caressing her cheek. "Trust me, love. It'll help you feel better."

"What about Sammy?"

"I'll keep an eye on him, as well as you, and I'll be downstairs just in case you need me. Right now, the best thing for you is sleep."

Her eyes opened halfway. "Will you be there?" she asked.

Surprised by her question, he smiled back. "Would you want me to be?"

"Maybe."

Silently pleased at her change of heart from earlier, he regretfully shook his head. "As pleasant at that might be, now's not a good time for that," he said. "But after you've rested, and once Crystal comes home to watch Sammy, I'll be happy to sit with you then."

"I'd like that," she said, just before her head fell back against the pillow, her eyes closing.

Smoothing her fever-dampened curls back from her forehead, Dominick shook his head again. What a cruel irony, he thought. When she still had her full memory, was well, and loved him, they were allowed only a brief time together in her dreams. When he arrived here to end their separation, she was injured and lost her memories of him, and when healed, appeared to despise him. And now, while they were together, and she was beginning to trust him again—despite her still missing memories—this damned fever was affecting her health.

Why *now*, of all times, when she was starting to accept him into her life again?

It was as if Fate held no end of obstacles to their love.

Shutting his eyes, he lifted her hand against his cheek. No matter. Fate or no Fate, **this** was real, and so was the love they'd shared and **would** share again. Nothing would stand in the way of that.

After all, as Julianna had mentioned earlier, he was indeed a most stubborn man... at least when it involved his future with the woman he loved.

*****

The hours passed slowly as Dominick managed to keep Sammy from finding mischief, while also checking on Julianna. As she slept, for a while he stayed downstairs to brighten her nephew's spirits with a game of dinosaurs. Admiring the plastic toys, he couldn't help being amused at the thought of Lendric's reaction to them.

Likely, he'd protest that dragons were just as worthy of being depicted by toy replicas, since at least **they** had much higher intelligence than dinosaurs.

Yet still, he'd probably be fascinated by these toys, even though he might not admit it.

He was reprieved from having one of his dinosaurs eaten by Sammy's T-Rex, when his mother came home later. After Dominick explained Julianna's sudden illness, Crystal took over watching her son, allowing him more time to care for his companion upstairs.

Awakening her gently to give her a dose of medicine, Dominick wasn't surprised to find her less than talkative, but when he would have left, she managed to grasp his arm.

"Please... stay with me, until I fall asleep again," she said quietly.

"If you like," he agreed, reaching across to dampen and reapply the cloth on her forehead. "Hopefully, your fever will break soon. Then you should really start to feel better." He stopped upon seeing her stare at him. "What's that look for?

Did Sammy stick a dinosaur on my back that I don't know about?"

"No," she laughed. "You just never seem to stop surprising me. The way you've taken care of me today."

"You would have done the same for me, if the situation was reversed."

Her eyes lowered. "Maybe. But when you were more of a stranger, and I was so angry with you..."

"Shhh," he soothed, touching her cheek tenderly. "That's all behind us now. Besides, we're not strangers anymore, are we?"

"No," she whispered, reaching up to rest her hand on his. "I'm glad that much is true now." As he gazed upon her, she continued, "You never finished your story earlier about dragons. You said you had a bond with one."

Dominick sat back, nodding in remembrance. "Yes, I do. His name is Roderlin."

Julianna showed no obvious look of disbelief. "Tell me of him."

"Roderlin is a blue dragon of my world. We've had a close bond from the day he first hatched."

Her eyes grew curious. "Is that a common ritual?"

"No, it's not," he said. "Although, there's another dragon, called Chaolyn, who resides with my grandfather in the palace..."

"A palace?" she interrupted. "You *live* in a palace?"

Dominick couldn't help chuckling at the way her eyes widened. "I did while I was growing up."

"You never mentioned you were a prince."

"That's because I'm not," he clarified. "Granted, my grandfather was the founder of Barokka, and is largely responsible for creating the island paradise we live on. And also, for the most part, we do oversee the majority of things there now. But despite our having a palace, we hold no claim to royalty.

"My brother Riff and I moved out of the palace several years ago, in favor of sharing a less congested home of our own. Although you might not realize it, life in the palace can get a bit stifling, especially at night when the guards shut that place up like a fortress."

Julianna laughed softly. "If my dreams of you are anything to judge by, I guess I can understand why they couldn't keep you cooped up in a place like that."

"I felt certain you would. Anyway, as I started to mention before, my grandfather Chaos is very close friends with a dragon called Chaolyn, who to the best of my knowledge has lived in the palace since before I was born. From what my grandfather told me, they met a short time after Chaos founded the island, but that's all he's ever mentioned. In any case, there's a very strong bond between them—despite their frequent verbal banter—which is why Chaolyn allowed my presence at a hatching of dragon eggs when I was about twelve. At this hatching, one of the blue hatchlings, Roderlin, broke away from the others to stand beside me, creating the start of a friendship between us. Although bonds like this are uncommon—making them even more precious—once established, they generally last a lifetime."

"You must have felt proud he chose you."

"Honored is more like it," amended Dominick, his eyes becoming pensive at the memory of his distant friend. "We've known each other for over fifteen years now, and during that time, we've shared countless adventures and soared to the skies above."

"It sounds wonderful."

"It is," he said, his expression peaceful as he returned his gaze to her. "Maybe one day, I could persuade you to go flying with us."

"Oh no," Julianna replied. "I'd have a heart-attack from

the height alone."

"It's not as scary as it sounds. I'll hold you to make sure you don't fall."

"You make it sound tempting," she said with a yawn, "but I'd have to think about it."

Dominick brushed his fingers along her cheek. "It looks like the medicine's finally starting to work on your fever. And if I'm not mistaken, you look more than a little sleepy now. Best not to fight it, love."

"I don't want to sleep just yet," she murmured. "I want to hear more about your life and your world."

He smoothed her hair back. "We have a whole lifetime for that, sweetheart. Besides, I can tell you more when you awaken again later. Right now, you need to concentrate on getting well."

Reluctantly she nodded, reaching out to squeeze his hand before drifting back to sleep. Tucking the covers around her, Dominick paused for a moment, unable to resist kissing her sleep-softened mouth just once.

"Sleep well, love," he whispered, shutting the lamp beside her before rising to leave.

When he got out in the hallway, pulling her door closed quietly, he was startled to find Crystal waiting outside. "She's gone to sleep again," he told her. "I'm afraid if you want to talk with her, you'll have to wait..."

Placing her arms about him, she stopped his words with a quick hug.

"Thank you for helping my sister," she said.

Understanding, he hugged her back. "I love your sister very much," he replied, "and I'll certainly always stand by her, well or ill."

"You've more than proven that, Dominick. I'm glad you're all she once said you were... and more than just a dream." Brightening, she added, "Now, I doubt you've given much thought to eating all day, so why don't you come downstairs to join us for a quick dinner while Julie rests?"

Feeling his stomach rumble slightly at her words, he couldn't repress a grin. "I guess I can spare a few minutes for that," he agreed.

*****

Dominick sat with Julianna throughout the night, comforting her whenever she awakened due to the fever. Each time, he held her with soothing words, reapplying cool cloths to keep her temperature down.

As he'd promised, he steered clear of visiting her dreams while she slept, only stealing a few winks of normal sleep himself when he could.

The next day followed a similar pattern as before, with him taking care of Julianna during the day. The only difference was, Crystal had consented to let Sammy play at a friend's house directly after school, so Dominick didn't have to watch him for as many hours while tending to her sister.

Due to his constant ministrations, it was early that evening when Julianna's fever broke. Since she was feeling considerably better, although agitated from being cooped up in bed for the past few days, Dominick helped her downstairs so she could watch television for a while.

She started to protest when he picked her up to carry her down, but seeing as he wasn't willing to take 'no' for an answer, she finally surrendered to the comfort of his strong arms, nestling her head against his chest.

"Aunt Julie!" exclaimed Sammy, running over with one of his dinosaurs.

"Hello, Sammy," she responded, still sounding a bit nasal as Dominick placed her on the sofa, moving to sit beside her. "Something tells me these dinosaurs are here to stay."

"They sure are," he said. "And Dominick says that when his friend Lendric comes back, they might even find me a dragon to go with them."

"Why am I *not* surprised?" she laughed, facing Dominick.

He merely stared at the ceiling innocently, moments before the doorbell rang, startling all three.

"Was your family expecting company tonight?" Dominick asked her curiously.

"No, not that I know of." Abruptly, Julianna remembered. "Oh, great," she said, her head falling against her hand. "That must be Roger." At Dominick's questioning look, she continued, "The other day, remember when I agreed to go out to dinner with him tonight? I completely forgot to cancel it due to being sick."

As she pushed away from the sofa to stand, Dominick's eyes narrowed with alarm. "And where do you think *you're* going?" he demanded.

She turned to him, bewildered. "What does it look like? I have to go explain things to Roger."

"Right," he replied, "so you can get a chill, and then a relapse, so you'll be right back where you started." He shook his head. "No, Julianna. I'm just as capable of explaining things to your 'friend'."

"I'm not so sure of that," she said hesitantly. "The last time you and Roger were both in the same room, you nearly started a fistfight with each other."

"That was before, when you were proclaiming war on me. Why should I seek to threaten the new bond between us now?" She looked skeptical, until he clasped her hand. "You said you trusted me the other night, Julianna. Give me a chance to prove your faith well-founded."

Slowly, she exhaled a sigh. "Just... don't throw him off the porch, all right?"

"I'll be the perfect gentleman," he assured her.

As he left the room, Julianna remained doubtful. Maybe

he was a gentleman around *her*... but Roger? She could only hope there were spare bandages in the house, just in case of an emergency.

If she could have read his thoughts right now, she might have found cause for concern. Bearing a calm look, Dominick wasn't about to break his word to Julianna... although inwardly, he might *like* to break Roger into little pieces! But even though he might be forced to bear false civility towards his despised rival, he couldn't mask how glad he was to have *any* reason to get rid of Roger.

The doorbell rang again, just before Dominick pulled the door open. Sure enough, Roger was standing there in well-dressed attire, a fresh set of flowers in his hand, while his smile quickly faded.

"Not bad, Collins," chuckled Dominick. "All decked out, complete with flowers to bribe the lady. And isn't that fancy cologne 'Eau de Skunk'?"

Roger's eyes darkened with rage. "A pleasure as always to see you too, Westbrooke," he growled. "I'm surprised Julie agreed to let you off your leash to answer the door." Dominick's amusement never faded. "Now, I don't feel like wasting my time exchanging insults with you, so if you'll just tell her I'm here..."

"Oh, she knows already. Why do you think she's not present at the moment?"

At his flippant attitude, Roger gritted his teeth. "Look, Westbrooke, I'm not in the mood for games with you. *Where* is Julie?"

"To tell you the truth, Collins," he began dramatically, "my poor sweetheart came down with a cold as of yesterday morning. Complete with coughs, sneezing, and a fever. The bottom line is, Roger..." He spread his hands innocently, offset by his devilish grin. "Julianna *can't* go out with you tonight."

"You're lying, Westbrooke!" snarled Roger.

"You want lies?" Dominick snapped back, his eyes flaring angrily. "Try remembering the platefuls of *garbage* you fed Julianna the other day. Fortunately, we managed to work things out though, so she won't be as receptive to your lies the next time." Struggling to maintain his calm, he added, "As to Julianna's current illness, I *did* tell you the truth, not that you *deserve* it."

"I demand to see her," declared Roger.

"That's not your decision to make. Julianna's not up to seeing *any* visitors at the moment, and I respect her wishes foremost over anyone's... *especially* yours!"

"And who are *you* to be here?"

"That's really none of your concern, *Roger*," countered Dominick, his tone subtly threatening. "If you're so desperate to see her, you can wait a week until she's better. Although by that time, I imagine she might remember the truth you've lied about regarding your so-called *cousin* Marilyn. I'll bet Julianna's friend Marybeth could clear this up quite easily, if we contacted her."

Alarmed at how much this man obviously knew, Roger still wasn't a man easily deterred. Abruptly, he tried to push past Dominick, but his rival wasn't about to let him get anywhere.

"This *is* private property, Collins," he warned, amused at his growing chagrin. "You'd do best to remember that, lest Julianna's family press charges against you. And we both know that her sister Crystal would be *more* than happy to do that."

Roger was forced to admit privately that he was right about that much, damn both him *and* her sister! Clenching his teeth, he hissed, "You can tell Julie, I'll be back in a few days for a raincheck on our dinner tonight. Because for some reason, I don't believe she's as sick as you claim."

"Believe what you want," replied Dominick. "Personally, I'm not too surprised she got sick so suddenly. Just thinking about going out with you tonight must have made her stomach turn."

"Damn you, you'll pay for your insults, Westbrooke!" yelled Roger, crushing the flowers he held as he stormed back to his car.

"Nothing more than you've earned, Collins," said Dominick, slamming the door behind him.

Julianna glanced up immediately as he reentered the family room, her gaze expectant as it fell upon his. "It looks like you actually didn't kill each other," she remarked with admiration.

"What more could you expect of me, my lady?" he asked, with a gallant bow.

She nodded with an accepting smile, just before it faded into skepticism as she folded her arms. "All right, Dominick... now let's have the truth. I heard the shouting match going on between you two."

He grinned. "Who were you rooting for?"

"Never mind *that*! Just give me the brief rundown of what happened."

"If you insist," he sighed, explaining it to her quickly. Surprisingly enough, his story *did* seem to coincide with the bits and pieces she'd heard, which eased her mind. "I told him not to come back for a week, but I'm afraid he'll be back sooner than that."

"That sounds like Roger," she agreed. "He isn't that easy to dissuade."

"I'll say. And I must admit, when we argued in your room the other day, I came very close to tossing Roger out the window, like your father considered once."

Her eyes widened at his words. "How do *you* know about that?" she asked.

Dominick eyed her seriously. "I visited your sister once in her dreams to help prove my reality at the time, so you'd have someone here who trusted your belief in me. She told me of how Roger turned to another girl when he couldn't get what he wanted from you that night."

Briefly, he explained what Crystal had told him. Julianna looked stunned. "This is news to me. I don't remember Roger going to someone else, after that time he disappeared for several weeks."

Although it *was* possible, her mind concluded.

"Even if your memory comes back, you won't remember *that* part of it, since your family never wanted to hurt you with the truth. Crystal can back me up on this, if you need proof of it. I just felt I could tell you now, since given recent circumstances regarding Roger, you'd have a better understanding of what he's like, despite his words to the contrary."

"What circumstances are you talking about?"

He gladly would have answered her question, including the truth about Marilyn, but knowing how she'd quickly jumped to Roger's defense before, he wasn't sure whether she'd believe him at this point.

"Since you're still recovering, it's not something you need to deal with right now. But I can tell you that Roger hasn't been as saintly as he's been acting lately." At her curious look, he said thoughtfully, "I've noticed you and your sister Crystal are very close." She nodded. "All right then. When you're feeling better, I'd advise asking *her* what happened over the past few months regarding you and Roger. She can give you a more objective explanation."

Julianna shifted her gaze to the floor in confusion. *What could Roger possibly have done?* she wondered. Shaking her head, she decided he was right in that she wasn't ready to deal with whatever it was.

"When I'm better, I'll do that."

"So... now that I've told you all," Dominick continued, "I suppose you're about to rail at me again for how I handled him tonight."

Prepared for her anger, he wasn't expecting her to lean forward to hug him instead. "Thank you," she whispered.

"I don't understand," he murmured. "Have you remembered something I don't know about?"

"No," she replied. "But I'm thanking you for all that you've done over the past few days. You took good care of me when I needed help, as well as watching over Sammy, and I'm truly grateful."

Embracing her back, Dominick kissed her forehead. "I'll always take good care of you, love," he promised. "Well or ill, you're stuck with me."

Julianna smiled. "Then I'll thank my lucky stars."

No more than I'll thank mine, he thought, with a smile of his own.

Chapter Eleven

"It's too soon," Dominick protested a few days later. "I don't care *how* warm it is outside."

"I'm better," insisted Julianna. "And if I'm forced to be stuck in this house for one more day, I'll certainly be sick again. From boredom. Besides, I promised Sammy this afternoon I'd take him to the park."

Folding his arms with a scowl didn't help, since she'd come to understand this look was only a surface threat. Especially when Sammy ran into the room, several dinosaurs tucked under one arm.

"Can we go now, Aunt Julie?" he asked.

She knelt down to his level. "We sure can. Tell T-Rex to lead the way."

As the boy ran outside, Julianna was about to follow, when Dominick cleared his throat behind her. Before she could question this, he'd placed her coat around her shoulders, earning a thankful smile from her.

"Since it's obvious I can't talk you out of this, I'll go with you," he decided. "I just hope you don't have a relapse."

Patting his shoulder, she said confidently, "I'm stronger than I look."

"Yes, and much more stubborn," he added as he followed her out, closing the door behind them.

*****

Leaning one arm against a tree, Dominick was unable to suppress a smile as he watched Julianna play with Sammy on the swings. *This* was the woman he remembered, he thought. Thank the stars her fever hadn't been too serious and she was better now.

Yet the more he watched Julianna, the more he felt the sting of their present situation. In truth, nothing was resolved between them. She hadn't told him of any other flashbacks, although at least she seemed to be warming up to him now, memory or no. Seeing her so content with Sammy triggered memories of his own, reminding him of the times they'd discussed the possibility of children.

"Look out, T-Rex!" screamed Sammy, when his dinosaur fell from his hands to bounce along the ground. Climbing down from the swing, he ran to retrieve it.

Grinning, Julianna turned to Dominick. Surely, he'd want to join them. She was unprepared for the solemn look in his eyes as he seemed to be staring right through her. Uncertain what it meant, she walked over to him, taking his hand to break him free of his vacant look.

"Care to join our dinosaur war?" she asked. "T-Rex may have a bit of a headache after being dropped, so we might have an advantage over him yet."

Regardless of his dampened spirits, her pleasant invitation worked its own magic. At least she wasn't pushing him away anymore, he reflected, even as Sammy climbed back onto the swing.

"Dom, can you give me and T-Rex a super push?" he asked.

"A super push, huh?" chuckled Dominick. "Well, let me see what I can do." Moments later, Sammy was soaring towards the sky, cheering happily, while his aunt laughed in the background. "We'll make a dragon out of you yet, Sammy."

"Make sure you don't tell his mother that, or Crystal will evict us both," she warned.

"She won't. After all, she didn't evict Lendric, knowing *he's* a dra..." Julianna gave him a gentle jab with her elbow, gesturing towards Sammy while shaking her head. "Oh... I forgot. Sorry about that."

When Sammy seemed to be going high enough, Dominick stepped off to the side with her. "It's all right," she told him. "But since Crystal doesn't want Sammy to know *everything* about this situation just yet, including your story about Lendric being a dragon, we really should respect her wishes. She's been gracious enough to allow you to stay at our house while you're here, but don't push it too far."

"I understand," he agreed. "If I were in her position with a son like Sammy, I suppose I'd..."

At his sudden silence, Julianna turned to him. "You'd what?" He shook his head with a somber look, renewing her earlier suspicions. "Something's bothering you, isn't it?"

Getting no response, she followed his gaze to where another couple was leading several children towards a different set of swings nearby. Surely he couldn't know them, since they were a new family in the neighborhood, and he wasn't from around here.

"We discussed having a family like that," he whispered in remembrance, facing her again slowly. "You mentioned how fond you were of children, and seeing you with your nephew today only confirms it. I remember how we used to hold each other at night as we spoke of plans for having a child of our own someday, after we could be married on one of our worlds. I just wish..."

Shutting his eyes, he sighed regretfully, knowing he probably shouldn't have spoken of this to her. But how could he not when confronted by images of their future children that might never be now?

Sensing his feelings, Julianna squeezed his hand, recapturing his attention. "You seem so honest when you speak of these things," she said softly, "and I want to believe you, Dominick. But I just *can't* remember any of it."

"I know." Abruptly, his eyes filled with new

determination as he placed his hands on her shoulders. "Julianna, I have a favor to ask of you."

She tensed. "You're not about to ask me to bear your children, I hope."

"No, sweetheart. I wouldn't ask that unless it was something you wanted too. And even then, only if we were married first."

"Dominick..."

"But I'm not asking that of you," he continued. "What I *am* asking is this. Would you be willing to let us try starting over again?"

"Starting over? But why? We seem to be doing all right as things stand now."

"Very much so, and I'm grateful for that. To be more specific, I'm asking you to give me a chance to win your heart again as I did once before." He reached out to hold her hand. "I'm certain that if you'd be open to this, you'll come to understand what we shared before, and maybe want that again."

Julianna absorbed his words slowly. "You mean, you want us to try dating?"

"More accurately, love, I wish to court you, in the hope I can persuade you to consider a more permanent future between us."

She didn't need to ask what he meant by *that*.

A bit uncertain, she thought for a moment. "I can't remember anyone ever wanting to 'court me' as you put it," she said, staring at the sky as she considered the ramifications of his proposal.

If she accepted, she wouldn't be agreeing to marry him necessarily, or promising her body to him. Yet surely he'd want *something* out of this. The question was what.

He didn't need to be a mind reader to grasp her thoughts, squeezing her hand reassuringly. "No strings attached, love," he promised. "You have my word I won't force you into anything, although I will certainly make every attempt to convince your heart of how strong our love was, and can be again."

He presented a tempting offer, she thought, having already fantasized several times of their one romantic evening together... and what might have happened afterwards had they not been interrupted. In addition, Dominick had captured her interest with his stories of Chavernos, and he was the type of man with whom she could somehow see sharing more stories with, perhaps even ones that she'd told no one else.

Heaven knew she was attracted to him by new things every day.

Why not? her mind decided.

"I can't promise anything," she said finally, "but if you wish to 'court me,' then I won't turn you away. Actually, I think I'd like spending more time with you."

Dominick's smile became a full-fledged grin as he pulled her close to kiss her passionately. Surprised, Julianna had no chance to protest, since he moved away moments later. If his goal had been to leave her speechless—and breathless too—he'd succeeded.

"I promise to give you the utmost courtship, love," he responded, running his hands through her hair, while the warmth of his blue eyes mesmerized her. "Until stars willing, the day comes when you agree to marry me again."

Julianna's eyes refuted this, shaking her head. "Wait a second, Dominick. I said you can court me. I never said I'd marry you afterwards."

He lifted her hand to his lips to kiss her palm. "Perhaps not yet, my lady. But time will tell." As he placed further kisses along her wrist, Julianna felt a warm shiver run through her, privately wondering if she'd just sealed her fate with this man after all.

Yet surely, there were worse fates than *this*!

From Dream to Reality

*****

"Another bouquet of roses," said Julianna, inhaling their sweet fragrance, before glancing at the accompanying card which bore a tender message from her suitor.

Crystal smiled. "Red ones this time," she noted. "They go well with the white ones which arrived yesterday. You know, I think that man's in love with you, Julie."

Her sister could only blush.

Having silently observed from the staircase, Dominick escaped upstairs unnoticed, bearing a most satisfied smile of his own.

Over the past several days, with help from Julianna's family—as well as Lendric, who returned briefly before spending more time with the Dragends—Dominick arranged for Julianna to receive various gifts, including more bouquets of flowers.

Crystal and Vicki helped him choose a bottle of her favorite perfume, while Jerry helped him find a box of her favorite candy. Even Sammy helped, letting him know of Julianna's liking for stuffed animal tigers. And of course Lendric helped too, supplying some of the gold they'd thoughtfully brought along on their journey. With this, Dominick arranged for purchasing a few very special items, which he planned to give her later.

Throughout all of this, Julianna found that Dominick's idea of courtship didn't involve mere material things. Instead, he spent almost every waking hour keeping her company. He took long walks with her, and accompanied her to various places of interest, sharing memories of past and present with her.

One night, Jerry and Crystal went along with them to a dance club. For one who was unfamiliar with Earth's type of dancing, Dominick caught on quickly, cutting a dashing figure on the dance floor. Something that drew the attention of many envious women, Julianna noticed, especially during the slow dances, during which she hugged her partner closer.

Late the next afternoon, Julianna was presented with a far different surprise than the other gifts.

Three boxes of different sizes arrived, which she and Crystal carried in.

"What do you think they are this time?" asked Julianna. "We already have a kitchen sink, so I hope he hasn't included *that*."

"Don't be silly," replied her sister. "Just open them."

Choosing the largest box first, Julianna's hand flew to her mouth as she opened it. "Oh my," she said, pulling forth a beautiful floor-length, ivory-colored satin dress. "Dominick's outdone himself this time," she murmured, running her hands along the soft fabric. It reminded her of the dress she'd worn when she'd dreamed of him. Something that hardly seemed like a coincidence now.

Taking the initiative to open the medium box, Crystal pulled out a matching pair of ivory-colored shoes with low heels. "I think these must go with that," she said.

"But what are they for?"

"Maybe the last box has the answer," suggested Crystal.

Feeling like a child during the holidays, Julianna tore the ribbons from it, finding something wrapped in layers of tissue. This last gift made her catch her breath. It was a diamond, emerald, and gold bracelet!

"Where on Earth did he get the money for this?" she asked.

Not quite from Earth, her sister thought, remembering how she and Jerry had gone with Dominick and Lendric to exchange some of the gold they'd brought with them. Since Julianna's companion swore that it was mere pocket change to his family, Crystal could only assume her sister would never have a worry moneywise with him.

Reaching within the box, Julianna withdrew a white card that she'd missed before, and read it aloud. "*'My dearest*

Julianna, I would be most honored if you would accept these humble gifts... '" More like priceless! she thought, overwhelmed. *"'along with my invitation to a romantic dinner tonight. Love always, Dominick.'"* She turned to Crystal suspiciously. "Did you know of this?"

Smiling, her sister nodded. "As a matter of fact, I did. He made me promise not to give it all away."

"I have to thank him," she replied, moving to stand.

Grabbing her arm, Crystal shook her head. "He left with Jerry a short while ago to take care of some things, but they'll both be back in a few hours."

"Oh." Julianna looked disappointed. "Then I guess I'll have to thank him later."

"I'm sure you will. In the meantime, why don't you put that sparkling jewelry upstairs, so you don't lose it before he comes back?"

"Don't worry. I'm not about to do *that*."

Running upstairs to her room, Julianna immediately looked around for her jewelry box. That was funny. She knew she had one, yet she couldn't remember where it was. Good heavens, if this was yet another memory gap, it was getting really irritating!

Opening the closet door, she let out a soft cry as several boxes fell towards her feet. Slightly annoyed, she kicked them aside temporarily to uncover something in the far corner. Feeling about, she identified the rectangular edges of the object of her search.

"Bingo!" she said, pulling the box free.

Taking it over to her bed, she sat down to find a suitable place for the new bracelet. Dominick must have spent a fortune on those diamonds and emeralds. Maybe he wasn't a prince where he came from, but if this bracelet was any indication, he was no pauper either!

Opening the bottom drawer of the jewelry box, she

looked affectionately at the many trinkets she'd collected over the years. Her mood ring shaped like a heart, which shone blue when her hand was warm... reminding her of the warmth of Dominick's eyes.

She picked up a long rope necklace next, remembering how she used to pretend it was a lariat as a child. In another corner of the box, there was a locket she'd gotten from her mother, who had once received it from her grandmother. Gripping it tightly, she sighed. There were times like this when she missed her mother.

She thought of the times as a child when they used to play with the trinkets in this box, as well as when her mother allowed her to play 'dress up' on occasion. She'd been so kind and loving. If only she hadn't died so young. Her father had died not many years afterwards. Almost as if they couldn't bear to be parted, not even by death.

All her life, she'd prayed to find a love like they had known, and how they'd cherished one another when they'd both been alive.

Could Dominick give her that love she sought? she wondered.

And in heaven's name, what was she to do about Roger?

He'd called a few days ago, asking to postpone their raincheck for dinner, since once again he had to head out of town on business. He assured her he'd call her when he returned to follow-up. Although he'd voiced being disappointed, Julianna surprisingly found she wasn't, though of course she kept this to herself.

During the time she'd spent with Dominick, she'd come to appreciate being with him much more than her former friend. Especially since Roger's ridiculous accusation that Dominick was mentally crazy.

It was so hard to believe that she and Roger had started to have a relationship before she'd lost her memory. Strange...

she thought, even as her hand brushed against something at the bottom of the box. Puzzled, she flipped the box upside-down, emptying the trinkets onto the bed, along with a small book which fell into her lap.

"My journal!" she exclaimed, her eyes brightening.

She'd wondered where she'd put it, since it wasn't in her dresser drawer where she usually kept it. Since she didn't remember placing it in her jewelry box, it must have happened recently. When she tried to open it, she was surprised to find the book locked. She hadn't generally done that, knowing her family wouldn't invade her privacy. Hopefully, the key was somewhere on the bed.

Sifting through the trinkets, a familiar flash of gold caught her eye.

Success, she thought happily, using the key to open the journal. Flipping through the most recent pages, she was a bit disappointed to find she hadn't written anything about Dominick. In some ways, that made sense, since if his words were to be believed, they'd initially met in dreams. Not something she might have written of at first.

However, she noticed there were entries mentioning Roger from a few months ago. Going back a bit further than the last one, she was curious to see if anything he'd said was true.

"*I'm so glad that Roger came back into my life. He does so much to make me happy,*" she'd written. "*I just can't understand why my family ever mistrusted him.*"

A fact that was still true today, she thought, though curious why. As she read a few subsequent entries, she was surprised that they had indeed started a relationship together. There was a time when that would have pleased her, as it clearly had then, but now that Dominick was a part of her life...

Shaking her head, she read on, but noticed the tone of the writing was changing.

"*I know I wasn't comfortable with the notion of*

spending the night with Roger, but for him to get so angry at my wanting to wait really upsets me. It's a big step in a relationship, and I want the timing to be right. Why can't he understand that?"

Flipping another page, her blood ran cold by the words. Especially since the words had obviously been blurred by the telltale stain of tears.

"'I feel like the biggest fool in the world. I went to Roger's apartment tonight to work things out and maybe spend a romantic evening with him after all. But instead, I found him with an 'old friend' of his called Marilyn who obviously was giving him what he wanted in my absence.'

"'He hasn't spoken so coldly to me since I wouldn't spend the night with him last week, and when he closed the door in my face, I realized there really is nothing left of us. I wish I could disappear where the pain of seeing him and Marilyn together wouldn't hurt me anymore.'"

The words of the last entry echoed in her mind as she shut the journal.

Marilyn was Roger's former *lover*? Whom he'd apparently left her for?

The thought made her feel nauseous.

Dominick had been right after all! Her 'dear friend' of the past *had* lied to her. Oh yes, they'd started a relationship... one which he'd ended because she wouldn't sleep with him within his timeframe, so he'd turned to another woman instead. A woman he blatantly lied was his *cousin*! All the while *knowing* she couldn't remember where his lies were coming from.

Feeling even sicker at the thought, she jumped when Crystal suddenly called for her downstairs.

"What is it?" she managed to shout back.

Her sister's voice was ice cold as she spoke. "You have a *visitor* at the door, Julie. Roger's here."

Roger? she thought. *Here? Now?*

He'd bypassed calling her this time. It wouldn't surprise her if he'd waited until Dominick wasn't home.

Narrowing her eyes, her anger mounted. No wonder she'd locked the journal and buried it in the closet. Not to mention, it explained why she hadn't written of Dominick afterwards, since she'd likely wanted to forget the journal altogether.

Stormily, she placed the book and key back in the jewelry box, and quickly covered it with the trinkets again.

When she got to the bracelet Dominick gave her though, she paused to hold it tenderly, placing it off to the side before slamming the box shut, her hands shaking from how angry she was. Not only was Roger a deceiving liar, but one who had the *worst* timing! A fact he'd soon regret.

Walking downstairs, she found him waiting by the front door. "Julie," he said cheerfully. "I just got back this morning, so I thought I'd surprise you."

You certainly did, she thought angrily, though she kept silent.

"I'm sorry work preempted our dinner date again a few days ago, but at least it looks like you've conquered your supposed fever."

"Oh, didn't Dominick tell you?" she asked icily. "I was *very* ill the other day, which is why I had him cancel our dinner date." *And my being ill from your **lies** now, is reason enough to cancel our friendship as well!*

Roger missed the change in her tone.

"That's why I'm here today. Julie, I have a wonderful evening planned for us to make up for the other night. Prepare to be wined and dined, sweetheart."

"I'm sorry, Roger," she replied, trying to control her disgust, "but I'm afraid I have a previous engagement with Dominick this evening."

His eyes widened. "Just what do you mean by an engagement?" he asked suspiciously.

It would serve him right if I let him believe just that! she thought grimly. "We're going out to dinner later."

The shock on his face earned minor satisfaction from her, but it was short-lived. "It would seem I underestimated Westbrooke, if you've become such good friends so suddenly," he murmured. "But I didn't come here to discuss him. If you're busy tonight, we can go out tomorrow night instead."

Oh, we can? After all your lies, you'd better think again, buster! She nearly shouted this to him, along with the revelation that she'd caught on to his lies... but abruptly she reconsidered.

No, maybe she *would* take him up on his offer.

It would provide the perfect opportunity to end this charade once and for all, and wipe that grin off his face!

"Hmmm, we could do that," she replied, "but we'll have to keep the evening short, since I always tuck Sammy in by eight o'clock."

There, she thought. *That much is true, and it should help keep things from getting complicated later.*

"I am working a bit later than I'd like tomorrow, but I suppose we can plan around it." Nodding, he smiled. "All right then, why don't we go to the nightclub tomorrow instead of dinner? Maybe you'll be inspired to sing again."

"Sing?" she questioned in genuine confusion. Was that yet another lie? she wondered, nearly scowling.

At her blank look, he realized the implication. "Okay, you might not remember that, but don't worry, it's not important. I'll pick you up tomorrow then."

Her eyes betrayed sudden concern. Hmmm, that could present a problem. How would she get home later, since she wouldn't be leaving with him afterwards? Jerry and Crystal were both working late, and Dominick couldn't drive a car—or at least he claimed he couldn't. Ah, but Vicki was supposed to be home early, from what she'd overheard. That would suffice.

Now only one nagging detail remained.

"There is one last thing," she said evenly. "I may have a few memory gaps, but I don't like being forced into things, so no more foisting kisses on me like the other day. Understood?"

He looked about to protest, but her determination held firm until he nodded. "Fine," he conceded. "Just so long as you give me a chance to make up for that night you weren't feeling well."

"Tomorrow," she agreed. "Now if you don't mind, I have a few things of my own that need attending to."

"I'll pick you up around six-thirty." Eyeing her casual attire, he added, "Can I count on you to wear something pretty?"

"Oh, I guarantee I'll find something," she said coolly as he waved before leaving. *I've already **found** proof of your deceptions, you two-faced liar!*

Almost slamming the door from her silent rage, Julianna stormed back upstairs, certain that after tomorrow—one way or another—she'd get Roger Collins out of her life once and for all.

*****

"Want to talk about it?" asked Crystal, having come upstairs after hearing her sister's door slam.

Glancing out the window, Julianna pressed one hand against the pane. "I can't believe I fell for that man's lies," she said.

Crystal's eyes narrowed in confusion. "Dominick?" she questioned.

"No, not Dominick," replied Julianna, sighing regretfully. "Good Lord, **he's** the one person I should have trusted all along, and instead..." She paused, before hissing, "I trusted that bastard who was **supposed** to be my friend!"

Crystal understood instantly. "What has Roger done now?"

"It's not only what he's done now, but what he did before which he lied about!" she snapped. "I found entries from my journal I've kept that say *exactly* what he did when we were seeing each other a few months ago, and he had the nerve to try and pretend otherwise!"

Knowing Julianna kept a journal, though she'd never read anything from it, she could only be glad that her sister finally knew the truth on her own. "Does Roger know you're aware of this?"

Julianna shook her head, as she turned. "No. For once, I decided to leave *him* in the dark, although I fully intend to remedy this when we're out tomorrow night."

Crystal's eyes widened. "You're going *out* with him?" she asked incredulously. "Julie, I really don't think that's a good idea."

"I think it is!" she exclaimed. "Crystal, what kind of man would take advantage of a woman's memory loss by attempting to reprogram her head with lies?"

"The kind of man *you* shouldn't be dealing with anymore," her sister retorted. "Julie, I've seen you over the past few days with Dominick, and you've been very happy together. Why jeopardize this by seeking some pointless form of revenge on someone you should forget entirely?"

Julianna's voice lowered. "I know you can't understand," she said, "but I can't just *forget* what Roger tried to do to my life. I *need* to finish things with him tomorrow, because only then will I be able to move forward with my life, and to have any possibility of a future with Dominick, if one is meant to be."

Folding her arms, Crystal's expression was grim. "I can't say I agree with you, but I know you're too headstrong to argue with." Thoughtfully, she asked, "You will tell Dominick though, won't you?"

Without hesitation, Julianna nodded. "Yes. There have

been enough lies surrounding us, and I'm not going to add one more to the list." Glancing at the bracelet shining from the bed, she then turned to Crystal. "But not tonight. I don't want the evening he's planned to be ruined because of Roger. I'll explain things to him early tomorrow at the latest. In the meantime, can I get your agreement that you won't...?"

"I'll leave *you* the honor of telling him," she interrupted. "I just hope he can talk you out of it, when you do."

Julianna tried to look reassuring, although her sister was *far* from convinced by this. "Don't worry about me, Crystal. I can take care of myself tomorrow. And now that I know the truth of Roger's lies, I fully intend to confront him about each of them. Now... if you don't mind, I need to talk to Vicki."

Nodding, her sister followed her out.

*****

Alone in her room again a short while later, Julianna couldn't see anything wrong with her plans. Although Vicki said she already had her own evening plans to go out to dinner with her fiancé the following night, she promised to be back in time to pick Julianna up at the nightclub at a quarter of eight. That way, she'd be home in time to help put Sammy to bed.

While things were all arranged to her satisfaction, it wasn't easy for Julianna to put aside her anger over Roger so easily. But upon running her hands along the satin of the dress Dominick had presented her with, she was determined to do just that.

Seeing how late it was getting, she donned it quickly, along with the matching shoes, and of course the shimmering bracelet. Brushing her hair until it shone, as she glanced in her mirror, she found herself unexpectedly nervous about this evening. True, it wasn't her first date with Dominick, but her formal attire did seem to give it a different significance.

For the umpteenth time, she checked her reflection in the mirror. The dress certainly seemed to enhance her in all the right ways, but would Dominick think so?

She wasn't given long to ponder this, as she heard Jerry's voice. "Cinderella, I think the prince has arrived to escort you to the ball!" he called out.

Grabbing her purse, Julianna would have run downstairs, but the dress wouldn't allow her that luxury. Instead, her appearance at the staircase left her brother-in-law whistling.

"Really, Jerry!" she exclaimed. *"Cinderella?"*

"You do look like a princess," he said seriously as she came downstairs.

She glanced towards the front entrance, but saw only her sister and an oddly transfixed Sammy who was staring out the open door.

"Where's Dominick?" she asked, puzzled. "I thought..."

"Aunt Julie, I think Dominick won the lottery!"

Julianna grinned at her nephew. "I don't think he'd know much about that, Sammy."

"But he must have!" the boy insisted, staring at her with shining eyes. "Look!"

Intrigued, she joined a beaming Crystal at the door. "Care to explain?" she asked. Her sister only pointed outside, prompting her to look. As she did, Julianna's eyes widened.

A white limousine was now parked out front!

Maybe Sammy was right after all.

The front door of the limo opened, revealing the chauffeur, who then opened the rear door for a shadowed figure. In the best formal attire Earth could offer, Dominick stepped out, striding towards her. Stopping but a few feet away, his eyes quickly appraised her before meeting hers again.

"Thou art most beautiful this night, dear maiden," he said softly, bowing before her.

Julianna had no idea how long she stood there gaping at him, until Crystal deftly gave her a slight nudge forward, jarring the blank look from her.

"So are you, Dominick," she murmured, just before shaking her head. "I mean... handsome, of course."

Smiling broadly, his blue eyes glittered, mesmerizing her all over again. She barely noticed when he held out his hand for her. "Our evening awaits us, my lady."

As she took his hand in acceptance, he placed his free arm about her shoulders, leading her towards the awaiting limousine.

"Do you suppose she'll regain her speech before the end of the evening?" Crystal asked her husband.

"I suppose her companion will manage either way," replied Jerry, raising one hand to his mouth. "Just make sure you have her back by midnight, Dominick!"

Gaping at him, Crystal swatted his shoulder before turning to the exiting pair. "Never mind him!" she told them. "You just have a good time!"

Julianna smiled with a wave as Dominick helped her into the limo, joining her afterwards. Shutting the door for them, the chauffeur got back in and started the engine.

Placing an arm about his wife, Jerry was certain Crystal was as pleased as he was over this turn of events. During his brief stay, they'd both taken to Dominick, and certainly preferred his company over Roger's.

"If all goes well, something tells me Dominick may become a new addition to our family," he said.

Crystal hugged her husband. "For my sister's sake, I certainly hope so, sweetheart."

*****

At a hotel dining room high above, overlooking the town below, Julianna's brown eyes glowed like stars as Dominick led her to a candlelit table. When he held out her chair for her, she couldn't help feeling like a fairy tale princess, especially with the way her companion had seen to every detail being perfect this night.

Over the past several days, she'd come to realize just what must have captured her heart so swiftly regarding this man. Everything he did for her was done out of love. From the time he'd taken care of her when she was ill, to the time they'd shared a wonderful night together by the ocean, in her dreams.

Regardless of how true everything he said was, there was no denying the way her heart raced just being with him now.

"I have a present for you," he said, reaching across the table to squeeze her hand.

"Another one?" she asked. "Dominick, you're going to end up spoiling me with these presents of yours. Wasn't the diamond and gold bracelet expensive enough?"

"A mere trinket compared to the jewels I'd gladly give you if we were back on my homeworld."

For once, she simply smiled, not minding his mention of Chavernos anymore. Wherever he was really from, it must indeed be a wonderful place. While she was lost to her musings, she abruptly realized he'd left his seat to stand behind her.

"Dominick, what is it?" Her eyes widened as he placed a shimmering gold necklace about her neck. At the end of the delicate chain rested a gold heart, the edges of which were lined with tiny diamonds and emeralds. Touching it reverently, Julianna gasped. "Oh, Dominick... I'm not kidding. You *really* shouldn't have."

"Well, of course I should," he chuckled, kissing her neck. "I happen to regard this courtship very seriously. So... do you like my gift?"

Julianna clasped the heart as she faced him, her eyes shining. "Of course I do. How could I not? It even has my favorite gems in it, just like the bracelet."

"Emeralds," he agreed. "Something you told me once before." His expression brightened. "But you obviously haven't taken a very good look at it yet. Otherwise, you'd have noticed the inscription within."

"It's engraved?" she asked with wonder. As he nodded, she opened the locket gingerly to read what was inside, written across both halves. "*To my dearest Julianna. Love eternally, Dominick.*" Tears welling from her eyes, she shut the heart slowly, gripping it tightly.

Dominick knelt by her side anxiously. "By Chaos, sweetheart, the last thing I meant to do was to make you cry," he said. "I'm sorry, Julianna. If I'd known you'd react this way, I wouldn't have..."

"No," she interrupted, brushing a hand across her eyes. "I love it, truly I do." Seeing his features brighten again, she opened her arms to him. "And right now, I would really like to hug you."

Standing to pull her close in an affectionate embrace, Dominick glanced up with newfound hope. Things were going better than he'd planned. If the evening continued on this note, perhaps he'd have the opportunity to present his final gift to her.

He just needed to be patient a little while longer.

*****

Before their dinner arrived, they took advantage of the dance floor across the room, joining the other couples who were slow dancing to some appropriately romantic music. Leaning her head against Dominick's shoulder as his strong arms held her close, Julianna couldn't remember a time she'd been happier.

He seemed to share her thoughts, never losing the tender smile he wore, while occasionally stroking one hand along her back, making it clear to any onlookers that he wasn't about to relinquish his partner to anyone.

*Memories of Daffordshire could attest to **that**!* he thought privately.

Afterwards, all throughout dinner the pair shared stories and laughter, often exchanging subtle glances at each other when the other wasn't looking. Upon ultimately realizing this, Dominick reached out to take Julianna's hand, and this time she held his in return.

To others in the restaurant who watched them, they looked very much like a couple in love.

The pair were so wrapped up in each other that neither noticed when the plates were cleared away. "This was a beautiful evening, Dominick," said Julianna. "No matter what happens, I'll never forget it."

"Nor will I, love," he replied, glancing out the window for a moment before his smile broadened. "But the night isn't over just yet," he continued, facing her again. "Since we still have some time left before your family wonders where we are, how would you like to see a dinner show tonight?"

"I'd love to. Did you have a particular one in mind?"

"Hmmm..." he considered, as his gaze was drawn back to the window. "Ah, we're in luck. There's a theater below which might have an interesting show playing. Care to have a look?"

Leaning forward, Julianna read a few names aloud, just before the lights abruptly blinked out. "What?" she gasped. "Looks like they're having some kind of problem." Moments later, the lights came back as new letters scrolled across the screen. "Oh, wait, there it is. 'Will You...'" She paused, her eyes widening. "'Marry Me, Julianna?'"

Turning slowly to face Dominick as her words trailed off, she found him gazing at her lovingly as he withdrew a small velvet box. "I knew someday I'd manage to leave you speechless, one way or another," he said, lifting the lid to remove the ring within.

Composed of an emerald encircled by diamonds, in a pure gold setting, it was identical to the one he'd given her in the dream-state upon originally asking her to marry him. Having chosen it carefully for just this reason, Dominick hoped it would bring the same response from her as he'd received before.

As Julianna stared at it, transfixed, Dominick took her

hand gently to place the ring upon her finger. "Will you marry me, Julianna?" he asked softly.

More than speechlessness kept her from replying.

Upon seeing the ring, it triggered a memory she'd forgotten. Of a night not that long ago when she'd received a ring just like this one, and accepted the marriage proposal it offered, from the one man she truly loved.

As more memories flooded her mind, taking her back on a swift journey of all she'd forgotten, Julianna blinked rapidly, feeling a surge of emotion well through her heart. Her eyes lifted to face the expectant gaze of her companion.

"I remember," she whispered, almost in disbelief.

Dominick's expression became confused. He'd expected a 'yes' or a 'no', but not... "You remember?" he echoed, feeling a glimmer of hope. "What do you mean, you remember? Remember what?"

"I mean I remember *everything*," she said excitedly. "I remember when you once gave me this ring. I remember our engagement. And most of all, dear heaven above, I remember *you*, Dominick!"

"By the stars, love, you don't need to tell me twice," he breathed, bounding from his chair to pull her into his arms, kissing her with all the pent-up desire he'd felt since their ill-fated reunion. Julianna was no less enthusiastic, tangling her hands in his hair as Dominick fairly devoured her mouth with his, pressing her back against the table, both blissfully ignorant to the outside world.

"Ahem!" came an urgent voice, gradually breaking through to them. Dominick raised his head first, to find the headwaiter staring at him questioningly. "Excuse me, sir, but we do have rooms..."

Both Dominick and Julianna broke into laughter before he cast a somewhat sheepish look at the waiter. "Point taken," he said. "My apologies. I'm afraid since my companion and I have been separated until this evening, we let the heat of the moment get to us."

"Hmmm, so it would seem," concurred the waiter, not masking a smile. "But please, since you *are* in our dining hall, do try to keep your, er... 'enthusiasm' down to a reasonable level. All right?"

"We'll do our best," Dominick agreed, gently leading Julianna back to her seat. Nodding, the waiter left them alone again, while the other spectators in the restaurant resumed their own dinners. "I apologize for that, sweetheart," he said, his eyes still bright. "You just surprised me, that's all. Do you really remember everything now?"

"As incredible as it seems, I really do," she replied, holding his hand. "As soon as you brought out the engagement ring, all the memories came back in a flash. I even remember what happened during the accident."

Dominick's mouth tightened grimly for a moment before he shook his head. "Let's not speak of that just yet," he said, raising her hand aloft. "Instead, I believe we still have some unfinished business regarding this ring."

"Unfinished business?" she asked.

He fairly groaned, although his hopeful expression countered this. "You still haven't answered my question yet. Will you marry me, Julianna?"

"Oh," she exclaimed. "Yes. Yes, of course I'll marry you!"

"We have a 'yes'!" Dominick announced happily, earning applause from several other tables, just before he drew Julianna close again.

Her joy was matched by his, while Dominick could only wonder if he wasn't dreaming this unexpected happy conclusion to this most special evening. In which case, he wasn't taking any chances, kissing her *now* with still more fire than before.

As the pair leaned back against the table again, knocking

over their wine glasses in the process, the headwaiter came running, wringing his hands in frustration. Eyeing the irrepressible newly betrothed couple wearily, he could only hope the cleaning crew wouldn't have a fit over *this* one.

More importantly though, he hoped he could convince the pair to move their 'engagement celebration' to a secluded room elsewhere, before the observant spectators saw more than they bargained for.

*****

As they rode back in the limousine later, Julianna leaning against Dominick's shoulder as he held her, she gazed at her cherished ring happily, glad that at last it was as tangible as she was... and Dominick too, of course.

"I had it engraved as well," he told her, piquing her curiosity.

Removing the ring to see for herself, she found the beginning of the words, and read, " *'To Julianna ~ Love, Dominick.'* "

"To my future wife," he whispered, placing the ring back on her finger. "Now that you know what it says, I hope you'll wear it always."

"You can count on it." Smiling, she touched the sparkling ring. "Julianna Westbrooke... I like the sound of that."

"I'm glad to hear it, since I intend to marry you as soon as possible."

Liking the sound of *that* even more, Julianna leaned closer to kiss him, not minding when Dominick lowered her back against the seat... although when the chauffeur coughed meaningfully, it did crimp their style a bit.

"Things are less complicated in dreams," she remarked.

"More than I ever expected," he agreed, giving her a seductive grin. "But perhaps when we get back to your house..."

"Perhaps, Mr. Westbrooke," she said, kissing him again.

"We'll see."

*****

"Hmmm, the others seem to be asleep," said Julianna, glancing up the stairs when they arrived home. "It looks like..."

She gasped as Dominick's arms encircled her waist, while he pressed a few kisses along her neck. "It looks like we're alone, my sweet bride-to-be. No more hotel waiters, no more restaurant spectators, and no more chauffeurs. It's just us now."

She turned with a smile. "Noticed that all by yourself, did you?"

"Mmmm, you'd be surprised what I'm capable of noticing," he murmured. "For one thing, you seem to be very warm, despite the cool autumn evening."

"I can't imagine why."

"You seem to be shivering though," he observed, trailing his hands down the length of her to prove his words. "Maybe you're having a relapse of that fever, and I should carry you over to the couch."

She laughed as he did just that, bringing them into the other room. "But you might catch the fever then," she protested as he lowered her back against the pillows.

"Sweetheart," he breathed, "I'm afraid we've both got it this time."

Lowering himself against her as they kissed, Dominick reached beneath her back to arch her closer, while his other hand remained free to roam. Tugging at the tie around his neck, Julianna cast it aside, reaching her arms about his neck while moaning against her companion's intimate touch, even through the layers of clothing separating them.

Upon hearing her soft sounds of yearning, Dominick's eyes abruptly sprang open.

Groaning with a steel will he knew he barely possessed now, and couldn't much longer, he reluctantly broke away from her, resting his head against her chest with a heavy sigh.

Julianna sensed the abrupt change in him, stroking his hair comfortingly. "Dominick, I know we've been apart for roughly a week, but this constant romantic tug-of-war is getting a bit frustrating."

"You have no idea how much," he replied, shaking his head, before entwining his hand with hers. "But I do think we should wait on this anyway."

"But why?" she asked. "You don't seem to be suffering from any... physical problems."

He gave her a mischievous smile. "Very astute, darling," he agreed, kissing her nose. "Obviously, there are some things one can't deny. But still, as much as the rest of me wants to consummate our love right now, I'd rather wait until we're married."

"Now that *is* a switch," said Julianna, not masking her surprise. "Don't you think your theory's a bit belated, all things considered?"

"Perhaps," conceded Dominick. "But remember, those times were all in dreams. Since we're both together in reality now, it's different, and I have my reasons for wanting everything to be perfect."

Blushing, she knew he was referring to her inexperience. This soon faded however, replaced by acceptance. "All right," she sighed. "If you insist on taking the chivalrous approach, I guess I'm amenable to however long you want to wait."

"Don't think me a saint, love." He grinned as he stroked her cheek. "Naturally, this only means I plan on marrying you tomorrow to keep our waiting to a minimum."

"Oh, I should have known with you!" she replied, picking up a pillow to swat him with. Deftly removing it from her grasp, he only looked more amused. "So *now* what do we do? Say a chaste good night, and go back to our separate rooms?"

Sensing their shared reluctance to being parted, Dominick shook his head. "Not on your life, sweetheart," he said, leaning back while gently pulling her across him. "We can sleep just as comfortably right here, and the others won't think any less of us for it."

"But *you* won't be comfortable this way. I could suffocate you in your sleep."

Chuckling, he pulled her closer while cradling her head against his chest. "You don't weigh *that* much, Julianna," he told her, kissing her once. "Now close your eyes and relax. The sooner we get some sleep, the sooner we can make plans for our wedding tomorrow."

Tomorrow... her thoughts echoed.

Remembering Roger, Julianna's head nearly bolted up. "Dominick, that reminds me, I need to tell you something..."

"Shhh," he interrupted, placing one finger against her lips. "Tomorrow, love," he whispered.

Knowing she should press the matter, but not wanting to disrupt this perfect evening with mention of Roger, Julianna gradually relaxed against him, feeling his hand stroke her hair in a gentle caress.

There *would* be time tomorrow, she decided, shutting her eyes. As soon as she did, Dominick allowed his own eyes to close, both drifting off to sleep, content with the knowledge that nothing could separate them now.

Neither noticed a hidden dark light in the corner, which abruptly disappeared.

Chapter Twelve

"Your spell failed," snarled Dual, now back on Chavernos in Dark Haven.

"You didn't seem so displeased when the girl lost her memory, leaving her lover distraught!" retorted the dark mage.

"It proved amusing at the time, but the wench got her memory back, and *now* she and my hated enemy plan to be married on the morrow. Shade, I paid you to arrange for your spell to *kill* one of them, and it obviously didn't, so I now demand retribution!"

Shade's eyes narrowed. "Don't threaten me," he warned with deceptive quiet. "The spell *would* have killed the girl, if that meddling dragon Lendric hadn't interfered. Since that was beyond our agreement, I owe you none of the money you paid me."

"I don't want the money," Dual hissed. "But I think you owe me *something* in exchange. Otherwise, I might easily inform some of your other prospective clients of your *faulty* spells." The dark mage's cheek twitched, but he remained silent. "Therefore, I propose an alternate arrangement to call it even, so I won't need to carry out that ugly rumor."

"And *what* would this arrangement be?"

A calculating smile replaced Dual's anger. "After having watched the girl carefully over the past week, I think I've found a suitable weakness to exploit," he replied. "She plans to meet with a man from her past tomorrow, in order to cast him out of her life. Rather cold-hearted, although not surprising since she consorts with Westbrooke." His smile changed into a dark grin. "But with *my* influence as a dreamphaser, I intend to alter the man's thoughts towards his 'innocent' companion, so that afterwards, I can use him as a tool to exact my own revenge. Which is where you come in."

"Wouldn't sending this man after her be revenge enough?" asked the mage. "Filling his head with dark thoughts should suffice."

"Not this time," said Dual, shaking his head. "He is to be the instrument, but *I* personally intend to pay the wench back myself. Since I'm a dreamphaser like my enemy, unfortunately I can't materialize on her world to do this. But if I could possess the *body* of my enemy's rival, that would present the perfect means for my revenge."

The dark mage gave his words consideration. Having received endless requests from assassins over the years—along with endless volumes of treasure in payment—this one was different than he usually dealt with. Not that he cared what Dual planned to do with the girl, since he preferred to keep a distance from his clients' dealings.

What *did* matter to him was that granting Dual's request would make up for his last spell's deficiency. Vindication for one's work was important for a mage assassin of his caliber, since assassins could never afford to allow others to witness mistakes or signs of weakness.

"I do have an *extremely* rare amulet of temporary possession, which when properly charged, would work with your powers as a dreamphaser to bring about what you desire," Shade informed him. "It can grant the bearer its use for several hours before losing effect."

"Perfect," agreed Dual. "When can you have it ready?"

"Ah, ah... not so fast, my impatient friend," Shade replied. "There are a few conditions attached to this valuable item."

"Which are?"

"First, you must return it to me immediately upon

returning to Chavernos. Second, regardless of what happens, I demand your word that this last *favor* will conclude our bargain." Dual nodded to both conditions. "A wise choice, since I'd hate to have to take this to my master Zmalyrithe, should you become a greater thorn in my side."

"Fine. Is that all?"

Pointing a finger at Dual sharply, Shade added, "There is one last thing of prime importance that I must *insist* upon. You must *not* inhabit that other man's body while Lendric is present."

Surprised, Dual began to laugh. "I see no reason why he would be, but why on Chavernos should that matter?"

"Never mind *why*!" he snapped. "Just make sure you remember to follow this last rule, or else!"

"Very well," sighed Dual. "*Now*, is that all?"

Shade's mouth curled into a smile. "Well, since I *am* going out of my way to charge this device for you in such a hurried manner, I would think a small added compensation would suffice."

Dual gritted his teeth. "You'll have your *compensation*," he said, earning a triumphant look from the other man. "But only after *I* receive compensation for your former bumbling tomorrow night!"

Snarling, the dark mage swirled his cape around his shoulder. "You'll have what you seek first, assassin," he growled. "But if you don't pay your dues afterwards, you'll have my master to reckon with. And I assure you, you *don't* want that!"

As he vanished, Dual looked after him icily. If not for the threat of Zmalyrithe and his need of the amulet, he'd put a knife through the mage for his insolence. Something to be considered *after* he claimed his revenge on Julianna and his besotted enemy.

Grinning slowly with satisfaction, he decided to head back to Earth to pay a dreamphasing visit to someone else first… Roger Collins.

*****

Realizing she was downstairs in their dream castle, Julianna was certainly glad she could remember it again. She'd never realized how maddening it could be to lose parts of one's memory, and shuddered at how it could have been worse. She might have lost her memory completely, or worse still, **never** have regained it at all.

Fortunately, that was all behind her now.

As she stared absently at the cold fireplace, she was startled when it abruptly flared to life. Clutching her throat, her surprise soon faded into suspicion. Crackling fires didn't spark **that** fast under normal circumstances, which seemed to indicate she wasn't alone.

Gasping as she found herself pulled to the velvety rug, she glanced up to find Dominick smiling at her. "You're too clever for me, love," he chuckled, just before he began to kiss her neck.

"Wait a second!" laughed Julianna, trying unsuccessfully to hold him back at arm's length. "Whatever happened to all your honorable intentions, and your desire to wait until after our marriage tomorrow?"

"Tomorrow's too far away," he murmured. "We've already been apart for what feels like an eternity." Before she could say anything, he added, "I've missed you so much, sweetheart."

"I've missed you too."

"Let me love you tonight, Julianna. For in this realm, it will still only be as it always was… a dream. Why deny ourselves what we've already known here before? Please say 'yes', love."

Julianna's eyes grew misty as she touched his cheek. "Yes, Dominick."

As if a match had been dropped between them, sparks ignited. Embracing with all the repressed longing they'd felt over the past days, Dominick rained kisses over her, while she returned them in kind. "Chavernos, you're beautiful, my dear sweet love," he whispered, his hands traveling up and down her back, as if to re-memorize everything he'd missed about her.

"You're not so bad yourself, my dream knight."

Her words trailed off as he kissed her mouth again, parting hers eagerly to accept his more intimate touch. *How could I have forgotten this?* she thought.

"I hope they can arrange for an early wedding," said Dominick. "Heaven knows we've waited long enough."

As he spoke, Julianna's bliss faded. "Dominick... I've been meaning to ask you about that," she began. "Would you mind terribly if we had an evening ceremony instead?"

His eyes grew puzzled as he gazed at her. "Why?" he asked, kissing her neck again. "I think your sisters would understand."

"Actually, I want to postpone it for a few hours, because I have to take care of something first."

"What on Chavernos could be more important than our wedding?"

"I arranged to meet with Roger."

She could feel Dominick tense against her, slowly drawing away. "You have your memory back, and we're getting married... yet you're still going back to that bastard again?"

Julianna sighed at her dream companion's anger, glancing towards the warming flames of the fireplace so as not to face him directly. *Damn!* she thought. *If only I hadn't mentioned this tonight.*

"Dominick, please let me explain. Do you remember how things were with Roger when I **didn't** have my full memories, and how he wanted a raincheck for that evening I was too ill to go out with him?"

"I remember," he said grimly. "But that's changed since your memory's returned—not to mention, we're getting **married** tomorrow—so you can cancel any plans you made with him before."

"For my own reasons, I'd rather not."

"So I see," he retorted. Before she could say anything more, he turned away to stand, leaning against the mantle above the fireplace. "Once, you claimed you went out with him for purely work-related reasons. Then of course, you lost your memory, and remembered him as a friend that you might have gone out with before. Yet now, what excuse will you justify it with this time?"

"Try, earlier I found my journal, including an entry I'd written regarding Roger's betrayal with his *lover* Marilyn, and I wish to confront him regarding his *lies* which helped keep us apart!"

At her vehement tone, Dominick turned to her, remaining where he stood. She looked so enchanting sitting there, a light turquoise gown hugging her curled up form, while the firelight cast a warm glow on her face. Spirited fire and soft innocence wrapped into one... which Roger could easily destroy.

Shaking his head, his irritation rekindled. "That isn't necessary. If all goes well, we can leave for my world tomorrow after our marriage. There's no need for you to deal with Roger anymore."

"To *me*, there is," she said angrily. "Dominick, the man *used* my weakness to try and destroy *our* relationship! Not to mention, the countless other times he's hurt me. This time, I will *not* just walk away without a word!" Folding her arms, she stared at the floor. "Heaven knows I've let others walk over me in the past, including my boss Almira who demanded I go out to that business lunch with Roger, knowing I *had* to hold my tongue with her or lose my job."

Sensing her inner pain softened Dominick's anger. "This Almira you speak of never treated you very well, did she?"

"Not often," Julianna agreed, brushing her hair back

before facing him again. "But where I live, jobs are hard to find these days, and I couldn't afford to give mine up lightly. Not all of us have the luxury of being the grandchild of a wealthy island ruler."

Dominick's jaw flexed, but finally he nodded. "True enough," he said, moving to sit beside her again. "Which is why I understood your putting up with Roger before, but I can't help being skeptical about your dealing with him now."

"It's not like it once was. After everything he's done, our friendship is over. You have nothing to worry about."

He stared into the glowing flames for long moments before replying. "You loved him once," he reminded her. "I'd say that's something."

"Dominick... that was so long ago. Now..."

Before she could continue, he interceded. "You know, it's easy to say you hate someone who's wronged you in love when they're many miles away. But when you're suddenly confronted with facing that person every day, things can change."

She tried to interrupt, but he wouldn't let her. "Before I came here—when the distance of our worlds kept us apart—it looked like you were starting to let Roger back in your life, when you once swore you'd never want that again. And considering how you seemed to feel about him when you'd temporarily lost your memories, it couldn't be impossible that you might have fallen in love with him again too."

"It was impossible then, and it certainly is *now*!" she protested, leaning forward to hug him, pressing her cheek against his shoulder. "You're the only man I've ever *truly* been in love with. I love you more than I ever loved him, and I'd rather spend the rest of my life with you than anyone else. Dominick, please... after everything we've been through, you must know that!"

Feeling her tears, he turned to face her slowly, seeking

the truth in her eyes. "Julianna, I..."

She cut off his words with a passionate kiss, before pressing others against his cheek. "I'm in love with *you*, Dominick Phaser Westbrooke. I won't *ever* let you doubt that." Not giving him a chance to reply, she kissed him again, loosening his shirt to steal her hands within to rest against his chest, while her eyes sought his. "Please... don't shut yourself away from my love."

The power of her touch alone would be all it took to push him over the edge, but her words sealed his fate. With a passion equal to hers, Dominick pulled her to him, his eyes smoldering as they held her gaze. "I could never do that with you, Julianna," he breathed. "*Never.*"

Covering her mouth with his, he pressed her back against the soft rug, tearing his shirt free as he went. Joyfully she responded, all traces of their argument melting into consuming desire, the flames of the firelight only mere sparks compared to the flames of passion that ignited.

"My sweet temptress," he murmured, "how I've missed you."

"And I you. Deep down, even when I couldn't remember you, a part of me knew something was missing." She shook her head. "I don't ever want to lose you again."

"I won't let you," he replied, taking her face in his hands. "We're soulmates, Julianna. Nothing and no one will ever change that. Not Roger, nor anyone else."

Lowering his mouth to hers again, Dominick's kisses held a greater urgency this time, kindling desire as Julianna clung to him fiercely. His hands stroked and caressed through the fabric of the gown, pulling her closer.

Julianna wanted more, moving restlessly against him. Giving a low groan in response, Dominick eased the gown from her, before resuming his earlier ministrations.

"You can't know how hard it was," he said, feeling her

tremble beneath his touch like rippling waves. "Wanting so much to touch you like this, and knowing I couldn't."

"We both suffered," she whispered, touching his cheek. "But that's in the past, and I won't deny you again, my love. Especially not this night, when we can finally heal each other."

Needing no further confirmation, Dominick pulled her into his embrace, branding her mouth with heated kisses. She melted against him, a low moan escaping her as she met his passion with her own.

Feeling the same desperate need for each other, they mutually dematerialized their remaining clothing, allowing their hands to relearn each other by touch.

As he kissed and caressed her warmly, taking his time even now, her heart felt renewed happiness at how he always made her feel cherished. Something that she enthusiastically reciprocated, feeling his own happiness match hers.

Their thoughts entwined, only deepening their desire.

Dominick...

I hear you, love, his thoughts replied. *And I'm with you.*

Amidst their kisses, Dominick's hand found and clasped hers, their grip slowly tightening as he smoothly sheathed himself within Julianna's welcoming warmth, her legs hugging him tighter in grateful acceptance. Shutting their eyes with soft cries of fulfillment, both reveled in the ancient promise of two souls becoming one.

As he bestowed melting kisses upon her, she wrapped her free arm about him, arching back as Dominick kissed the quickening pulse at her throat. At her ecstatic response, his thoughts again reached for hers.

By Chavernos... I'll love you forever, Julianna.

Her heart filled with joy at his words, heightening what she felt. *I'll always love you too, Dominick.*

Then all thought receded as his mouth closed over hers, and it wasn't long before they soared through rapture. Breathing as one, they continued to hold each other, as the soft cloud of sweet repose covered them both.

Smiling languorously, Dominick kissed her deeply. She smiled back, comforted by the warmth of his arms surrounding her like a soft blanket as he hugged her close, pressing a kiss against her forehead.

This time, he preferred to remain where they were, and she had no objection, their legs loosely entwined.

He mused that if they'd been together like this in reality, they'd surely have begun a child this night. He could already see the vision in his mind. A daughter with curls like her mother, or a bright-eyed son like exuberant Sammy.

"Our child," he murmured.

Having overheard, Julianna turned towards him. "Reading my mind again, are you?" she asked.

Stroking her shoulder, he raised up to look at her incredulously. "Would you truly like us to have a child now? Even though we're to be married tomorrow, it would still be so soon."

She gave a gentle laugh. "It *does* take nine months before a child's born," she reminded him, as her expression became serious. "I myself don't need to wait," she added tenderly. "After all, the only thing that could make my life any more perfect than it is with you, is to have the pleasure of holding our son or daughter in my arms."

"Oh, my dearest," he replied, kissing her joyfully. "'Tis indeed a desire we share."

"Besides," she said practically, "there's no guarantee we'd have one immediately anyway. We'd better get started trying tomorrow. Although, I get the feeling you want to practice right now."

He chuckled through a kiss. "*This* was why I preferred to break us apart every now and then. My body doesn't stand a chance against your endless temptation."

"Oh, and am I to understand that you'd rather not do that anymore tonight?"

"Hell, no!" he laughed. "We can break the world's record tonight for all I care. However... are you *sure* you have your memory back completely? Because it looks like you may need more convincing."

"Hmmm, it couldn't hurt," she agreed. "As long as you don't wear us both out before tomorrow, if we're to see to having this child we both want."

He shrugged. "Well, if takes another month's practice, we can make the sacrifice."

Shaking his head, while his gaze held hers, he lazily stroked her cheek. "Dear heaven, I never believed I'd ever love anyone as I love you, Julianna." Before she could question how he meant this, he continued quickly, "In *all* ways, although I won't deny I do enjoy when we're truly one together." Julianna was grateful for his understanding.

"Mmmm, I feel the same about you," she said, snuggling closer as she rested one hand against his chest. "I hope you believe that now, and know that I could never have any feelings for Roger anymore. For the longest time after we broke up, I thought myself unworthy of love."

His expression sobered, clasping her hand which he still held close to his chest. "You're more than worthy, so don't ever tell me otherwise again. I'm not a fool like Roger. If I didn't hate the bastard so much for how he's hurt you, I'd almost feel sorry for him, since thanks to his idiocy I've gained the most beautiful treasure he lost. One I'll be sure to keep from him or any other man. Thankfully in reality as well now."

"Believe me, I'm glad of that," said Julianna, hugging him tighter.

"No more than I, love," he replied. "But for this night..." His words trailed off as he swooped her into his arms, his eyes twinkling seductively. "I'll be content with any way I can have you all to myself, my precious bride-to-be."

As he carried her towards the stairs, she hugged him close, infinitely glad he was a man of his word.

*****

"Just how far do you think you can run in one castle room?" chuckled Dominick, engaged in the ritual of being on one side of a large table, while his fiancée stood opposite him. A bit different only in that the pair were wearing minimal clothing. "Give in, love. According to the rules of the game, you lost the last poker hand, and therefore have to forfeit that pretty negligée you're wearing."

"Not likely," she sing-songed. "You cheated by using your powers to read what cards I had, so the hand is forfeited."

Dominick gave her a smile of warning, despite a playful look. "I'd take back that false accusation if I were you," he replied, "or I'll make you wish you had once I catch you."

"*If* you catch me, and I will *not* take it back." She gave the hint of a smirk. "Are you calling *me* a liar, Mr. Westbrooke?"

"Oh, I don't believe in using such appellations, Miss Sherborne." A mischievous gleam caught his eyes as he rested both hands on the table. "After all, as my mother would have put it, there's more than one way to handle a situation."

Sensing his thoughts, she shook her head.

"Dominick... Don't you dare..."

Before Julianna could blink, he'd leaped across the table, successfully catching her in his arms before she could flee. As she gave the expected amount of token protest, Dominick ignored it to carry her to the bed, sending playing cards everywhere.

"Now then, my dear wife-to-be," he said enticingly, leaning on one arm while toying with the satin strap on her shoulder. "I believe it's payback time, and you still have to relinquish this tempting distraction of white lace." He leaned closer to kiss her ear, his breath a mere whisper against it. "But if you give in graciously, I promise I'll be a most generous man and grant you a passionate loving you won't forget."

"Oh, really?" she replied, eyeing one of the pillows. "How would you like it, my *dear* husband-to-be, if I..."

His fiery kiss stole the unspoken words from her, slowly erasing all else. Long moments later, he pulled back to caress her cheek with his hand. "You were saying, love?"

"I like your idea better," she breathed, earning a chuckle from him as he kissed her again, more cards falling from the bed as he moved closer to her.

A sudden knock on the door interrupted them.

Both turning towards it, their reverie faded instantly. "It couldn't be that bastard Dual again, could it?" whispered Julianna.

"Since this a dream, and no one *I* know would dare disturb us tonight, I can't think of a likelier candidate," hissed Dominick. Materializing a dagger, he slid it into his startled fiancée's hand. "Keep this hidden beneath the covers, and don't be afraid to use it if you have to. Remember, a fatal wound here will only dematerialize a person, not kill them." She nodded quickly, although judging by the way she was shaking, she still hoped it wouldn't be necessary.

Dominick materialized a sword, holding it close as he heard another knock on the door.

"Phase, I know this is awkward, but I have to speak with you."

Exhaling sharply through a curse, Dominick opened the door a bit to reveal his brother. "What the hell are you doing here, Riff?" he growled. "Are you planning to be here during our wedding night too?"

Riff shrugged with a grin. "Hmmm, I have nothing planned right now, so there's an interesting notion," he considered, just before Dominick raised his sword threateningly.

"Hey, watch your temper, Phase!" he protested, holding his hands up in defense. "To be honest, I just came to see how Julianna's doing. I noticed how cozy you looked together at her house, so I wondered if that meant she got her memory back." Glancing at her, he flashed her a quick smile. "Apparently so."

Blushing under his appraisal, she pulled the blankets higher, thankful that she was still wearing the negligée.

"How's he treating you, my little sister-in-law-to-be?" Riff continued cheerfully, with a wave. "Brought out the whips and chains yet?"

At her gape, Dominick pulled his brother into the room and slammed him against the wall, holding the sword up to his chin. "Give me one good reason why I shouldn't send you out of here the hard way!"

His brother's eyes never lost their amusement. "Look, for once I truly apologize for interrupting, but you know how Chaos is. By now, he was wondering if you were coming home at all, so he sent me to check." His gaze trailed back to Julianna buried beneath the covers, admiring anew what a pleasant sight she was... just before Dominick placed himself before his line of vision.

"Get your disrespectful eyes off my future bride," he snarled in a deadly voice, "before I think twice about using this sword on you. You can tell Chaos that Julianna's fine now, and after we're married tomorrow, we'll head back to Chavernos. In the meantime, *you* go home!"

"Oh, fine!" retorted Riff. "*Be* that way!" Casting a last look at Julianna, he said regretfully, "Alas, fair maiden, I suppose the next time I meet you, you'll be my sister." A wolflike grin spread across his face. "Although in your case, I may gain a new appreciation for my relatives."

As his brother raised his sword again, Riff vanished through echoing laughter. Swearing quietly, Dominick dropped the sword with a clang, returning to his amused fiancée.

"Maybe we should stay on Earth," she suggested.

"It wouldn't matter," he sighed, rejoining her on the bed. "As long as he's a dreamphaser, he'd find a way to bother us. Although if he doesn't curb that habit soon, he may face an early grave in the near future."

"Don't worry about him," she replied, touching his cheek. "If he gets to be a problem, we can always ask your friends Roderlin and Alysadaria to carry him off somewhere."

He couldn't help laughing at the suggestion. "If 'Lysa gets her talons on him, she'll likely drop him in the nearest swamp."

"You see? Problem solved. Which reminds me. About *our* dispute over that poker hand..."

Dominick stifled her words with a searing kiss that sent pleasant sparks through her with its intensity, lowering her back against the pillows, and leaving her moaning softly in protest as he broke away. As she opened her eyes to find his glittering with passion, he murmured simply, "*What* poker hand?"

"You're right," she agreed. "Game over."

He shook his head and grinned. "The game's just beginning, love," he whispered, kissing her again.

*****

This new sports car is indeed a beauty, thought Roger, brushing away the last of the water from its shiny red surface with a soft cloth. Just the thing to cruise around town in, with his beautiful companion by his side. Surely, Julianna wouldn't resist an invitation to ride in it.

"A logical notion if this car really existed," said a sarcastic voice, jarring his thoughts. Glancing up, he saw a dark stranger standing by the tail end, his arms folded. Thinking quickly, Roger couldn't place his identity, since rarely had he met a person with such gray eyes.

"What do you mean *if* it really existed?" he asked, knocking on the car's finish, before leaning against it. "It's as real as we are."

"Not quite," amended the stranger, snapping his fingers. Instantly the car vanished, throwing Roger off balance so the cloth fell from his hands. Catching himself, he could only gape. "As you can see, we're not meeting in the conventional reality of your world. This is merely a dream." At the other man's dubious expression, he continued, "I'd believe it if I were you, Mr. Collins."

Roger's amusement faded. "How do you know my name?"

"Oh, I know you well enough, **Roger**," the stranger replied. "Although I could easily have found out your name by reading your mind, since I do have that useful ability in dreams."

Roger laughed doubtfully, before the stranger interrupted. "I can see you require further proof, which I'll gladly supply." Waving his hands, he vanished, replaced by a full-height black dragon. Grabbing hold of Roger's collar before he could flee, the stranger lifted him effortlessly. "*Believe me now?*" he hissed, acid dripping from his mouth and singeing the pavement. Hearing the sizzle of the acid, Roger could only nod mutely. "*That's better.*"

Dropping him to the ground, the dragon abruptly vanished, replaced by the stranger's human form. Trying to mask his wariness, Roger picked up his car cloth, still absorbing the fact that this was supposedly a dream.

"But I didn't come here as an enemy," the stranger professed, gesturing good-naturedly. "Although we haven't been formally introduced before, we do share a common interest in one respect... our mutual interest in Julianna Sherborne."

Eyes narrowing, Roger crumpled the cloth in his hand, his teeth clenched. "And *how* is that?"

"Quite simply, neither one of us want to see her wind up with Dominick Westbrooke. Am I correct?"

Roger's expression hardened. "I'll agree on that point,"

he conceded. "But she's *not* going to end up with him. As a matter of fact, I have an evening planned with her later."

"Do you?" the stranger asked in a mocking tone.

"Just who *are* you anyway?"

Dual wasn't about to give this simpleton any means to unravel his plans. "That's unimportant," he replied. "But as to this *evening* you speak of with Julianna, you're fooling yourself if you believe she'll be thinking of you while you're with her. In fact, don't be surprised if your 'dear Julianna' loses interest in you altogether to be with her lover instead."

Roger's eyes turned cold at his words. "You're lying," he growled. "Just because she went out to dinner with Westbrooke last night doesn't mean she's forgotten their earlier altercations, let alone become his *lover*. I know her better than that."

"You underestimate Dominick," Dual stated in annoyance. "He plans to have your Julianna to himself at all costs. You, my friend, don't know her as well as you think. In fact, they've consummated their relationship again this night, even as we speak."

Turning away from him, Roger sought to find a reason to refute his words, but instead found the memory of when he'd overheard Julianna and Marybeth talking at the club. When Julianna had been perpetually yawning, Marybeth had questioned if Dominick wasn't responsible for her tiredness, and her friend merely smiled without answering.

At the time, he'd discounted this, since Dominick hadn't actually been seen with her. Now, with the truth proven that he *did* exist, the stranger's words hit home.

"Your meeting tomorrow night only masks a charade by her," Dual persisted, sensing his growing irritation. "She plans to pretend nothing has changed to mar your recent relationship, just before she'll conveniently drop you out of her life afterwards."

"Damn you, Julie wouldn't do that!" snarled Roger.

Dual laughed openly at this, only infuriating him more. "I must admit, I haven't dealt with those of your world very often, but even so, I thought your kind had *some* shades of intelligence." He continued with a sarcastic drawl. "The most clever actresses can play innocence convincingly enough to fool a saint, or those who choose to be fooled."

Before Roger could turn away, he reached out to grab his arm painfully. "Hear me out," he demanded. "There are other things you'd best get through your thick skull, regarding her other deceptions. Or are you going to tell me you believe her false pretense of having amnesia as well?"

Roger shoved him away roughly. "What do you mean *false* pretense?"

"Think, Collins! Do you believe she's *really* forgotten your past history?" He shook his head. "Oh no, my friend. That's why Julianna has planned out this elaborate scheme of revenge against you. Both her *and* her lover Westbrooke."

"Stop calling him that!"

"Why shouldn't I?" replied Dual. "It's true. Unless, of course... you choose to alter this reality, by taking charge of the situation tomorrow."

Sensing Roger's lingering hesitancy to accept all he'd said, Dual played his trump card. "If you're still doubtful," he said, "then perhaps you'll believe *this*!"

Waving his hand in an arc, a dark framed mirror appeared, just before an image came into view within. Roger's eyes widened in shock upon seeing Julianna standing on a balcony, wearing surprisingly little, leaning against a waist-high wall as she stared up at the stars.

Before Roger could voice his curiosity as to what *this* was supposed to prove, someone else appeared. Reaching his arms around her waist, Dominick hugged her close, kissing her neck as she smiled against him. Roger's blood turned cold, since although unable to hear their brief exchange, there was no mistaking what had gone on between them.

Further proven, moments later, when Julianna appeared to be laughing as her companion spun her about, kissing her again.

Roger's shock changed to angry disgust at the sight, his fists clenched tightly, while Dual sent the mirror back into oblivion.

"As you can see, I do know of what I speak," he emphasized. "But as I mentioned before, there is still time for you to get back at Dominick, and gain what you've been cheated of with your precious Julianna, if you'd care to hear more."

Roger's gaze became fully attentive. "I'm listening," he replied tonelessly, barely masking his underlying anger. "What do you suggest?"

Dual grinned, knowing he'd won. With Roger's shattered beliefs about Julianna's honesty, which he'd easily break down further before this evening was out, his anger would make his mind that much easier to control with the amulet later.

Setting in motion his plans for revenge, which would see fruition tomorrow night.

*****

Stirring as the rays of the morning sun struck her eyes, Julianna lifted her head to gaze at her companion's peaceful expression as he slept. Not too surprising he should be tired **now**, since he'd been so full of energy during their shared dreams.

As if afraid she'd suddenly disappear, Dominick had certainly been insatiable last night with their loving.

Thank heaven theirs was a private beach! she mused with a blush.

Almost immediately, she felt his arms tighten around her, a telltale smile proving that her companion was awake now too. "Hmmm... I could get used to waking up like this with you from now on," he murmured.

"You'll have ample opportunity for that," she replied, giving him a quick kiss.

Unwilling to let her go, Dominick prolonged it, rewarded by an enthusiastic response from her. When he finally pulled back, his gaze meeting hers, the blue in his eyes was warm with passion and love.

"Good morning to you too, sweetheart," he whispered.

Unable to resist, she kissed him again, feeling her senses reel as he hugged her tighter, molding her against him.

"I suppose this means things went well last night," came Crystal's amused voice.

Both turned towards her abruptly, Julianna feeling a bit embarrassed by their compromising position on the sofa. Fortunately, they were still in their formal attire, although said clothes were now slightly rumpled, not meant for nightwear.

Before either could reply, Sammy appeared out of nowhere. "Can I play too?" he asked, grinning as he exuberantly joined the pair on the sofa, landing unceremoniously on Dominick.

"By Chaos," he breathed, glancing up at Julianna. "I know I said you didn't weigh that much, but both of you?"

"Sammy, come over here!" Crystal intervened, going over to pick up her laughing son when he pretended not to hear. "I'm sorry about that, Dominick."

"I wasn't really complaining," he assured her, sitting up while shifting Julianna to his lap, resting one arm around her waist instead. "So, what's new in the business world, Jerry?" he asked casually, when the other man walked in.

"Never mind that," he replied, folding his arms with a curious look. "Now, how did the evening go?"

"Shall we tell them?" asked Dominick. Julianna nodded, holding up her hand with the ring.

"We've decided to get married."

Jerry clapped his hands, as Crystal stepped forward to hug her sister. "I knew it would work," he said, earning confusion from his sister-in-law.

Julianna turned to Dominick, who cast her a knowing look.

"You have to admit, you certainly played hard to get for a while," he explained, unable to resist a smirk. "So... I employed the help of your family and Lendric to try and persuade you otherwise last night. But since you unexpectedly went against our plans by getting your memory back first, I suppose we'll never know if you would have accepted anyway."

"You got your memory back?" exclaimed Crystal, grabbing her sister's hands, just before her expression turned chiding. "Julie, why didn't you tell me that to begin with this morning?"

"I didn't have a chance, with Sammy using Dominick as a trampoline," she laughed. "But yes, I did get my memory back last night." Gazing at her ring, she smiled. "As soon as Dominick showed me this, it reminded me of the first time he proposed, and brought back all I'd forgotten. So now we're going to get married as we once planned to."

"Today," said Dominick.

"*Today?*" the other couple echoed in shock, turning to one another questioningly.

"That *is* a bit sudden," remarked Jerry.

"Yes," agreed Crystal. "Besides, I have to work late again tonight, so I don't really have time today to arrange all the details. Since tomorrow starts the weekend, can't you wait one more day?"

Glancing at her companion, Julianna could easily read the disappointment in his eyes. No doubt there was more behind it than merely wanting to legally bind them. Guessing what that might be, she squeezed his hand before facing the others.

"Tomorrow's fine," she said softly. "But could you give

us a few moments alone?" Seeing no problem with this, the others quickly acquiesced, although Sammy gave a minor protest upon being escorted out by his father. Looking after him fondly, Julianna returned her gaze to Dominick.

"I know you must be anxious to get back to Chavernos." At his surprised look, she continued, "It was written all over your face. I can only imagine what it must have been like for you over the past week, being cast into a strange world with only your friend Lendric, leaving all your family and friends behind. I only hope I can adjust half as well, since I'll be going to your world without anyone I know."

"*I'll* always be with you," he said reassuringly, hugging her close. "And you've already met my grandfather and brother, whom you know have both accepted you as family."

"Yes," she said, suddenly feeling foolish. Here she was trying to comfort *him* for being away from his world, yet she'd only awakened her own doubts about leaving *her* homeworld.

Sensing her thoughts, Dominick kissed her forehead. "Forgive me, sweetheart," he murmured. "I should have realized how this change of events would affect you too. But take heart. Remember that group of friends you met in the dream-state, whom I frequently get together with?" She nodded. "As we speak, they're all looking forward to our arrival so they can formally adopt you into our group. Kiri and the gals told me to let you know that they'll help you make the adjustment, just as if they were your sisters as well."

Thinking back to his last conversation with his dragon friends, he added, "Roderlin's mate Alysadaria told me she was especially glad you'd replaced Chaos's prospect of Sionne as my future wife, and she's also looking forward to being your friend. Then of course, there's Roderlin, Chaolyn, and Zantarl, along with Alarius and Laelea, the parents of your namesake..."

"Okay, I'm convinced!" she interrupted with a laugh.

"I just want you to know, you'll never be alone on

Chavernos. Besides, the island is one of the safest places on our world, so you need never worry about that either."

Thinking about her job, Julianna said, "I suppose I won't mind leaving my irritable boss behind. But what will I do on your world? Do they even have secretaries there?"

"Hmmm, not exactly. But I could certainly use a partner to help with the responsibilities of the island. That is, if you wouldn't mind our being together most of the time while we work."

"Let's see... a job where I can travel about an exotic island with you instead of dealing with Almira?" she considered, with a broadening grin. "Looks like you've got yourself a new partner."

"I'm glad to hear that," he chuckled. "I'd much rather travel across the island with my beautiful wife, rather than have constant disputes with my brother. And when we're not busy with the island duties, I'll gladly give you a grand tour of all the entertainment spots, as well as our new home."

"I can't wait. By the way, regarding what you said earlier, about never knowing what my response would have been to your proposal had I not regained my memories afterwards... I can answer that for you." She met his curious gaze tenderly. "As we spent time together that night, I'd already decided with my heart that if you proposed again, I would have accepted. When I saw the marquee, I felt the same, even before you showed me the ring which brought it all back."

His ensuing embrace confirmed without words that the last was all he needed to hear.

Even as a startled Vicki walked into the room. "Did I miss something?" she asked.

Breaking away from Dominick's hold, Julianna turned to her sister. "Does announcing an engagement count?"

Chapter Thirteen

Resting her head against her arm, Julianna couldn't resist being amused at the memory of her sister's shock over the announcement of her engagement to Dominick. To Vicki, it must simply seem like a whirlwind romance.

Wait until she learned the whole truth!

Well, she considered, remembering her evening with Dominick last night. *Maybe not **everything***.

"Daydreaming?" he asked.

Gazing at her fiancé across the breakfast table, she shook her head. "Why would I need to do that? You're already here."

"Very happily so, my wife-to-be," Dominick agreed, leaning forward to kiss her.

The phone ringing stopped him.

As Julianna sighed, he glared at the offending device. "Do these things have any use other than interrupting romantic moments?"

"Doesn't seem like it," she replied, getting up to answer it. "Hello." While she listened, she felt Dominick's arms steal around her waist. "Yes, this is her," she answered, happily distracted as he brushed her long hair aside to kiss the back of her neck. *I might not mind answering phones with a response like that*, she thought.

Abruptly, she stiffened. "No, I didn't realize they expected me to contact them this week." As Dominick stopped to eye her questioningly, she mouthed the word, 'work'. He nodded silently. "Well, you see, my memory only fully returned last night. Thank you, I do feel much better. Miss Thompson wants me to come in this morning?"

Dominick shook his head. "We have to get our marriage license shortly," he reminded her.

She nodded. "Well, I already have an appointment scheduled for this morning." After a pause, she shut her eyes, sighing again. "I understand. She's inconvenienced as it is this week. All right. I'll try to be there shortly. Thank you." She hung up the phone, looking drained.

"What did they say, love?"

"Almira needs me there this morning. She's apparently not happy with the temp they got to fill in for me in my absence for the week."

"Well, she'd better get used to it," he said. "After this weekend, you won't even be on this world anymore."

"Yes, but I can't tell *her* that."

"Why not?" he chuckled.

"Because my family and my friend Marybeth would never hear the end of it. That's why."

"Good point."

"Though honestly, I think I'd rather go to Chavernos now than have to deal with Almira again."

He stepped forward to embrace her, and she hugged him back, resting her head against his chest. "Hey, you don't have to worry about her anymore. You're not alone. If you need to go speak with the woman, I'll go with you."

"I appreciate that, Dominick. But I'm not so sure that's a good idea."

"I am," he replied, kissing the top of her head. "No dread female is going to upset my future wife while I'm here."

She only hugged him tighter.

*****

Almira shook her head at the growing pile of papers on her desk. Although she'd never admit it, Julianna was more useful around here than she'd once thought. The temp they'd hired hadn't lasted the full week—professing it wasn't what she'd expected—and Almira was all too happy when she left, since she didn't get half the things done Julianna would have.

Unfortunately, the workload had gotten out of control in the meantime, forcing her to get Human Resources to contact Julianna to come back in immediately. The projects needing mailing alone would take all day, if she had to do it herself.

Seeing the telltale look on her face, Marybeth smiled for long moments before knocking on the doorway of her office to get her attention.

"Miss Thompson, there's a Miss Sherborne here to see you," she said pleasantly.

Glaring at her, Almira bit out, "Just send her in, Miss O'Neill." Another reason to get Julianna back. That friend of hers made no effort to hide her amusement whenever the temp had had difficulty following her instructions, which had been often. Hearing quiet laughter as she left, Almira called after her, "Keep it up, Miss O'Neill, and you'll find yourself transferred to the mail room!"

"Sounds good to me!" came Marybeth's pleased reply

Sighing, Almira went back to sorting papers, just as Julianna appeared in the doorway.

"You wanted to see me?" she asked.

For a moment only, Almira came close to smiling. However, desperation could only do so much with a person's inner nature, and her expression stiffened. "I hear your head injury has finally healed."

"Yes," agreed Julianna, "and my memory's back to normal."

"And just in time too," retorted Almira. "Do you have any idea how much work hasn't gotten done in your absence? I've had people complaining all week that their deadlines aren't being met."

"I'm sorry to hear that. They told me you'd hired a temp, so I assumed…"

"You assumed *wrong*, whatever you thought," she snapped. "That temp barely knew how to answer phones, let alone prep mailings for overnight delivery." Gesturing to the stack of papers on the desk, she continued, "Now that you're back, I need you to get these projects taken care of. If you get started now, you can probably get the majority finished by six."

"I'm afraid that won't be possible."

"Of course it's possible," Almira insisted. "Oh, and in addition to the papers here, there's another set of projects on your desk."

"I meant... I've just come here from Human Resources. They told me I should give you this." Holding out a paper, not surprisingly Almira snatched it from her hand, reading it quickly, only to look up in disbelief.

"This is a letter of resignation, effective immediately, stating you're moving from the area." Julianna nodded. Almira's composed look faded again. "You can't just walk out like this! Who's going to get these projects taken care of?"

"I don't know," she replied, shrugging. "The only other person I worked with on most of those was my coworker Marybeth O'Neill. You might want to ask her help in sorting it out. She's already spoken with most of the contacts, so they're familiar with her."

Almira's eyes narrowed. "I wouldn't ask for her help if my own job was in jeopardy!"

"Funny that. Because if you don't get her help, you may lose your job by default, and Human Resources might just move Marybeth in instead. She passed me on her way downstairs to fill out an application for the mail room, but I think they can find her a position she's more qualified for." The older woman's mouth tightened, but she didn't answer. "It's up to you, but you might want to reconsider your position... before you lose yours."

"I suppose you think this is as amusing as your friend,

don't you?"

Julianna looked up in consideration, and then smiled. "You know, part of me *really* does." Almira silently glared at her. "But all of me is just happy I won't have to tolerate your verbal abuse anymore."

"You'll never find a better job out there. Mark my words, you'll be back!"

"Mark *my* words... I won't."

Dominick chose that moment to stride in, stopping Almira's tirade. Her eyes widened, obviously wondering who he was, and showing even more interest than that which she'd shown Roger.

"Can I help you?" she asked.

"No, thank you," he replied. "I just came to collect my fiancée." Placing an arm about Julianna's shoulders, he said meaningfully, "Darling, we don't want to be late at the courthouse for our marriage license. Are you all finished here?"

Julianna gave him a nod, linking her arm around his waist, as she turned to her former boss one last time. "I can't say it's been a pleasure, Miss Thompson. But good luck anyway."

Both waved, arms still about each other as they left, and Dominick pulled the door shut.

As they walked away, they heard a telltale shriek behind them. This startled the nearby workers briefly, although some looked amused. Squeezing Dominick's hand gratefully, Julianna walked with him to the elevator, glad to finally be free.

*****

Leaning on her arm once more, much later, Julianna's thoughts weren't as serene as they'd been this morning, now wondering what she was doing here at the nightclub.

With some assistance from Lendric, she and Dominick had managed to get their marriage license without much difficulty. Afterwards, Lendric departed for a farewell dinner with the Dragends, while they enjoyed sharing the rest of the afternoon together. They even got into an enjoyable game of dinosaurs with Sammy, when he returned from kindergarten. He decided that his T-Rex should be able to breathe fire like a dragon, which made the pair smile.

However, when Sammy was watching his cartoons later, they'd had a much different 'heated' debate over her meeting Roger tonight.

"For the millionth time, I can take care of myself!" she'd protested, earning a stubborn look of defiance from Dominick.

Folding his arms, he replied, "Maybe in most cases, love. But with Roger, I'm not so sure. And as I told you before, you don't need to prove **anything** with him."

"For myself, I do."

"**Why**?" he countered angrily.

"You of all people **know** why!" she retorted, slowly calming down. "Look, I'll only be out for an hour or so. Vicki's going to pick me up well before eight, so you don't have to worry. I'll be back in time to say good night to Sammy, and after that, we can discuss the plans for our wedding tomorrow." Seeing his jaw clench, she added, "We couldn't have gotten married this evening anyway. You remember, Crystal said she'd be late getting home. And on my world, you can't just drag someone out to perform a marriage at all hours of the night."

She was certain he'd continue to fight her on this, but after hesitating, he nodded. "You'll be back by eight o'clock at the latest?"

"Not a minute later," she agreed. "And after tonight, I'll try not to mention Roger's name again. All right?"

He paused before replying. "All right," he said, giving her a hug. "Just be careful tonight."

"I will," she promised, feeling his arms tighten around her.

As her thoughts returned to the present, Julianna shook

her head regretfully. Dominick had been right all along. She didn't need to prove anything.

Turning to watch other people dance as she sat alone at her table, waiting for Roger to return with his drink, she wished she was home with Dominick now. Glancing at her watch, she was very glad Roger had picked her up later than planned. Vicki would be here soon to take her home, and she could put this behind her.

In fact... maybe the best thing *would* be to forget her plans for confronting him, head back home to Dominick, and just go ahead with their future instead.

"I'm back," Roger said cheerfully, sitting beside her.

Shutting her eyes wearily, Julianna managed a smile. "You were gone so long, I thought you'd been sidetracked by a woman at the bar." *Wishful thinking!* she thought.

"Now, would I do that to my favorite girl?"

"I'd have to ask Marilyn to know that one," she mumbled, the memories painful.

"What?"

"Never mind."

Despite Roger's further attempts to spark a conversation, Julianna said little. Her lack of attention wasn't lost on him, only fueling his suspicions as he sipped his drink.

He'd retained his memories of the vivid dream regarding the dark stranger who'd showed him those very disturbing visions of Julianna. Was she really pulling an act tonight, merely feigning friendship while she planned to break off their relationship completely instead?

True, Roger *had* sensed a subtle change in her yesterday when they'd spoken, but was it *that* drastic?

Remembering how he'd seen her in the mirror, wrapped in Dominick's embrace, seemed answer enough.

Even after witnessing the condemning scene, the stranger certainly hadn't relented afterwards, relaying further sordid details of Dominick's relationship with Julianna to fuel his vexation. Thinking of his constant jabs at how they were mocking him all this time only kindled his anger towards his rival, as well as the woman sitting across from him now.

Had she and her supposed lover been duping him all this time with a false act of amnesia?

He wouldn't put it past Dominick.

Julianna's faraway look didn't ease his thoughts. He wondered how true everything the stranger said was, and if in fact, she was thinking of Dominick right now. Angered at the thought, he found it hard to smile.

"Sure I can't convince you to use that pretty voice of yours again?" he asked.

"Not tonight," she replied. "I'm really not in the mood for singing now."

His eyes narrowed. "But you would be if Dominick was here?"

She sighed heavily. "Roger..."

"Never mind," he interrupted. "The answer's obvious. I just wish your sister would wise up and send him packing. He's certainly overstayed his welcome as a guest."

Her eyes darkened. "As if it's any of your business who my family is friends with."

"Friends!" he sneered. "Considering how close he seems to be with your sister, it wouldn't surprise me if Westbrooke had a hidden agenda to his moving in so suddenly. Maybe the two of them are using you as a smokescreen so they can see each other openly."

"How dare you say something like that about my sister!" she snapped, storming to her feet. "I'll have you know, Crystal is very happily married and she has no interest in Dominick!"

He stood as well, his own eyes filled with anger. "Maybe not, but you've just proven you do. The guy I spoke with last night was right. You probably *have* been sleeping with him despite all your protests."

His words sparked her curiosity. "What guy?"

"It's irrelevant. The point is, I'm wise to your game. I know now that your supposed loathing of Dominick was just a façade to cover up what's really been going on between you two. There are some things you can't hide."

"Oh, really?" she replied angrily. "As if you're any stranger to hiding things from *me*." At his questioning look, she added, "You know, I was going to let this go, but since you so *kindly* brought up the subject, I've been meaning to ask you. How is your sweet *cousin* Marilyn doing these days?"

His expression sobered instantly, easily reading the anger in her own. She remembered their break up. Blast it all! What lousy timing with that Westbrooke bastard obviously more than willing to 'comfort' her.

"Julie... let me explain."

"Why? So you can lie to me again?" Before he could reply, she reached for her purse, slamming the journal on the table. He wasn't sure what was in it, but he could guess, his eyes confirming this when he flipped through a few pages. "Yes, I found out the truth of how you left me for your supposed *cousin*, who was no relative of yours. Funny how you were more than happy to sleep with her when I said I wanted to wait. And if that wasn't bad enough, she moved in with you!"

"Julie, I know that what happened before was a mistake. But anything that happened between me and Marilyn is *over*," he protested. "That's the absolute truth. You've got to believe me!"

"*Do* I?" she asked, as she stuffed the journal back in her bag. "I don't think so, Roger. You also wanted me to believe Dominick was crazy, some ex-patient from an institution, insisting that *he* was the one telling me lies."

"How do you know he isn't?" he retorted.

Bracing her hands to lean forward on the table, she

glared at him. "Because I remember that there really *is* a past history between us, and we really *are* engaged."

His own anger escalated. "You never *once* mentioned that to me! How was I to know?"

"Maybe you didn't know *that*, but you knew I wasn't seeing you just before my accident and chose to lie about it." Wanting only to leave, she reached for her purse. "In any case, I see now who I *can* trust... and who I can't trust anymore." Giving him a cold smile, she added, "But you know what, Roger, it doesn't matter. Because by this time tomorrow, I'll be Dominick's wife. Now, if you'll excuse me, I have someone waiting for me at home."

Julianna strode towards the exit, leaving a fuming Roger behind. Slamming his fist against the table as he sat, nearly spilling his drink, he ignored the startled looks from those nearby.

His worst suspicions were confirmed. So the stranger in his dream had been right. Julianna *had* been stringing him along while dallying with Westbrooke behind his back.

Downing his drink, moments later he nearly jumped upon hearing a familiar voice in his mind. *"The question is... what are you going to do about it?"* it asked.

Shaking his head to clear it, Roger stared down at his glass. No doubt the voice was a delusion brought on by the drink. *"I'm no delusion!"* snarled the voice. *"Haven't I already proven the girl's deceit to you?"*

"Yes," Roger murmured. "But what *am* I supposed to do about it? She's gone back to Westbrooke."

"Apparently not just yet, since her ride seems to be late."

Considering this, as he saw Julianna standing at the exit, the somber man shook his head. "What good will *that* do?" he answered quietly, so as not to be overheard. "She won't go anywhere with me now."

"Not unless you're man enough to persuade her otherwise," sneered the voice. *"Or would you rather she continue her liaisons with him?"*

The thought of Julianna being with Dominick did grate on Roger's mind. And without question, he would like to take her home with him instead. Yet... deep down, he knew whatever chance they might have had to rekindle their relationship was gone. It was clear whatever was between her and Dominick had survived her amnesia and looked unbreakable.

At his hesitation, the voice continued taunting him. *"Come on, Collins, we both know the wench only went out with you tonight to laugh at your weakness! Are you the kind of man to meekly accept being browbeaten by her, or are you going to wipe that smug look off her face* **and** *her lover's by taking her home with* **you** *tonight?"*

Roger was silent for long moments while Julianna's last words regarding his deceptions replayed in his mind. He didn't want to see her with Dominick, but neither did he want to see her hurt. The latter won out.

"No," he whispered finally. "I won't do that to Julie."

"Oh, for demon's sake!" hissed the voice. *"Don't tell me you're giving in to weak-willed sentiment."* Glancing up towards the door, Roger saw Julianna pacing by the exit, a puzzled look on her face. *"Well... if you're not going to cooperate, then I think it's time I take the reins from here, Mr. Collins. Thank you for being such a cooperative drone."*

As the dark presence exerted its will through the amulet of possession, Roger's eyes widened in shock, just before he emitted a few choking sounds, his head then slumping forward.

Moments later, Roger's eyes blinked open... but no longer due to his own will.

"At last," said Dual, flexing his hands menacingly. "And now, to business."

His eyes filled with malice as his gaze rested upon

Julianna.

Oblivious to this, she looked at her watch, noting it was past eight o'clock. Sammy would be upset, as would Dominick. *What in heaven's name is keeping Vicki?* she wondered.

"I could take you home," Roger called out, causing her to jump as she turned to him. "Since you're waiting for a ride," he added.

"Thanks, but not this time," she replied, as she faced the door again, shivering against the cold air.

"Come on, Julie. It's dark and freezing out there," he persisted. "No matter what you think of me, or what I think of Westbrooke, I wouldn't want you catching cold again, would I?"

Shooting a quick glance back at the table, Julianna wouldn't reply.

"I'm not asking for your forgiveness," he said. "I know we're beyond that. But for old time's sake, can't we at least sit here civilly for five more minutes before you leave for good with your fiancé?"

Hearing him admit Dominick was that eased some of her ambivalence. At least he was finally accepting the truth. Sighing as she rubbed her hands, Julianna nodded. "All right," she agreed. "My sister will be here soon anyway."

As she sat again, he smiled, while twirling a coin on the table. She turned at the sound, beginning to watch it absently, while he spoke several unfamiliar words, waving his hand over the spinning coin. Her look became still more vacant.

"You know, Julie," he said evenly, lifting her chin to gaze into her eyes, "you really *should* reconsider letting me drive you home myself."

She shook her head, but felt unable to speak.

"Julie..." he continued in a soothing voice, his eyes still gazing into hers, "I'm not such a demon that I'd leave you stranded here. Let me take you home." He smiled with sudden inspiration, adding, "Home to Dominick."

Blinking her eyes through heavy lids, she lifted a hand to her temples. "Home," she whispered, her breathing becoming labored.

"Yes, home. You want me to take you home right now, don't you?"

Her eyes were now so heavy, she barely noticed as he waved a hand in front of her eyes. His hand emitted a red glow and he pressed his palm against her forehead. Trying unsuccessfully to fight the lethargy encompassing her, Julianna called out weakly, "Dominick..."

"That's right, my dear Julie," he said, patting her cheek. "You just keep thinking of Dominick... for now."

Never losing his amused expression as he stood, he clicked his tongue. "Poor thing," he crooned in mock sympathy, as he picked her up to carry her. "Time to get you home."

As he carried her towards the exit, several onlookers only now looked up. The man who ran the karaoke section walked over, having recognized Julianna from the other night.

"Is she all right?" he asked concerned.

"Yes," said Dual. "We were celebrating, and she just had a bit too much to drink tonight, I'm afraid. But not to worry. I'll see she gets home safe and sound."

"She looked fine when the last singer performed. Can I see some ID?"

Irritated by the man's interference, Dual searched Roger's thoughts, and found something useful. "Of course," he replied, grinning. "You were the announcer that called Julianna up the other evening when she sang."

"What's your point?" the man pressed.

"Well..." he said, with a sheepish look, "although I didn't expect her to openly announce who she was singing that song for, I happen to be the 'Dominick' whom she mentioned."

Stirring slightly, Julianna echoed, "Dominick..."

"You see?" Dual replied. "If you'll recall, I was sitting at a table with both her and a friend of hers that night." The man did remember that much. "And since we recently got engaged, I decided to take her out to celebrate. Is that so strange?" As he muttered something else under his breath, it caused a white mist to cover the other man's eyes. The man blinked a few times but was unable to clear them.

"That makes sense, doesn't it?" Dual asked persuasively.

"Yes," he said. "I'm sorry for bothering you, sir, and I hope your fiancée feels better tomorrow."

"Don't worry. I assure you I'll take care of her," he promised, carrying Julianna outside, cleverly concealing his dark, satisfied expression. *I'll certainly take **care** of her tonight!* he thought, nearly laughing aloud. Who would have thought feigning Dominick's identity would prove so useful?

But mustn't keep the girl waiting to take her 'home', Dual thought. How convenient that he had access to Roger's memories and could make use of this to not only get revenge, but to leave the simple-minded fool to take the blame afterwards.

As the oblivious Julianna slumped against him, completely unconscious now, Dual successfully exercised the amulet anew to use Roger's memories to assist in finding his car. Placing Julianna within, and then utilizing the possessed man's thoughts to drive them to his house, Dual could sense Roger's mind trying to fight him to no avail, and smiled darkly.

This night, he would finally pay Dominick back.

*****

"Where's Aunt Julie?" wailed Sammy. "She **promised** to be home on time to tuck me in."

Dominick patted the boy's shoulder. "Maybe she and your Aunt Vicki just ran into traffic," he replied, looking up as he heard the front door open. "It's about time," he said, having started to worry a bit himself, striding to the entrance. When he got there though, he was surprised. "Crystal... Jerry?"

"When last we checked," said Jerry. "Why?"

"I just assumed you were Vicki and Julianna. They were supposed to be back by now."

Crystal immediately looked concerned. "Wait a second. Wasn't Vicki supposed to pick her up from that nightclub tonight?"

"Exactly," said Dominick.

"She might have run late, but if that was the case, Julianna would still have called to let us know."

"Does either one of you know how to contact the club?"

"I don't have their phone number off hand, but let's find out," said Jerry, leading them into the kitchen. Grabbing the phone book, he flipped through the pages until locating the number they needed. Dialing it quickly, he paused before replying, "Yes, I was wondering if you could help me. I'm trying to locate someone in my family who should still be at your club. What does she look like...?"

Taking the phone from him impatiently, Dominick explained, "Her name is Julianna Sherborne. She's of average height, with reddish-brown hair and brown eyes, and she's there with a dark-haired man by the name of Roger Collins." The man on the other end of the phone asked him to wait while he checked.

"Maybe we should go down there in person to see for ourselves," said Jerry.

"We will, if necessary," assured Dominick, just before a different voice came on the line. "Is this the same person I just spoke with?"

"No," the man answered. "But I do recognize the name of the woman you mentioned. She was here a short while ago, but she left with her fiancé."

"Her *what*?" he exclaimed, startling the pair beside him. "That's impossible!"

"Well, that's who he said he was. A dark-haired guy who claimed his name was Dominick. He carried her out earlier when she apparently passed out from too much alcohol."

Feeling a surge of anger, Dominick managed a quick 'thank you' before hanging up. "Damn that bastard!" he hissed, turning to the others. "Roger's got Julianna. We've got to find him, before it's too late."

"Hold on," said Jerry. "What makes you so sure?"

His eyes narrowed. "The man at the club thinks that Julianna left with her fiancé Dominick!" At Jerry's stunned look, he nodded. "On top of which, he said he carried her out of there unconscious, due to her having had too much to drink."

"And Julianna *never* drinks," murmured Crystal, grabbing the phone book. While the others watched her, she dialed another number, pausing only a short time before slamming the phone down. "There's no answer at Roger's house," she informed them.

"Care to drive?" Dominick asked Jerry.

"As if I have a choice?" he replied, jotting down Roger's address, before both ran out.

*****

Upon pulling up to Roger's house, the pair found it dark, although his car was parked outside.

"This is the right address, but there aren't any lights on," said Jerry. "I don't like the look of this."

"Neither do I," replied Dominick. "I've dealt with enemies in the past who've relied on darkness to cover for them. We need to get inside."

As he leaned forward to open the car door, Jerry caught his arm. "Hold it, Dominick. I know we're both worried about Julianna, but this isn't the way to handle it on our world. We can't just break in without proof she's in there, or we could both be arrested."

He considered this for a moment. "There *is* a way I can check."

"And how pray tell can you do that?" challenged Jerry.

"Do you suggest we hold a glass up to the front door?"

Dominick shook his head. "No," he decided. "I have a much better method. Wait here for a moment, and don't do *anything* to jostle my concentration."

"You mean you're going to use that dream power of yours?"

"If I could reach your sister-in-law with it across the solar system, I can certainly infiltrate Roger's house," he agreed, shutting his eyes. While Jerry watched silently, Dominick's head quickly fell back against the seat, his astral form escaping its confines.

Glancing over his shoulder, Jerry caught a glimpse of a star-like light disappearing towards the house, just before it vanished through the front door. Blinking in amazement, he couldn't help wondering what other powers existed on this other world of his future brother-in-law's.

Floating through the walls of the house, Dominick found nothing initially, but his concern only grew as he headed upstairs. With each passing step, he prayed that his suspicions were wrong and that Julianna was safe somewhere else, yet his heart grew heavier with worry.

Waiting outside the first closed door he came across, the faint sound of rustling movement caught his attention, just before he heard someone's quiet laughter.

Dimming his light before passing through the door, the sight that met the dreamphaser made his blood run cold.

Sure enough, Julianna was there, unconscious on Roger's bed. Kneeling beside her invisibly, Dominick reached out a hand to touch her cheek, even as it went right through her. She was totally oblivious to his presence, and even her breathing seemed irregular.

By Chavernos, what has that bastard done to you? his thoughts asked. His curiosity about Julianna's strange physical condition was halted suddenly upon hearing low laughter from across the room again, causing him to eye the man standing only several feet away.

Leaning against the wall as he refilled a glass he was holding, Roger took a long swallow before grinning as he stared at Julianna.

"A toast, Julie," he drawled, walking over to her. "To an evening together long awaited."

She never moved.

He must have drugged her, Dominick thought. So much for friendship! Eyeing the bottle in Roger's hand, he thought quickly. *Hmmm, so he's been drinking, has he?* he considered. Well then, perhaps a little astral magic might distract him from Julianna temporarily.

Brightening his astral light until it formed the outline of his body, Dominick instantly earned Roger's attention. To his surprise, he didn't even blink. He merely put the bottle down and walked towards the light.

Cleverly, Dominick passed through the door, dimming his light afterwards. Roger missed this though, opening the door to give a cursory glance down the hall in both directions. Finding nothing, he simply smiled, walking into the hallway while closing the door behind him.

Back in the room with Julianna, Dominick returned to her side, wishing she could hear him. But no matter. At least now he could confirm her whereabouts with Jerry.

Before he could leave though, a slow clapping sound from across the room drew his attention. Bolting around, he saw the dark presence of his familiar enemy. Something only he could see clearly, since Dual was in his astral dreamphaser form.

"A most interesting diversion," he said. "Too bad it won't work a second time."

His surprise becoming a deep molten anger, Dominick's fists clenched. "I might have known you'd show up. One can always sense your slime oozing up from a mile away."

"Ah, but apparently you couldn't tonight."

"Get out of here if you value your life!" he yelled.

"Why, Dominick, such possessive behavior," Dual replied, striding forward menacingly, arms folded. "As if you could cast a blow in astral form. Tsk tsk. You know, for a minute there, you sounded almost jealous as if someone was about to ravish your future wife."

His words sparked an even deeper hatred as the realization of Dual's words sank in. "You played a part in Roger bringing her here, didn't you, you cold-blooded demon?"

Dual shrugged, spreading his hands. "And how would I do that?" he queried.

"I have no idea, but I wouldn't put anything past you."

"You know, Westbrooke, it's almost a pity what's going to happen to her," he said, still with a hint of amusement. "But what can I say? She's a rather striking woman. And as you know, I wanted to sample her beautiful body's luscious charms before." His eyes narrowed, with an ominous grin. "How fortuitous that thanks to some powerful magic I obtained, I fully intend to tonight."

"What in blazes are you talking about?" snapped Dominick. "You're still on Chavernos!"

"Only partially true," replied Dual. "Or haven't you ever heard of amulets of possession?" Dominick's face drained of color. "Ah yes, so you have. Then surely you understand how easily I've gained control of that simpleton, whose body only awaits for me to animate it again." His expression darkened with satisfaction. "You never did consummate your relationship with your lover last night, did you?"

Dominick's eyes widened angrily. "You were *there*?"

Not answering this, Dual cast him a cruel smile instead. "Ah, then it's true," he whispered. "I wasn't completely sure, but now your actions have proved my suspicions. So irony of ironies, your precious Julianna is truly still a virgin after all, despite your meaningless trysts in the dream-state."

At Dominick's pained expression, he continued icily, "Not that she'll be one much longer thanks to the abilities the amulet's power grants me. Of course, your presence here means that naturally I can't have you interfering at the last minute, so I'll make sure not to spare any gentleness when I use his body to take her. In fact, it should be quite interesting to see her let out quite a different set of screams this time than her usual ones with you."

"I'll see you in hell before that happens!" yelled Dominick, striding forward. His fist went through Dual's visage.

"You first," he hissed, as he turned to leave.

Dominick's eyes blazed. "You'll pay for this, Dual!" he swore. "Nothing will stop me from finding you on Chavernos and breaking your miserable neck in two!"

"Feel free," mocked Dual, gesturing at Julianna. "The demonworld knows it won't help her now."

Grinding his teeth as Dual walked through the door to take possession of Roger's body again, Dominick vanished from the room.

*****

Nearly jolted back into his body from his hasty return, Dominick blinked his eyes rapidly. Jerry clasped his shoulder immediately. "Is she up there?" he asked.

"With the worst demon alive!" agreed Dominick, opening the car door to jump outside.

Following him, Jerry's eyes grew curious as the other man withdrew the orb his friend had given him. Biting his lip, Dominick glanced at it briefly. "Dammit, Lendric, this had better work!" he shouted, tossing it to the ground full-force. The device shattered, making no other sound.

"What was that?" asked Jerry.

"Something he gave me to summon him back in an emergency," said Dominick. "Now come on. Lendric or no, we've got to get in there to rescue Julianna."

Striding after him to the front door, Jerry gaped as he saw Dominick withdraw a small piece of metal from his pocket, just before he held it up to the door. "Not that you should take this the wrong way, but does Julianna know you pick locks?"

Dominick warded this off. "Don't worry, Jerry," he replied. "I'm not a professional thief on the side. But on my world, I have run into a few of them in the past. So while I wouldn't use the knowledge I gained from them for stealing, it has come in handy on occasion."

Shaking his head in disbelief, Jerry could only hope this was one of those occasions.

*****

"Time to wake up, sweetheart," someone crooned, tapping Julianna's cheek gently. At first, since her last thoughts were elsewhere, she murmured absently, "Dominick...?"

Annoyed at her response, Roger's eyes narrowed abruptly, just before he slapped her hard.

Jolted to her senses, Julianna shook her head, her eyes opening wide. Through her scattered thoughts, she heard a sharp laugh, prompting her eyes to flutter. "Roger," she gasped, still half dazed from the spell and unable to move from where she was, apparently lying in his room and on his bed. Swallowing hard, she tried to clear the hazy images in front of her and saw Roger stand up.

"So good of you to remember me, Julie," he said. "And now that you're awake, I think it's about time I saw to it that you never forget me again."

Before his words could sink in completely, her vision cleared enough to see him remove his shirt, sending a sickened feeling of fright surging through her. "Roger, wh-what are you doing?" she stammered, cursing her weakened limbs as she backed up as far as she could before the wall stopped her.

If she could have, she'd have gone through it.

A sneer further twisted his expression. "Don't play the innocent with me anymore, Julianna. I know all about the countless nights you spent with Dominick, and I fully intend to experience you as he has."

"You'd resort to rape?" she yelled, her voice high-pitched from her fear. "Roger, we were friends once! How could you?"

His hand closed over her mouth, cutting off her words. "No, Julianna, how can *you* call something between us rape? After all, you used to tell me how much you loved me. In a way, I'm only giving you what you've always wanted since that night your father interrupted us."

"Bastard!" she spat. "I could never love you again after what you put me through. And if you lay one finger on me, my family will shoot you!"

"Not when they hear from the club that you'd passed out drinking, and that you practically threw yourself at me when we got back to my place. I am only human, you know." She started to protest again, but he shushed her in the same manner as before, his eyes taking on a dark gleam, while his voice deepened. "But this talk is becoming most tiresome, and I can't wait any longer to claim you at last, my jewel."

Feeling telltale chills course through her, Julianna was confused. "Your voice," she whispered. "It doesn't sound like you, Roger."

An eerie grin spread across his face. "Maybe because it's *not* him," he hissed. "Although we have met in the past, if you remember."

Her eyes widened in shock. "Dual?" she gasped. "But that's impossible!"

"Is it really, my fair *wench*?"

At his laughter, Julianna tried to reach out to slap him, but her arm only got halfway up before Dual easily caught it, pressing it against her side again. Panicked by her lack of strength, she looked up at him with mixed anger and fear. "What have you done to me?" she demanded. "And to Roger?"

"Oh... I merely controlled his mind, as I'm now borrowing his body. As for you, I used a very helpful hypnosis spell to persuade you to come here with me, combined with a debilitation spell. One that takes some time to wear off, but at least you'll be awake for our forthcoming union."

"No!" she exclaimed. "Damn you, Dual! I won't let you do this!"

"You have no choice," he replied darkly.

*****

"This isn't getting us anywhere," Jerry said, shortly after.

"Damn this thing!" snarled Dominick, tossing the pick down. "It always worked on *my* world."

"But this *isn't* your world," he reminded him.

Clenching his teeth, Dominick nodded. "All right then," he decided. "I guess this door's hinges can't be too strong."

Before he could follow through with his intent, Jerry blocked him. "Whoa!" he shouted. "Before you break your back, I'd better warn you that the doors probably aren't as easy to break down as they might be on your world either."

"You're right," said Dominick, focusing his attention as his hands began to glow. "So let me try this instead." Before Jerry could question this, he hurled a blast of blue-white light at the door. It made a loud noise as it struck, but the door remained intact. "Blazes!"

"See what I mean?"

Sighing with frustration, Dominick turned to the side of the house. "Then I suppose there's only one thing we can do. We'd better smash a window to get inside." Before the other man could protest, he interrupted. "Jerry, I know it may not be the preferred method on your world, but right now, all I can see is that Julianna's trapped up there with a man who's apparently drugged her! *That* takes precedence over all else."

Pausing only a moment, Jerry replied, "There's a tire iron in my trunk. We can use that."

Clapping a hand against his arm gratefully, Dominick followed him back to the car.

*****

All during Julianna's continued protests, Dual ignored her with a knowing smile. As he removed his clothes, she tried to move away from him, but he kept her pinned where she was, gripping her chin painfully.

"It's too bad I had to borrow another identity this night," he murmured in irritation. "I would have found greater satisfaction in bearing my true form this night, the same as when we met at your castle."

"I remember," she hissed, twisting in his grasp. "You showed your true colors as a demon!"

"Why, thank you," he replied, amused. "Actually, I *am* part demon, now that you mention it." He ran one hand along her arm, grinning. "My enemy was right on one count. You are indeed a beauty, my jewel," he said, stroking from her shoulder downward. She pushed the intruding hand away, but he merely laughed, leaning forward to kiss her.

At least able to turn her head away, she interjected, "What would Caralei say if she could see you now?" Dual froze. Struggling to maintain calm, Julianna continued, "Would the woman you loved condone your punishing those who never hurt you?"

Growling, he gripped the sides of her face painfully to stare daggers into her eyes. "How do you know that name?" he demanded. "You've never even met her!"

"I heard what happened to her. Dominick told me."

Dual shook his head angrily. "He hasn't the right to speak Caralei's name, much less to discuss her death so freely!" Pulling back, he stared at the wall. "That pampered brat knows *nothing* of life beyond his palace walls. It's because of him she died!" Picking up his glass from the nearby desk, he cast it against the wall, smashing it.

"That's not true!" she protested.

"Yes, it is!" he insisted. "Furthermore, Dominick never saw his mother and surrogate father murdered before his eyes by his biological father! Nor was he present to see the innocent one he loved most get her throat slashed!"

"So you would teach him at the expense of another innocent's life?"

Dual turned to her with an unreadable expression. "You ceased to be innocent when you got involved with Dominick."

"Just like Caralei with you?"

"Enough!" he yelled, anger filling his eyes, as he slammed her head back against the wall. "Anyone who speaks ill of her deserves to die. And whether I kill you or not, by the end of this night, I'll see to it that your precious Dominick will never want you again."

Grinding his mouth against hers, Julianna shut her eyes in revulsion. Knowing how much Dominick hated both Dual and Roger, she feared that could very well be the truth. *If only I could fight back!* her thoughts raged, but the spell still rendered her too weak.

As Dual covered her body with his, her breathing quickened, trying desperately to think of a way to escape. "Dual... don't do this!" she pleaded.

"Save your protests, fair wench. If you're cooperative, I may let you live after all."

Knowing he was lying, her pleas were nonetheless crushed into silence as Dual's mouth recaptured her own. He tore at her clothes, amusement in his eyes at her continuing attempts at resistance. So much so that he was caught off-guard when she bit him, as she had before in the dream-state.

Drawing back furiously, he slapped her hard. "She-devil!" he snarled, holding her with one arm as he pulled forth a knife. "You'll pay for that, wench... dearly!" As she struggled to free herself, he was suddenly distracted by a loud crash from below. "What was that?" he snapped in irritation, turning towards the noise.

"Julianna!" a voice rang out.

Sudden hope clouding her features, Julianna managed to knock the knife from Dual's hand, screaming back, "Dominick! I'm...!"

Ignoring the clatter of the knife, Dual clamped his hand against her mouth to stifle any further sounds from her. "Too bad, fair one. But if I can't have you, at least he won't either." His hands were on her throat too quickly for her to let out more than a gasp, squeezing hard like a vise.

Choking with pain, she clawed at his grip, but especially in her weakened condition, he was too strong. Feeling life ebbing from her, memories of Dominick flooded her mind. She could see herself being pulled away from him as darkness replaced his visage.

"Say good-bye, fair jewel," Dual hissed, his eyes glittering as her resistance faded.

A thundering crash split the silence of the room.

Dual turned abruptly, just as a bolt of magic slammed into him.

Numbly, Julianna felt sudden coldness replace the pain at her throat, her thoughts swirling incoherently as darkness still pulled at her consciousness.

As she felt a pair of hands on her back gently lifting her, awareness returned and she started to scream, just before a familiar voice quickly shushed her. "Julianna, it's me, love. Dominick."

Cognizance returning, Julianna's eyes opened as she whispered faintly, "Dominick..."

Weakened as she was, she hugged him as best she could as he pulled her into his strong embrace. She murmured his name over and over, as if a litany to ward off what had just happened. Kissing her forehead, he felt moisture sting his eyes. "It's over now, sweetheart. He'll never come near you again."

"Dominick, look out!" shouted Jerry.

Pulling Julianna down with him from the bed to narrowly avoid Dual's knife, Dominick shielded her as he cast another energy bolt in Dual's direction. As the glittering light stunned his opponent, Dominick turned to Jerry, who was by his side instantly.

"Get her to safety, while I settle the score with *this* demon."

Nodding, Jerry lifted Julianna easily to carry her from the room. She protested, afraid to leave Dominick with the assassin, but her brother-in-law wouldn't be argued with.

Satisfied she was out of harm's way, Dominick's eyes narrowed with hatred. His focus shifting, he knocked Dual from his feet when he attempted to stand. Immediately clamping one arm around his neck, the latter struggled and clawed for oxygen, much as Julianna had done before. Glancing at his enemy's telltale lack of attire, Dominick's grip tightened even more, eliciting a grunt of pain from him.

"If anyone gets strangled here, it'll be you, demon-spawn!" he swore. "When I get done with you, so help me Chaos, there won't be enough pieces left of you to feed to the piranhas!"

Casting a spell of his own, Dual sent a powerful blast towards Dominick, breaking free of his hold. Rubbing his throat, to Dual's chagrin his adversary quickly recovered. "How the blazes did you get in here?" he demanded.

"Never you mind," Dominick replied. "All that's important now is breaking your neck, even if this *isn't* Chavernos!"

Before Dual could move, Dominick leaped forward to smash his fist into his enemy's jaw. Allowing no respite, he rushed forward to grab Dual by the neck and deal him more punches.

Roger's body wasn't completely defenseless though, as Dual rapidly demonstrated. Ducking free, he struck back. Throwing several blows at Dominick's stomach, temporarily winding him, a carefully placed kick by Dominick sent him backwards.

Lifting a hand to his mouth to find it smeared with blood, Dual clenched his fist. "Do you think *I* won't have your head on a spear for this? And just because I failed to kill your fiancée with that Staff, don't believe I'll fail a second time!"

Dominick shot him a smug look. "I always knew it was you. Which only gives me one more reason to end your life. Prison would be an insult to your kind."

"The only true *insult* around here is your continued existence, which I intend to remedy!" replied Dual, lunging at him again. Knocking Dominick to the floor, he sought to clasp his hands around his enemy's throat to strangle him, but his adversary was quicker, rolling away from him to stand.

Dual looked past Dominick's shoulder, catching sight of the bottle of alcohol he'd left on Roger's desk. His eyes bearing a furtive gleam, he began circling around his opponent to edge towards it.

*****

"But Dominick may need me," Julianna insisted.

"You're in no condition to help him," Jerry reminded her downstairs. "But since *I* can, just stay here, while I see what I can do."

"Jerry, wait!"

Shaking as she huddled within a blanket as he went back to help, Julianna could only hear the fighting going on. She gazed towards the room above, while praying for Dominick's safety.

Her gaze was so intent, she flinched when she felt a cool

hand suddenly touch her arm. Looking up, she saw an unexpected stranger—fortunately in his elven form—whom she gave a hug.

"Lendric," she breathed. "How did you know to come here?"

"Dominick used a device I gave him to send for me in an emergency." Glancing at her torn clothing, his expression was grim. "Apparently, he had good reason. Are you all right?"

"I am now," she agreed, "but I want to see what's going on upstairs, though something's left me weakened."

"That presents no problem for a dragon," he replied with a grin, lifting her to carry her up the staircase. Halfway up, he halted momentarily upon overhearing a crash.

"What in the name of Chavernos?"

"Lendric, you've got to do something," she said. "Dual's somehow taken control of Roger's body, and Dominick's fighting him as we speak."

Not needing to be told twice, the dragon sorcerer hurried on, stopping within the doorway. As the dragon lowered her to the floor, allowing her to lean against the doorframe, Julianna's eyes widened upon seeing a familiar form lying still on the floor.

"Jerry!" she screamed.

Quickly kneeling beside the man, Lendric saw a broken bottle close to his head, no doubt a 'present' from Dual. Checking his pulse quickly, he then turned to Julianna reassuringly.

"He's just unconscious."

Both fighting men remained oblivious to him, just before Dual hit the wall with a thud, while Dominick's hands pressed against his throat. "For my future wife's honor, I'll see you burn in the demonworld!" he snarled.

As his adversary's face began to take on a strange pallor, Julianna managed to grasp Lendric's sleeve. "Please do something. I despise Roger, but I don't want his blood on

Dominick's hands. He's fighting Dual, but he could end up accidentally killing Roger. He's just too blinded by anger to see this now!"

Lendric patted her hand. "Take courage, sweet lady. I'll take care of the matter right now." Stepping forward, just before he was about to break up the fight, his eyes narrowed abruptly. Wait just a second... There was the unmistakable aura of foreign magic. The full meaning of Julianna's words sank in. *Dual's taken control of Roger's body?*

An amulet of possession, he realized.

His eyes began glowing red, seeing the outline of Dual's astral form within, along with the amulet against his chest. Perhaps there was an alternate means to end this struggle. Raising one hand towards Roger, he recited a powerful incantation, the final word sending a beam of light at him. As the light engulfed him, the other man let out a blood-curdling yell in Dual's voice, as the amulet's glow brightened. The same light that struck Dual channeled through him, traveling swiftly through the ceiling.

Less than a minute later, there was a sound akin to shattering glass as the amulet disappeared, just before Dual's cry faded back into Roger's own voice.

Dominick shifted back, but wouldn't release the man's neck.

Lendric breathed a sigh of relief. That was one problem solved. Now for the other. Waving his hands in an arc, abruptly his elven form vanished.

Even having seen a dragon only a short time ago, Julianna was awed anew at the sight of the dragon that appeared, whose head reached the height of the ceiling, even as he let out a room-shaking roar. From Roger's startled vantage point, he glanced up with widening fear-rimmed eyes, while Dominick merely glared at the man with disgust, pushing him roughly to the floor.

Backing against the far wall, Roger gasped for breath, even as Lendric moved to stand beside Dominick, placing a scaled hand on the dreamphaser's back that expressed its own silent message.

"Dual's gone, Dominick. It's over."

Realizing by the confused look in Roger's eyes that this was true, he relaxed. But remembering what the other man had done, especially during the last week, his expression darkened again. "You're right, Lendric. The Rogers of this world aren't worth anyone's time or effort."

He hissed the last, while his rival merely cowered where he remained, only now realizing with growing puzzlement that he was wearing next to nothing!

"I'll watch him," said Lendric, his voice deep with its dragon tones. *"For now, see to your companion, while I see to her brother-in-law."*

"Julianna..." whispered Dominick, turning to her immediately. Her face was tear-streaked, but she was smiling now as he knelt beside her. Pulling her into his embrace, he kissed her forehead. "Thank Chavernos you're all right, love."

"I'm so sorry," she choked. "I had no idea Dual would use Roger against me. I thought..."

"Shhh, you couldn't have known," he replied, shaking his head. "Your being safe is all I care about."

"H-how did you get here so quickly?"

A smile smoothed his features as he leaned forward to touch her forehead with his own. "If I have to remind you forever, Julianna," he said softly, "you really shouldn't underestimate me."

Then there were no more words as he pulled her close, their hearts beating in unison. He kissed her passionately, feeling a hundred emotions, as she happily reciprocated. Until finally, tenderness overwhelmed this need, and they merely clung to each other.

"I love you," whispered Julianna, as his arms hugged her tight.

"And by Chavernos, I love you too, my darling," he replied thankfully as he stroked her long curls. Slowly, his eyes held a look of mock reprimand. "I won't say I told you so, but now do I have your word that you'll never stir up trouble with Roger anymore?"

"Never again," she promised.

Helped to his feet while rubbing his sore head, Jerry was clearly relieved at the sight of the happy pair.

Roger, on the other hand, had recovered enough to scowl at them. Lendric merely smiled warmly, while his dragon eyes kept a careful watch on the man against the wall. It was only when Roger growled audibly that Lendric replied in kind.

"I wonder what a barbecued Earth human tastes like," he said, licking his chops for emphasis.

Eyes widening again, Roger lapsed into unconsciousness.

*****

Jerry returned to the room, after calling home to relay the news. He found Roger looking strangely subdued in one corner of the room, even though some of this could stem from Lendric's unnerving constant observance.

"I can't remember any of that happening," Roger said quietly, earning a glare from Dominick.

"Don't give us that!" he snapped. "You still held your own mind when you kidnapped Julianna!"

His rival clenched his jaw at that, staring at the floor. "I don't remember leaving the nightclub, let alone with her." Turning to Julianna, his gaze softened. "I know I was angry, but I never would have hurt you."

"I find *that* hard to believe!" Dominick replied, with a sneer.

Clearing his throat, sending an unintentional low rumble

through the room, Lendric interrupted. *"I'm afraid on that count, he's probably telling the truth, Dominick. When an amulet of possession is used to give complete control to its bearer, as Dual demonstrated tonight, the person controlled rarely remembers anything that happened during that time. And since he doesn't remember leaving the club with her, it's likely that Dual was exerting control even then."*

"That would explain the voice I kept hearing," confirmed Roger. "It sounded like the stranger I dreamed of last night, who does match your description of this Dual. It sounded like he wanted me to seduce her, but I refused. That's when everything went black."

Lendric nodded. *"That sounds like Dual. And knowing him, he searched your memories in order to be able to bring Julianna to this destination."*

"That does make some sense," she murmured, staring down at her folded hands.

Worried by her uncharacteristic quiet, Roger strode towards her, just before Dominick stepped forward to push him back. "Lay one finger on her, and I'll change my mind about letting you live," he warned.

"I wasn't about to," said Roger, turning to meet Julianna's gaze. "Julie, I swear I wouldn't have treated you like that monster did. We may have had our differences, but I've always cared about you. Please believe me."

Swallowing once, she replied, "I know it was Dual's possession overall that caused this, and I'll forgive you for that much, because you've never hurt me physically." He sighed with relief, just before she shook her head. "But as to caring about me, I can't believe that. Because if you truly did, you wouldn't have tried to break up my relationship with Dominick, nor lied to me left and right when I didn't know what to believe."

"You've got to understand why I did that, Julie."

"No," she said, leaning closer to Dominick. "I'm afraid

this is one time which your excuses can't make up for, Roger. I wish you happiness with your life, despite everything you've done to interfere with mine... but tonight is good-bye forever."

"Wait a second," he protested. "You can't..."

Once again, Dominick intervened, holding Roger back with one hand, his eyes blazing. "I think Julianna's made her feelings *quite* clear, Collins," he replied with deceptive quiet. "But I would add one thing, which you'd best remember after we leave. If you *ever* set eyes on my future wife again after this, it will be the *last* time."

Roger made no further argument, sensing Dominick was determined, and fully capable of carrying out that threat, if provoked. A meaningful low growl from Lendric added his own agreement, as he teleported outside, and Jerry walked out to follow him. Afterwards, Dominick then led Julianna from the room as well.

"Julie," Roger called after her. She stopped, but didn't turn. "Although you might not want to believe this... I am sorry, about everything." Seeing she wasn't about to answer, he added, "And I do wish you well. Even though I wish you might reconsider..."

His words trailed off as she resumed walking out with her companion, neither one looking back.

Chapter Fourteen

"Roger kidnapped Julianna?" exclaimed Vicki. "I know I was delayed getting back with Luke, but I figured she'd be fine until I got there."

Sitting on the sofa while Sammy played with his dinosaurs, Crystal sighed. "It wasn't exactly Roger who kidnapped her. It just seemed that way, although it was really someone else. I'll explain the full details later when there's more time."

"More time?"

"Listen to me. That was Jerry on the phone before. The important thing is, Julianna's safe and she's coming home right now, but there are a few things I do need to explain. First of all, there's a possibility she may be going away tomorrow."

Sammy's eyes widened. "Forever?" he shouted.

Crystal rushed to his side, giving him a hug. "No, not forever," she said comfortingly. "Goodness, where did that come from?"

"Well... since Uncle Dominick's from another world..."

"Another world?" laughed Vicki. "Are we back to *that* again? Maybe I should ask Luke if he can dig up any alien relatives, so we can join in this game."

"It's not a game," Crystal replied. "The only reason we didn't explain all of this sooner was because of Julianna's injury."

Her sister folded her arms. "You know, *that's* something else I never understood either. For someone who supposedly lost part of her memory, she seemed to remember *us* well enough. Just because she couldn't remember your visiting friend Dominick..."

"He's *not* really a visiting friend of mine. He's..."

"Don't tell me," Vicki said. "He's Julianna's man from *Mars*!"

A bright flash of light appeared, from which several figures emerged.

"Actually, I'm from Chavernos," chuckled Dominick.

As Vicki turned in surprise to find Julianna clinging to his hand, Sammy's excited cry interrupted anything she might have said.

"Daddy!" he yelled, even as Crystal ran forward to hug her husband. Not wanting to be left out, Sammy jumped up to join them.

"I'm glad you're all right," she whispered, looking a bit puzzled upon seeing no mark upon his forehead. Running her hand across it, she shook her head. "Wait a second. I thought you said you were hit with a bottle."

"I was," Jerry replied, tousling Sammy's hair affectionately. "But Lendric certainly surprised me with his capability for magic. They should have healers like him on this world."

Seeing Vicki's building curiosity, Julianna stepped forward. "I suppose Crystal's started to tell you the truth about Dominick," she said quietly. "Although you might not believe this, he happens to be the same man I told Sammy about, who really did visit me in my dreams."

"What?" gasped Vicki. "It can't be. It..."

"I understand," said Julianna. "The portrait I drew of him that day couldn't have done him justice, but I would hope that some of it resembles him."

Before she could reply, Sammy ran over to hug Julianna too. She knelt down to hug him back, feeling a sudden wave of sadness that she'd be leaving her dear little nephew for a long time once tomorrow came. Still, she was consoled by the fact that Dominick and Lendric promised her that she could return on occasion to visit Earth.

"Aunt Julie, we didn't know where you were," Sammy told her, pouting now. "Did that green slimy gooberhead Roger really kidnap you?"

"Sammy," she said, amused, "you've been watching too much television. Green slimy gooberhead?"

"Well, you once called him a gooberhead too," he protested.

Dominick lifted an eyebrow at that, and Julianna shrugged. "After Roger left me for Marilyn, I had to substitute for Sammy what I *really* wanted to call him."

"You were definitely onto something even then," Dominick agreed, as he smiled down at the pair. Sammy looked up.

"Can I call you my Uncle Dominick now?" he asked.

"Hmmm, well, let's see," he replied, reaching down to pick him up. "Since I intend to marry this fine lady who's your aunt before we leave, I guess that sounds about right." Conspiratorially, he leaned closer to add in a whisper, "And you're right, Sammy. Roger *is* a green slimy gooberhead."

"Purple slimy too," laughed Sammy.

Dominick grinned as Julianna stood beside him again. "You were certainly right about your nephew, dearest. He's a very bright lad for his age."

"Can I go with you to Chavernos?" he asked.

The couple sobered instantly, exchanging uneasy glances. It would seem Sammy might be a bit *too* bright in some ways. Seeing their difficulty, Crystal stepped forward to retrieve her son, Jerry placing an arm around her shoulders.

"No, sweetheart," she said gently. "You have to stay here with us, but they'll come back to visit." Realizing the uncertainty of this, she turned to her sister slowly. "You *will* come back, won't you, Julie?"

"Of course I will," she replied, earning a cough from her

companion. Linking her arm with his, she added, "Or rather, *we* will."

"I don't get any of this!" complained Vicki.

A loud noise just outside prompted her to whip about, in time to see another bright flash of light. When the glare died down, a most unexpected sight met everyone's gaze, which left Sammy gaping and Vicki screaming. Immediately, Jerry and Crystal tried to calm her, but to little avail.

Still in dragon form, Lendric looked about worriedly. *"What? What? Are we being attacked by poisonous ranorgians?"* It only took him a moment to realize what she was *really* afraid of. *"Oh dear... I forgot to change back to my elven form, didn't I?"*

"Unless elves have suddenly sprouted dragon scales," Dominick sighed, turning to the shaken Vicki. "Don't worry, it's the same Lendric you met before, and he won't hurt any of us. He sent us ahead first with a spell, so he could teleport Jerry's car afterwards. In teleporting himself here, I'm afraid he must have gotten a little side-tracked. Obviously, he's really a dragon."

"S-so I see," Vicki said, still clutching her sister and brother-in-law.

Escaping his mother's grasp, Sammy stepped towards the dragon sorcerer with a puzzled expression. "Are you *really* Lendric?"

In reply, the dragon raised his arms, just before transforming back into his familiar elven form. "I believe this should answer your question."

Sammy's eyes brightened. "Wow! Can you breathe fire too?"

"Certainly," he replied, casting a quick glance towards Crystal. "Er... although I doubt your mother wants me demonstrating this in your house." She nodded in agreement. Patting the boy's head, Lendric turned to Dominick. "This child reminds me of you when you were younger," he said with admiration. "My dragon form never frightened you either."

Tugging at Lendric's shirt, Sammy regained his attention, holding up his toy dinosaur. "Uncle Dominick said you can make me a dragon to go with T-Rex. Could you please show me before you leave?"

"Hmmm, so 'Uncle' Dominick said that, did he?" he murmured, eyeing the man in question, who then whispered something to him with a beseeching look. "Well, I suppose I can manage to figure something out."

"Gee thanks!" exclaimed the boy, giving him a hug.

Upon witnessing Sammy's acceptance of Lendric—as well as seeing the dragon sorcerer in his elven form again—Vicki felt more at ease with the situation. Giving them a brief smile, she asked, "*Now* will someone please explain to me just what the heck is going on around here?"

"Mass confusion?" Lendric supplied helpfully.

While the others filled Vicki in, Dominick tapped his friend's shoulder, leading him off to the side. "Since you're still here, and this explanation might take awhile, I was wondering if you'd help me with a favor while we're waiting."

Lendric frowned. "I hope you're not about to ask for more gold coins. I'm afraid those gifts you bought Julianna expended most of it."

"Oh no, nothing like that." He cast a furtive smile towards Julianna, who was wrapped up with her family, oblivious to their conversation. "Actually, I had something else more important in mind."

"Well then, by all means, just tell me and I'll see what I can do. I'm all ears... er, no elven pun intended!"

*****

"The things a dragon does in the name of friendship!" grumbled Lendric, striding into the house, while another man followed him curiously.

A dragon? he wondered. The man who brought him here didn't seem to fall into that category. He was by no means old—given his blond hair bore no streaks of white—reasonably tall, and altogether quite human. All except for his peculiar shaped ears of course.

"Here's your justice of the peace," announced Lendric. "I just hope you *appreciate* the great lengths I went to..."

"Over here!" Crystal interrupted cheerfully, gesturing to where Dominick waited beside her. The dragon sorcerer gave a low growl, but moved aside without further comment.

It hadn't been easy to find someone to perform a late night ceremony, but Lendric had his methods of persuasion. Having already procured the necessary marriage license earlier in the day, the couple were almost ready.

Just a short time ago, Julianna had been pleasantly surprised when Crystal brought out a beautiful white dress fully adorned with lace which she'd had prepared secretly, on the off chance that her younger sister might need it one day soon. It could still be used as a regular dress for a formal occasion after the wedding itself, and a gauzy veil complemented it. For Dominick, Jerry let him borrow one of his suits, and since they were roughly the same height, the arrangement worked well.

Crystal called Julianna's name, and she appeared moments later from the upstairs hallway, descending slowly. Jerry took her hand at the bottom of the staircase to lead her to Dominick. When the engaged pair were reunited, they were speechless for long moments, holding hands and gazing into each other's eyes with love. The touching sight even had Vicki in tears, earning a smile from Crystal.

Dominick squeezed Julianna's hand. "I told you I'd find a way to see us married by the end of this night," he murmured.

"Thanks to some unexpected help from Lendric," she said. "I'm just glad you don't mind having a ceremony here as well as on your world, to prevent my sisters from complaining about it for the next fifty years."

"I can understand that. My own family and friends will be even **more** adamant about our having a second ceremony to satisfy **their** not being present at this one. Speaking of friends, are you sure it was a good idea to phone your friend Marybeth at this hour? She looks asleep on her feet."

"Don't worry, she looks the same way when Almira gives speeches, until things get going," Julianna replied playfully, looking over to her friend. "Can you stay awake for a few more minutes over there?"

Marybeth yawned loudly, but nodded. "You bet I will," she said. "No best friend of mine gets married without my being here. Just do me a favor and don't ask me to throw any rice, or I'm liable to miss and break a window."

"Only if you do me a favor to be careful going home."

"Fear not. I'll make sure she returns home safely," Lendric promised Julianna, as the couple turned to the justice of the peace.

"Now that all are present and accounted for..." the justice began, yawning once himself. "Please excuse me. I'm not used to being rousted out of bed so late for emergency ceremonies."

"*Emergency* ceremonies?" Julianna whispered in confusion.

Dominick turned to Lendric suspiciously, tugging at his arm. "Just what **did** you tell this man to get him here."

Lendric shrugged. "Nothing too extraordinary," he replied quietly. "Just pretend you've only got a week to live, and we'll do just fine."

"*What?*" he shouted, just before Julianna pulled his attention back to the ceremony.

Trying to keep the sympathy from his eyes, since the groom was obviously distraught about his tragic condition, the justice of the peace continued.

From Dream to Reality

"Dearly beloved, we are gathered here today..."

*****

"I hope you're not going to complain about the merits of Lendric's idea all night," said Julianna, leaning on her elbow as she reclined on her bed. "It probably would have been harder otherwise to find someone to perform a last minute marriage this late at night."

Dominick kept pacing, occasionally glancing out the window, and muttering his irritation with the dragon sorcerer.

"A week to live," he said aloud. "I'll give *him* a week to live after this!"

"Now, Dominick, aren't you forgetting that if it wasn't for Lendric, we wouldn't be together at all?" He stopped pacing at her words. "And if it wasn't for his timely intervention, I might not have survived that blast from the Teleportation Staff. You know that."

"Yes," he sighed. "I suppose given the circumstances, I can let this minor 'idea' of his go."

"I hope so. Now, do you mind if we could postpone any further discussions until tomorrow? I'm all tired out between having to fend off Roger—or I should say Dual—explaining everything to my sister, and then participating in a very rushed marriage ceremony, although a beautiful one nonetheless."

Dominick moved to sit beside her, running one hand lightly along her arm. "*All* tired out?" he asked softly. At the questioning look in her eyes, he added, "Well... this *is* our wedding night, isn't it?" Seeing her expression turn into a smile, he leaned closer to kiss her...

And found himself smacked in the face by a pillow.

"That's for the poker game last night," she told him, though her tone was amused.

"Oh, you'll pay for that, my impertinent minx," he laughed, recovering instantly to pick up a pillow to reciprocate.

Laughter escaping her as well, it wasn't long before the

ensuing contest left the same result as a similar incident around a decade ago. An incident that both now knew, since she'd told him the whole story after Crystal mentioned it.

"Feathers everywhere, you said?" he chuckled, picking up a handful and tossing them in the air.

Blushing at the full realization of their antics, Julianna turned to bury her head against what was left of the two pillows. Fortunately, they'd neglected the two others, which were still intact. "I don't believe this. Why do I *always* get myself into these things?" Feeling Dominick's hands on her shoulders, she slowly looked up at him again.

"Because you're a playful spirit who revels in doing the unexpected," he replied, brushing a feather from her cheek. "Which is part of the reason I love you so much. Don't ever change that, dearest."

"I won't," she said, reaching up to embrace him. She eyed him meaningfully. "And don't *you* ever change your endlessly romantic nature."

"Believe me, I won't," he replied emphatically. Both kissed each other, discarding their clothes quickly to dive beneath the covers together. As the enthusiastic groom pulled his bride closer, he glanced about them dubiously. "I don't think this bed of yours was intended for more than one person."

"It's a small single," she agreed.

"Hmmm," he said thoughtfully, shifting to cover her body with his, leaning on his elbows above her. "I think we can fit if we squeeze together."

She gave a murmur of enthusiasm, resuming their kisses, passion igniting between them. Even so, Dominick wasn't about to rush this special night.

His mouth stole endless kisses as his hands slowly traveled from her shoulders to her neck, and beyond, where he could feel her heartbeat racing beneath his touch. He kissed her deeply, stroking and caressing as he fanned the flames of her desire.

He could sense her breathing quicken when his hands moved lower, chuckling seductively as he felt Julianna shiver helplessly beneath his touch.

"I wouldn't have thought it possible, but it's even better in reality," he breathed against her ear, nuzzling it with kisses. At her sounds of pleasure, he could feel her body trembling as his touch became more insistent. "But first," he whispered, "I need to make sure you're ready. Just relax, love... and let your senses go where they will."

She found it impossible to relax, but had no choice about her senses running wild. Especially not when Dominick was murmuring soft seductive words of love. Staring down at the passion building in her glazed eyes, he smiled, kissing her neck as he continued his silent ministrations.

Instinctively, Dominick's mouth closed upon hers to capture her passion-filled sounds. His own senses were equally inflamed as he closed the distance between their bodies. Effortlessly, he shifted position, feeling her body's invitation.

Julianna's insistent hands gently beckoned him onward in acceptance, while their kisses grew more urgent, until he finally embraced her tightly in answer to a silent promise. Having been denied the reality of being together like this until tonight, he knew it would be impossible for them to hold back for long.

Yet still, remembering the reality of Julianna's remaining innocence, Dominick managed to slow them down so he wouldn't hurt her unnecessarily. As understanding dawned, her eyes widened.

"I almost forgot. We never really..."

"I wouldn't forget, love," he said, caressing her cheek. "I wish there was some other way this first time, sweetheart... but I promise to guide you through it. Just trust me."

"I always will," she replied. "But would you mind kissing me, while you..."

He kissed her lovingly, answer enough, as Julianna's arms reached up to hug him. Forcing control on himself, amidst her sweet response, Dominick slowly joined them with the full consummation of their marriage.

At his complete possession, she did cry out softly, gripping his shoulders. But for all the times she'd spent with Dominick before, the memories protected her and it was the most fleeting sensation. In a way, it was symbolic between them. Having cast aside this last obstacle, it signified that they were finally together as they were destined to be in reality, and this truth brought its own happiness.

Kissing away the few tears in her eyes, Dominick immediately saw to replacing them with loving caresses, tender words, and promises of the future. As she shared her love in return, he could sense her relaxing beneath him, removing his hesitation towards continuing.

Brushing a few loose strands of her hair back, he kissed her deeply then, even as they began to share the intimacy they'd known so well in the dream-state. Gladdened at Julianna's enthusiastic response, Dominick devoted his full attention to finding and sharing the glorious heaven he sought with her.

Gazing into the radiant eyes and flushed face of his beautiful bride, he saw the deeper pleasure of their union reflected in her blissful expression.

"Julianna, I love you so very much," he whispered.

"No more than I love you, my Dominick."

Julianna hugged him as she returned his gaze, smiling at the sweetness of it all, even as Dominick clearly felt the same.

"Always, love," he said.

His expression was so tender, it brought tears to her eyes again, even as he kissed her passionately and she warmly reciprocated, their joyful union soon culminating in an explosion of passion.

Heightened by the sweet triumph of knowing that this

time they were truly one... heart, mind, body, and soul.

It took some time for their breathing to return to normal. They remained together in their embrace, sharing unequalled happiness. Dominick stirred first, one hand lazily stroking Julianna's shoulder as he held her.

Her eyes fluttered open as she looked into those of her husband, and she cuddled closer. As she felt his arms tighten about her, she felt safer than she ever had before in her lifetime, and was infinitely happier. They were finally married in every sense of the word. In an ever-changing world of constant uncertainty, she knew that his unfaltering love was the greatest gift she would ever know, and one she intended to hold onto forever.

As if reading her thoughts, Dominick kissed his weary companion, stroking her hair gently. "So dreams do come true," she said.

Smiling in remembrance of those countless memories which had led to their being together now, he brushed a hand against her cheek.

"Aye, love," he replied softly. "And are you happy, dearest?"

"Aye, my dream knight. Very much so," she told him, laughing as a stray feather wafted upon them. "This is one encounter you never thought of in the dream-state."

"Perhaps not, but there'll be others," he said with a chuckle. "From now until the rest of our lives, love."

"Mmmm, I like the sound of that," she responded happily.

Cradling her face in his hands, he kissed her again, not too surprised at the rekindling of passion between them. Somehow, he doubted such flames would ever fade.

"My sweet Julianna..."

"Yes, Dominick..."

"Oh, blast and blazes!"

Julianna cried out in shock, while Dominick looked up sharply. "What the...?" An immediate scowl crossed his expression. "Lendric!" he yelled. "What the hell are *you* doing here?"

The sorcerer was now hovering above the far edge of the bed in dragon form—held aloft only thanks to his wings—and looking very surprised indeed.

"*Oh, my word. I meant to teleport to my room from the kitchen. I guess this isn't it. I didn't think... Oh, by Chavernos, this is embarrassing!*"

"You're damn right it is!" exclaimed Dominick, pulling the bedcovers higher to reach his startled wife's chin. "Now would you please get out of here before I consider turning you into dragon shish kebab?"

"*Right away!*" agreed the flustered dragon, abruptly halting his wings just long enough to drop onto the bed with a thud, missing the pair by inches.

Followed by a loud **CRASH**, as the bed collapsed.

Moments later, Dominick dropped his head against his hand with a groan of frustration, while Julianna struggled to get her shaken senses back. Lendric stared down at the bed, clicking his tongue regretfully.

"*Oh dear,*" he said quietly. "*I don't suppose a simple apology would count for much right now.*"

"For waltzing in here on our wedding night?" growled Dominick. "No, I really don't think so! Lendric, so help me, in spite of all your help, if you don't get out of here in five seconds, I'll..."

His words trailed off as the dragon vanished.

Dominick turned back to his bride, silently cursing Lendric's rather irksome—and ill-timed—habits. Understanding completely, Julianna calmed her distraught husband.

"He didn't mean any harm, Dominick," she soothed.

"I know," he said, "but by Chavernos, for him to show

up when we were..." Unable to complete the thought, he pressed his head against her shoulder, shutting his eyes with a sigh. "I just hope Riff doesn't hear about this."

"He won't, or I'll personally help you clobber Lendric."

Her words brightening his mood, Dominick hugged her again, resting his forehead against hers. "A secret just between us then?"

"Just between us," she agreed. Kissing him with a smile, she added thoughtfully, "All things considered, at least this time my father won't be breaking the door down to reprimand our feather war and the rest."

"Thank goodness."

As they leaned forward to kiss each other, the door flew open.

"Julianna, what on Earth?"

If not for the unmistakably female voice, Julianna would have sworn it was her father having returned as a ghost.

The startled newlyweds met Crystal's gaze with surprised and rueful expressions. *Could anything else go wrong?* they wondered.

Then again, better not to know. Julianna's father might still show up yet from beyond.

"Crystal," she said, "it's not how it looks. We aren't responsible for this." At Dominick's cough, she blushed. "Well, okay, maybe the feather part was our fault... but not the bed." Realizing how this sounded regardless, she covered her eyes with her hands. "Oh, blazes," she groaned, earning quiet laughter from Dominick.

Glancing once at the feathers, the collapsed bed, and the compromising look of the pair, Crystal put two and two together and came up with the expected five.

Smiling, she said, "It's all right, Julianna. You won't be the first couple in history to be subject to a bed collapsing on your wedding night for obvious reasons." Julianna shook her head in protest.

"It wasn't *us*," she explained. "Lendric..."

"Oh, don't worry about him tonight. I'm sure he'll be fine. Now why don't you get back to sleep... or whatever else, and we'll forget this little incident since you're leaving tomorrow anyway. You're just lucky Dad wasn't around to see this." Julianna mumbled something under her breath, just as Crystal stood in the doorway to add mirthfully, "Oh, and Julie... please make sure you and Dominick pick up all those feathers in the morning."

There was a moment of silence as the pair heard her pull the door shut quickly, locking it behind her.

"Oh, that does it!" exclaimed Julianna. "I'm going to send that dragon into orbit for this!"

As she started to move from the bed, Dominick laughed and held her back, ignoring her demand to let her go. "I'm sure that would amuse Lendric no end, to see a lovely but angry bride railing at him, with the added fact that she has no clothes on."

Blushing at this, part of her wished *she* could head to orbit right now!

"Don't worry about it love," he added. "It really doesn't matter what they think. All that matters is that we're together. Although I'll admit, this wasn't *quite* the way I'd pictured our wedding night on Earth."

"You had something else in mind?" she asked.

"Come here, love, and I'll show you," he chuckled.

Neither voiced another complaint that night.

*****

"Thank you for everything, Crystal," said Julianna.

Tears threatened her sister's eyes as she hugged her one last time, still finding it hard to believe that Julianna was really leaving for another world with her husband. A world that precious few knew of on this world, and one that might never be known by the general population. Even as Vicki embraced her sister as well, she too found it difficult to grasp.

Understanding their feelings, Jerry turned to shake Dominick's hand, telling him firmly, "You be sure and take care of Julie out there. It's not often that a family relinquishes one of their own to leave for another planet."

"You need never worry on that count," he replied seriously. "I'll always protect her with my life."

"After the events of last night, I think we have no doubt of that," Jerry said, looking off to the side to see Julianna hugging his son good-bye.

"Be a good boy while we're gone, Sammy," she whispered.

Having temporarily released his new toy dragon, he hugged her back. "Please come back soon, Aunt Julie," he replied. "Fireball, T-Rex, and I will miss you."

"I'll miss you all too," she said, "but I'll try to return for long visits when I do." Giving him a kiss before letting go, she gave Jerry a hug too, and then moved to stand beside Dominick again. Clasping his hand, she took one last look at her family, smiling at them through her tears.

"All set?" Lendric asked. Glancing down at the several suitcases she'd packed, and then back to her family, she nodded. "In that case, would the rest of you please step back to the far end of the room? This spell works within a relatively small radius, but let's not take any chances."

As the others complied, Dominick eyed the Staff warily. "Are you *sure* that thing's safe now? The last thing we need is to end up cast adrift in space."

"I ran several tests of magic to check, and it seems the curse upon it was a one-time spell. There should be no repeat of the malfunction again."

"I certainly hope not," he said, hugging Julianna close against his side. Mollified, the dragon sorcerer turned to the curious eyes upon them.

"Don't worry, folks," Lendric said cheerfully. "I'll have them back to visit before you know it." Looking towards Sammy, he added, "Remember your promise to show me this game of dragons and dinosaurs you mentioned, when we return."

"I will," the boy laughed.

Beforehand, the dragon sorcerer had instructed the others to remain silent, so as not to interfere with the necessary incantation. Now, as he spoke it, colored lights began to swirl around the trio, glowing brighter by the moment.

Feeling Julianna's grip tighten, Dominick said reassuringly, "Remember the times I teleported us within the dream-state, love. Our travel will be just like that."

Smiling up at him, she fought down her silent fears. "Just don't let go."

"I have no intention of ever doing that."

Their last view was of each other's eyes as the lights grew too bright to see, and the room faded around them.

*****

"Welcome to Chavernos," said Dominick, prompting Julianna to examine her new surroundings.

Nearly breathless, she immediately felt the sense of serenity around her. In the near distance, she could see the ocean, and several people running along the beach. In another direction, past a haze of mist, she saw the darker shadows of the mountains Dominick had told her of. They did indeed seem a dark shade of purple, although perhaps the distance only cast an illusion of this.

The sun shone above, as warm as she remembered it from Earth, but the beautiful shifting colors of the sky were a welcome addition. Watching the colors play off the clouds, it would be easy to be mesmerized by their tranquility. Scattered people moved about their homes. Children played outside—much as they had outside her former home—while several adults watched them, talking leisurely. From a building not too far away, she could hear the hint of music, but it was one particular sight that caught her attention.

A palace unlike any she'd seen, except in movies, greeted her. All throughout it, people bustled about with their daily tasks, although none seemed to find this stressful as they chatted amongst themselves.

"Is this where you live?" she asked.

Dominick laughed, shaking his head. "I used to," he replied, "but I moved out to share a new place with my brother instead, remember?" Before she could question this, he continued, "However, since we're married now, this situation will obviously be changed. When I last spoke with Chaos about it, he insisted we reside in the palace temporarily, until our *own* home can be built. In fact..."

Leading her forward to another spot, he pointed towards a not-too-distant site. "As we speak, they're working on it now. Look there."

Upon following his gaze, she inhaled sharply. "Dominick... that almost looks like..."

"Our dream castle?" he chuckled. "It should. I helped my grandfather's architect design the plans for it. But unlike our dream castle," he added, hugging his arms around her waist, "this one won't disappear each day."

She smiled as he kissed her cheek. "It's more wonderful than any dream," she said, holding his hand.

"I'm glad you think so. But awake or asleep, I look forward to spending many happy years together," he assured her. "And I'm certainly glad to know that from now on, you'll not fade from my arms when we awaken each morning... as we did this day, my precious wife."

"Mmmm, I remember," she murmured, as he spun her about to kiss her.

"Ahem!" Lendric coughed meaningfully, breaking them

apart. "Not to be a fuddy-duddy dragon, but don't you think you should save that for later? After all, your grandfather still believes we're on Earth."

"Yes," agreed Dominick. "He'll want to be the first one to know we're back, and it's about time he got to meet Julianna in reality."

"Wait," she interrupted, eyeing them both. "Speaking of reality, what about Dual? He's still *here*, and I'm sure he's fuming over having his plans for revenge ruined last night. He could come after us again, even easier than before, since we're on Chavernos in reality now."

Her husband's jaw tightened. "A threat I'd nearly forgotten. Something's got to be done about that demon once and for all."

Stepping forward, Lendric rested a hand on Julianna's shoulder. "Fear not," he replied, meeting the gaze of both. "After his last stunt of wielding an amulet of possession, I personally intend to see to it that Dual never bothers you again."

"But how?" asked Julianna.

He smiled. "Leave that to a wise dragon sorcerer, who has considerably more years of wisdom than that upstart."

Before more could be said, their attention was drawn to the front of the palace, as the doors opened to reveal a familiar figure striding out.

"Confound it, must I do *everything* around here?" snarled Chaos, pushing past the palace butler.

"Well, you *are* the head of the island."

"Stop reminding me!" he interrupted, glaring at him. "If Riff would stop gallivanting about with his endless paramours, long enough to put his mind on business..."

"An unlikely prospect," replied a knowing voice, causing him to turn instantly. Grinning, Dominick chuckled. "I take it you remember me."

"Blazes, boy, it's about time you came back!" exclaimed

Chaos, rushing forward to give him a hug. "After what happened the last time with the Staff, I thought you might have..." Looking over his shoulder, he stopped, pulling away to face the auburn-haired woman smiling at them. "By Chavernos, I need not ask who this is." Stepping towards her, he took her hand with a cordial kiss. "Seeing you here at last, I understand why my grandson would not return without you."

"Thank you, sir," she replied. He raised one eyebrow, eliciting a blush from her. "Oh, sorry. I mean, Grandfather."

With a deep laugh, he pulled her close, patting her shoulder. "Welcome to your new home, Granddaughter."

"The thanks I get these days..." grumbled Lendric. "Ignore the helpful dragon. Rail at him for the minor things."

"I have **not** forgotten you, dear friend," said Chaos, releasing Julianna to shake his hand. "Lendric, our family owes you a great debt this day, for bringing both my grandson and his bride to our world safely. We'd be honored if you'd remain at the palace while arrangements can be made for their wedding, and of course you're invited."

Glancing over at the couple, Lendric remembered the awkward events after their *last* wedding, not disguising his uncertainty about Chaos's invitation. Sensing this, Dominick swiftly intervened. "Julianna and I wouldn't be together right now if not for you," he said, "and we'd **both** be honored if you'd attend our wedding."

Lendric's eyes widened in surprise, while Dominick gripped his shoulder, giving him a wink. "Just let's not have a repeat performance of last night, all right?" he added in a whisper.

Chaos's eyes showed curiosity. "Excuse me?"

"Er... nothing needing mention," replied Lendric, shaking Dominick's hand. "As to your wedding, I accept your invitation gladly. And I'm sure nothing will go awry this time."

Dominick and Julianna smiled knowingly, glad that

Lendric had the discretion to keep certain things a secret.

*****

There was an equally happy reunion among the rest of Dominick's family, including his parents, who insisted on meeting their new daughter-in-law. Riff welcomed the couple with his usual irrepressible nature, while Kiri and Chaos strove to keep this to a minimum. The rest in the group arrived to welcome Julianna with open arms too, soon wiping away her last feelings of insecurity on this new world.

Word spread quickly across the island of the upcoming wedding, finally getting around to Dual, who had been in hiding for several days to avoid the dark mage Shade who was demanding the return of his amulet. Knowing how strong his vengeance would be upon finding out the truth, he was surprised when he was found by someone else.

In elven and human form respectively, Lendric and Roderlin burst into the palace, dragging Dual in with them. Even upon facing the entire Westbrooke family, he remained spitefully defiant.

"And what do *you* cretins want of me?" he spat.

Dominick stepped forward, with a malicious look. "Your head on a pike." A muscle in Dual's cheek twitched at the animosity in his voice. "But fortunately for your pitiful life, the decision was made differently. Quite simply... you're banished from Barokka permanently."

Dual laughed sharply. "And what makes you think your pathetic edict will stop me from returning?" he sneered, eyeing Julianna vindictively. "Let alone haunting your dreams for the rest of your lives, and finishing what I started with your wife."

Before Dominick could retaliate, Lendric and Roderlin switched into their dragon forms, digging their talons into Dual's arms, until he was forced to grimace.

"You'll desist on your tirade against Dominick, Julianna, and their future descendants," hissed Roderlin.

"*Because if you don't,*" continued Lendric, "*both we and our several hundred dragon kin will see to hunting you down to rip your miserable carcass to shreds and incinerate the pieces!*" To emphasize this, Chaolyn and Alysadaria made use of their dragon forms, sending warning flames into the air.

Clenching his jaw, Dual knew that dragons could be every bit as vengeful as assassins and demons, if not more, uniting against an enemy to strike swiftly and efficiently. Yet ironically, their ruling might be in his best interest, with the dark mage out for his blood while he lingered.

"*Furthermore,*" added Lendric, "*before you leave, you'll return the jewels which you've wrongfully stolen from we the dragons.*" Dual's eyes widened. "*Yes, dolt! Those treasures belonged to us!*"

Inwardly, Lendric couldn't help being pleased by the assassin's stunned reaction, although having no use for the jewels himself, he planned to give them to Alarius and his family later.

"*And should anything befall this couple, in the dream-state or otherwise,*" he growled, tightening his claws meaningfully, "*we shall hold you accountable, and deal with you accordingly.*"

"All right!" Dual snarled, glaring at Dominick. "Yours is one face I won't miss, upon leaving this place."

"On that count alone, I'll agree with you," he replied.

As the door burst open, all turned to find Sireni, her expression less than bright for once as she ran to Dual.

"What are you doing here?" he demanded.

"I heard what they said, and I'm going with you."

"The hell you are!" he protested. "You're staying on the island where you belong."

"And leave you to all those other females out there?" she sneered. "I think *not*."

Despite his best attempt otherwise, a smile broke

through his anger. "You always were a stubborn one," he murmured, as she linked her arm with his, her familiar cat-smile upon her face as the dragons escorted them out.

*****

Jarissa looked out the window of the bride's dressing room, whistling at the endless people who'd chosen to attend this once-in-a-lifetime occasion. For not only was this the first time a dreamphaser had brought back a bride from another world, but due to the fact that the groom was Dominick Westbrooke—one of the most renowned bachelors of the realm—it was an especially rare event.

"Everyone in Barokka must be here today," the guardian devil told the others, allowing the curtain to fall back as she turned to them. "You may think you've led a quiet ordinary life back on Earth, Julianna, but you've certainly written a new chapter in dreamphaser history this day."

"Maybe so, but it's my fiancé—or should I say my husband-to-be again—who actually went to great lengths to make this possible," she said, facing the mirror as the last alterations on her dress were completed. "From what I've heard mentioned during the past week, regarding Dominick's former history as a bachelor, I just hope he's not regretting giving that up for me."

"How could he?" asked Psych, squeezing her hand. "After all, he traveled across the solar system to bring you here, not to mention he already married you once on your world, did he not?"

True enough, Julianna reflected.

Everyone gathered around her with appraisal, as she stood resplendent in the midst of never-ending white satin and lace. Frills of this trailed along the back of the gown, winding about in a circle of ruffles at Julianna's feet, with allowance for a small train. In every sense of the word, her bridal gown was like a dream.

"Be assured, the groom has no doubts," confirmed a voice from the doorway. Turning in that direction, Julianna gave a warm smile to Chaos as he stepped into the room. In a rare expression of emotion, he gave her a hug. "You're a most beautiful bride, needing no enhancement of magic to prove this."

"Thank you," she whispered, gladdened that he'd come to accept her as family. "I'm just grateful Dominick doesn't mind undergoing two marriage ceremonies, so both our worlds will recognize this."

"Our world already accepts your Earth marriage as valid," he assured her. "Nonetheless, all who know Dominick here are certainly glad for this second ceremony. When you and my grandson marry this day, you'll be legally married in everyone's eyes and minds here as well. And if anyone has any qualms regarding this, I'll see to... What the blazes?"

The interrupting voices outside only grew louder.

"I really don't think this is a good idea," Inferno warned. "After all, I once heard from a dreamphaser that on Earth, it's customary..."

"Customs be damned, why the hell wouldn't it be a good idea to see the bride?" argued Riff. "After all, if Julianna's done the smart thing and skipped out on him, he should be the first to know, right?"

The sound of a loud jab, followed by Riff's unmistakably winded response, gave indication of at least one other man present. "One more insult out of you, Riff, and I swear I'll find myself a substitute for my best man."

During his brother's grumbled reply, the bride-to-be quickly gathered up the edge of her gown to head towards the back room.

"Julianna, what's wrong?" asked a bemused Kiri.

Whirling about to see the others bearing much of the same expression, including Chaos, Julianna nearly laughed at the mistaken thought that their world's views on marriage were entirely similar.

"Nothing's wrong," she explained. "Only some regard it bad luck for the groom to see the bride in her wedding dress on the day of their marriage, just before they're actually wed."

Jarissa shook her head. "Does that mean they use blindfolds during the ceremony?" she asked.

"Likely not," said Kiri. "I think I understand. You go hide, and we'll try and keep your future husband at bay."

"Good luck," sighed Chaos, knowing his grandson very well.

In a swirl of white, Julianna disappeared into the next room, shutting the door behind her as the other women stood waiting at the outer entrance. All the while with folded arms, Chaos began muttering his usual opinion of the impetuosity of youth, sitting down comfortably in a chair off to the side to prepare for some possible fireworks.

"What if her three demoness guardians are hiding in here with her?" sneered Buddy, especially earning Jarissa's instant anger.

"Simple," decided Riff. "We'll just conjure up a few demons to chase them away."

Kiri's eyes narrowed, as she hissed, "Why those sons of..." Jarissa and Psych shushed her, just before she gestured for them to follow her behind the door where they wouldn't be seen. Just in time, as it opened.

All in formal attire, the four men glanced about the room, earning Riff's immediate amusement, albeit the groom didn't look too pleased. "I was right, Phase," said Riff, slapping him on the back. "Not only are you the first dreamphaser to marry an Earth woman, but you're also the first one to be left standing at the altar."

"I heard that, Riff, and you're a hundred percent wrong!" Julianna yelled from the other room. Dominick's friends smiled at the groom's apparent relief. "Maybe you're having premonitions of what'll happen if *you* ever choose to get married, but not us!"

Chaos couldn't help chuckling at the chagrined look on his elder grandson's face. A look that never lasted long.

"No thanks," replied Riff. "I have no intention of being similarly shackled like my starstruck baby brother. But while we're on the subject, why are you secluding yourself back there? Poison ivy get you?"

"No, you idiot!" said Kiri, stepping out of hiding with the other pair. "It happens to be customary on Earth that the bride isn't supposed to see the groom before the wedding! Don't you know *anything*?"

"I know that in your case, that'd be a damn good custom," he answered, just before the fiery copper-haired woman began swinging punches at him.

"Ah... happy weddings," chimed Inferno, turning to Dominick. "I salute you, my friend. Congratulations on finding a bride to marry you in spite of who her brother-in-law will be."

"I heard that, fireball!" Riff returned sarcastically, while dodging Kiri.

Ignoring this, Dominick leaned against the wall beside the door concealing Julianna. "Are there any other unexpected Earth customs that I should know about, such as the groom not being allowed to touch the bride on the honeymoon?"

"A custom I'm sure you'd ignore if it existed," said Julianna.

"You'd better believe I would," he said adamantly. "Now, what other customs are there to your Earth style weddings?"

"Simple things really," she explained. "A wedding veil worn over the bride's face, until the groom removes it when they're standing at the altar; the bride tossing her bouquet to eligible females, and the groom removing a garter from her leg to toss the lace to available bachelors; the groom carrying the bride over the threshold when they're alone..."

"This is getting interesting," murmured Riff.

"That's enough, Julianna," interrupted Dominick, eyeing his brother meaningfully. "You can give me the further nightly details later. In any case, be it as you wish, love. I'll await you outside if you insist. Although since this *is* Chavernos, would you consider altering the rules slightly?"

"Some fates shouldn't be tempted," she replied softly. "But, Dominick..." she continued in a more seductive tone, "if you allow me these few minutes now, you'll find the wait more than worthwhile when we're alone."

"Hmmm... maybe I can get used to these customs after all," Dominick said with a smile. "Just don't keep me waiting too long at the altar, love. I'm most anxious to see to our making an early escape later."

"Or in Julianna's case, perhaps she merely wants to escape in general," snickered Riff. Dominick was about to reply in kind, only managing to give his brother another jab, as Chaos rose from his seat with a fist slam to the armrest.

"All right, you two," he growled, clapping a strong hand on each of their shoulders to lead them out. "I'm beginning to see the logic of that Earth custom regarding the groom and his brother not seeing the bride beforehand."

Julianna smiled behind the door, knowing that in Riff's case, that was a fairly accurate restatement of the custom. A few minutes later, Chaos returned to collect the bride.

"At least that incident proves how strongly my grandson loves you," he said. "Not to mention, how impatient he can be." He shrugged in resignation. "Ah well, youth. Anyway, I brought the finishing touch." From behind his back, he revealed a tiara, which had diamonds sparkling about its circular frame, and a long gossamer veil flowing from it.

Gently placing it upon Julianna's head, Chaos arranged for the veil to fall behind her, earning a curious look from her. "I know... you spoke of a tradition for the bridal veil to cover her face from view initially, but I'm afraid my grandson has never been the conventional type."

Seeing tears in her eyes, he took her hand, linking it to his arm, and held it strongly with reassurance. "No tears, my new granddaughter. This is a day for happiness."

As the ceremony began, and he led her to the awaiting groom, Julianna could only agree.

A special blend of harmonious music filled the air, more beautiful than anything she'd heard before, played by some musical instruments that she couldn't yet name. One by one, her new friends and bridesmaids joined their companions.

Only Riff did the unexpected, giving a wink to a dark-haired woman, that Kiri didn't miss. Narrowing her eyes, she swatted him with the flowers she held, while some of the spectators laughed.

Dominick shook his head at his brother, earning an innocent look from him.

"What?" Riff protested. "I've got a date with that one later."

"Isn't that her **husband** beside her, threatening to kill you with a look?" he inquired.

Glancing in that direction, Riff shrugged. "I must have gotten her confused with her sister," he said, returning his gaze to Dominick. "Hey, you know how I am, Phase. Just because you're getting tied down, don't think I'm going to share in..."

His words trailed off as he followed his brother's sudden stare. As Chaos appeared to lead Julianna down the aisle, she looked very different in her complete bridal attire, and so breathtakingly beautiful that several men expressed their envy of the fortunate groom.

Covered in white satin and lace while carrying a bouquet of white flowers, her reddish-brown curls streamed all about her shoulders, with the veil only partially concealing them.

Dominick couldn't tear his eyes from her. In her simple gown, for their Earth marriage, he'd been more than content. But now, in this new gown, she looked like a veritable princess. No wonder Earth custom had it that the groom couldn't see the bride like this beforehand, or they might never have gotten to the ceremony.

Stopping just before him, Chaos placed their hands together as the music quieted, smiling at Julianna. "Welcome to the family again, Granddaughter," he said softly, before turning to Dominick. "You take care of this one. I still want those great-grandkids one day." His grandson smiled as Chaos moved to take his seat.

Julianna turned her attention to Dominick, who took her hand with love shining in his eyes. Then both turned to the awaiting justice of the peace, as he began speaking.

"Friends gathered, it is not uncommon that two people choose to wed on Chavernos, yet there must indeed be a true bond of love between a pair who have met across the span of different worlds. A joining of two souls is ever a joyous event to behold, thus may both of these young people know the greatest joy to come in their years together. If you will both raise your joined hands please."

Curiously, Julianna followed Dominick's lead as he raised their hands. The justice of the peace held out a silken cord which he wrapped around both their wrists. "As this cord binds your hands, may it be symbolic of the binding of your hearts, lives, and souls."

As the cord was gently tied, the pair held each other's hands tighter as the man continued, barely hearing what he said, until the time came to speak their marriage vows.

"I, Dominick Phaser Westbrooke, take thee Julianna Sherborne to be my wife, to love, honor, and cherish, from this day forward, for as long as we both shall live."

Squeezing her hand, he added, "Julianna, I never thought

I would find the one I was searching for on another world so far away, but not a day goes by that I don't thank Heaven for helping me to find you, my dearest love. You've brought a meaning to my life that wasn't there before. Wherever the future takes us, I swear I shall always walk beside you, and you'll always have my deepest love."

Tears glistening in her eyes, she spoke next. "I, Julianna Sherborne, take thee Dominick Phaser Westbrooke to be my husband, to love, honor, and cherish, from this day forward, for as long as we both shall live."

Smiling up at him, she continued, "Dominick, I've never known what real love was until I met you, but more importantly, you always make me feel loved and cherished. I too thank Heaven for helping you to find me, so now we can spend the rest of our lives together. And I look forward to all that the future brings, as long as you'll share it with me, for you shall always have my deepest love as well."

"What poetry book did they swipe those lines from?" mumbled Riff, just before Kiri deftly stepped on his foot to silence him.

Ignoring this, the justice looked past the marriage couple. "The rings please." Kiri readily had hers in hand, while Riff took an extra moment to produce his.

"Didn't mean to worry you," he told his brother, handing him the ring.

"Like Chaos you didn't," replied Dominick, giving him a tolerant smile.

Shortly after, the man gestured for him to proceed. Dominick placed his ring on Julianna's finger. "With this ring, I thee wed, and henceforth pledge my heart."

Glancing at it with a smile, she then placed the ring she held on her awaiting groom's hand. "With this ring, I thee wed, and henceforth pledge my heart," she repeated.

"And people really go through ceremonies like this

willingly?" murmured Riff. This time, it was the justice of the peace who leaned forward to swat him with his book, earning more amused laughter from the crowd,

Clearing his throat meaningfully, the man placed his hand upon the couple's joined hands again, as he continued speaking. "Then by all the powers of Chavernos, I hereby pronounce you husband and wife." Giving an added smile to Dominick, he removed the cord and released their hands. "I would presume you might want to kiss your new bride."

"Clever man," replied Dominick, pulling Julianna close to give her a most lengthy passionate kiss.

So much so, that as the crowd broke into applause and cheered, Chaos finally stepped forward to gently coax them apart. "Slow down, you two. The great-grandkids can wait another day." They both laughed, giving him a hug just before he turned to the many happy guests. "On to the reception, everyone!" he called out jovially, in one of the rare times he displayed his emotions.

Taking Julianna's hand, Dominick ran with her back down the aisle, dodging the endless confetti tossed by the well-wishers, while jubilant music filled the air. Both could only hope the rest of their lives would be filled with such unequalled happiness as they felt now.

*****

Much later, as Dominick carried her over the threshold of their palace room, Julianna reminded him, "You know, the groom *can* put the bride down afterwards."

"Is there no end to these Earth customs?" he sighed, with mock disappointment, as he set her back on her feet.

Resting his arm about her waist, he led her over to the outer balcony, revealing the view of the moon and the stars, as well as their unfinished new home. Chaos's promised gift was definitely starting to resemble their dream castle, which only brought fond memories to their minds.

From Dream to Reality

"It's a bit more distant than it seems from here, since it's closer to the ocean," Dominick told her. "Just like our other dream castle."

Hugging his side, Julianna glanced up. "Even the night sky doesn't look that different from my world," she replied softly. "In a way, it's as though I haven't really left Earth behind."

"We'll return on occasion," he promised, kissing her cheek. "Both you, and I... and one day, our child."

As he touched her stomach gently, she couldn't stifle a laugh. "That sure of yourself, are you?"

Dominick shrugged. "One never knows," he replied. "After all, it's not impossible, considering the past several nights."

"Hmmm. Does that mean there's no point in having the rest of our honeymoon?"

"I never said *that*, my temptress," he chuckled, picking her up again as he carried her over to the nearby bed. Lowering her against the pillows as he followed her down to kiss her, he murmured with a seductive smile, "As a matter of fact, beginning this night, I have no intention of *ever* ending our honeymoon."

Epilogue

A year later…

"So you're planning to stay on Earth yourself, after they return?" asked Chaos.

"Only briefly initially," replied Lendric. "As I did before, when I visited the Dragends, I'll carefully alter my appearance so their son won't recognize me later. But in a few more years, when the time draws near for his return to his true homeworld, I do plan to appear as I am now and to remain on Earth for an extended stay. I hope to make the transition easier for him by gaining his friendship first."

Chaos shook his head thoughtfully. "I can't imagine how he's going to react upon finding out he's part dragon, when the time comes."

"Nor do I," sighed Lendric, "but it's the way his parents wanted it, so he could grow up with a normal human life on Earth. I can only hope all works out for him." His somber expression lifted as he patted his friend's shoulder. "On a lighter note though, you must be pleased with how things have turned out with Dominick and Julianna."

"Yes," he agreed. "Hard to believe, it's really been a whole year since their marriage." Glancing towards the back room, he added, "Which reminds me, where *are* those two?"

"Patience," said the dragon sorcerer.

Chaos glared.

Patience was never considered one of his virtues.

As he paced about the room, he wondered for the millionth time what was taking the pair so long. That is, until he heard the sound of voices coming closer. By the time Dominick and Julianna came in, laughing as they each cuddled a child in their arms, Chaos had managed to put on a brighter smile.

Brightened even more as his gaze fell upon his two great-grandsons.

Seeing the couple for the happy parents they were, it was hard to believe that little over a year ago they'd had their own share of never-ending problems in order to be together. But even in comparison to the dreamphasing magic and Lendric's which had brought them together to begin with, their love had proven to hold a far stronger magic all its own.

Fortunately, as Chaos saw it, everything had worked out for the best, since they'd chosen to live on Chavernos. The only stipulation was that Julianna wanted the freedom to visit her homeworld at least twice a year to be reunited with her family on Earth.

Once again they were to make this trip, and as before, the elder man was sorry to see them go, even though Dominick and Julianna's stay would only be for a few weeks, and then they'd return.

He knew he shouldn't have minded this situation, but since they were taking the children with them, he suddenly felt an air of loneliness hit him. Not that his son Discord wasn't somewhere else on Chavernos, nor his other grandson Riff here, but Chaos couldn't help feeling a special kinship to Dominick and his little family. A family that might not stay so little at the rate the pair was going.

He'd been pleased just upon hearing the news that the pair were expecting their first child, an announcement that occurred only a few months after their marriage on Chavernos. But then the pair surprised him again by being doubly blessed with twin sons! The older twin Dash had received his name from the letters of his father's two known names: Dominick and Phaser. Chase, on the other hand, received his name because of its similarity to his great-grandfather's. A fact that tickled Chaos no end, although he loved both his great-grandsons equally.

Yet even that didn't seem to deter the surprises Dominick and Julianna had for him, for only yesterday, they'd announced that they were expecting yet another child. And another great-grandchild for Chaos.

He couldn't have been more pleased!

Admittedly, the expectant couple were hoping for a daughter this time, but that was a matter that only time would reveal. If it was a girl, they'd decided to name her after Dominick's grandmother Ylana, bringing tears to the elder man's eyes. Keeping his thoughts private, although he did visibly give a smile to the skies above, Chaos hoped his dearly departed wife could somehow see her grandson and his family now, for surely she would have been as happy as he was.

His thoughts were interrupted by hearing the couple engaged in discussion over something. During Chaos's brief musings, the couple had handed the children to Inferno and Psych who doted on them as much as everyone else did, and he caught the second half of Julianna's words to her husband.

"All I can say is, after this one, I want us to get off the baby carousel for a while. I don't mind your idea for more kids, but certainly not all at once."

"You'll get no argument from me, love," replied Dominick, wrapping his arms around her waist to pull her closer in order to kiss her. "And after this one, what say we indulge in a nice long second honeymoon?"

"Isn't it a bit soon for one of those?" she inquired mischievously.

"It's never too soon for a romantic getaway," he decided, kissing her again. "As long as we have some time to ourselves. I doubt Chaos would mind assisting in the babysitting while we're gone." As he spoke, he and Julianna took the children back from their friends, walking over to him.

From Dream to Reality

"Speaking of which, why don't you simply leave the children with me this time?" Chaos suggested enthusiastically, his features brightening anew.

"We would," explained Dominick, "but under the circumstances, Julianna and I don't want to be separated from them for this trip. You see, her family is still waiting for word of our first... child?" A pleased smile crossed his face as he glanced down at the twins.

This would certainly surprise Julianna's family!

He could still remember the day he and Julianna had gone to her doctor and received the news. At first, the doctor had worn a rather somber expression, earning their instant concern.

"Well, how can I say this?" the doctor began. "It appears we missed something."

"Surely nothing's wrong," Julianna said worriedly, as her hand came to rest on her more than rounded stomach. Ever protective, Dominick calmed her gently and then turned to the doctor.

"But if nothing was wrong, you wouldn't be talking to us like we were about to face execution," he said sternly. "Now tell us what's wrong with our child?"

The doctor quickly shook her head. "Oh no, I assure you everything's fine... with both of them."

It took a moment for the second part of her statement to sink in, but when it did, the young couple's eyes widened, Dominick finding his voice first. "You're saying we're going to have twins?"

"I believe that's the proper diagnosis," said the doctor, just before she was called for by another nurse. "If you'll excuse me, I'll be right back."

When the door closed behind her, the pair turned to each other with surprised elation. "Twins," breathed Dominick, reaching forward to hug his beaming wife. "Oh my dearest love, you've made me the happiest man alive this day."

"Then I'll match you for being the happiest woman alive," she replied, "although if you'll remember, I did have some help from my rather devoted husband in this being possible to begin with." She added, "Unless of course, you've forgotten how it occurred."

He pulled her close with a seductive growl. "Just you wait until I get you home, Mrs. Westbrooke, and I'll prove to you just how good my memory is... among other things."

"Oh, how I do love being married to a man of action," she sighed contentedly. He kissed her deeply before releasing her. When he did, she smiled and took his hand to hold it against where their children slept, filled with happiness upon seeing the adoration and reverence in her husband's expression as his hand caressed her stomach.

"Our children," he repeated, still adjusting to this unexpected revelation. "By Chavernos, this will certainly surprise Grandfather no end."

And of course it had.

Resting one arm about his wife's shoulder while he kept young Dash tucked safely within the crook of his other arm, Dominick looked to Chaos like the embodiment of true happiness, echoed by his radiant wife. A fact which brought a single tear to the elder man's eye, although he would have throttled anyone who might have noticed the fact. After all, he still had a reputation to uphold as the stern authoritative ruler of Barokka.

A sharp crash jostled everyone from their pleasant thoughts, followed by loud curses, some male and some female. Chaos dropped his head against one hand, cursing the approaching pair for the millionth time. Of all the guardian angels and devils on Barokka, Buddy and Jarissa were the most impossible to deal with.

"One more word out of you, hothead, and I'll tear those

wings from your back!" snarled Buddy.

"You try it, and I'll strangle you with that halo of yours!" retorted Jarissa.

Some things never changed, thought Chaos, even as Psych and Inferno tried to separate them from beating each other senseless.

"I can't say I won't mind some peace and quiet at your family's house for a while," Dominick murmured to his wife.

"Don't expect that," said Julianna. "The twins are still bound to wake us up in the middle of the night, and I bet their doting aunts Crystal and Vicki will raise a stir of their own when they're finally introduced." She continued thoughtfully, "Vicki's husband Luke will appreciate the added incentive to convince her to have children of their own. And Jerry is certainly thrilled now that they're going to be parents again, while Crystal's happy they're expecting a little girl."

"Which reminds me. Do you think your nephew's adjusted to the fact he's going to have a sister?"

She shrugged. "I certainly hope so," she replied honestly. "Sammy had mixed feelings the last time we saw him, when we found out, but that was many months ago. Although either way, I think you helped when you talked with him, since he seemed to be considering the merits of being a protective big brother."

"In that case, I wouldn't worry." With amusement, Dominick added quietly, "And I'm certain Sammy will be a more agreeable older brother than a certain other one around here."

"I heard that, Phase!" snapped Riff, striding over from the rest of the group to join them. Rolling her eyes with a sigh, Kiri followed. "You know, it's not like I've been causing you trouble lately."

"I see... and what would you label the dancing girls that 'coincidentally' showed up at our wedding reception?"

"That was a year ago," his brother protested.

"Hmmm, all right," replied Dominick, "then explain the time we caught you throwing a party in our home the last time we were away."

Riff shrugged. "Well… your place does accommodate more people."

"Not to mention, the time you were roasting marshmallows in our fireplace, just before nearly setting our house ablaze afterwards," said Julianna.

"It was just an accident."

Dominick nodded. "And how about the time you sneaked into our house in the middle of the night to escape Kiri's wrath, making enough of a commotion to wake us up thinking you were a prowler?"

"Okay, so I made a few mistakes," mumbled Riff.

"A *few?*" both chimed in unison.

Folding his arms in chagrin, Riff presented a wounded expression. "That's still no reason to denounce me as a role model," he retorted, glaring at Dominick. "And if you think I've forgotten the times you've interrupted *my* liaisons with some very pretty maidens, you're..."

Kiri abruptly stifled his tirade with a cleverly timed kiss, earning a wide-eyed look of surprise from Chaos when it actually worked, leaving Riff speechless!

"Don't forget," she said in an overly sweet tone, "we're a couple now, sweetheart. Those 'pretty maidens' had better be history."

Changing his ire to amusement over her jealousy, he replied, "Yes, dear."

While everyone was distracted, the butler strode over to Lendric, whispering something before the dragon sorcerer excused himself. Heading outside, he found a couple waiting for him.

"Carilya," he said in surprise. "I haven't seen you in many months. What brings you here now?"

"We can't stay long. I just wished to see you off," she said, her husband Devon one step behind her. "And your nephew wished to do the same." Stepping forward, she handed him their newborn son.

Startled into silence as he took the child, Lendric could only gape. He'd heard his sister was expecting a baby, but didn't know she'd actually given birth to him. "When?" he gasped.

"Nearly a month ago. We didn't have the opportunity to tell you sooner, which was why we made the effort to be here today." At her brother's curious look, she added, "We've named him Rydarizon, for the fabled sun dragon, although we usually go by his human nickname, Ryder."

Tickling the boy's chin, Lendric was rewarded by the child smiling, just before his eyes opened. Feeling his blood turn cold, the dragon sorcerer faced his sister again.

"He has violet eyes."

"I know," she said softly, biting her lip. "But we're doing everything in our power to hide this fact from becoming widespread knowledge."

"One *can't* hide something like this forever," he retorted. "I don't suppose you'd consider leaving Chavernos to raise him safely on Earth, as the Dragend family are doing?"

She shook her head. "Chavernos is our home. We couldn't possibly leave it."

Before Lendric could reply, Devon interjected, "You need have no worries about Ryder. Carilya and I have no intention of allowing the dark forces of this world to get their hands on our son."

"No one ever intends for an assassin to sneak past one's defenses, until it's too late," Lendric argued. "As I'll be on Earth to settle a few things with the Dragends, I'll be gone for a few weeks. But as soon as I return, we're certainly going to have to create some strict measures to protect your son, if you insist on remaining here while he grows up."

Carilya sighed wearily. "Zaruldar and Pyro have already said much the same thing, and *refuse* to take 'no' for an answer."

"A wise decision," her brother replied. Devon didn't seem to agree on this count, as he retrieved his son, but then Lendric doubted he understood just how his son's violet eyes could drastically affect his life.

In any case, they'd just have to pray for the best.

Back in the castle, looking over Julianna's shoulder at the baby she held, Riff felt Kiri's hand upon his own. "I doubt fatherhood would agree with me," he said quietly. "All that constant responsibility. Running an island carries more than enough of that."

"Are you sure you aren't simply afraid we might have a child that takes after you?" she teased.

Grimacing, he eyed the child again. "Very funny, Kiri. Just don't count on my brother's children convincing me that we should have one of our own. If anything, mention of those two o'clock feedings stops any paternal instincts I might have had."

"Really?" she said, leaning against his shoulder with a devious smile. "I think I might be able to change your mind sometime down the road." At his responding growl, she backed off, folding her arms. "Well, if *that's* the way it's going to be with you, Mr. Westbrooke, maybe I'd be better off looking elsewhere for a more amenable boyfriend."

At her jibe, he quickly used her own method to cut it short, pulling her close with a passionate kiss that would convince *any* woman of her boyfriend's devotion. Seeing her uncharacteristic dazed look, he grinned.

"Still wish to look elsewhere, sweetheart?" he asked.

"Well, I guess I could be persuaded otherwise," she amended happily, as he entwined his hand with hers.

Lendric returned, gesturing to the others that it was time to leave.

From Dream to Reality

"Come back soon," said Psych, waving to the couple who moved to stand beside him with their children.

"We will," said Julianna.

"Considering how often I shuttle people back and forth between worlds, I ought to start charging for this," Lendric murmured to Chaolyn. The other dragon merely snickered as he stepped back with the rest, allowing the dragon sorcerer to focus on the Teleportation Staff while chanting the necessary incantation.

Hugging one arm about his beloved wife, while holding young Dash within the cradle of his other arm, Dominick couldn't resist kissing her cheek. "What was that for?" she asked.

"For the anniversary of what will always be remembered as the happiest day of my life," he replied, "when you became a permanent part of mine, a year ago today."

"I remember," she whispered, her brown eyes shining. "Although you certainly never give me cause to forget, my dream knight."

"Will you still be calling me that fifty years from now?" he laughed.

"Hmmm, I don't see why not," replied Julianna. "After all, you still visit my dreams on a nightly basis." She began to smile, with a courtly nod. "Or should that be a *'knightly'* basis?"

"Ah, well... that's what happens when a dream knight falls in love with a temptress," he sighed, squeezing her waist. "A fate I wouldn't have changed for anything on Chavernos."

"Or Earth?"

"Or anywhere else in the solar system, love," he agreed with a grin, his warm blue eyes capturing hers as he pulled her closer to kiss her again.

Lendric smiled as he caught sight of this, the lights of his spell growing brighter to encompass them all.

Jen Robyn

Just before they vanished from the room, bearing the magic of a dream come true.

*****